*For Sue, who makes it all possible and
Jenny and Andy, who make it all worthwhile.*

REGULATION OF
INVESTIGATORY POWERS ACT 2000

Section 26(8)

a person is a **COVERT HUMAN INTELLIGENCE SOURCE (CHIS)** if—

(a) he establishes or maintains a personal or other relationship with a person for the covert purpose of facilitating the doing of anything falling within paragraph (b) or (c);

(b) he covertly uses such a relationship to obtain information or to provide access to any information to another person; or

(c) he covertly discloses information obtained by the use of such a relationship, or as a consequence of the existence of such a relationship.

PROLOGUE

Seeing them go, that's what really did it for Joey. The moment of death, if he could just glimpse it. But the eyes had to be open; he liked it best when the pupils were wide with terror. Then, one click, the screen went blank. They were gone and that vacant stare shot through him like two hundred and fifty volts. Better than crack, better than charlie, way better than shagging. It was the ultimate hit. It was the power. Game over, you'd won. They were meat, you were the butcher.

Joey stood over Marlow, nerve ends zinging, his cock stirring in anticipation. Marlow fingered his broken nose, blood dripped onto the concrete floor. Joey unclenched his fist, rubbed his knuckles. He was in no hurry. He enjoyed a bit of foreplay.

'So you gonna tell me the truth now?'

Marlow looked up at him, trying to gauge his mood. He had to make his next words count.

'Seriously Joe, what is this about? Someone's got their wires crossed here.'

Joey smiled. He seemed relaxed, unconcerned even.

'You reckon?'

Built like a bruiser, face like an angel, Joey Phelps had charm to spare. Even as a small boy he had drawn people to him; those hypnotic baby-blue eyes under thick sandy lashes, his quirky smile. Joey reached into his jeans pocket, pulled out a neat wedge of folded tissues, squatted down beside Marlow.

'Here. Clean yourself up.'

Marlow took the tissues warily, wincing as he pressed them to his nose.

Straightening up, Joey thrust both hands in his pockets and took a leisurely turn about the lock-up. The night air seeping under the door was chilly and dank. He gazed up at the vaulted arch of the ceiling, row upon row of blackened bricks, laid maybe a hundred and fifty years before to carry the railway from the smoke to the suburbs. Joey peered around; he knew he could take his time, savour his power.

'Look at this place. You ever think about the blokes that built the railways?'

The remark hung in the air. Marlow glanced from Joey to Ashley. Ashley, as usual, was waiting on Joey's next move. He was picking his teeth. He'd seen some actor do this in a clip from an old film he'd streamed, thought it looked cool.

'All them millions of bricks to lay. Now *that* was grafting.'

Marlow eased himself up into a sitting position and rested his back against the wall. He could feel the dampness through his shirt; icy cold, it seeped through his flesh, chilling him to the heart. He knew that Joey was toying with him. He'd suspected for almost a week now that his cover had been blown. But when Joey and Ashley had called for him that evening, full of laddish high spirits, his fears had been allayed. They'd been clubbing, done a couple of lines, had a few beers. They were going on to a party, some soap actress Joey had been shagging. Then Joey announced he needed to make a quick stop.

Marlow cursed his own stupidity, he really should've guessed. He was twenty-nine years old, he had parents, retired now to Swanage, two older sisters. How would they cope with all this? Should he cry? Should he beg? He sucked in a few deep breaths to calm himself; exhaust fumes from the nearby main road, rancid fat from the kebab shop on the corner. The smells of London were suddenly all there, flooding his senses in both reality and in memory. And he was sure of one thing: he didn't want to die.

'Listen Joe, I dunno what lying bastard's been telling tales about me, but—'

The silver toecap of Joey's handmade boot caught him squarely in the temple. His head jarred with the impact and ricocheted back against the wall. Joey gazed at him calmly.

'The Net's a wonderful thing, innit? I got a couple of illegals who're dead clever with all that. Hack into anything. They hacked into your file ... Detective Sergeant. A Commissioner's commendation. Ash was impressed. Weren't you Ash?'

Ashley, intent on quarrying with his toothpick, simply nodded. Dazed from the blow, Marlow lurched forward and vomited on the floor. Joey watched, a smile of amusement and expectation spreading across his face, as if he were waiting for the punchline to a joke.

'You ain't gonna deny it then?'

Marlow wiped a shaky hand across his mouth, raised his head slowly. His gaze was watery but unflinching.

'You're a psycho Phelps. A real nut-job.'

'Yeah?' Joey laughed. 'Hear that Ash? I'm a nut-job.'

Ashley slipped the toothpick in his pocket, glanced at Joey, the blue eyes shining iridescent, sweat beading on his upper lip. Joey smiled.

'Nah mate, you're the sucker here. No one plays me.'

Ashley pulled a pair of vinyl gloves from the back pocket of his jeans and calmly drew them on. Now it was really going to kick off. Joey selected a tyre iron from the tools on the workbench, weighed it in his hand. Marlow swallowed hard, glanced at the door and the tantalizing chink of neon beyond; it was worth a shot.

As Marlow scrabbled to his feet Joey slammed the tyre iron down on top of his skull, cracking it open. He lifted the iron and blood gushed up over splintered bone and the ruptured pearlescent membrane of the cerebral cortex. Joey seized Marlow's jaw, twisted the face round to look right at him – the eyelids drooped. Marlow had already slipped into unconsciousness. Joey shook him with frustration. He wanted to see, but it was too late. Shoving him away Joey took another couple of swings. Ashley watched in annoyance. He was going to have to clean this lot up. He huffed.

'Yeah all right. I think that's done the trick.'

Joey paused and turned. Ashley caught a look of feral rage and quickly stepped back. Joey's breathing was fast and shallow. His heart thumped. He closed his eyes. Ashley had seen this enough times before, yet still he never knew how to react. He focused on the blood puddling out round the lumps and bumps in the concrete.

'I'll get them bin bags out the car, shall I?'

Joey ignored him, the tyre iron clattering to the floor. He let his arms hang loose. He inhaled slowly. His shoulders sagged as the tension in his muscles slackened. Ashley stood rooted to the spot; he wasn't going to risk the noise of the door. After a couple of moments Joey opened his eyes. Ashley held his breath then Joey grinned broadly.

'Fuck me, what a blast!'

Ashley's nerves evaporated. He grinned too and laughed. 'Yeah! Wow!'

Joey filled his lungs, hooted with joy. 'Fucking bastards! They think they can get me. Send all the fucking shit-eating filth you like. I'm Joey Fucking Phelps. And you'll *never* get me!'

1

A pair of brown eyes stared directly at Kaz. Not solid brown, more muddy spiked with flecks of amber. The look itself was harder to read; some anger, resentment certainly, but behind that a void, a hollow of despair.

Kaz returned the look with her own searching gaze. Then she selected a pencil from the battered tin box, a 2B, she always started with a 2B. Opening the sketchbook to a fresh page she rapidly plotted out the main features. The eyes first. Her hand moved across the sheet of one-twenty gram cartridge with practised assurance. Her own eyes darted from the face in front of her down to the drawing and back again.

Yasmin's brow furrowed.

'Dunno why you don't just take a picture.'

'This is better. You see more.'

The contours of the head, the nose, the planes of the cheek were quickly taking shape. Kaz paused and forced herself to look harder. She was missing something. Was it in the angle of the chin? Somewhere deep in the gene pool below the whores and the drug mules, the servants and slaves, there lurked a Nubian princess, mistress of all she surveyed. And that pride was still there in the tilt of Yasmin's battered jaw. Kaz smiled to herself, adjusted the line.

A key clanked in the lock and the cell door swung open. A

prison officer stood there. It was Fat Pat. A short bundle of venom, she'd always had it in for Kaz.

'You ready then Phelps?'

Kaz closed the sketchbook and slipped it with the tin of pencils into the plastic carrier at her feet. She stood up and smiled awkwardly at Yasmin. Yasmin rose stiffly and opened her arms.

'Be lucky babe . . .'

Kaz stepped into the hug.

'You be out yourself soon.'

'Yeah and he be there waiting for me. Nah, I'm better off where I am. Least I got no broken bones.'

Fat Pat marched Kaz down the corridor. Being escorted was an all too familiar routine: walk in front, wait, the body odour and rasping Lycra as Pat waddled along behind. Kaz stopped at the door to the block and stood aside for Pat to unlock it. She towered over Pat by at least five inches. At first the daily sessions in the gym had been an outlet for her pent-up rage. Later it had become part of her discipline, the way forward, the way out. At twenty-five she was certainly the fittest she'd ever been; more importantly she was four years clean and sober. And she planned to stay that way.

Pat glared up at her. Kaz returned the look with a steady gaze.

'Y'know Phelps, you may fool the shrinks, your offender manager and the parole board. But you don't fool me. You're pure evil. Clever, I'll give you that. But underneath it all, evil.'

'Well you know better than any of them, don't you Pat? All them smarmy gits with degrees that get paid shedloads more than you.'

Kaz could see Pat rising to the bait, she always did. Her neck flushed, her cheeks reddened.

'The Lord will smite thee Phelps! He will cast down the ungodly into the pit of hell!'

'What's that bit in the Bible, Pat? Something about more joy in heaven over one sinner that repents? You should check it out.'

Pat's eyes glistened with hate.

'You'll be back on crack in a week. You won't be able to help yourself.'

Kaz smiled equably. Through the door her freedom was waiting. She felt almost high, suffused with the natural joy of being alive. She took a deep breath and wished she could hold on to this precious feeling, this golden moment. For she knew one thing for certain: it wouldn't last. Once she stepped outside there would be no respite, it would all begin again.

2

A fine drizzle was falling as Detective Chief Superintendent Alan Turnbull picked his way through the plastic bags, cans and tar to where SOCO had set up their tent on the foreshore. The river was still ebbing; steely grey, it stretched away into the morning mist. He could've stayed in the office twiddling his thumbs until the call came through from the SIO, but uncertainty made him nervous. If their suspicions were correct, he had to know. He had to know now because this could be the game changer he'd been waiting for.

He stopped at the outer cordon and as he signed the crime scene examiner's chit Detective Sergeant Nicci Armstrong emerged from the tent, suited, booted and gloved. She pushed back her hood, registered his presence without a flicker and headed towards him. Turnbull frowned. She had an attitude about her – chippy, arrogant – to his mind not an attractive combination in a young woman. Of course you couldn't say that nowadays, but he thought it anyway.

He surveyed the terrain with a professional eye; focus on the job, that had always been his technique for keeping uncomfortable feelings at bay. There were half a dozen people in protective gear, working quickly to stay ahead of the tide. He knew managing the scene, preserving every scrap of evidence, was important, nevertheless the rigmarole annoyed him. The cost of all this scientific expertise soon added up. In the end would it really tell them a single thing they didn't already know?

Armstrong looked flushed and irritable; the Velcro fastening on the suit had chafed her neck. Turnbull scanned her. She could've done with a touch of make-up. As she joined him she painted on a smile.

'Morning boss. Bit chilly.'

'Is it him?'

Armstrong swallowed hard; bile stung the back of her throat. She'd seen most things, pulled enough corpses out of the river. But this was different. A ghost of familiarity remained in the face even with lamprey eels feasting on the brain. She gave Turnbull a curt nod.

'Yeah we think so. We'll need to run a check on DS Marlow's dental records and DNA to confirm though.'

Turnbull nodded. 'Still got his teeth then?'

'The lower jaw's intact. Well just about. Obviously the body's been in the water for some time.'

Turnbull wiped a film of rain from his face, turned to stare at the cranes sedately swinging over the shell of some luxury apartments rising up on the far bank of the river. He wondered what the asking price would be; north of a million certainly. Then he caught Armstrong's eye. Her face a rigid mask, she was waiting for him to speak. He shook his head.

'Confident bastard isn't he? But this time he's overreached himself.'

Armstrong shifted her balance from one boot to the other. She could feel the squelchy silt sinking beneath her. She'd been up since six. This was hard enough, finding a colleague, a mate like this; she wanted to get on.

'Can I organize you some kit boss, so you can take a look?'

Turnbull exhaled, he was wet and certainly not about to

11

scrabble into a clammy plastic suit in the cramped confines of a SOCO van. He gazed out across the river, avoiding her eye.

'No, I'm due at a meeting with the Assistant Commissioner. Email me a preliminary report by lunchtime.'

Armstrong nodded. 'Do you want the digital recording as well? We've got some three-sixty spherical images on R2S.'

Turnbull shot her a belligerent look as he wondered what that load of high-tech kit was costing his overstretched budget. He sighed. 'No, a written summary's fine.'

She dipped her head. He could see she was struggling. Had she been close to Marlow? He had no idea. This whole thing was a grade-A fuck up. But he was certain of one thing: he wasn't about to carry the can.

He reached out to pat her arm, felt her body stiffen, retreated into a perfunctory smile. 'I realize this isn't easy Sergeant, but ... we'll nail him. Don't you worry about that.'

Armstrong watched him trudge back to his car. She didn't know why he'd come. Maybe it was guilt; she supposed it was possible that behind the slick facade there lurked a conscience. As a rule the boss didn't concern himself with actual detective work – he delegated. Armstrong had never had that much direct contact with him outside of team briefings and her gut feeling was that she wanted it to stay that way.

Turnbull allowed his shoulders to sink into the leather upholstery of his chauffeured BMW as he considered the potential fallout from Marlow's death. Could he be accused of recklessness in placing an officer so close to a villain like Joey Phelps? There'd be an internal inquiry of course, but that was window dressing, he'd weather that. Undercover work was a dirty little secret and it was in everyone's interests it remained that way.

The one thing Turnbull didn't doubt was that Phelps had murdered his officer. Knowing Phelps it would've been a brutal end but it didn't do to dwell on that. DS Marlow had volunteered for the job. He'd been well trained, seemed tough enough. Turnbull tried to recall his first name; it was Phil, no, maybe it was Alex.

He stared at his BlackBerry, then tapped out a quick memo to his PA: make sure the DNA gets fast-tracked, set up a meeting with Marlow's family. It was important he do this right, break the news himself. They'd want details, which of course they couldn't have. He'd try to placate them with a speedy post-mortem and an offer of help with the funeral costs. He paused. He could put Marlow up for a medal, but then one of the broadsheets might start digging. That wouldn't please the Assistant Commissioner and keeping her onside was essential.

Turnbull gazed out of the window; on an open stretch of dual carriageway the car was cruising at speed before hitting London traffic. A small, private smile crept over his features. This was also an opportunity he could never have foreseen. He was sorry Marlow was dead, obviously he was. Still, it opened things up, put the Phelps inquiry on a whole new plane. Turnbull knew it was his moment but did he have the balls? *Carpe diem*, a Latin tag from school, flitted through his mind. He'd hated that place, being a poor kid in a rich kids' school. But the bitter memory galvanized him. He speed-dialled his office. His PA answered on the second ring. He didn't bother with any preamble.

'Who's that new DC . . . the pretty one?'

'You mean DC Forbes, sir?'

'No no, not her, the lad. Dark curly hair, looks a bit like a male model.'

'Oh, you mean DC Bradley.'

'Bradley! That's him. I want to see him as soon as I get back. And find out exactly when Karen Phelps is due for release. Ring the prison governor, say we want a delay so we can interview her again.'

3

It was over six years since Kaz had travelled on the tube. She'd been given a rail pass for the journey down to Euston but now she was on her own. She stood in front of the ticket machine like a tourist. The queue behind her was getting restive. People somehow seemed different, impatient, aggressive. The city was full of foreigners and snatches of languages she couldn't begin to fathom. Behind her some Slavic-looking type was jabbering away to her mate; as Kaz continued to dither, the woman glanced at her with contempt, asked if she planned to buy a ticket any time soon. Kaz turned. Inside she wouldn't have taken that kind of lip, she wouldn't have had to. She fixed the woman with a glacial stare.

'In a hurry are you?'

The woman caught her steely look, glanced nervously at her friend. Kaz smiled.

'Only I been in the nick. Armed robbery and GBH. They just let me out. Can't remember how you work these things. Maybe you could help me?'

Kaz had their attention now, she had the attention of the whole queue. The two women backed away, mumbling something in Bulgarian. A tall, sleek black dude behind them grinned to himself.

'You touch the screen, love. Don't matter where. Then it brings up your choices.'

Kaz followed his instructions. A list of options flashed up before her.

'Blimey, bit full on innit?'

The black dude looked her up and down. Tall for a woman, slender but with no hint of fragility; you could tell she worked out. The hair was thick, silky brown, grazing her collar. But what struck him most were the eyes, dark and watchful. She was fit and then some. He toyed with getting her number, but he was in enough trouble already with his old lady. He smiled wistfully.

'I had the same problem when I got out. Spent the first month feeling like a fucking Martian.'

Kaz selected a travel card, fed in the coins, collected her ticket and gave him an appreciative nod.

'Cheers mate.'

'You take it easy, eh.'

Their eyes met. She knew exactly what he meant. She wanted more than anything to take it easy, if only people would let her.

Kaz emerged from St Paul's tube station and consulted the scrap of paper in her hand. The offices of Crowley Sheridan Moore occupied a whole floor of a refurbished sixties block off Cheapside. Metal-framed windows and plastic cladding had been ripped away to be replaced with wall to ceiling smoked glass. The lobby was now a double-height atrium with what looked to be a full-sized palm tree in the middle. She gave her name at the desk and a chirpy receptionist suggested she wait in the coffee shop. Someone would be down to collect her.

Kaz skirted round the tree and wandered into the coffee franchise. Several earnest-looking suits sat at separate tables busy with their laptops. A boy with broken English and 'barista' on his T-shirt served her. She ended up with a huge corrugated cardboard cup of coffee and foam and not much change from a fiver. Inside, coffee came in white Styrofoam cups and tasted stewed and bitter. What she held in her hand now was three times the size, a sculpted artefact. She set it down on a table and was about to take out her sketchbook to draw it when she saw Helen Warner sailing towards her through the security scanners.

Dark tailored jacket, pencil skirt. Kaz had never seen her wear anything else. But today the shirt was dove-grey, reflecting her eyes. Helen grinned broadly, threw out her hands, palms upwards, as she clipped across the floor towards Kaz.

'Karen, this is a surprise. When I phoned the governor's office, they said your release had been delayed until tomorrow.'

Kaz shrugged and smiled. She'd waited too long for this moment. Now it felt really weird, finally being on the outside, no one watching every move, listening to every word, meeting in a coffee shop like anyone else. It floored her. She thought Helen was about to hug her, so she stepped back then immediately regretted it. They faced each other awkwardly. Helen took charge.

'Typical prison service. Right hand doesn't know what the left hand's doing. But hey, you're out! That's the important thing. Can I get you another coffee?'

'Nah, this one's big as a bucket. Hope you don't mind me just turning up. I sort of, I dunno, I came to say thank you . . .'

Kaz could feel her colour rising even as she tried to laugh off her embarrassment.

'Fuck, I had this all planned out! Proper little speech. I probably shouldn't have come.'

Helen shook her head and smiled.

'Don't be silly. It's great to see you.' She glanced around.

'Quite a change of scene, odd for both of us. Come up to the office and we can have a chat.'

Helen brushed Kaz's shoulder with the tips of her manicured nails and steered her towards the lift.

It was more than five years now since the elegant Ms Warner had strolled into the visitors' pen at Styal and informed Kaz that Fred Sheridan, the Phelps's family brief since the dawn of time, had succumbed to a heart attack and died. Helen introduced herself as a newly qualified solicitor in Fred's firm and explained she was now Kaz's legal representative.

At the time Kaz was puzzled. How did a posh bird like Helen Warner end up working for a renowned villain's brief, money launderer and rogue like Fred Sheridan? But she didn't ask. She didn't talk much back then. Little more than a kid, on remand, but with the prospect of serious time to do, she scored all the gear she could get and let the rest wash over her. Still, from the outset she was mesmerized by Helen.

As they stood side by side in the mirrored lift, with half a dozen others, Helen glanced at her and smiled.

'No family reception committee then?'

'Didn't tell them.'

Helen nodded. The lift doors opened at the fifth floor. 'Probably wise.'

From their earliest days Helen had trodden a fine line, never directly critical of the Phelps clan, yet always encouraging Kaz to look at her loyalty to the family. For the first year of her sentence Kaz refused to cooperate with the prison authorities in any way. She was hard then, rock-obstinate like her old man. She wouldn't talk about the robbery; an appeal failed because she refused to drop Joey in it, even though he was the one who'd given the cashier a murderous kicking. If he'd taken the GBH rap instead of her, her sentence would've been halved.

And Joey was barely seventeen at the time. A couple of years in a young offenders' unit. For him, it would've been a doss. But Kaz kept her mouth shut.

With infinite patience Helen finally coaxed Kaz into revealing why. In the first place it never occurred to her not to. She was the one who got nicked, that was just bad luck. But to have told the filth the truth, pointed the finger at her own brother, it was simply unthinkable. Everyone would've turned their backs. The old man himself would've been shamed into doing something about it.

At this point Helen had laughed; surely even a gangster like Terry Phelps wouldn't harm his own daughter. Kaz, still hollow-eyed then on prison crack, shook her head. They lived on different planets, her and her posh new brief. Kaz knew only too well what it felt like to have the old man's calloused paw leave a bruising imprint on her throat. And when he had plenty of whisky inside him, he had enough rage to kill anyone. At the age of five, through a chink in the door, she had seen with her own eyes what Terry did to her cousin Val. Val went on a date with a local plod who fancied her, drank a bit too much, talked a bit too much. Kaz's mum later explained that Val had gone away, to live abroad. They wouldn't be seeing her again.

Little by little Kaz began to trust Helen. The lawyer's visits continued and Kaz simply assumed she was coming every few weeks because the old man paid her to do so. Helen, by this time, had an agenda of her own; Kaz was her special project, her experiment. The girl had a razor-sharp brain if she could get clean for long enough to start using it. In the second year of her incarceration Helen persuaded Kaz to try out an art class. Kaz habitually and restlessly scrawled patterns with her finger in the spilt tea on tabletops, doodled in the margins of any form she had to fill in. Helen wondered what would happen if someone put proper drawing materials in her hands. The result had surprised everyone.

Helen shepherded her client into the office, a spacious glass-walled box. The desk was large but overloaded: neat piles of papers and a stack of files on either end. After six years in a prison cell, where they could spy on you any moment of the night or day, Kaz couldn't understand why anyone would choose to work in a goldfish bowl. But Helen seemed comfortable wherever she was. She removed a briefcase from the leather sofa and invited Kaz to sit.

'So you haven't been to the hostel yet?'

'Came straight here.'

'Well, I think you're going to like it. Of all the places they could've allocated you, I happen to know this one is five star. The Ritz of APs.'

Kaz smiled. Now she was relaxing, her eyes darting around, taking in every detail of her new environment. Helen watched, trying to ignore the tension in her lower abdomen as she noticed yet again how beautiful her client had become. The junkie that Helen first encountered had been painfully thin, avoided eye contact; a broken, hunted creature. The young woman in front of her now couldn't be more different. Athletic, alert, with a quiet confidence.

'Yeah, okay, I know you wangled me a good place. And I'm grateful for that too.'

Helen brushed this off. 'Down to your offender manager, not me.'

Kaz's gaze had come to rest on Helen's face and it was unnerving. Helen realized that her feelings, which she always kept carefully under wraps, were in danger of spiralling out of control. She glanced at her desk, grabbed the nearest file and opened it.

When Kaz was inside it had all been so simple. The formal structures of prison visiting had dictated the nature of every encounter. They also helped Helen avoid asking herself why, in a busy schedule when there was really no reason, she took time out to trek all the way up to Cheshire to visit this particular client. Now she was thrown off balance, she could feel her cheeks reddening; Jesus Christ, she was reacting like a bloody lovesick teenager, she needed to get a grip!

Kaz continued to look, mentally sketching her face, though truth be told she could draw Helen in her sleep. But the lawyer was resolutely avoiding her eye. Pulling another file from halfway down the neat pile, Helen sent the whole lot tottering.

'Oh honestly. The workload they expect you to carry in this place, it's bloody ridiculous!'

Kaz watched Helen struggle. She wanted to reach out, touch her hand; the sexual frisson zapping between them was unmistakable. But she held back.

'I'm taking up your time, I'm sorry. Shouldn't have come.'

'No no!' Helen flapped her hands about as if to bat away the uncomfortable feelings. 'Now tell me about college. When do you start?'

'Not 'til the autumn. That's if I get my grades.'

'Oh you'll walk it.'

'The art maybe, not so sure about the English and Maths.'

Helen gave her a confident smile, the blush in her cheeks subsiding. 'Karen, you'll get in.'

Now Kaz was the one having problems meeting Helen's eye. She started to pick at the loose sole of her trainer.

'Well, we'll see. Anyway I'm gonna do some courses over the summer, mainly drawing, get me up to speed.'

Helen nodded. She folded her hands neatly in her lap, took a deep breath. 'That's excellent.'

The excitement of Kaz's release had got the better of her, that was all. Now she was retreating behind the professional facade. Karen Phelps was just another client. Okay – her first real success story. Still, that was no excuse. Of course she was fond of the girl, and Kaz was grateful to her. But the boundaries between them had to remain clear.

Kaz continued to pick at her shabby trainers, they were coming apart, a small private smile crept across her features. Helen's reaction was telling her everything she needed to know. Inside, every meeting had been freighted with tension and longing. That was the nature of jail time, it distorted relationships, made equality impossible. Getting close to serious felons, that in itself could be a potent drug and Kaz had seen plenty of counsellors, volunteers, do-gooders and even screws who were hooked on the power, turned on by the sexual buzz of helping needy women and basking in their desperate adoration. But what had happened between her and Helen, Kaz knew that had to be different.

Getting clean was the most frightening thing Kaz had ever done. Stripping away the layers of protection had left her raw and exposed. She knew she'd never have set out on such a parlous course if it hadn't been for her desire to impress Helen, to retain her interest, keep her coming back. Every therapy group she attended was just a sideshow for the main event: reporting her progress to Helen.

In spite of the drugs Kaz had always been quick; whatever situation she found herself in, she soon figured out how to play it to her advantage. In the Phelps family, manipulation was the key to survival. Art classes, the gym, she poured her energy into whatever project Helen suggested to her. Then an odd thing happened. She found she was really enjoying doing all this stuff. She found she was hooked. And when she told the lawyer this, she could see from Helen's triumphant expression she'd hit pay dirt. From then on she morphed into the model prisoner. But really it was all about pleasing Helen.

Helen gathered up the papers from the spilt files and put them in order. She gave Kaz her standard professional smile; it was sympathetic but also detached, she'd spent years perfecting it.

'And what about the family?'

Kaz sighed.

'Come on Helen, we been through all this. I know Joey's into all kinds of villainy, but that's not my concern. I'm staying right out of it. I want my life back. I done my time, I'm going to college.'

Helen smiled. Yes, things were back under control, she could relax a bit.

'Have you met the new probation officer yet?'

'I got an appointment Thursday.'

'You understand the terms of the licence?'

Kaz gave her an irritated look. 'Well yeah, 'course I do. Behave or you're back in the nick.'

'There'll be random drug-testing at the hostel. The curfew's ten o'clock. But once the senior PO gets to know you I'm sure there'll be room for negotiation.'

Kaz cocked her head, a mischievous glint in her eye.

'Why? You gonna take me to the theatre?'

Helen looked puzzled. 'The theatre?'

'You don't remember? Few years back, I told you I'd never been to the theatre. You said when I got out, you'd take me.'

Helen gave her a wry smile. She rearranged her body in the chair, but still felt absurdly self-conscious.

'Well, we could always see a matinee.'

'Is that a date?'

Helen was used to fencing, the cut and thrust of legal repartee. But this wrong-footed her.

'I'd be happy to take you to the theatre. But let's be clear; I'm your lawyer. This is a professional relationship. Technically you're still serving your sentence, although you've been released on licence.'

Kaz huffed. 'Lighten up. I was only teasing. You don't have to hide behind the lawyer crap.'

'It's not crap.'

Helen's tone was far sharper than she'd intended. It found its mark. Kaz jumped to her feet.

'Okay, look, this was a bad idea. I shouldn't have come . . .'

'I'm not hiding. All I'm saying is we have rules for a reason . . .'

Their eyes met, but Helen looked away. She raked her fingers through her hundred and fifty pound haircut. Even in her sharp suit surrounded by all the trappings of the legal profession she had the look of a confused teenager. Kaz could see she was floundering and her anger evaporated. She loved this woman, there was no question of that and no other word for it. What had she expected though, Helen to jump her there and then on the office sofa? Kaz shook her head and laughed.

'This is mental. I didn't come here to upset you. What I wanted was to give you this.'

She pulled a large envelope out of her holdall and offered it to Helen.

'Go on, open it.'

The envelope contained a small pen-and-ink sketch of a woman, a back view of naked shoulders and tumbling hair. The drawing was elegant, the lines delicate with enough detail, but not too much. Helen gazed at it in amazement.

'It's beautiful. Thank you.'

'Just something I copied from a magazine photo. Anyway, you're busy, I can see that. Stuff to do. So I really should go and check out this hostel.'

Wrong-footed yet again, Helen started to get up.

'Oh, okay . . . but—'

Kaz hoisted the holdall on to her shoulder and was already halfway out the door.

'Don't worry. I'll find my own way out.'

Helen stared at her awkwardly, unthinkable scenarios cascading through her head.

'Well . . . if you need—'

Kaz flashed a smile at her. 'Yeah, I'll give you a call.'

Kaz strode through the outer office towards the lifts, a satisfied smile on her face. She didn't look back; she didn't have to. She knew Helen Warner was watching her.

4

Turnbull clicked his BlackBerry on, scrolled through the inbox. Checking texts, emails, any time he had a spare moment, this is what he did. He needed to keep abreast of things, that's what he told his wife. She told him it was an annoying habit.

Across the desk from him DC Mal Bradley had his head bent over the file he was attempting to speed-read. Turnbull studied him; his jacket was cheap and creased, his hair a mop of dark curls. But, as the father of three teenage daughters, Turnbull reckoned he had a shrewd idea of what young women went for and Bradley ticked all the boxes.

The young DC closed the file and looked up.

'She's quite a piece of work, sir.'

Turnbull smiled, slipped the BlackBerry back in his pocket.

'She's a candidate for sainthood compared with her little brother.'

Turnbull let his gaze rest on Bradley. The HR file displayed on his laptop made impressive reading: a 2:1 in Psychology, good evaluations throughout his training, plus he'd done the six-week basic for undercover work. But crucially he had the looks. He could be exactly what Turnbull needed.

'Ever work undercover Bradley?'

'Covert surveillance sir, but not the real thing, no.'

Turnbull allowed himself a rueful smile. The real thing? He wondered if Marlow would've called it that.

'I expect you've heard what happened to DS Marlow.'

Bradley nodded. Their eyes met. Turnbull scanned his face. What was he looking for? Nervousness? A hint of anxiety? He didn't find it. Bradley's gaze remained calm, respectful but not deferential. His body language was open and relaxed. Turnbull might be his superior officer, but Bradley's feeling was they were equals. Turnbull registered all this with pursed lips. Then he went on.

'He was a good officer. Very experienced in undercover work. You ever meet him?'

'No sir.'

'He spent nearly six months on this case, got pretty close to Joey Phelps.'

'How was his cover blown?'

'That we don't know. Unfortunately. We do know our target is a very dangerous individual. Which is why we're changing tack.'

Bradley inclined his head thoughtfully. 'Focusing on the sister?'

'She'll be your chiz.'

'Inform against her brother? Has she agreed?'

'No.' Turnbull rested his eyes on the young officer. 'But I'm hoping you'll find a way to persuade her.'

Bradley rubbed his chin as he absorbed this. He seemed slightly disappointed.

'Oh. I presumed I was about to become Joey Phelps's new best friend.'

'The Assistant Commissioner regards that as too risky. And I agree. That's why she's come up with this new strategy.'

Strictly speaking only the first part of this statement was true. The new approach was to use Bradley and that was entirely Turnbull's idea. What the Assistant Commissioner had in mind was a spot of political blackmail and she was relying on Turnbull to back her up by delivering Phelps. It was up to him how he achieved it.

A hint of a smile crossed Turnbull's lips; working for a woman boss wasn't all bad. He'd learnt a lot from Fiona Calder; in terms of the Met she was a consummate player. Her plan was simple: Marlow would be put up for the Queen's Gallantry Medal and as his proud but tearful parents received it, she would give an off-the-record briefing to selected media about the dangerous escalation in organized crime in London. She would blame the severe budget cuts imposed by the government. Blogs and editorials would follow; politicians on the law-and-order bandwagon would pitch in. Then as the media shit-storm gathered force, she'd extract a promise of extra funding from the Deputy Mayor for Policing and Crime. Marcus Foxley was a political creature, tooth and claw, but Calder knew how to twist his tail.

For Foxley the deal was a no-brainer: if he loosened the purse strings he'd get to share credit for the high-profile arrest of cop killer and drug baron Joey Phelps. But Calder's real aim was to prove publicly that when they were given the resources the Met could still do the job better than anyone, certainly better than any private security outfit. The Assistant Commissioner put a time frame of three or four months on the whole operation.

Turnbull couldn't help admiring the breadth of her vision. She thought like a politician not a copper and this was her pitch for the top job. She planned to be the first woman commissioner. Turnbull knew it was his opportunity too and that's what Calder was relying on. If he gave her Phelps he'd get to ride on her coat-tails, maybe become an assistant commissioner himself.

Turnbull considered the prospect. He was forty-eight; in a twenty-five-year career his record was outstanding, he'd put some nasty villains away. But what did he have to show for it? The QPM, a five-bedroomed house in Surrey, heavily mortgaged, and a couple of ISAs. In the scheme of things it was peanuts.

Turnbull scrutinized Mal Bradley. He reeked of inexperience. The education gave him a veneer of confidence, arrogance even. And it helped that the pressure was on. Turnbull's team had been after Phelps for months, but they'd been biding their time, giving Marlow a chance to get bedded in. Now all that was down the drain, tempers were fraying, the drive was to nail Marlow's killer. The question was, could Bradley deliver? On paper he was clever enough, but that counted for little out on the street.

Bradley gave a diffident smile. 'I can see that targeting the sister is certainly the sensible approach. But – hope you don't mind me saying this sir – if she's been in prison for six years, is she going to be close enough to her brother now to give us anything useful?'

Turnbull swivelled his high-backed desk chair to face Bradley. He smiled. He liked the fact the lad was a bit gung-ho, but was it just to impress?

'Point taken. But before he died DS Marlow was able to provide us with a lot of very useful intelligence about Phelps and his operation. And the first thing to understand is that Joey Phelps isn't just another thug. He's a thug with a brain. So I agree with the Assistant Commissioner. Phelps knows we're after him. Someone new turns up now, however plausible, he'll spot it a mile off. And I don't want to be fishing any more of my officers out of the river.'

Bradley nodded, but he knew he'd only have one shot at impressing Turnbull, so he ploughed on.

'Is Joey Phelps really that smart? Isn't it just that he's very violent?'

Turnbull reached across the desk and tapped the file in front of Bradley with his index finger. 'You need to study the rest of this. The family history. Terry Phelps grew up in the Bermondsey triangle, started out as an unlicensed boxer – Reggie Kray sponsored him for a while. He graduated to armed robbery, ended up inside. Came out in the mid-eighties and found the world had changed. So he shipped the family out to Essex and set up in the drugs business. Him and his nephew Sean Phelps ran a security outfit; Southend, Basildon, as far north as Chelmsford, they ran the doors on any club of any size. They supplied Ecstasy and cocaine.'

'I think I've read about Sean Phelps somewhere. Mid-nineties, drive-by shooting of a police officer? Witnesses changed their testimony because of intimidation?'

Turnbull sighed. 'That's been lying on file ever since. He finally went down in 1997, got life with a tariff of twelve for beating a rival dealer to death in a pub brawl. Parole Board have knocked him back twice, he's probably hoping third time he'll be lucky. But the important point in all this is that Terry Phelps was a small-time villain, he stuck to his Essex patch. Couple of years ago his son takes over and turns this small family firm into something far more ambitious.'

'How's he expanded so quickly?'

'Same as any businessman really. Takeover bids. He's rolled over every rival firm of any size in Essex, now he's moving into the East End.'

'Where's he get the muscle to do something like that?'

'Another tried-and-tested business strategy: outsourcing. He picks a local gang, usually young, hungry, desperate to move up. He's got plenty to choose from. He tools them up, gets them to clear a patch of territory in return for distribution rights.'

Bradley shook his head sceptically. 'I can think of a few London firms, like the Turks and some of the eastern Europeans, who'd start World War Three before they'd roll over.'

'So far he's been clever about picking his targets. Hasn't tried it on with anyone too nasty. But the real ace up his sleeve is supply. Everything he sells is top-quality product. He's become known for it. And his prices are reasonable. He's put reputation before instant profit. Very canny operator.'

'Sounds like you almost admire him sir.'

'No. No, I don't. He's also a cold-blooded killer. I just don't underestimate him and I don't want you to either.'

Bradley nodded. So they were back to Karen Phelps. He knew why it was him sitting there, not a more experienced officer. It didn't take a genius to figure out Turnbull's plan. Ever since he was a boy Bradley had been forced to accept that what people saw first were his looks. And he hated it. He had his Iranian mother to thank. Large liquid brown eyes, ridiculously long lashes. Even two days' stubble on his chin served to accentuate the cheekbones, the completely symmetrical features, the square jaw.

At school he'd been miserable. While the girls giggled and fawned over him, other lads were always wary. He'd tried to be sporty and tough, but on the rugby pitch he was the one targeted for a kicking. Was it racism because he was half Persian? Or did he unwittingly set off some kind of homoerotic vibe that scared other men? Even though he dressed down and walked around with a perpetual scowl, gay guys and women flocked to him. But other men generally kept their distance. And it was these men he wanted to impress. He knew that the only way to succeed in this world was to make sure other blokes took you seriously.

Being taken seriously was the reason Bradley had joined the police. He had lofty ambitions: to work undercover in counter-terrorism. He could pass for Arab, he was taking lessons to improve his Persian. The last thing he wanted was to get side-tracked into this sort of nonsense.

Turnbull gave the young officer a speculative look; he was maintaining a very proper facade, but underneath there was something niggling him and that bothered Turnbull. He took out his BlackBerry, turned it over in his hand like a talisman, then placed it carefully on the desk and leant forward.

'I'll be honest with you Bradley. I simply don't have the budget to mount a major surveillance operation on Joey Phelps for months on end. So we have to use our wits and ingenuity. We have to busk it.' He shook his head wearily. 'Nowadays a lot of policing involves that. You want to get ahead, you need to know that. Do you want to get ahead?'

'Absolutely sir. I've already passed my sergeant's exams.'

Turnbull glanced at the screen of his laptop.

'I can see that. On paper you look great. But, y'know, what I'm asking here . . .' Turnbull sighed, let his gaze drift as he pondered. 'No what I'm looking for is someone who thinks outside the box. There aren't any courses or exams for this. This is policing at the sharp end. Not many officers are up for it. You can say no . . .'

Turnbull let that statement hang in the air. He picked up his phone, clicked it on to check his messages.

To Bradley this change in attitude seemed abrupt. Was Turnbull signalling that the meeting was over? Bradley didn't know what to do. It suddenly felt as if he'd blown it and the opportunity was slipping away. He straightened up in his chair. Turnbull was tapping out a text with both thumbs. Bradley leant forward. 'I can think outside the box sir.'

Turnbull looked up, he gave the young officer a disinterested smile.

Bradley saw his chances fading and he panicked. 'Okay, I understand why you want to give Joey Phelps a wide berth. But, yeah, I can work on the sister. She's just out of jail, she's going to want to get out there, start living it up a bit. That's my way in I guess.'

Turnbull remained absorbed in his text. He sighed, tapped out a few more characters and pressed send. Then he let his gaze come back to Bradley. The young officer was looking decidedly anxious. Turnbull smiled to himself. A psychology degree was all very well, still the lad didn't realize he was being played. Turnbull frowned.

'You're confusing me Bradley. My impression was you had reservations. Are you saying you want to do this?'

'Absolutely. I can get close to Karen Phelps and I'll soon—'

Turnbull raised an admonitory finger, which stopped Bradley in his tracks.

'Bear in mind undercover work requires . . . delicacy. Now I don't believe in hamstringing my officers . . .'

Bradley looked surprised but he was on it straight away. Turnbull didn't have to say any more. 'Sorry sir. Just thinking out loud. I know there are boundaries. I don't want to . . . I'd never put you in an awkward position.'

The two men stared at each other for a moment. Then Turnbull smiled broadly. It had taken a while, but they'd got there. Bradley knew the score. Without Turnbull spelling it out he understood what was required to get the job done and he knew, since it was technically illegal, to keep his mouth shut about it. Turnbull leant back in his chair, placed his fingertips together, it was all looking good. He could assure the Assistant

Commissioner, keep her sweet. But more importantly his own project was launched, and anyone who thought Alan Turnbull was just another noddy cop sitting it out for his pension was in for a rude awakening.

5

At Stansted Airport, Joey Phelps was one of the first off the plane. He strode along the moving walkway to the Arrivals Hall rapidly tapping the screen of his iPhone with his thumb. In his grey silk shirt and pressed chinos he appeared in sharp contrast to the baggy Bermudas, flip-flops and hangovers being sported by most of his fellow passengers returning on the early morning flight from Ibiza. Keeping pace with Joey but two steps behind, Yevgeny, a mountain of muscle, carried two Italian leather holdalls and a slim attaché case. As Joey zigzagged through the meandering holidaymakers, his minder in tow, people turned to gawp. Well over six foot, handsome, expensively dressed; was he some famous actor or a footballer they couldn't quite put a name to?

Joey was oblivious to the ripples he caused in the crowd. The phone was now clamped to his ear.

'Yeah, Phelps. Karen Phelps. Well, is she there? Can you get her for me?' Joey tried to get a handle on his irritation. There was no point shouting at these bozos. Ashley had texted him the number of the hostel where Kaz was apparently staying. Some kind of scabby bail hostel. Why? He couldn't fathom it at all.

'Yeah right, well get her out of bed. I'll wait. Thank you.' Feeling the anger rising Joey started to count in his head. He'd read the books, sometimes it helped. He'd have postponed the trip to Ibiza if he'd known she was getting out. Then he could've taken her with him. It would've been perfect. They could've turned a business trip into a proper holiday. And it would've been a great way to ease her back into the firm.

Ibiza was one of his new operations. Mephedrone was the clubbers' current drug of choice and since the EU had helpfully made it illegal at the end of 2010, Joey had got in on the ground floor. He'd set up two labs on the island to synthesize the drug. He'd imported an old hippy chemist from Amsterdam, who used to make MDMA for his old man. Then he'd hired Yevgeny and a bunch of his mates, all former Russian soldiers who'd served in Chechnya, to handle security and discourage competitors. Joey was really proud of what he'd achieved and desperate to show it all off to his big sister. After what seemed like an age a sleepy voice came on the line.

'Joe?'

'Babe! Why didn't you tell us you was coming out? We'd've been there. The whole fucking family'd've been there!'

Kaz yawned; her first night's kip on the outside, she'd slept like a kid. Her mind was still wandering in some cosy dreamland. 'That's why I didn't tell you.'

'And what you doing staying in a fuckin' hostel?'

'It's a condition of my licence. But I got a place in one of the college halls of residence once term starts.'

'You're not going through with all this college malarkey, are you? I know you gotta give 'em the spiel, but now you're out . . . I mean, c'mon.'

Kaz stifled a yawn. 'Joey, I've told you. It's not some scam to impress the parole board. I'm doing it 'cause it's what I want.'

'Listen babes, you want it, that's good enough for me. Always has been, always will be. You know that. I know this geezer in the property business. Big warehouse conversions. Top end. He's got loads of stuff round Shoreditch, Hoxton, that way. Well, that's where all the artists and fartists live, innit. I'll get him to find something special for you.'

Standing in the hallway in pyjama bottoms and a vest, Kaz was jiggling from one bare foot to the other, trying to escape the chill of the tiled floor. 'What's the time for chrissake?'

'I dunno. Nine-ish. Trust me Kaz, he's a posh City boy, educated 'n'all that. He's got a good eye. It'll be really nice. You can talk to him yourself, fit it out how you want.'

'Okay, just listen will yer . . .'

'You wanna go to college, study, good luck to you, I say. Proper learning, that's one thing. But who in their right mind wants to live like a scabby bloody student? 'Specially when you don't have to.'

Kaz was shivering, she'd been dragged out of bed, still she couldn't help smiling wryly to herself. Joey's energy, his boyish impetuosity was like a steamroller. His enthusiasm simply flattened everything in its path. She could hear him sigh down the phone as he changed tack.

'All right, look, we can talk about this later. I'm coming to pick you up and we're gonna celebrate, my girl. So get yerself tarted up 'cause I ain't taking no for an answer.'

He checked his watch as he stepped out of the main terminal building. Ashley was waiting at the kerb in a black Range Rover Evoque. Yevgeny loaded the bags in the back as Joey climbed in the passenger seat.

'I'll be there in an hour, tops.'

Kaz set the phone on its battered cradle. She'd been a free woman for little more than twenty-four hours, but already it was beginning as she knew it would. She thought of Yasmin; for her, prison was a sanctuary, the only escape from a series of men who'd used and abused her. But Kaz was tougher than that. At least she hoped she was.

Her room was at the rear of the hostel overlooking the garden. It had been decorated to be cheerful. The walls were primrose with matching curtains in a lively abstract print. The small wardrobe, stack of drawers and bed were simple but well-constructed in bleached pine. It wasn't much bigger than the average prison cell, but the window opened and the toilet was down the hall, not a smelly stainless steel pan in the corner.

Kaz wandered back into the room and slipped under the plump duvet. As she pulled it up to her chin she smiled to herself. Helen was right about this place. Five stars definitely. She thought about Helen and the fantasies she'd had about her over the years. The age gap between them was probably only five or six years, but it had felt much bigger. Now she was out, Kaz could finally allow herself to wonder what might come next.

Inside she'd had relationships, although she wasn't sure she'd call them that. What they amounted to mainly was sex. But none of it ever conflicted with her feelings for Helen. Her passion for Helen was totally private, she never spoke of it to anyone. She couldn't. Being with women on the inside was how it went. But on the outside? She'd never thought much about whether she was a lesbian. Anyway it was all just labels. There'd been boys before, when she'd managed to escape the old man's oppressive orbit. And she assumed there'd be boys again. But also there was Helen, and for now that's all she could dream about.

She was dozing; warm, floating. She knew she should get up, but she couldn't be arsed. For six years she'd been forced out of bed every morning at seven. Fifteen minutes to wash and dress before the cell doors clanged open and you were marched down to breakfast. She was reflecting on the small things that freedom came down to when there was a polite tap at the door. She didn't have a watch but it seemed unlikely that an hour had passed since she talked to Joey on the phone. Puzzled, she flung back the duvet, stepped over to the door and opened it.

'Hiya. I'm Mal.'

He was probably about her own age, hands pushed in his jeans pockets, shoulders hunched, trying to look appealing.

'And?'

'I'm one of the support workers. Saw you in the hall on the phone. Wondered how you're settling in.'

'Look, I filled in all the forms last night, ticked all the boxes, pissed in a pot.'

He chuckled, which erased the crease between his eyebrows. Then he pulled his hands out of his pockets, straightened up and gave her a dazzling smile. 'Well, I'm not going to ask you to piss in any more pots this morning.'

'Good. I'm glad about that.'

Kaz allowed the smile to wash over her. With it he was unnervingly gorgeous. He had dark curly hair, looked vaguely foreign, but there was something else, another element and it didn't quite click. Inside Kaz had encountered a parade of professional helpers, they all had different titles and functions: offender manager, offender supervisor, probation officer, therapist. But to Kaz they all belonged to the same breed, 'the social', and you could spot them a mile off.

She scanned her visitor, he could be a support worker, his clothes were scruffy enough and he had that middle class, bleeding-heart air. But something was off-kilter and experience made her wary. She returned his smile. 'As you can see, I just woke up.'

'Yeah, well, y'know. I only wanted to introduce myself, touch base.'

She was aware of his eyes roving over her body, but not like your average perve. He seemed to be doing it more as an exercise, signalling that he fancied her. Then the penny dropped. Kaz gave him a sardonic grin.

'And how is Woodentop?'

'Sorry?'

'Detective Chief Superintendent Woodentop. I presume you're one of his boys.'

Bradley put his head on one side and sighed; he hadn't expected to be rumbled quite so fast. He thought about lying, but decided it was futile. 'They said you were bright.'

'Could be you're just crap.'

He smiled weakly. Of course she was right. He stood there, his cheeks reddening, his career as an undercover cop over before it'd begun. He blamed Turnbull for pimping him out this way. But mainly he blamed himself for agreeing. Kaz continued to stare at him, her expression unreadable. She probably thought he was a complete moron. He was a complete moron. He sighed deeply.

'Look . . . maybe we could . . . have a chat?'

'A chat?'

'Yeah, I could . . . buy you a coffee if you like. There's a place down the road.'

Kaz started to laugh. Was this really the best they could do? He was handsome in a sappy sort of way. But did they seriously think she'd fall for this? Still chuckling, she shook her head. 'Okay, this is the spiel I gave Woodentop when he came to visit me inside. Now I'll give it you. I'm stuck with my family, love 'em or hate 'em, just like you're stuck with yours. But I have no involvement any more and no intention of being involved in . . . what shall we call it, the family business.'

'We accept that.'

'Good. 'Cause I just wanna go to college and get on with my life. I don't plan on breaking no laws.'

Kaz's response provided Bradley with a few vital seconds to gather his wits. He decided to stop playing nice and go back to being a copper. 'You really think Joey's going to let you do that?'

Kaz cocked her head. Now he was being snotty and that didn't amuse her. 'Listen . . . Malcolm,' she spat the name at him, making it sound like an insult.

He jutted his chin. 'Actually it's Malik, not Malcolm. My mum's Persian.'

'So? I don't care if you just rode up on a fucking camel.'

'I was born in Basingstoke. Not a lot of camels down that way.'

'Whatever. You know fuck all about me or my brother.'

'I can give you a ballpark estimate of the number of people he's suspected of murdering or having murdered in the last three years.'

Kaz thought about slamming the door in his face. She knew what bastards they could be, now here was the proof. 'Yeah? Well I was in the nick, so I had nothing to do with it.'

'I've been reading your file quite carefully. The psychiatric evaluations – you're not like him Karen. He's a cold-blooded killer. And you don't have to cover up for him any more.'

Kaz folded her arms tightly across her chest; she knew he was lying, it was typical, they'd make up anything about anyone. But she wasn't about to let him push her buttons, she was determined to front this out.

'So why'd he pick you, eh? The prettiest boy in the office? I'm gonna shag you and tell all? Is that Woodentop's plan?'

Bradley had the grace to blush, he couldn't help it.

Kaz shook her head. 'What a bunch of tossers!'

Bradley sighed, this was going nowhere, it was a complete balls-up. He gave a diffident shrug. 'You're right, this is bollocks. Truth is the hats at the Yard don't give a monkey's whether you go straight or not. And Woodentop's not going to go away. They'll hound you Karen.'

'Tell me something I don't know.'

'But there is a way out of this.'

'Yeah? And, what, you're my fairy godfather?'

The door to the next room opened and a young African girl came out, she gave them a nervous smile.

Bradley's eyes didn't leave Kaz's face. 'Let me come in for a minute. Listen to the deal I'm offering. If it's not fair, then I'm on my way.'

Kaz glanced at her neighbour; they'd exchanged a few pleasantries the previous evening. Kaz gave her a nod. 'You all right?'

The girl was frightened and needy and too young to cope with all the trouble she'd landed in. But Kaz didn't want to adopt her, she'd been through plenty of that inside. So she turned to Bradley. 'You got two minutes. Clock's ticking.'

Bradley nodded and followed her into the room. He moved immediately over to the window, making sure to give her plenty of space. Kaz felt exposed in her skimpy vest and pyjama bottoms, but she wasn't letting him know that. She put her hands on her hips.

'Okay, let's hear the pitch.'

Bradley took a deep breath. 'Any information you pass to me is in the strictest confidence.'

Kaz spluttered at the hilarity of this.

'Karen, the CPS are not going to want to put you, a convicted felon, in the witness box. So that makes the whole thing simple. You tell me what's going down and when, the heavy mob arrive and nick them red-handed. No one ever need know of your involvement. You're my anonymous informant. I'll never reveal your identity.'

Kaz raised her eyebrows in disbelief.

'Is that it?'

'How you financing your belated education? Student loan? Believe me, that doesn't go far.'

'I'll get a part-time job.'

'You'll be lucky. Even shit jobs there are dozens of applicants for every vacancy. And you're an ex-con. Going straight is going to be harder than you think.'

Kaz gave him a baleful look. 'You don't say.'

He smiled like a magician about to pull a rabbit out of the hat. 'You'll manage much better with a totally legitimate monthly sub from the Metropolitan Police. We have a special fund for informants.'

Kaz shook her head. 'I'll bet you do.'

Bradley puffed his cheeks. He had that young male arrogance, like Joey in many ways. 'So? What d'you reckon? If you really want to go straight, go to college, this is the deal. It's a no brainer.'

Kaz had to smile, she couldn't help it. 'Don't take this too personally Malik, but there'll only ever be one answer: fuck off.'

He ruminated on this for a moment. 'Is that fuck off maybe or fuck off definitely?'

Kaz laughed, this was getting surreal. 'Even if I did fancy dobbing my own brother in, don't you think he, or some of his mates, might put two and two together? I know they haven't got your schooling Mal, no posh degrees, but they ain't daft.'

'We can protect you.'

'Yeah right.'

Kaz held out her hand to shake. She realized that the years inside had changed her. Sparring with cops now brought her a kind of wry amusement. She could see straight through him and out the other side. This relaxed her, made her feel confident. The anger had long since evaporated.

'Very nice meeting you PC Malik. Now if you don't fuck off definitely and conclusively I'll set my lawyer on you. She's a bit of an anarchist at heart, loves having a pop at the old bill. But Woodentop already knows that.'

Bradley took her proffered hand. His look was steady, the handshake firm with a gentle squeeze. She felt his palm soft and dry. He hooked into her gaze, treated her to the smile again. 'I'll see you around Kaz.'

Kaz stood at the door smiling to herself as he set off down the hall. He turned to give her a nod as Joey came bounding up the stairs towards him two at a time. Joey stopped, allowing Bradley to slip past. Then he paused at the sight of Kaz in her doorway. He didn't say anything but walked down the hall grinning like an idiot, arms wide open. Kaz had no choice but to be hoisted off her feet in a brotherly hug. Though he'd visited her regularly in prison the reality, the hard-muscled solidity of him, was a shock. Younger he might be, but there was nothing little about him any more. He held her at arm's length, tilted his head to one side, fixed her with those piercing blue eyes.

'Who's the fella then?'

Kaz didn't miss a beat. 'Social. Works here. He was just . . . well, y'know, seeing if there was anything I needed.'

Joey considered this for a moment then tipped back his head and howled with laughter.

'You slapper! You naughty naughty girl! Only been out five minutes and already you've pulled!' Tears of laughter coursed down Joey's cheeks.

Kaz smiled. 'Yeah. And?'

Joey turned and Kaz realized that someone had followed him up the stairs.

'Now you know where I get it from.' Still convulsed with mirth, he drew his companion forward. 'You remember Ashley.'

Kaz remembered a weedy boy with corrosive acne, who'd shadowed Joey all through school. Now she faced a smaller, shyer clone of Joey. He smiled nervously. Joey clapped him on the back.

'Actually, I brought him along in case you was in need of a quickie. Six years is a long time to be banged up with a load of dykes. He's a real studmuffin, ain't you Ash?'

Ashley reddened. Kaz gave him a sympathetic smile. 'I think I can sort myself out on that score little brother.'

Joey snorted. 'I can see that.'

Ashley, visibly relieved that he wasn't to be called upon to service the boss's sister, managed to open his mouth and speak. 'All right Kaz? Joey's been like a kid waiting for Christmas.'

Kaz gazed at her brother's beaming face. He slipped one arm round her shoulder, the other round Ashley's.

'Well boys and girls, Christmas has come early this year. I got the whole day planned. But first up we are going shopping!'

6

Nicci Armstrong had been hiding all morning. The women's toilet, the canteen, anywhere but the incident room. These avoidance tactics had nothing to do with laziness. She'd made DS in record time because she was smart and she was a grafter. The Job was her life, she loved it, which was probably why her marriage had gone down the pan. That and the fact she'd been promoted out of uniform way before Tim.

They'd met at Hendon as equals and mates and as she surged ahead her jokey, easy-going husband pretended that he preferred being a traffic cop, far more fun burning up and down the motorway. When she took time out to have Sophie he changed his tune though. He got his head down and got serious. He saw himself as provider and protector for his wife and baby and it became increasingly apparent that's how he thought it should be. He didn't want Nicci to go back to work, but she was never going to be a stay-at-home mum and that's when the rows had begun.

Nicci poured herself a strong black coffee and took it back to her desk. She clicked her phone on just to see her daughter's smiling face. Then she returned to her computer screen and tried to concentrate. She'd been hiding out to avoid having to accompany the SIO to the post-mortem currently being performed on Alex Marlow. This was a dead cop so they were going to town. The Home Office's most senior pathologist was conducting it himself. But Nicci knew what it would confirm: Alex had been bludgeoned to death, chucked in the river, and they had not a scrap of evidence to connect it to Joey Phelps.

She scrolled through the case notes. She'd been in charge of Marlow's backup and since he went off the grid two weeks ago she'd worked herself into a sleepless frenzy trying to find him. The trace on his phone hadn't been that accurate. Heavy traffic on the network caused it to ping off various masts in the vicinity of Whipps Cross Hospital. They'd done a search of the immediate area, every dumpster, wheelie bin and lock-up. They'd come up with a couple of dope dealers and a large stash of illegal cigarettes, but no sign of Alex or his phone.

When she and Tim finally split up, Alex Marlow had been her divorce buddy. He'd been friends with both of them but he took her side, which at the time felt like a moral victory. He'd listened to her rants, gone over the paperwork with her, accompanied her to the so-called mediation sessions, threatened to punch Tim's lights out on one memorable occasion and babysat Sophie. And Nicci had discovered that having a gay man in this role was perfect.

Her parents were disappointed with her; they basically agreed with Tim, she should be at home with her daughter. Her unmarried girlfriends seemed to relish her failure and the married ones gave her a wide berth in case it was catching. So bitching and drinking and clubbing with a gay bloke and his mates had got her through.

Alex didn't look or behave like anyone's idea of a homosexual. On a night out he could queen it up with the best, but the rest of the time, if he seemed to be anything, it was a copper's copper. Large, lean, gym-fit with a mordant sense of humour, he was always popular on the team. He made no secret of being gay, but he didn't advertise it either. He didn't join any organizations or carry any banners.

One of Nicci's frustrations, the question that had kept her up at night, that she was desperate to ask him, was how the fuck did he let Joey Phelps get the drop on him? He was a tough bloke, why didn't he fight back? Beat the shit out of the twisted little fucker. But in a way she already knew the answer.

Alex had jumped at the opportunity to go undercover. To the bosses he was eminently qualified, but it was probably only Nicci who knew that he had a thing for Joey Phelps. Phelps was handsome and dangerous, a fatal combination for Alex. As far as anyone knew, Joey was straight. His taste was fairly predictable: glamour models and actresses, anything fuckable that also looked good on his arm and confirmed his status. Alex never lost sight of what Joey was or the task in hand. But still there was part of him that loved hanging with the bad boys, worshipping at the shrine of testosterone-driven power. Nicci's private view, which she'd never expressed to anyone, was that Alex Marlow had fallen in love with his murderer.

Nicci sipped her coffee and scanned the office. There were few people about, leads were being followed, witnesses sought. She felt vaguely guilty; since she didn't have the stomach for the PM she herself should be out there working the case. But she was exhausted, close to breaking point and she knew it. All she wanted was to go home, hug her child and curl up on the sofa until the pain stopped.

She was staring into space, trying to pull herself together, when the new DC wandered across her eyeline. He was called Bradley and according to the DCI, he'd been asked by Turnbull to go undercover. Just the notion of this struck her like a slap in the face. It was an insult to even imagine that anyone could step into Alex Marlow's shoes. She knew this was an emotional reaction dictated by grief, but still what the fuck was some rookie DC going to achieve that Alex couldn't?

Bradley caught her eye and started to come over. He was smiling. Nicci reflected ruefully that his exotic Middle Eastern looks would probably have appealed to Alex. It had been a standing joke on the team that when a pretty new DC came along Alex would always try and take them under his wing.

Bradley seemed a tad nervous, gave her a diffident shrug. He looked like he was about to ask a question, but Nicci got up abruptly and walked away. She could feel the tears prickling her eyelids and she was damned if she was going to blub in front of anyone, least of all Bradley.

7

Kaz sat in the front seat of the Range Rover, Joey was at the wheel, Ashley tucked in the back next to various bags and boxes. They'd started out at Westfield, Joey insisted they do the posh designer shops. When Kaz expressed her discomfort with this, they moved on to Covent Garden. Okay, she needed some new stuff, that was clear. But she wasn't about to swan into her probation officer in Versace jeans.

Joey carried a clip of fifty-pound notes in his pocket and peeled them off to pay for each purchase. He was having a whale of a time. Kaz was less enthusiastic. A little voice in her head was whispering: 'Helen's not going to like this.' But what was she going to do, kick up, refuse to let her brother buy her a few grand's worth of gear? She'd persuade Helen just as she'd persuaded herself this was not the issue on which to make a stand. And trying on new stuff, getting out of trackie bottoms and sweatshirts after six years, well it made her feel like a proper person again. When she looked in the brightly lit full-length mirrors it was almost a shock; what she saw was a woman, not a scrawny kid. Somewhere along the line she'd grown up and now she was in the right gear, heads were turning.

They stopped off for lunch at a little Italian place in Soho and Kaz made it crystal clear that she was off the booze. It wasn't a problem. The boys had a beer apiece. She had an ice-cream milkshake and it was bliss.

Now they were cruising through the afternoon traffic headed out of town on the A13. Kaz had her feet up on the dash and she was frowning.

Joey glanced at her. 'Trust me babe, it'll be fine. They are gonna be so chuffed.'

Kaz gave him a baleful look. 'You reckon?'

Crammed in the back seat with their purchases, Ashley shifted his position and farted. He giggled with embarrassment. 'S'cuse I.'

Joey chuckled. 'Aww fuckin' hell Ash! Ladies present mate!'

Ashley glanced from one to the other sheepishly. 'I'm really sorry Kaz. Me mum's always saying I got no manners.'

'Got no control of yer own bum, that's what it is!'

Kaz listened to the banter, she was getting used to their antics. The designer shirts, the Rolex Oysters on their wrists, the platinum signet rings, the diamond ear-studs, these were their toys; they were two lads of twenty-three going on fifteen. She found it faintly reassuring; Joey hadn't changed. He was still a big kid, a bundle of infectious energy, and when he was in a mood like this, fun to be around.

She shook her head and grinned. 'And you expected me to shag him? I'd rather go down on Fat Pat.'

Joey laughed out loud. 'Who the fuck's that?'

'You don't wanna know.'

Three lanes of traffic snaked and dipped over makeshift flyovers until the A13 broadened into more of a motorway. Joey put his foot down as the elevated section carried them through Dagenham, past the wind turbines and messy acres of new and old industrial developments and on into the flat estuary marsh-land, the gateway to Essex. London had the buzz, and Joey liked that, but this was still his home turf. The city could be chaotic, full of strangers, ethnic gangs and constant change. But Irish, Jew, Bangladeshi or Somali, down the generations they all became English when they moved out to Essex.

Kaz stared blankly out of the window, pylons criss-crossed the landscape and she could see the flares on the oil refinery down by the river. Going home was not a prospect she relished; in fact the whole notion of home was something she'd ring-fenced in her mind. It was off-limits, a place she refused to visit mentally or emotionally however much various therapists had pushed her.

She was born in Bethnal Green nine months after the old man got out of jail and three months before her parents married. But she'd grown up in Essex. They started off in a council house in Basildon, then as the old man's business picked up their fortunes improved. Terry Phelps was obsessed with security, which in his line of work wasn't unreasonable. He bought a piece of land, a field really, out beyond Billericay and he got it dirt cheap because it had no planning permission and a semi-permanent travellers' camp next door. Terry fixed the local planning committee with a few bungs and saw off the pikeys with a JCB and a couple of sawn-off shotguns. Then he built his dream home.

As they pulled up in front of the electric, wrought-iron gates, Kaz turned to her brother. 'I don't know if I can do this.'

'They're expecting us. Can't bottle now.' Joey leant out of his window and pressed the intercom on the wall. 'Anybody home?'

There was a muffled reply, which possibly included a squeal of excitement, and with a clank the gates swung open.

Joey drove into the compound. The property was surrounded on all sides by an eight-foot solid brick wall topped with decorative but lethal spikes. The house itself was an imposing mish-mash of styles: a mock Tudor facade with a portico supported by Corinthian pillars. As the Range Rover pulled up, Kaz took it all in. The small leaded-light windows reflected the afternoon sun, making it impossible to see inside. But in Kaz's memory the interior was dismal, a place of shadows and unmentionable horrors.

Joey patted her knee and grinned. 'Well, we're here now.'

Kaz knew she'd been bullied, but it was hard to resist coming here without spoiling the mood of the day. Then the front door opened and there was Ellie Phelps beaming at them.

The last time Kaz had seen her mother was at Chelmsford Crown Court. As she'd been led into the dock, she'd glanced over at the public gallery and Ellie had been there, staring straight ahead, eyes glassy and blank. Valium had been Ellie's drug of choice for many years until Prozac came along, but she mixed it with a cocktail of gin, vodka, painkillers and anything else that came to hand. Life with Terry was a rollercoaster, his temper unpredictable at best. So Ellie had found escape and solace in the only way available to her.

Kaz took a deep breath and got out of the car. Ellie was hugging her son. Then she turned to her daughter with a huge grin. She was fatter than Kaz remembered and rosy-cheeked, but there was something else too. Kaz realized with a jolt that her mother had come alive. She was no longer the drugged-up zombie of Kaz's teenage years. Before her was a plump, middle-aged matron in a tight silk top. Her lipstick was shimmering pink, but behind it the smile was warm and the eyes had a definite twinkle.

Ellie flung her arms round Kaz and squeezed her tight. 'Lovey, we was gonna come and meet you. Stretch limo, the works. Joey had it all planned.'

Her words tumbled out in a torrent. Kaz had never seen her mother so animated.

'I've got your room all ready for you, we've had it completely redone. Pink – that was always yer favourite when you was little. I wanted to come and see you loads of times, but y'know them places they give me the heebie-jeebies. Then when yer dad was took bad I pretty much had me hands full and I thought she's a good girl, she'll understand.'

Kaz stared in frank disbelief. What had brought about this transformation?

Ellie rattled on as she steered her daughter into the house. Kaz got another shock when she saw how her childhood home had changed. The mismatched furniture was gone, so was the chaos and the mess.

Terry Phelps had owned two pitbulls, which it amused him to call Bill and Ben after some kids' TV show. They were savage beasts and pretty much had the run of the place. For security, Terry said. He didn't intend to be surprised in his bed by some rival hoodlum. Kaz and Joey had been mortally afraid of the dogs; they had bitten Ellie on more than one occasion. But now the formerly tiled and dog-shit-strewn hallway was covered in a deep-pile carpet. An ornately carved ottoman stood against one wall and on it a small tabby cat was curled up fast asleep. Kaz rapidly concluded that Bill and Ben were history.

The sitting room was in Kaz's memory a cold, depressing place. As kids they'd spent most of their time curled up in one corner watching a big old Philips television. As she stepped into the room now her eyes were assaulted by a riot of bright, warm colours. Heavy brocade curtains complete with pelmets and tassels covered the windows. Three enormous plush sofas were ranged around a glass coffee table. Lamps, ornaments, silver-framed family photos were spread liberally around the room. But the biggest change of all sat in one corner.

Terry Phelps's hulking frame was crammed into a neat, mechanized wheelchair. His chin was sunk low resting on his barrel of a chest and a small drool of saliva snaked over the edge of his slack lips down his chin and on to his cardigan. Kaz stood rooted to the spot. She stared into his black eyes. They were completely vacant. Ellie touched her daughter's arm.

'I know love, it's quite a shock. He can't move or talk or do nothing for himself really. It was a massive stroke. The doctors reckon it was a miracle he survived at all. But we keep him nice and clean and warm.'

As she spoke she went over and patted him, much as you would a dog. Joey strolled over to the drinks cupboard and poured himself and Ashley a Scotch.

'Mum has two full-time nurses to do all the lifting and that. And of course she's got Brian to help her out too.' Joey indicated the dapper man in his early sixties sitting on one of the sofas. 'You must remember Uncle Brian.'

Kaz turned to look at Brian, who was no sort of relative at all, but had been called that by Kaz and Joey as a sort of courtesy required of children to certain adults round their parents. Brian Mason had in fact been part of the Phelps firm, at various times Terry's driver, dogsbody and whipping boy.

He stood up and held his hand out to Kaz. 'Welcome home love. Must say, you're looking pretty fit.'

'So are you Brian.'

'Y'know, mustn't grumble.'

At this point Ellie sidled over to him and slipped her arm coyly through his. 'Brian's been a great comfort to me. I'd never have got through without him. He's my little treasure.'

Brian grinned and squeezed her hand.

Kaz looked around her, it was all starting to make sense. The inmates had taken over the asylum. She glanced over at her father in his wheelchair. He hadn't moved a muscle. You could almost feel sorry for him. But Kaz didn't. The vicious old bastard had got exactly what he deserved.

8

Kaz and Joey sat on loungers in the garden. He had a cold beer, she had apple juice. It was a summer evening, a scene so easy and normal that Kaz was still finding it hard to absorb. Brian was handling the barbecue, Ellie was fussing round him and giggling; they were playing house like a couple of newly-weds. Kaz watched them, she wasn't certain if her mother's current happiness pleased her or whether she resented it. She certainly resented all the years when Ellie had checked out and left her kids to fend for themselves.

Joey caught the direction of his sister's critical gaze. 'Bit of a turn-up, eh?'

'How'd it happen?'

'Dunno really. When the old man had his stroke, Brian was driving her, y'know, taking care of things generally.'

'I didn't imagine it started before that. He'd've killed 'em both.'

Joey didn't reply, he didn't have to. Their father's violence had always been part of their lives, it didn't merit any discussion.

Kaz turned to her brother and scanned his face. 'So when's someone gonna tell me about Natalie?'

Joey avoided her eye at the mention of their sibling. Natalie was their baby sister, twelve years old when Kaz went down.

'Ain't no secret babes. She and Mum had their ups and downs. Nat moved out last year.'

It sounded innocuous enough, but Kaz could sense from his tone that there was more to it than that.

'Where's she living now then?'

'Down Southend.'

Kaz nodded, she could see this was going to be hard work, but she persisted. 'On her own?'

Joey's jaw visibly tightened. 'With some fella.'

He jumped up, strode over to Ashley, who was patiently guiding Terry's mechanized wheelchair round the garden. 'Go on mate, get yourself a beer. I'll take over.'

Joey pointed the wheelchair in the direction of the shrubbery. Kaz watched them go, Terry's inert bulk hunched in the chair, Joey walking beside him, controlling the joystick with one hand but staring straight ahead, completely ignoring his father.

Ellie was laying the table so Kaz got up too and went to help her.

'Bet you don't recognize this old garden. Joey knew this lad from school, got his own landscape gardening business. He done the whole thing. They brought in plants by the lorry load.'

Kaz smiled at her mother's pleasure. 'It does look great.'

'Cost a fortune. But Joey didn't care, paid for the lot. Y'know, since your dad was took bad and with Sean inside, he's stepped up to the mark has Joey. I think quite a few people have been surprised. Truth be told, I was meself a bit. You seen these?' Ellie held up a fine porcelain plate. It was a good fourteen inches in diameter and had a gold band round the circumference. 'I love these plates. Got a whole set from John Lewis.'

She chattered on, laying out the plates, arranging knives, forks, napkins, on the table. Everything matched, most of it looked new. One thing was clear to Kaz: Joey had decided to give his mother the life that Terry had promised but never really delivered.

'You see much of Natalie then?'

Ellie's busy hands stopped. She shrugged off the question. 'Now and then.'

'So what's she get up to down in Southend?'

Ellie became preoccupied with adjusting all the place mats. 'How the bloody hell should I know? She's eighteen, she don't talk to me. And if I recall, you was the same at that age.'

Kaz did recall. At eighteen she'd been strung out on a cocktail of crack, coke, booze and a myriad of other drugs. Being the daughter of Terry Phelps had carried one advantage: when it came to getting your hands on illegal substances no one said no to you. More often than not they just gave you the stuff for free.

Brian carried a huge platter of meat from the barbecue over to the table. 'Who's ready for a nice juicy steak? Come on, 'fore it gets cold.'

Kaz helped Ashley set chairs round the table. Ellie flapped her arms and shouted, 'Joey! Come on lovey, we're ready to eat.'

Joey steered the wheelchair back in the direction of the patio area and parked Terry up at the head of the table. Finally they all sat down.

Ellie looked round beaming, her face flushed. 'I been so looking forward to this day. Kaz coming home. The family all together. It's as it should be.'

Kaz looked at her father, his empty carcass still a baleful presence. She thought about Natalie, her absent sister. Then she glanced at her mother, happily forking massive sirloin steaks on to her precious plates. Ellie may have managed to escape her own drug-fuelled hell. But to Kaz's mind she was still playing the same game.

Kaz sat in her childhood bedroom and stared at the new pink walls. They were loud, screaming pink, only the curtains were worse. A selection of gonks and cuddly toys that she'd never seen before were lined up on the windowsill. The duvet cover had a pink frilly border all the way round and the bed was piled high with furry cushions. It was the kind of girly boudoir that might've delighted a ten-year-old. Kaz reflected that she was probably about that age when Terry first started making moves on her and her mother checked out.

The door opened a crack and Joey popped his head in.

'You all right?'

Kaz glared at him. 'No. Ten o'clock, that's my curfew at the hostel. How the fuck am I s'pose to get back for that?'

Joey shrugged. 'You come to see your family. Anyway, ain't like you to worry about stuff like that. You used to bunk off school all the time and stick two fingers up at the social when they come round.'

Kaz stared at him in disbelief.

'I'm not a schoolkid any more. Twelve years Joey. I got twelve years 'cause that bloke at the garage that you whacked in the head ended up in a wheelchair.'

Joey scowled, stepped into the room and closed the door.

'Yeah well, it was his own fault. He should've handed over the cash. I mean, what was his problem, he only worked there. And anyway twelve don't mean twelve, does it? It's only really six.'

Kaz got up, hands on hips and faced him. 'Yeah six inside, six on licence. Break the licence, you get recalled. Banged up straight away, no discussion. So for the next six years of my life I ain't gonna be sticking two fingers up at no one.'

A look of contrition spread across Joey's features. 'Babes I'm sorry. I dunno, I didn't think about the time.' He sighed. 'I just wanted you to come home. See how things are now.'

'See what exactly? Him? The shedloads of stuff you've got Mum?'

Joey sat down on the bed. He fixed her with an intense, mesmerizing gaze. This had always been the thing with Joey: the look. It was hard not to be drawn in. He put her in mind of a little boy, innocent, appealing, as he struggled to find the right words.

'Listen, when you went down, I was completely gutted. Twelve fucking years – I mean, it was like a bullet.' He put two fingers up to his temple and pulled the trigger. 'And I know . . . well, I know it should've been me, not you. I was running round like a blue-arsed fly, doing completely mental stuff.'

Kaz exhaled, plonked down on the bed next to him. 'Think we both were mate.'

'Part of me wanted to turn meself in. Then the old man got hold of me. Well . . . you don't need me to spell out how that went.'

Kaz shook her head sympathetically.

'When he'd finished beating the shit out of me he said you knew the score, you'd never grass. And there was no point both of us going down. But it was my job to take care of things while you was away. That was my part of the deal.'

Kaz shifted uncomfortably. 'Joe, a lot's changed in six years. I'm not the same person. I'm not out of my box on crack, for a start.'

Joey seized her hand. 'I ain't the same either. I mean I know I muck about. But even back then I started to do some thinking.

I mean proper thinking. Took me a while, but I got me head straight. Bunking off school, getting wasted – why did we do all that?'

'To escape all this?'

'Yeah well I started to think, at school they was on at us all the time to read books. Okay, I thought, I'll read some fucking books, see what all the fuss is about. I was amazed, it's all out there once you start looking. And on the Net you can find out about anything. I never took an exam in my life, but in the last six years I've learnt how the world works.'

'Believe me little brother, I'm impressed.'

'I knew nothing'd change while the old man was running things, so I kept me head down, waited. Then he had his stroke.' Joey's eyes lit up at the memory. 'I went down the hospital with Mum. We thought he'd bought it. Then the doctors pulled him through.'

Kaz gave him a cynical glance. 'Bet that cheered everyone up.'

Joey smiled. Then the warmth faded out of his face. 'I dunno what made him survive. Bloody-mindedness probably. All that bastard ever cared about was having his own way. He's a fucking monster.'

A tear welled up in the corner of Joey's eye, Kaz took both of his hands in hers.

'You think I don't realize you got the short straw. I was the lucky one – least I got away from him.'

Joey let her hold on to him for a moment. Then he stood up, angrily brushing the tears away.

'All the stuff he done to you and Mum over the years . . . when I see him in that chair I think, yeah mate, I hope you're still in there, trapped inside your own bonce, screaming to get out.'

Kaz watched her brother pacing the room, fuelled with inner rage. She got up and went to him. 'Joe, I know how much it hurts, but . . . you gotta let it go, put it behind you.'

He turned, seized her by the shoulders, his grip so powerful she winced.

'Yeah, I know. I know!' His eyes glistened with tears and fervour. 'And now you're out babes, I can. It's gonna be me and you together, like it used to be. I been waiting, I been planning.'

Kaz eased herself free, rubbed her arm.

He looked mortified. 'Sorry, did I hurt you?'

'Don't matter. Look, there's a lot we need to talk about. I got some plans of me own.'

'Great. Whatever. Bring it to the table.' Joey gave her a wide smile, pulled out a tissue and blew his nose; his rage had evaporated as suddenly as it'd come.

Kaz watched him, the same rapid mood swings as when he was a kid. Always sunshine and showers with Joey, that'd been the family joke. Now he was bouncing round the room, he picked up one of the gonks, tossed it playfully in the air.

'Right, sod this.' He tossed aside the toy and checked his watch. 'Half nine, we'll never make South London by ten, not even the way I drive. I'll call the lawyers, get them on it with the hostel. We pay 'em enough.'

Kaz shook her head. 'It's all right, I sorted it. Phoned them earlier. I've got to see my probation officer tomorrow anyway and he's in Basildon. So I got permission to stay over.'

A knowing smile spread over Joey's features. 'You're a little tinker, 'n't you? You just wanted to give me a bollocking!'

Kaz gave him a hard stare. 'No, I wanted you to see my point of view.'

'I do see it babes.' Joey nodded sagely. 'They get you every which way, the bastards, don't they?' He scanned the room and started to giggle. 'As for this … Still, kept her happy doing it I guess.'

'She lives in fantasy land Joey. She always did. This is just a different fantasy.'

'You don't wanna stay here, come back to my place tonight.' He raised his hand to pre-empt any objection. 'I'll take you to Basildon tomorrow myself. You'll be on time I promise. Less you wanna sleep with the gonks.'

He waggled one of the pink furry creatures in her face. She smiled, the day had exhausted her. Why shouldn't she stay at his place? Who'd know?

'What's it like then, your gaff?'

'It's all right. Don't worry, it's got two bathrooms, so you ain't gonna be grossed out by Ash. Also it'll give me a chance to bring you up to speed with the business—'

Kaz held up her hand. This was what she'd been afraid of: his assumptions and the unstoppable tide of his enthusiasm.

'Look, don't get me wrong, you've done really well for yourself, but …'

Joey stood stock-still, his face a picture of boyish incredulity. 'Not for myself. No.' He shook his head emphatically. 'For *us*. I done it for us. My part of the deal, like the old man said. Half the business is yours babes. You served the time for both of us, so you've earned it. We're partners.'

9

Helen Warner told the taxi driver to drop her in Birdcage Walk at the edge of the park. From there she walked round the corner to the conference centre giving herself time to calm any nerves and focus. She was used to meeting people from all walks of life, getting up and speaking, she did enough of that in court. But this was a new departure for her, the first tentative steps in what she hoped would lead to a parliamentary career. She was thirty-two, a successful lawyer, she had all the right credentials, it was time to get moving.

She entered the QEII conference centre by the main entrance, passed through security and saw that the event she was attending was in the Churchill Auditorium, an interesting choice, she thought, given the subject matter.

The room was about half full, maybe a hundred or so people. She was handed a glossy brochure at the door emblazoned with the title 'Broken Britain – A Way Forward'. Taking it she reflected that if they spent the money laid out on this shindig in some of the daggy neighbourhoods that had been the tinderbox for the riots, that might be a step in the right direction. She glanced round the room, saw a couple of Labour Party policy wonks she recognized; they gave her a friendly nod, and she took a seat towards the back.

On her feet at the podium Assistant Commissioner Fiona Calder was presenting her opening remarks. It was all pretty standard stuff: alienation, gangs, poor role models, bad parenting, exclusion from consumer culture. Calder was a small woman, but made up for that fact with a large presence. She also looked good in the uniform, not all women did. Helen tried to listen, but she'd heard it all before, read it, regurgitated it herself. Since the August riots of the previous year she'd acquired a roster of new clients. The crackdown on criminality promised by the government had brought her firm a twenty per cent upturn in business and a slew of juicy appeals.

Helen leafed through the brochure, admired the spectacular photos of London burning. Then she let her eyes range around the room, checking out who she recognized, who was on her networking list. It took her a few moments to become aware of the man sitting close to the podium on the Assistant Commissioner's right-hand side. She realized with a start that he was staring straight at her. It was Detective Chief Superintendent Alan Turnbull and as soon as he caught her eye he smiled.

Helen spent the coffee break on the fringes of a group she vaguely knew; some lads from Labour HQ were baiting a fat Lib-Dem, who was unfortunate enough to have a very junior role at the Home Office. She saw Turnbull bearing down on her, but there was nowhere to run. As usual he was immaculately turned out: a tailored suit, silk tie with platinum tiepin. As he held out his hand to shake, Helen reflected he dressed more like a high-priced corporate lawyer than a policeman.

'Ms Warner! I thought it was you.'

It was impossible to ignore him. His handshake was a grip, a subtle demonstration of his hidden physical power.

'I see the Feds are out in force today Superintendent.'

He smiled, crinkling the flesh round his eyes as if her quip had really amused him.

'I'm only here to give the Assistant Commissioner some moral support. But I'm glad I ran into you.'

'Isn't that what these things are for, running into people?'

He smiled again, Helen found him hard to dislike. He was certainly a cut above the average senior cop. As a lawyer Helen had dealt with quite a few, mostly they were snotty and arrogant. But Turnbull had an easy manner.

'How's your client?'

'Which one? I've got over fifty.'

'I was thinking of Karen Phelps. She's a special project of yours, isn't she? Bit of a poster girl for the rehabilitation of offenders?'

There was only a hint of sarcasm in his tone. Helen painted on a smile. Did he have any inkling of just how special or was he simply being a cop? She concluded the latter.

'She's fine, but she'd be even better if you lot'd stay off her case.'

Suddenly the smile vanished. Turnbull sighed and fixed her with a serious look.

'Something you don't know, but probably should, is that we had an undercover officer who got pretty close to Joey Phelps. We've just pulled his body out the river. Looks like Phelps murdered him.'

He scanned her face, waiting for the reaction this news would bring. But Helen wasn't about to give him the satisfaction. She shook her head.

'C'mon, what's that got to do with Karen? She's been in jail and she has no involvement in her brother's criminality. I'm sure she knows nothing about it.'

Turnbull inclined his head to one side as if dealing with a recalcitrant child.

'My point is, Joey Phelps has murdered a police officer. What do you think he's going to do to his sister when he finds out she's been talking to us?'

Helen raised her chin. This was really beginning to piss her off. 'She hasn't been talking to you, you've been badgering her and she's made her position very clear. She's not prepared to act as an informant and you can't force her to. And if you continue to harass her . . .'

'One of my officers went to visit her at the hostel. He even bumped into Joey. Now I wonder how Karen will have explained that away? If she lied, that could be tricky. Joey Phelps is not stupid, he sees the same officer hanging round Karen a couple more times, he's going to get curious. In a paranoid individual like him, who knows how that'll play out?'

Helen stared at him in disbelief. 'What is this? You're setting her up? You're hoping to provoke him into attacking his own sister?'

'Not at all. I'm merely trying to point out to you the dangers of her situation. She's not going to be safe to get on with her life until her brother is behind bars. You need to persuade her Ms Warner. It's for her own good. I'm not the enemy, you need to tell her that.'

Helen met Turnbull's gaze directly. He exuded a confident masculinity. Crossing swords with him was exhilarating, at the same time Helen felt at a disadvantage. Some men seemed to be able to do that to her and she hated it.

He produced a business card from his pocket. 'Let's keep in touch.'

Helen took the card, but she wasn't about to let him think he'd won. She eyeballed him, gave him the tough stare that had put the fear of God in more than one CPS lawyer.

'Two things Superintendent. Karen Phelps has served her time and provided she abides by the terms of her licence she's entitled to get on with her life free from police harassment. And if I have to go to the IPCC and lodge a formal complaint, I will. Secondly, even if I tried to persuade her, I don't think I could. She's given you her answer, she's not going to change her mind. So back off.'

Turnbull smiled, inclined his head. 'Sooner or later he'll turn on her. You know that, I know that. You really want that on your conscience?'

It was a hit, Helen's face remained a mask but they both knew it. Helen had expressed exactly that fear to Kaz on several occasions. But Kaz had simply dismissed it; Joey would never harm her. Helen wasn't convinced.

Turnbull knew he'd made his point. He gave her a lop-sided grin. 'Come on Helen, are we that different, you and me? I'll tell you how I look at it. Justice system can't cope, the government's got its head up its arse, police morale's the lowest it's ever been. But still the likes of us, we soldier on don't we? Why?' He glanced over her left shoulder with a faraway look in his eye. Then he sighed. 'Fact is, we get on with it, don't we. Do the job as best we can. Surely we're on the same side you and me?'

Helen inclined her head and laughed. 'Nice speech. I'm still not buying.'

Turnbull let his gaze travel round the room, then he zoned back in on her. 'Well no one comes to these things for fun, do they? So my guess is you're planning a career move. Politics is a whole new ball game. You'll be needing a few friends and allies. And as you said yourself, Karen Phelps is one client.'

Their eyes met, he seemed completely relaxed, which was maddening.

'Good to talk to you.'

Helen watched him snake his way across the room. He homed

in on Marcus Foxley, the Deputy Mayor for Policing and Crime. Foxley grasped his hand and gave him a blokey pat on the shoulder. Helen let her annoyance escape in a breathy hiss; bastard was just showing her how well connected he was. Rubbing her nose in it.

She turned and walked away. She strode down the first corridor she came to until she found a quiet spot. Then she took out her phone, clicked it on and anxiously scanned the text she'd received earlier from Kaz: *scuse mistakes jus getting hang of this been staying at mum and dads all ok b in touch K.*

Helen sighed as she clicked the phone off; on a personal and professional front this was all getting way too complicated.

10

Kaz stood before the wall-to-ceiling plate-glass window gazing out. Joey's place was on the south bank of the Thames close to the Tate Modern. In one of the upscale new developments, which clustered behind the gallery, it commanded a river view with the dome of St Paul's as a backdrop. She strolled over to the kitchen area and poured herself another coffee. She'd made a whole pot of Blue Mountain Arabica using the state-of-the-art coffee-maker. She wandered round the room letting the caffeine hum through her veins. Having given up cigarettes during her last year inside she was delighted to discover that there was still one hit she could legitimately indulge in.

She'd slept like a log cocooned in a vast double bed in the apartment's spare bedroom. It had its own en suite plus there was a shared bathroom with a massive Jacuzzi. The place was remarkably clean and tidy, she thought, considering it was occupied by Joey and Ashley. She later discovered a couple of Polish blokes in neat blue overalls turned up every afternoon at three, blitzed through the whole flat in less than an hour and disappeared again.

As Kaz sipped her coffee her eyes roamed around the minimalist space. A large 3D, flat-screen TV dominated one wall with a stack of Blu-ray discs and a PlayStation on a shelf underneath. She was surprised to see a dozen or so books next to the discs. The titles ranged from self-help manuals about how to succeed in business to a couple of heavy-looking economics tomes. She pulled one out of the neat row: *The Seven Habits of Highly Effective People*. It didn't strike her as being very Joey, but then what did she really know about him now? Six years of prison visits had only provided a series of snapshots of a boy turning into a man.

The front door opened and Joey bustled in with a couple of carriers of shopping. He dumped them down on the kitchen counter and beamed. 'Great. You're up. But it is only half eleven.'

Kaz yawned. 'Think my body clock's up the creek ever since I got out.'

Joey unloaded his bag. 'We got pastries, some oranges to juice' – he pulled out a pack of bacon – 'plus, you ask me nicely, I'll make you the best bacon butty you've had in your entire life.'

Kaz grinned. 'Okay, I'll give that a go.'

Joey pulled out a frying pan from the pristine bank of cupboards. 'I sent Ashley on an errand, give me and you a chance to talk business.'

'Thought Ashley was part of the business?'

'Up to a point. He's a good lad, don't get me wrong. Totally loyal. But when it comes down to it, he's not the sharpest card in the pack.'

Kaz absorbed this. She'd been hoping to persuade her brother that while he had a sidekick like Ashley he didn't really need her. 'But he is your best mate.'

'Yeah, but you're my sister.'

'Don't give me that family first crap. 'Cause I'd run a million miles to get away from our lot.'

Joey laughed. Kaz watched him slapping the rashers in the pan, he was a complicated boy, always had been. She remembered him as a small child, clinging to her when the old man went on the rampage. Usually they'd hide in one of the many cupboards in the house and frequently Joey would wet himself. It always made him cry, tears of rage and shame. But Kaz would tell him it didn't matter, she'd clean him up and then she'd cuddle him until he fell asleep.

As the delectable aroma of frying bacon rose up from the pan, Joey glanced at her. He raised his index finger, ticking off a mental list. 'So . . . number one, let's start with Ibiza.'

Kaz took a deep breath, it was now or never. 'Hang on, I got some stuff I need to say first.'

He stared at her. His expression was hard to decipher. Joey didn't like to be thwarted, Kaz knew him well enough to read impatience behind the look. But he simply shrugged. 'Fire away.'

Kaz sighed, she positioned herself on the opposite side of the kitchen counter to him. 'Thing is Joe, I don't ever wanna go back inside. Six years of my life, swallowed up.'

He opened his mouth to butt in, but she ploughed on. 'And I ain't blaming no one but myself. Drugs and a stupid bit of villainy, that's what put me there; I ain't going back to that. Which is why I can't be involved in the business. I appreciate what you've done. Truly I do. But if I get recalled, I'm fucked. I can't take the risk.'

Joey beamed at her. 'What if there is no risk?'

Kaz shook her head in disbelief. 'Are you being dense or what? Last three months I've had the old bill on my back, visiting me inside, trying every which way to get me to grass you up.'

Joey chuckled. 'Plonkers! If you was gonna do that, I don't reckon you'd've waited six years.'

'The point is they are after you little brother.' Kaz flung her arms wide. 'All this, the house that charlie built? It's a red rag to them. They are on your case and they ain't about to give up.'

Joey smiled. 'You worry too much babes. If they had even a shred of evidence to nail me, you think they'd be knocking at your door? Just proves how desperate they are.'

'What if this place is bugged? They could be listening in even now.'

Joey grinned. 'They'll be lucky. Not with the kit I've had installed.'

Kaz folded her arms protectively; she took a turn round the open-plan living room. This was never going to be easy. 'What I want is to go to art college. Learn to be a proper painter.'

Joey flipped the rashers over a couple more times. 'I got no quarrel with that. It's a good cover.'

Kaz faced him, stared him down. She had plenty of her own brand of angry defiance. 'It ain't a cover, it's what I wanna to do with my life.'

He gave her an amiable grin. 'Great. I could do with a few pictures round here. Get some plates out. I don't want this to get cold.'

Kaz watched him cut doorsteps of bread and carefully load each slice with bacon, mayo and a handful of salad leaves. It was all a bit messy, but he ended up with two gut-busting sandwiches. He plated them up and carried them to the table.

'Tuck in then.'

Getting their mouths round the erupting, dripping slabs of bacon, mayo and bread put paid to any further discussion. Joey demolished his in canine gulps. He got up, tore some sheets of kitchen paper from the roll on the counter and wiped his mouth and hands.

'So am I right or am I right?'

Kaz was only halfway through hers. 'About what?'

'Best bacon butty you've ever had?'

Kaz gave a wry smile as she chomped her way through another mouthful. 'It's not for wusses, I'll give you that.'

Joey poured out two fresh mugs of coffee from the pot on the hob and brought them to the table. 'Can I have my say now?'

Kaz shot him an acerbic glance. 'Can I stop you?'

He strolled over to the vast window, coffee mug in hand. 'Look out there. What d'you see?'

Kaz took a mouthful of coffee. 'Buildings? London?'

'Yeah London. One of the biggest financial centres in the world. You know what's at the heart of it? What makes it tick?'

'Money?'

Joey shook his head. 'That's how it functions. That's like the wheels. Nah, at the heart of it all there's one truth. Only one truth: everybody's at it. Everybody's on the take. Laws don't matter, nothing matters. You're smart enough, you grab your share. How do I know this? 'Cause I got lawyers, accountants, bankers – posh boys with degrees down to their bums – who've never seen the inside of a nick or the back of a police van. And now they're working for me.'

Kaz watched him, his eyes shone with that same fervour she'd seen the day before.

'And I ain't exaggerating.' He put down his coffee mug and laced his fingers together. 'Nowadays villainy and business are like this. 'Cept we don't call it villainy no more, 'cause as I say everybody's at it. We're all players in the market. I'm no different to the rest, I'm just a businessman.'

Kaz shifted in her chair. 'What d'you call selling cocaine then? 'Cause I call it drug dealing. Last time I looked so did the old bill.'

'It don't matter what the product is. If people wanna buy it, there's a market. Recreational drugs is a billion-dollar industry. And don't talk to me about harm – fags and booze and stuffing their guts with junk food is what kills more people in this country than anything else.'

Kaz laughed. 'You got an answer for everything, haven't you?'

Joey took another slug of coffee. 'Let's talk about risk. You don't wanna go back inside, 'course you don't. Thing is babes, there is no risk, 'cause now we got technology on our side.'

Kaz extracted a shred of bacon from between her teeth.

'Technology? Don't try feeding me a line, I ain't daft.'

Joey returned to the table and sat down facing her. His expression was deadly serious and she could sense his excitement.

'Look, it's gonna take less than a year, but I'm scaling right back on all face-to-face dealing. We're gonna do it all on the Net.'

'On the Net? How's that gonna work?'

'Punters place their order online using an anonymous market. It's like a website that the authorities can't get to or trace. It's just out there in cyberspace.'

Kaz frowned and gave him a sceptical shrug. 'Then how do the punters find it?'

'People are getting savvy to how this stuff works, it's not only for techies and nerds. All you need is special software to conceal your IP address and make you anonymous. We been using a site called Trade Winds to try it out, but I got some of my own people building a site exclusively for us. It's beautiful, you sell anything you like, any kind of contraband, collect the dosh using bitcoins – no way it can be traced to you.'

'Bitcoins?'

'Cybermoney. Change it for dollars on the Net, straight into an offshore company.'

'Someone's still got to deliver the drugs.'

'Ordinary postman. Vacuum-sealed plastic pouch. No one's any the wiser.'

Kaz stared at him. 'It's still dealing. They'll find a way to get to you eventually.'

'In a few years maybe, but by then we'll have moved into the mainstream: property, equities, other legitimate investments. We'll be untouchable. Very rich and totally legit.'

Kaz puffed out her cheeks. 'Sounds great. But I ain't stupid Joey, you still got to get the drugs in the first place. And that's a very dangerous business. What about the people that get in the way? What d'you do about them?'

Joey lifted both arms and turned his palms upwards. 'I'll be honest, if you have to, you kill 'em. I ain't saying it's ideal. But it's the way of the world. Governments do it all the time. Bunch of ragheads give you grief, you don't like the way they run their country, send over a couple of drones, blast 'em all to buggery. You can dress it up with fine words, comes down to the same thing.'

Kaz smiled. 'You really have got it all worked out, haven't you?'

He got up from the table and shovelled his hands in his jeans pockets. 'The rich get richer and the rest get screwed. I don't wanna be a villain Kaz. I just wanna join the club.'

Kaz gazed up and around her at the vaulted ceiling, the spiral stairway and balcony leading to the bedrooms. 'I'd say you already have.'

Joey scratched his head. 'Nah, this is nothing. This is profit from a few smart deals. But you and me together babes, we're gonna be invincible.'

She could feel the power, the absolute belief in his voice.

'Why me? I don't know nothing about the Net, business, any of it.'

'You're smart, you'll pick it up. Plus you're the one person in this world I can really trust.'

Kaz considered this. 'What about Sean?'

Joey's lip curled. 'What's he got to do with anything?'

'Oh come on Joey, him and Dad, they was the firm. Once he gets parole—'

Joey didn't let her finish. '*If* he gets parole. Him and Dad was a couple of second-rate villains with no imagination. He wouldn't even understand what I'm talking about. The firm – what's that even mean? The firm is us.'

'Sean might have other ideas.'

He fixed her with those hypnotic baby-blue eyes. It put her in mind of the little Joey, always gazing up at her with a mixture of need and adoration.

'Listen to me, we don't owe him a fucking thing. 'Specially you don't.'

'I know that.'

'I need you in my corner, that's all I'm asking. I don't expect you to get involved in none of the rough stuff. I got people for that now. Ex-military. I keep all that at arm's length. The old bill can't touch us, I promise you.' He squatted down beside her chair, took her hand, cradled it in his own. 'We deserve it, don't we? We've earned it. It's our time babes.'

She held on to his huge paw, stroked it. 'Look, I know what you're saying, but I can't go back Joey. Not to jail, not to the old life, not to any of it.'

He encompassed the room with a sweep of his hand. 'This look like the old life to you? You can have your own place just the same. Do your painting. Go to college. Okay you're out on licence. But all you gotta do is give 'em the spiel, keep 'em happy. You're dealing with a bunch of two-bit, underpaid civil servants. They ain't that smart. Long as they can tick their boxes. Any problems, the lawyers sort it out.'

Kaz looked into his eyes, his conviction was captivating. He was a lot cleverer than she'd ever imagined. She thought about Helen, the woman she so desperately wanted to impress. Helen had no idea of the world she and Joey had grown up in. Helen could walk away tomorrow and leave her high and dry. Whereas she'd always be bonded to Joey and it wasn't simply blood. It was everything they'd suffered together and that they'd survived. Maybe he was right: it was their time.

She gazed at him, her huge little brother. 'Look I'll always be in your corner, no question, you know that.'

He gave her a big grin. 'That's all I'm asking.' He went to the kitchen drawer and pulled out an envelope. 'I'll get you a proper bank account sorted, something they won't be able to trace. Meantime you'll need some walking-round money.'

He emptied the envelope on to the table, five neat bundles of fifty-pound notes tumbled out. Kaz's eyes widened, he smiled.

'Don't worry, it's all clean.'

Kaz gave him a sceptical look. 'Yeah but where am I s'pose put it? They can search your room any time.'

'Keep it here. I'll give you a key. Take what you want, whenever.' He checked the Rolex Oyster on his wrist and grinned. 'Well, that's sorted. Better get showered and dressed. Don't want you to be late for your probation officer, do we?'

11

The wine bar was off Gresham Street, but there was a small French brasserie attached. At one o'clock it was packed to the gunnels with thirsty City workers and Kaz had to shoulder her way through to the restaurant at the back. She saw Helen, already seated at a table in the corner, sipping mineral water and reading some documents in a folder. Kaz paused to watch her. Almost a week out of jail and the euphoria had given way to confusion, a sense of dislocation, punctuated by moments of dread. She had half a mind to turn tail and flee, then a waiter was at her elbow, a big bloke in a waistcoat with half a tablecloth wrapped round his middle. He said something that Kaz couldn't quite catch because of the hubbub from the bar. Helen looked up, caught her eye and smiled.

The waiter escorted Kaz to the table, pulled out the chair for her and thrust a menu into her hand. Helen could see that Kaz was uncomfortable with the way she was being marshalled by him.

The waiter inclined his head; his accent was French, but sounded fake. 'Something to drink mademoiselle?'

Helen dived in. 'Could you give us a moment?'

The waiter dipped his head again. 'Of course.'

He slid away and Helen beamed at Kaz.

'Sorry. They're a bit overenthusiastic in here, but the food is good.'

Kaz shrugged.

Helen scanned her face with concern. 'You look a bit stressed.'

Kaz sighed. 'It's the crowds. Tube was packed. Guess I'm not used to it.'

'You do need to give yourself time to adjust.'

They gazed at one another awkwardly across the table. Helen had deliberately chosen lunch and a busy restaurant near her office; she hoped the formal surroundings would help re-establish some boundaries. Now, witnessing Kaz's discomfort, she felt guilty.

'I'm sorry, this was a bad idea.'

'Nah, it's fine. I gotta get used to London hassle again.'

'How did it go with the new probation officer?'

'Okay. Except he's about fifteen.'

Helen smiled. 'Pity you lost Becky.'

Kaz simply nodded in agreement. Becky, the offender manager who'd handled her case for about two years prior to release, had left to have a baby. Kaz liked Becky. She was astute, low-key and had recognized immediately the importance of Helen in Kaz's rehabilitation. Kaz had never revealed how she felt about Helen, but Becky had seemed to understand. Doing her GCSE's, applying to college, Becky had guided her through the whole process.

Her replacement was an earnest, nervous young man called Jalil Sahir. He was rake thin and wore a short-sleeved, polyester shirt. Kaz found it impossible to imagine discussing anything personal with him. She was beginning to think Joey was right, she just had to smile, give them the spiel and watch them tick their boxes. Joey had driven her to Basildon and waited twenty minutes while she and Jalil had a pointless conversation. Then Joey had treated her to a milkshake.

Kaz's eyes darted round the restaurant. The hustle, the confidence needed to navigate London was wearing her down. There were too many people. She exhaled, allowing the breath to gently hiss through her parted lips.

Helen watched her with a sinking feeling. 'Things turning out tougher than you expected?'

Kaz gave her a scornful glance. 'No, I knew it'd be tough.'

'What about Joey?'

'Haven't really seen him to talk to.' Kaz avoided Helen's eye, she didn't want to go there. And anyway Helen wouldn't understand.

Helen nodded, she sensed the need to tread softly instead of hammering Kaz with the concerns and questions that had been keeping her awake the last few nights. If Turnbull was right and Joey had murdered a police officer, then he could well turn on his own sister. Helen had every reason to fear for her client. But tackling that now? Helen decided to bide her time.

'How are your art classes going? I need another drawing so I can hang the two of them together.'

Kaz had been waiting for this. She hesitated, she felt awkward enough, she didn't want to lie to Helen about everything. 'Missed the first couple. Next week I'll get to one though.'

Helen inclined her head. She wanted to reach out, a simple pat on the arm, but she didn't trust herself. She repeated the mantra for the umpteenth time: boundaries. She was a lawyer lunching a client. In reality that was pretty unusual too, she met most of her clients at a custody suite or in a police cell. But she decided not to dwell on that.

There was a strained silence. Helen sighed. 'If this probation officer's no good I could always—'

Kaz shifted abruptly in her chair then erupted. 'Fucking cops!

You know what they're up to now? First morning I was at the hostel this cop comes knocking at my door pretending he's some support worker.'

'Why didn't you ring me and tell me?'

'I told him to fuck off.'

'You should've rung me.'

'But he's still hanging round. Saw him when I got back from . . . from Mum and Dad's.'

'You said you'd been in your text. Did you stay over?'

Kaz felt as though she was in a bubble and she was drifting further and further from Helen. This was turning into a nightmare. Helen was the one person she wanted to be open with, she wanted that desperately.

She took a deep breath. 'Yeah, well actually . . . I stayed at Joey's.'

Helen merely raised her eyebrows. 'Did you agree that with the SPO at the hostel?'

Kaz gave her a sheepish glance. 'They thought I was at my mum and dad's.'

Helen unfolded her linen napkin, dabbed the corner of her mouth. She didn't want to give Kaz a lecture. She doubted anyway if it would work. Still she pursed her lips.

Kaz could feel her disapproval. It stung. 'I went to my mum and dad's and y'know what she's done to my room? Painted it bright fucking pink. I couldn't stay there. It's like a paedo's wet dream.'

Helen cracked a smile, she couldn't help herself. She gave Kaz a wry glance. 'Maybe it's an unconscious acknowledgement of the sins of the past?'

Kaz cocked her head. 'I doubt it. She's not that bright my mum.'

'What was it like seeing her again?'

Kaz dipped her eyes, evading the question. 'Didn't really want to go. But I thought Natalie might be there.'

'Was she?'

Kaz shook her head.

The waiter was hovering and looked ready to swoop. Helen glanced from him to Kaz. 'Shall we order?'

Kaz stared at the menu. Predictably it was in French, with explanations in small print underneath. She scanned it in annoyance. 'I dunno. I'm not that hungry.' She swivelled round in her chair, caught the waiter's eye. 'Oi tosh! Bring us a glass of wine.'

'The house wine mademoiselle? Red or white?'

'White.'

He nodded and moved away. Kaz realized that Helen was staring at her.

'What? I can't have a glass of wine?'

Helen painted on a smile. 'You do what you please Karen. It's not up to me.'

'Then why you looking at me like I just chopped out a line on the table?'

Helen's face dissolved into a grin. 'Even if you had, it wouldn't exactly be a first in here. That's why they have those nice little booths at the back.'

Kaz returned the smile, licked her finger and raised it. 'Yeah all right, one up to you.'

Helen gave her a tepid smile. They relapsed into silence.

The waiter placed a one hundred and seventy-five centilitre glass of wine on the table in front of Kaz. Beads of moisture sweated round the chilled bowl. Kaz gazed at it. Four years. A long time sober. She wasn't sure she even wanted it. She'd only ordered it to prove a point. But what point? That she could? That she was in charge of her own life now? That was a joke.

Her freedom was contingent on playing the game, on abiding by the rules. Joey was right, the bastards had you every which way.

The waiter returned with his pad to take their order. Kaz stared at him balefully. 'I asked for a glass, not a fucking bucket. Why does everything come in fucking buckets? You can take it away. And I'll have fillet steak, medium rare, with chips.'

The waiter made no comment, he was used to being abused by the City's finest. He blinked, scribbled, turned to Helen. She ordered fish; he picked up the glass of wine and hurried off.

Kaz huffed out a sigh then she gave Helen a tentative smile. 'Sorry. I'm being a right fucking pain in the arse, aren't I?'

Helen smiled. She blamed herself for this. Kaz was obviously struggling and she'd just made it worse.

She reached across the table and placed her hand over Kaz's. 'No you're not. I'm the one owes you an apology. Bad choice of venue.'

They sat for a frozen moment, both completely absorbed by the feathery caress of skin on skin. Then Helen used the excuse of pouring Kaz a glass of mineral water to remove her hand; as she concentrated on this, Kaz scanned her face.

'I told the new probation bloke about the cop.' Kaz smiled at the memory. 'Said I was being harassed, needed to leave the hostel. Really put him off his stroke, he didn't know what to say. Said he'd speak to his supervisor.'

Helen raised her glass of mineral water. 'Yeah and so will I. And Turnbull. And the IPCC if I have to.'

'If I get into college maybe I can move into the student residences early. I don't want to stay at Joey's, that was never the plan. But that pink – seriously, it was an emergency.'

Helen sipped her water, smiled. 'I can imagine. But you have to tread carefully. You can't give them any excuse.'

'I know that.'

Helen gazed at her client and sighed. Her relationship with Karen Phelps was different, there was no disguising that fact. The important thing was that feelings didn't get out of hand. So it was up to Helen to manage the situation, to keep any unruly emotions contained. It was all about control and that was Helen's forte.

She gave Kaz the detached professional smile. 'Well, let's enjoy our lunch. Though there was something I wanted to ask you . . .'

Kaz shot her a suspicious glance. 'Now what?'

'The BP Portrait Award is on until the end of the month. I usually try and go. The reviews have been very good this year. I wondered if you'd like to come with me?'

Kaz cocked her head, she didn't bother to conceal her surprise. 'To an exhibition? What, we friends now?'

Helen took another sip of water. 'We've always been friends.'

12

Ashley gunned the Range Rover Evoque down the hill past Chalkwell Park and turned left on to Southend seafront. A disgruntled Joey sat beside him.

'Speed cameras, mate! I don't want a fucking ticket.'

Kaz sat in the back; she gazed out at the Estuary, a vast expanse of mudflats, low tide, the water was maybe half a mile distant. It was a breezy day and the kite surfers were out in force bobbing and leaping over the choppy waves. The pier sat long and low on the grey horizon as Ashley drove more sedately along the front towards it.

Joey had taken some persuading, but Kaz realized she had quite a bit of leverage with him if she cared to use it. They were finally going to visit Natalie. Kaz had tried calling a few times, but the phone always went straight to voicemail. So their visit was probably unannounced. Kaz had spent a lot of time wondering about what had happened to her baby sister. She had a few theories, but none of them were good so she kept them to herself.

Ashley negotiated the speed bumps from the Pier Hill to the Kursaal, passing the neon strip of arcades and bars, which late morning were largely empty. Back in the eighties this had been Terry Phelps's stamping ground. Kaz remembered trips to the arcades with a fistful of coins to keep them quiet and amused whilst the old man conducted 'business'.

They turned up into the town and headed for the rundown sixties tower blocks where Natalie lived, apparently with a boyfriend. His name was Jez and he was a toerag; that was all the information Kaz had been able to prise out of her brother. Ashley pulled off the road on to a patch of tarmac lined with council wheelie bins, which served as a car park to the flats.

Joey leant between the two front seats and eyeballed his sister. 'You sure you wanna do this?'

She returned his gaze with equal determination. 'Yes.'

He shrugged and got out.

The lobby to the flats had entryphone access. Joey stabbed at a random series of buttons until someone got fed up and the door clicked open. The entrance was tiled, grime in the corners and a pervasive smell of disinfectant and piss. Joey pressed the call button on the lift.

'Hope to Christ this fucker's working, 'cause they live on the thirteenth floor.'

Ashley giggled. Both Joey and Kaz cast him questioning looks.

'Thirteen? Well, it's sort of . . . well I dunno. Just thought it was funny.'

Joey scowled at him. 'You have to be such a moron?'

'No I . . . sorry Joe.'

The lift arrived and as the steel doors trundled open Joey gave Ashley a shove. 'Get in you stupid tosser and keep your lame jokes to yerself.'

'Ain't a tosser.'

'Yeah you are.'

Kaz watched their antics with mild amusement as she followed them into the lift.

Natalie's flat was towards the end of a long corridor; a kid's pushchair, a broken bike, a couple of bin bags of rubbish all had to be negotiated before they reached the front door. Joey hammered on it with his fist, the thin plywood reverberated with the force.

Joey sighed. 'They'll probably think it's the social or the council.'

Abruptly the door opened and a tall, scrawny lad was blinking at them through round granny glasses. He was white, but his head was a mass of dirty bleached dreadlocks. He seemed confused, Kaz concluded he was simply wasted. Then recognition dawned and he beamed.

'Joe! All right mate?'

Joey glared at him. 'You letting us in or what?'

'Yeah yeah . . . come in.'

Joey pushed past him into the narrow hallway. Kaz and Ashley followed. It was oppressively hot and when they got to the sitting room they could see why: the gas fire was going full blast. Joey turned to him. 'Fuck me Jez, it's like a bleedin' sauna in here. Stinks 'n'all.' He went straight over to the glazed door, which opened on to a small balcony, and flung it open.

Jez twisted the dreads between his fingers. He was struggling to focus on his visitors. 'Nat, she feels the cold.'

Joey pointed at the gas fire. 'Turn that bloody thing off.' Jez looked at it blankly so Ashley obliged.

As Kaz rapidly took in the room all her worst fears were confirmed. Drug paraphernalia littered the table and the floor, together with takeaway cartons, bottles and beer cans. Joey booted an empty pizza box across the room at Jez.

'Don't you ever clean this place up?'

Jez raised his head slowly and gave Joey a dreamy smile. 'Nat, she feels the cold.'

'And where the fuck is she?'

Jez looked around and a puzzled expression crept over his

features as if he'd mislaid something, his keys maybe, and couldn't quite recall where he'd left them. The whole performance served to wind Joey up all the more; he elbowed Jez aside. Jez landed on the sofa in a heap like a rag doll.

'I hate fuckin' junkies.'

The flat was a maisonette on two floors. Kaz followed her brother up a short flight of stairs to the two bedrooms above. One was empty, bare boards and a tatty old pair of jeans forlornly abandoned in one corner. In the second, larger room there was a mattress on the floor with a duvet and some blankets heaped on top. Joey gave the room a cursory glance and slammed straight out.

'They do my fuckin' head in.'

Kaz hesitated in the doorway, scanning the room more closely. There was a can of beer by the bed, a loaded ashtray, a lighter and a crack pipe. Her chest felt tight, she was conscious of having to make an effort to breathe. Days lost, waking up with sore, parched lips, it all came flooding back. Kaz had been here, she'd done all this. As she moved across the room towards the bed she noticed a tiny nugget of crack still nestling in the foil wrap next to the pipe. The desire exploded in her brain before she was even conscious of the thought. Just one hit, just the one, it screamed. For old times' sake, what harm could it do?

She squatted down beside the bed, picked up the wrap and the pipe; the glass was discoloured, the edge broken, it was well used. Then the mound of covers moved and two eyes, pale and blue as Joey's, were staring straight at her.

'You nicking that?' The voice was a barely audible croak.

Kaz put the pipe and the wrap down. 'No.'

Kaz lifted the grimy corner of the duvet to reveal her sister's face. Natalie's blonde hair was also braided into short stubby dreads that gave her a fuzzy halo. The face was drawn, the lips and chin covered in sores. Kaz painted on a smile.

'How you doing Nat?'

Natalie pushed back the covers and struggled to sit up. She wore a thin vest, which provided no disguise for her emaciated form.

'What you doing here?'

'Came to see you. Didn't anyone tell you I was out?'

Natalie ignored the question as she focused on manoeuvring herself into an upright position.

'Got a fag?'

Kaz shook her head. 'Sorry.'

Without warning Natalie took a deep breath, opened her mouth and hollered, 'Jez!' The volume of sound took Kaz by surprise, it seemed impossibly loud for her sister's frail form.

Natalie glared at her impatiently. 'Where the fuck is he?'

'Downstairs. You getting up?'

Joey appeared in the doorway. He glanced from Natalie to Kaz. His jaw was set, his gaze came to rest defiantly on Kaz. His point was made, now he wanted her to acknowledge it.

Kaz smiled equably. 'I'm gonna help Natalie get dressed. Perhaps you and Ashley could make some coffee?'

Joey stared at her mutely, gave a curt nod and disappeared.

Natalie's eyes remained fixed on the empty doorway where he'd been; her brain seemed to be functioning on a time lapse, it took several seconds to catch up with events. 'Has Joe got a fag?'

'I dunno. You get dressed and come downstairs, maybe we can find out.'

It took Kaz the best part of half an hour to coax Natalie out of the bed and into a pair of jeans and an over-large hoodie, which looked as if it belonged to Jez. As she descended the stairs she hugged the hoodie round herself.

'Always fucking freezing in here.'

Joey was pacing the room, television remote in hand, channel-hopping. Ashley perched on the sofa, Jez stared into space.

Kaz shepherded her sister through the door. 'Here she is.'

Natalie booted Jez's outstretched foot. It jolted him out of his daze, he turned and smiled in recognition. 'All right babe?'

'Got a fag?'

Jez pondered the request, then his attention drifted away.

Kaz piloted Natalie towards the table. 'Drink your coffee first.'

Natalie hovered uncertainly in the middle of the room; she was practically Kaz's height, but her shoulders were bowed, her body rake-thin. She started to scratch.

'I want a fag.'

Kaz picked up a tepid mug of black coffee from the table and held it out to her. 'Have some of this first.'

Natalie eyed the mug and her sister with disdain. 'I want a fag.'

Joey had ceased to pace, he was watching the battle of wills between the sisters.

Kaz painted on a smile. 'The coffee'll help.'

Natalie balled up both fists and shut her eyes. 'I want a fag.'

Kaz watched, blankly, calmly, as Natalie started to chant. 'I want a fag. I want a fag. I want a fag—'

This was too much for Joey. He hurled the remote at the sofa, narrowly missing Ashley's head.

'Christ almighty, will someone give her a fuckin' fag!'

Kaz shot him a look and inclined her head towards the doorway. 'Can I have a word?'

Joey stomped down the hall to the small kitchenette. It was worse than the sitting room, a narrow galley, cartons of congealed food furred with mould littering both counters. Kaz followed him in and pulled the sliding door to. Penned in he turned to face her.

'Now you seen it for yerself. Satisfied?'

Kaz looked at him, tears were welling up in her eyes. 'How could you let this happen?'

Joey stared at her in disbelief. 'Me? Ain't nothing I could do!'

Kaz erupted, the tears were coursing down her cheeks now. 'This your idea of taking care of things while I was away? It's all bollocks Joey! She didn't get like this overnight. Where the fuck were you?'

Joey's lower lip quivered. Kaz's dark gaze was boring right into him. 'I . . . we . . . she wouldn't have it. Mum tried—'

'*Mum* tried? Mum! And gave up after five minutes no doubt, soon as it got a little bit awkward or inconvenient.' Kaz jabbed her index finger in his chest. 'So you all closed your eyes, turned your backs, walked away.'

'No! It weren't like—'

'You tell me how it was then. How did a bright twelve-year-old kid turn into an eighteen-year-old crackhead?'

'I don't know.' Joey started to cry too. He booted one of the kitchen cabinets, caving the door right in. 'I don't fucking know! It's not my fault.'

Kaz stared at him and she saw her father, his shadowy bulk filling her bedroom doorway. Once she'd been removed from the scene it was easy to imagine how he'd transferred his attentions to Natalie. If only she'd been there, she could've stopped it. The anger and bitterness rose in Kaz and like a filthy black bile engulfed everything. Joey and his tears, his excuses, seemed pathetic to her. He was flinging his arms about now like a petulant child; he punched a cupboard door, swept dirty crockery on the floor. Kaz stood stock-still, indifferent to his childish fury.

'Look at you Mr Big Business.' She laughed sourly. 'You reckon you know it all? Gonna become rich and successful. You couldn't even sort out your little sister. You stood by and let her turn into a junkie. What use are you?'

Joey stopped in his tracks. He stared right at her, the intense, hypnotic gaze. His voice was cold and detached. 'That what you really think?'

Kaz stared right back at him but she didn't reply. She was miles away, years away, before, if there ever was a before, searching her mind in vain for a time of childhood and innocence.

Joey pushed past her, practically yanked the sliding kitchenette door off its runners. He stormed into the sitting room, seized Jez by the throat and lifted him bodily off the sofa. Jez's glasses tumbled to the floor, he looked like a startled fawn; Joey had one arm round his neck, trapping it in a vice-like grip, the other under his flailing legs. He strode across the room to the open balcony door and holding Jez's gangling body horizontally he stepped through it, hoisted him up to shoulder height and threw him off the balcony.

Kaz returned to the room in time to see Jez disappearing. He made no sound, he was simply gone.

Joey stepped back into the room with a satisfied smirk on his face. He met Kaz's astonished look. 'You wanted it sorted, it's sorted. Okay?'

He scooped the car keys from Ashley's hand, marched down the hallway straight out of the flat, slamming the door behind him. Kaz rushed out on to the balcony and looked down. Thirteen floors below, Jez's broken body was splayed face up across one of the council wheelie bins, neck and shoulders dangling limply over the edge, one leg twitching. Kaz stared in disbelief. Inside the flat Natalie started to scream.

13

Kaz had to admit she was impressed by the way Ashley simply took charge of the situation. He whacked Natalie round the chops just hard enough to stun her into silence. Then he rooted round the debris of the sitting room and found a pair of flip-flops for her to put on.

'Right, we need to get out of here.'

Kaz was still so flabbergasted by Joey's actions she didn't reply. Grabbing Natalie's hand, she allowed Ashley to shepherd them both towards the front door. They reached the lift and he pressed the call button. Kaz glanced at him anxiously.

'Wouldn't the stairs be better . . . less obvious?'

Ashley dismissed this with a shake of his head. 'We're already on the CCTV, if it's working. Stay cool, act normal, pretend like nothing's happened.'

The lift arrived and they stepped inside. Natalie was snivelling then a low keening started to rumble through her emaciated frame. Kaz put a comforting arm round her shoulders. 'It's okay babes, it'll be okay.' She didn't believe this herself, her brain was reeling, but the immediate priority was to deal with Natalie.

Ashley reached in his pocket and pulled out a plastic grip-seal pouch of about half a dozen pills. He held it up.

'Could try giving her a couple of these?'

'What are they?'

'Benzos. They're ace for chilling you out. I give them to Joey when he has a freak out.'

Kaz stared at him, she was beginning to see Ashley in a whole new light. He tipped a couple of pills into his palm, offered them to Natalie.

'There you go Nat. Make you feel better.'

Natalie didn't hesitate for a second; pills, powders, this was what she knew. She hoovered them up like Smarties, even managed to give Ashley the ghost of a smile. 'Cheers.'

Ashley tipped out a third pill and handed it to her. 'One more for luck, eh?'

Natalie gobbled it down.

The lift doors opened at the ground floor, Ashley stepped out into the lobby and did a quick recce. A crowd of people was gathering outside round the wheelie bins, someone was on a mobile, several kids were using their phones to take pictures of the corpse. People were milling about in an atmosphere of excitement and prurience. But that made things easier.

A battered-looking CCTV camera was mounted on the wall facing the entrance, Ashley considered it. Then a gang of lads on bikes rode up, eager to see what was going on. This gave Ashley the chance he was looking for. He grabbed Natalie's arm and, using the lads as cover, slipped through the outer door and along the wall until they were out of the camera's range.

No one gave them a second glance as they skirted round and back to the car park, but the Range Rover was long gone.

Kaz stared at the empty parking space and huffed. 'Oh that's just great.'

Ashley was on alert, his eyes scanning in all directions. 'Don't worry, he'll be fine.'

Kaz snorted. 'He'll be fine? *He'll* be fuckin' fine! What about us?'

Natalie was standing, face upturned, blinking at the sky. It occurred to Kaz that she might not have been outside in full daylight for a while. Suddenly a shaft of sunlight burst from behind the scudding clouds and drenched them and the scrubby tarmac in blinding sunshine. Natalie pulled up her hood to shield her eyes and started to squirm. 'Need a pee.'

Kaz glared at her; the determination to rescue her baby sister had worn decidedly thin in the last half-hour. 'You'll have to wait.'

Natalie pressed her knees together, she was bent almost double, her face contorted. 'Need a pee.'

A wailing siren announced the imminent arrival of a police car. Ashley put a guiding hand on Natalie's elbow. 'Let's get out of here.'

'Need a pee.'

Kaz and Ashley propelled Natalie down the road between them. Once they were out of sight of the flats, they allowed her to squat behind a parked car and take a piss. As she relieved herself Ashley got out his phone and made a call. Kaz paced the pavement and tried to get her jumbled thoughts in some kind of order. Two weeks out of prison, how the hell did she land herself in this unholy mess? She cursed her own stupidity. She should be sitting calmly and safely in her life drawing class, not running from a murder scene. Getting hooked up with her family was always going to be a mistake. How many times had she told herself that? She'd sworn never to go down this road again, but here she was, up to her neck in shite, courtesy of Joey.

Natalie was fumbling to refasten her jeans, she couldn't seem to coordinate her fingers. Kaz grabbed her by the waistband and hoicked up the zip none too gently.

Natalie gazed up at her, her watery blue eyes met Kaz's angry gaze. 'Got a fag?'

Kaz considered clumping her, but she held back. What had she expected anyway, when she came looking for her baby sister? Natalie was no baby any more, she was an eighteen-year-old drug addict whose life had gradually and inexorably spiralled out of control over the last six years. She needed help and she needed treatment. She needed someone who cared about her enough and was prepared to persist for long enough to see that she got those things. Their mother clearly couldn't give a toss, Joey had issues of his own. That left her, Karen, playing the big sister once again, a role she'd vowed would have no part in her new life.

Ashley clicked his mobile off and smiled. 'Right, got things sorted. We need to head down to the front, wait for a pick-up.'

A stiff breeze was blowing up the estuary, they walked away from the primped and paved esplanade until they found a shelter facing the beach. It was wrought-iron, much painted, a random piece of Victoriana left over from Southend's glory days. Kaz swept abandoned chip papers from the seat and sat down. There were few people about aside from a Muslim family, the women wearing hijab, laughing and teasing each other as they attempted to keep the ends of their scarves from blowing in their ice creams. They seemed happy in each other's company, the children buzzing one another on their scooters, one of the men swinging a toddler up on to his shoulders. An ordinary family on a day out at the seaside, Kaz felt envious.

Natalie curled up in the corner of the shelter and stared into space. She seemed a whole lot calmer now. The benzodiazepine had kicked in. Ashley positioned himself with a view both up and down the promenade. The funfair was one way, the Sea Life Centre the other. Kaz watched him.

'You knew what he'd do, didn't you?'

Ashley gave her a shifty glance. 'Nah not really. Joey's always full of surprises.'

Kaz returned his look with her own searching gaze. 'Thirteen? Unlucky for some? Ain't that what your joke was about?'

'I was being a prat.'

'Strikes me Ash, you pretend to be a prat. That's your cover. But you're a lot more canny than you let on.'

Ashley's grin was lopsided but he seemed to appreciate the compliment. 'Well, y'know what Joey's like.'

'I used to. But I reckon you got the drop on me now.'

Ashley smiled. 'Nah, ain't no one matters to him as much as his sister.'

Kaz snorted. 'Yeah? Which one?'

Ashley didn't reply. They both knew the answer and it wasn't Natalie. He spent the next quarter of an hour fidgeting, continually glancing up the road. Kaz left him to it. She needed time to gather herself and figure out a viable strategy to keep her from going straight back to jail. And Fat Pat would be waiting.

Kaz felt her gut contract. She was imagining the screw's gleeful greeting, when she noticed Ashley raise his arm at a big black BMW X5, which promptly drew up kerbside. A bloke, well over six foot, got out of the passenger door and strode towards them.

Ashley smiled at him. 'All right mate?' The man nodded. Ashley glanced at Kaz. 'Don't know if you two have met?'

Kaz looked him up and down. He was solid muscle with sleeve tattoos up both arms, head shaved to a dark stubble.

'Kaz. Yev.'

Yevgeny gave her a curt but respectful nod.

'You do some serious time for a woman.' His accent was thick as treacle, to Kaz's untrained ear it could've placed him anywhere east of Krakow.

She smiled. 'Yeah. Reckon I did.'

He nodded again, pondering this. Then he glanced at Natalie in the shelter. 'Want me to carry her to the car?'

Kaz looked at her sister. 'She'll be all right.' She held out her hand. 'Come on Nat, time to go.'

Natalie got up and meekly took Kaz's hand. She allowed herself to be led to the four-by-four. Ashley held the door open and she climbed in the back. He buckled her in as you would a child.

Kaz glanced at the driver, he was a younger version of Yevgeny. He wore tight leather gloves, with the backs cut out. Yevgeny himself was still sizing her up. He smiled.

'My brother. Tolya.'

Tolya gave Kaz a friendly salute.

'His English ain't so good.'

Kaz returned Tolya's smile, then glanced at Yevgeny. 'Little brothers eh? They can give you a lot of grief.'

Yevgeny pursed his lips and gave a curt nod. A man of few words, Kaz reflected, though it was hard to say if this was because of his language skills or his temperament. Kaz looked at him, then at Ashley. She resented the fact that she was being rescued and protected by Joey's minders. Yevgeny was holding the rear door of the Beamer open for her. She was a female relative of the boss; organizing her, controlling her, that was his prerogative, he was simply doing his job. Fuck this, thought Kaz. She folded her arms and stood her ground.

'Right, well one of you two lads had better get that miserable little fucker on the phone, 'cause I want a word with him.'

Ashley met her look nervously. Her gaze bored into him. 'You heard me Ash. Now.'

Then she opened the front passenger door of the car and climbed in beside Tolya.

14

Mal Bradley placed himself strategically at the very back of the room in the hope that Turnbull wouldn't notice him. He'd spent the last three days attending a life drawing class at the Slade School of Fine Art, part of a summer school course that Karen Phelps had signed up for. She'd signed up but so far she hadn't shown up and Bradley's pathetic attempts to put charcoal to paper had earned him some sympathy and a slew of patronizing advice from his fellow students. Initially he'd assumed that sitting in on the class would be a doddle, staring at naked young women all day, he could manage that. But the model turned out to be male, muscular with a periodically tumescent penis, which embarrassed Bradley, although no one else in the class seemed to notice.

Bradley spent the rest of his time hanging round the hostel in his assumed role of support worker. Only the SPO knew his true identity, everyone else simply accepted him. Karen's stuff was still in her room, he knew that because he'd used the pass key to take a snoop. But Karen herself was proving evasive. She'd checked in with the SPO, the story was she was visiting her sick father.

If Bradley was honest he didn't know how to move forward or who to ask. When the boss had summoned him he'd been on the team barely a week. He'd had only nine months out of uniform, done a couple of courses, but mostly he'd been sitting on his backside all day listening to phone taps. The new skipper was DS Nicci Armstrong and he'd made the mistake of calling her 'Skip'. She'd given him a disbelieving glare.

'I'm not your bloody dog Bradley.'

'Sorry Skip.'

It was nervousness pure and simple, but she hadn't seen it that way. She thought he was trying to be smart. Some of the other lads had laughed and that made it worse. Armstrong was one of these don't-fuck-with-me women, she'd have your nuts in the wringer as soon as she looked at you. She was early thirties and had a kid, he only knew this because he'd overheard her bitching to one of the others about the cost of childcare.

Turnbull had called everyone in for an emergency briefing, but all Bradley could glean from the rumour mill was there'd been 'developments'. The boss walked into the room flanked by the DCI; Bill Mayhew was maybe ten years older than Turnbull and perpetually harassed.

Turnbull surveyed the room with a thin smile. He was seriously hacked off, but not about to reveal that to his assembled officers until he was good and ready. Sharply suited, the tip of a white handkerchief peeping out of his top pocket, Bradley admired his style. Beside him the pot-bellied, scurrying Mayhew looked like a down-and-out. Turnbull continued his leisurely scan as Mayhew and another minion prepared the PowerPoint presentation. His eyes came to rest on Bradley for a second, then they moved on. A mugshot of a young man in round glasses with a mass of unruly dreadlocks came up on the projection screen. Turnbull glanced up at it then he turned to address the room.

'Afternoon everyone. Jeremy Mark Harris, known as Jez. Twenty-two years old, known drug dealer and the former partner of Natalie Phelps. I say former, because this morning he plunged to his death from the thirteenth floor of a tower block in Southend. Question is did he fall or was he pushed?'

Turnbull's eyes roved around the room and settled on Nicci Armstrong, who shifted uncomfortably. Turnbull stared at her. He was pissed off because events had overtaken him, they'd moved out of his control. In his position that was dangerous at the best of times.

'DS Armstrong, you were in charge of the surveillance team on Joey Phelps. Perhaps you'd take up the tale from here.'

Armstrong cleared her throat. 'Yes sir, well . . .'

'Come up to the front Sergeant, so we can all hear you.' Turnbull's tone betrayed his anger and there was sympathy in the room for Nicci as she edged round the desks and her fellow officers. She took up a position with her back to the screen, as far away from Turnbull as she could manage. He didn't smile.

'In your own time Sergeant.'

The sarcasm in his voice served only to galvanize Nicci. She glanced at the smug fucker and raised her chin defiantly. She was hardly the first person to have blown a surveillance and she wasn't about to take the rap for this fuck-up.

'Essex Police logged Jez Harris's death at eleven-o-five this morning. Myself and DC Payne were in a surveillance vehicle which followed Joey Phelps's Range Rover Evoque into Southend at approximately ten a.m. Unfortunately we were involved in an incident at some traffic lights and we lost Phelps. The Range Rover was clocked by an ANPR camera on the A127 heading out of Southend at eleven seventeen.'

Nicci shot a look at Turnbull and waited.

'Presumably you did get a look at who was travelling with Phelps in the vehicle?'

Nicci nodded. 'Ashley Carter was driving. Karen Phelps was in the back.'

Turnbull's gaze shot down the room and zoned in on Bradley. 'Did you know about her trip to Southend DC Bradley?'

Bradley felt like a rabbit caught in the headlights.

'No sir.'

'No sir?' Turnbull raised his eyebrows. 'How is it that not one of you was up to the mark on this? Karen Phelps gets out of jail and goes with her brother to visit their junkie sister in Southend. Within an hour of their arrival her sister's boyfriend has taken a dive out of the window. And we know nothing about it until I get a call from Essex Police.'

Bradley focused on a loose thread fraying from the cuff of his denim shirt. He sensed Turnbull was just getting started. 'Come up here Bradley.'

Bradley raised his head, jutted his chin to bolster his confidence and made his way to the front. He still felt like an errant schoolboy, which he knew was Turnbull's intention.

'Stand next to Armstrong. Now, tell me, what is going on here? Have we got a communications problem? Did your mobile run out of juice Bradley?'

The young officer blinked. 'No sir.'

Nicci Armstrong took a deep breath, she'd had more than enough of Turnbull's crap. She wasn't about to be turned into a scapegoat to cover his arse.

'Can I speak sir? Because there's a hell of a lot more to this than meets the eye.'

Turnbull put his hands in his pockets. 'Okay, let's hear it.'

'First of all the surveillance. We're trying to keep tabs on someone like Joey Phelps using one car, which is ridiculous. We follow him into Southend, we're two vehicles behind at the traffic lights and we get rear-ended by a bloody great BMW four-by-four. It's got French plates, which, when we finally get a trace on them, turn out to be false. It's got two blokes in it, who speak not a word of English and from their tattoos look like they've been demobbed from the Russian army. The whole thing was no coincidence. Add to that the fact the tracker we placed on Phelps's vehicle turns up at a motorway services on the M25 on a Tesco's lorry. Phelps is running rings round us and will continue to do so until we're provided with adequate resources to carry out a proper, professional surveillance operation.'

The room was completely silent. No one moved a muscle. Bradley was close enough to Armstrong to feel the tension and the fury burning off her. A dozen pairs of eyes were focused expectantly on Turnbull. He pursed his lips, inhaled. He decided to go with the flow, in this instant it seemed the best option.

'Well . . . glad someone's got the balls to speak up.' He swivelled round and focused on the unfortunate Mayhew. 'One-car surveillance Bill? How was that ever going to work?'

Mayhew sucked in a mouthful of air and hunched his shoulders. He could've announced to the whole room that in trying to manage with one vehicle they'd been following Turnbull's earlier instructions. But he knew better than to challenge the boss in public.

Bradley followed the exchange intently; clearly when Turnbull had said they often had to busk it he hadn't been lying.

Turnbull gave Nicci an apologetic shrug. 'What can I tell you Sergeant? The cuts are the bane of all our lives. Unfortunately we must soldier on with the resources we have.'

Nicci smiled to herself, she knew she had him on the ropes. 'Can I finish sir? Because this is not simply an issue of resources.'

Turnbull folded his arms, she was an ambitious little bitch, but he was beginning to think that might work to his advantage. He gave her a smile, inviting her to continue.

'DC Bradley is new to the case, we gather he's been tasked

to work undercover. But so far as I'm aware, there's been no attempt to bring him up to speed with the rest of the operation. Okay, if he's running a chiz I can appreciate that he must act independently and maintain a sterile corridor. But we still need a formal mechanism for the exchange of intelligence.'

Bradley glanced sideways at her. She was the last person he expected to ride to his rescue. Turnbull rubbed a finger over his chin and pondered as if he were giving her words the most serious consideration. Then he nodded sagely, glanced at Mayhew. 'Fair comment Bill?'

Mayhew took a deep breath and ran his fingers round the inside of his trouser belt, easing the pressure on his paunch. There was an undercurrent of resentment in the room and everyone knew it. Alex Marlow wasn't even in his grave and Bradley had been parachuted in.

'Well of course boss, I think the whole team has been upset by the loss of Alex Marlow. He did a lot of good work. A number of officers, including Nicci, provided excellent backup. It was all running like a well-oiled machine. Which makes what happened this morning doubly unfortunate. But we need to learn the lesson, reorganize and regroup.' He nodded to himself as if struck by the good sense of his own advice, then he glanced at Turnbull and waited.

Turnbull was leaning against a desk, jingling his change. He knew what Mayhew was telling him: he'd pissed people off. But frankly he couldn't give a toss, he needed to get the show back on the road. He nodded his head thoughtfully several times.

Bradley caught Nicci Armstrong's eye; she was still steaming and was shifting impatiently from foot to foot. Turnbull stepped forward placing himself centre stage.

'Right, this is a bloody shambles.' He shot an accusing glance at Mayhew. 'But here's what we're going to do. Bradley clearly needs help. Armstrong, you'll become his handler, work closely with him from now on. It's quite likely Karen Phelps became an accessory to murder this morning. So I want you on her case. Relentlessly. Threaten her with recall, do what you have to. She is going to be our chiz. And I couldn't give a monkey's uncle about maintaining a sterile corridor between her and the team. We don't have the time or resources for that.'

Turnbull was warming to his theme. What he was saying was obvious, but somehow the pitch and delivery made his words sound momentous, even epic. He raised a finger, pointed it decisively at Mayhew.

'Bill, Joey Phelps is our target and I don't want Essex Police muscling in on the act. They want us to put details of our investigation up on HOLMES so they can access it. Well bugger that. Phelps murdered a police officer and that takes precedence over some two-bit drug dealer. Surveillance is key, we need to up our game.'

Turnbull paused and scanned the room. Most eyes were on him, although there was a bit of fidgeting, so he lowered his voice, adopting a softer more personal tone. 'I don't need to remind any of you that we've lost a valued colleague, not to mention a friend. So I want a hundred and fifty per cent from everyone. Time we nailed this bastard, so let's get out there and let's do it.'

Turnbull took a deep breath and smiled. That was it, briefing over.

As Turnbull sailed off through the swing doors and down the corridor Bradley turned to Nicci.

'Thanks for that Sarge.'

She gave him a cursory glance and started to walk away. 'Didn't do it for you.'

Nicci joined Mayhew, who was pouring himself a coffee.

'Sorry boss, but I wasn't going to let him mug me. Not in front of the whole team.'

Mayhew smiled, patted her arm. He was a slow, benign bloke, nothing ruffled his feathers. 'Don't fret Nic. I'm his designated bum-boy, not you.'

Nicci ran her fingers through her hair wearily. 'He blames everything on the bloody cuts. More like his lousy management.'

Mayhew shrugged this off, wiped a hand across his sagging face. 'He's been acting odd, I don't know what he's up to. Still, least you nailed him on the surveillance, which should help. Now I can insist on two units.'

Nicci poured herself a coffee. 'So what was this bollocks about anyway? Why an emergency briefing?'

Mayhew gave a rumbling laugh. 'Essex Police got him on the blower. Assistant Chief Constable no less. Started to throw his weight about. They plan to pull Joey Phelps in and they expect our full support and cooperation. Want it to be their collar. Turnbull went apeshit.'

Nicci grinned. 'I'll bet. Does it never occur to any of them that we're on the same side?'

Mayhew sank half a cup of coffee in one gulp. 'Turnbull's got to keep an eye on his score sheet. Days like this I just think about my pension.'

Nicci topped up the mug for him. 'I've been trying to get a line on these bastards in the Beamer. I got Payne trawling the Hendon database for more sightings. But they're totally off the radar.'

Mayhew sighed. 'Would be. Foreign, ex-military – smart move on Joey's part. There are plenty of Russians in London, better to have them working for you than going into competition.'

Bradley came to the coffee station behind them, poured himself a mug. Then he sidled forward. 'Listen, can I have a word?'

Mayhew and Nicci both turned to look at him.

'Okay, so I'm Turnbull's boy, that's how everyone's got me pegged . . .'

Mayhew chuckled. 'You're his Exocet missile, lad. The Assistant Commissioner is relying on you. 'Course we can't admit it's a honeytrap, 'cause they're illegal. So it's all very hush hush, eh Nic?'

She nodded.

'Which is why we're all running round fucking clueless, including you I suspect.'

Bradley shifted restlessly. 'I've spent the last three days at a bloody art class.'

Nicci looked him up and down, somehow his obvious good looks annoyed her. But she was working hard to keep her personal emotions in check. The only way she could do that was to focus relentlessly on the job. And that meant dealing with Bradley. She milked her coffee. 'You tried approaching her yet?'

Bradley looked a bit sheepish. 'Yeah well I went to the hostel. Posed as a support worker. Unfortunately she made me straight away.'

Nicci laughed out loud. 'You mean she didn't swoon into your manly arms? Well there's a fucking surprise! We've got a murderous gangster out there, killed a police officer. And we're relying on an airhead. A fucking rookie airhead!'

She took her coffee and strode off.

Mayhew gave Bradley a sympathetic look. 'Nic and Alex Marlow were good mates.'

Bradley huffed. He knew he'd made a mess of things and

that was starting to panic him. He didn't want to plead, that would make him look more stupid. But what was the alternative?

'Look, I'm not trying to replace Alex Marlow. All I want is to be part of the team and do my job.'

Mayhew nodded, eased the belt on his paunch. He'd seen plenty of versions of Mal Bradley, impressive on paper but not an iota of useful experience. Still, he felt for the lad and he knew Turnbull. If things went wrong, Turnbull would need a scapegoat and Bradley was perfect. He wondered if the young DC had figured that out yet.

He put a hand on Bradley's shoulder. 'I know you do. So back to square one, eh. Come in my office and let's see if we can sort out a way forward with this.'

'Thank you sir.'

Mayhew laughed. 'Don't call me sir. Everyone will think you're a bloody rookie.'

Bradley hung his head. He shot a baleful look across the room to where Nicci Armstrong was lounging at her desk, phone to her ear.

Mayhew followed his gaze. 'And you need to get on with her. When you're undercover, your backup is your lifeline. Plus she's probably the best copper on this team.'

15

Karen was pacing her mother's kitchen. Her attempts to take control of the situation had been a dismal failure. Joey wasn't answering his phone, Ashley and the Russians had simply dumped Kaz and her sister back here and driven off.

Ellie had fussed over Natalie like a mother hen. Kaz discovered that her sister's bedroom had received a makeover very similar to her own, except Natalie's colour scheme was yellow. Kaz had watched as Ellie settled her daughter under the plump duvet and rearranged the cuddly toys around her. Ellie cooed over Natalie as if she were a small child who'd come home from school with a tummy upset and just needed a bit of extra TLC from Mum. The charade simply annoyed Kaz; their life had never been like that.

Now Kaz faced her mother across the sleek granite worktops. Ellie was pouring boiling water from the kettle into a smart spotted teapot.

'Nice cup of tea, that's what we need. I don't mind a cappuccino or latte when I'm out, but I've never been much of a coffee drinker. As your nan used to say, good strong cuppa, always sets you up.'

Kaz watched her mother as she rattled off this litany of nonsense. She'd rarely heard Ellie speak of her own mother. Their 'nan' had never been more than an abstract concept in their lives. Ellie was the youngest of five in a family of dockers, who'd shown her the door when she hooked up with Terry Phelps. The 'nan' in question took a dim view of her daughter's attempts to better herself by marrying a villain, and Terry was not the sort of bloke to tolerate criticism from his mother-in-law. As a result Ellie became completely estranged from her family and didn't attend her mother's funeral. Kaz had never met any of them.

Ellie took down two flowery mugs from the cupboard. 'You still take milk and sugar? Joey still spoons it in, like when he was a little boy.'

'Mum, I don't want a cup of tea.'

Ellie was already pouring, but she paused mid-flow and gave Kaz a critical glance. 'Suit yourself lovey. But I think it'd make you feel better.'

Kaz wanted to scream at her, but she reined herself in, focusing on the greenery out of the kitchen window. 'What would make me feel better is to have a sensible conversation about the state Natalie's in and what we're going to do about it.'

Ellie picked up her mug, cupped her hands round it. 'Oopsy, bit hot! Silly me.' She put the mug back on the counter.

Kaz crossed her arms and huffed in disbelief. 'Mum?'

Ellie was intent on carefully lifting the hot mug by its handle. She balanced it between thumb and index finger, took a tiny sip of tea.

'Well I don't know what to say about it lovey. You'll have to have a word with Doctor Iqbal yourself when he gets here.'

Kaz glared at her.

'What? Who the fuck's Doctor Iqbal?'

'Oh he's very expensive. But Joey sees to all that. He's helped us before when Natalie's been bad.'

'Hang on, who's called him? You?'

Ellie gave her a blank look, as if it should all be quite obvious.

'No, Joey's called him. Then sent me a text. Came just before you arrived.'

Kaz digested this. She wanted to scream at her mother. She could see what Ellie was up to. It was all a deliberate wind-up designed to put Kaz in her place. But Kaz refused to rise to the bait.

'What is he then, some kind of addiction specialist?'

Ellie stirred two large sugars into her tea. 'Oh yes, he's very specialist. Nice manners too. Speaks perfect English, you can understand every word.'

'Why did no one mention him before?'

Ellie gave her an aggrieved look. 'You never asked. You jump to conclusions, my girl, always did. You come home, start throwing your weight about. You think we ain't tried to get Nat off the drugs?' Ellie fingered the small gold crucifix at her neck and a tear welled up in the corner of her eye. 'We tried everything. As God is my witness, I spent nights sitting up, crying over that child.'

This was about as much of her mother's shtick as Kaz could take. She turned on her heel and walked out of the kitchen.

Kaz stomped through the sitting room and found refuge in the newly built conservatory. It was awash with exotic plants. She had wondered who in the Phelps clan had the patience or the skills to nurture anything and make it grow. Then she'd learnt the secret from her mother:

'Couple of illegals that work for Joey – Vietnamese I think. Always very polite. They pop in twice a week, do everything. Joey reckons they're dead clever, can make any sort of plant grow. They grow stuff for him. Suppose it's all them rice paddies.'

Kaz found herself a chair between lush greenery, sat down

and took out her mobile. Joey had bought it for her on their shopping trip and she'd nearly got the hang of it. She clicked onto Helen's number, chose office over mobile and let it ring. She didn't know what the hell she was going to say. She wanted to scream help, but that wouldn't be cool. In spite of the panic that was tearing up her insides Helen's good opinion still mattered.

The phone rang several times then went to voicemail. Kaz checked her new watch: Gucci, gold and platinum – another 'essential' picked up on the shopping trip. It was half past six, so Helen must've left for the day. Kaz was about to try her mobile, when she became aware of a low snuffling whimper. She peered through the foliage, it was coming from the other side of the conservatory and it was getting louder. It sounded like an animal, a stray dog maybe that had got shut in. But that didn't make any sense. As Kaz got up to investigate, the whimper became a feral whine; she looked around for some kind of stick. She didn't fancy confronting a trapped animal empty-handed.

Having armed herself with a cane from one of the rubber plants, Kaz stepped forward. Then she saw the source of the noise. Tucked away in a corner between some delicate orchids and a large yucca, Terry Phelps sat slumped in his wheelchair and an angry moan was rising up from his chest into his throat, causing saliva to bubble on his lips. Kaz stood and stared, though it was all she could do not to turn tail and run. His glassy black eyes seemed to bore straight through her, but if there was any recognition in them she couldn't discern it. The hairs on the back of her neck started to prickle, maybe this tale of a stroke was all some elaborate scam of his and he was about to leap up from the chair and seize her by the throat. She could almost see him start to rise then the fear engulfed her. She stumbled backwards, turned desperately to find the door and fell straight into the arms of Brian.

He caught her by the elbows. 'Hey, what's up?'

Kaz pushed him savagely away. Her heart was thumping in her chest. 'Fuck me, Brian! You scared me half to death!'

'Sorry, didn't mean to creep up on you. I come for your dad. Heard him carrying on. Bit past his teatime. He gets hungry, he makes his feelings known – don't you Tel?'

Brian patted his arm and reached for the joystick to put the wheelchair in motion. Kaz sucked in a couple of deep breaths as she fought to appear normal. Fortunately Brian was more intent on manoeuvring the wheelchair out of its corner. His attention was on Terry, who was still whining, but now it was more of a low grumble.

'I know I know, teatime's a bit late today. But we got a nice lasagne, you like that.'

Kaz glanced down at her hand, still grasping the cane, realized it was visibly shaking much like the rest of her. So she focused on returning the cane to its slot next to the rubber plant.

Brian was guiding the wheelchair out through the door-way then a thought struck him, he paused and glanced over his shoulder at Kaz. 'Oh, I nearly forgot – your mum said to tell you Joey's arrived.'

16

Once Kaz had composed herself she entered the kitchen to find Joey cracking open a beer he'd taken from the fridge. He gave his sister a sunny smile. It was as if nothing had happened.

'All right babes?' Then he turned back to Ellie and threw an arm round her shoulder. 'But the important thing is I don't want you to worry, Mum.'

Ellie's expression was petulant, her cheeks were pink and tear-stained. Her fingers were busy shredding a tissue.

'Ain't I had enough to contend with? Your dad in a wheelchair, your sister in jail . . .' She shot an accusing glance at Kaz. 'Now all this trouble with Natalie. I don't think my nerves can take it son.'

Joey drew her into a hug. 'It'll be all right, I promise.'

Ellie briefly returned the hug, then edged away from him and cast a baleful look in Kaz's direction. 'She blames us y'know. Thinks we din't keep a proper eye on Natalie.'

Joey shook his head. 'No she don't Mum. 'Course you don't, do you Kaz?'

Kaz took a deep breath and opened her mouth to speak, but Ellie didn't give her the opportunity. She started to wail.

'I know I ain't been the best mother in the world. But I loved my babies, all three of them . . . as God is my witness Joey . . .'

Joey pulled her into his arms again, then over her shoulder he mouthed at Kaz: 'Say something.'

Kaz snorted contemptuously. 'Like what?'

She glanced through to the dining room where Brian was patiently shovelling liquidized lasagne into Terry Phelps's slack mouth. It was a messy process, Terry gagged on almost every mouthful and half the food ended up on his improvised bib. Kaz reflected on the years of bullying Brian must've endured at her father's hands. Now he was his part-time nurse, yet there was no resentment. Or there didn't seem to be. But behind closed doors? Brian had all the power. Kaz rather hoped he abused it.

She looked back at her mother and brother, still locked in each other's arms; she'd forgotten what a clever manipulator Ellie had always been. Terry had thumped her often enough – that was his way, he thumped everyone – but he wasn't an out and out wife-beater. Ellie knew how to play him, just as she was playing Joey now. And it came to Kaz in a blinding flash that that was why she hated her mother so much. Ellie had known only too well what Terry Phelps was doing to his young daughter when he went up to tuck her in every night. But she'd turned a blind eye. Her priority was to keep Terry sweet and stop him from bothering her all the time.

Kaz remembered those long ago desperate attempts to get her mother's help and protection, and she remembered Ellie's response: 'What a lot of nonsense! Your daddy loves you, so don't you go making up wicked stories 'cause he gives you the odd clout now and again.'

The 'odd clout', Kaz thought ruefully. That she could've coped with.

The entry system intercom buzzed, Joey went to answer it. Kaz watched from the kitchen window as the heavy wrought-iron gates swung open and a silver Mercedes luxury people carrier with darkened windows drew up in front of the house. A small, sharply suited man in rimless glasses climbed out, flanked by two middle-aged women. Joey already had the door open. He held out his hand.

'Doctor Iqbal, thanks for coming.'

The doctor smiled politely as his small, neat hand disappeared in Joey's paw.

'I'm sorry you have need of my services again Mr Phelps.'

The women wore matching pale mauve nurses' tunics and one of them carried a black medical case; they followed the doctor into the house.

In the kitchen Ellie glanced resentfully at Kaz, dabbed her eyes with a tissue and swept out into the hallway.

'Oh Doctor Iqbal, we've been having such a time of it. My poor baby, I been so worried.'

Doctor Iqbal gathered both Ellie's hands in his compact capable clasp.

'Where is Natalie now Mrs Phelps?'

'I'll take you up.'

Then, as an afterthought, she glanced at Kaz, who was hovering in the kitchen doorway.

'Oh, this is my other daughter, Karen. She's been abroad.'

Doctor Iqbal's keen gaze rested briefly on Kaz and he inclined his head politely. But Ellie was already dragging him towards the stairs. The nurses followed.

Kaz and Joey were left in the hallway.

Joey clapped his hands together and grinned. 'He's a great bloke. Lifesaver. I called him soon as I left. He's driven down all the way from Yorkshire y'know. That's where his place is. Fucking amazing, looks like a stately home. He took care of Nat before, got her clean. And she would've stayed that way if it weren't for that toerag Jez.'

Kaz watched her brother, he was completely hyper, pacing the hall, the nervous tension burning off him.

'And you was dead right babes, I should've done something about it before. But, y'know, I was busy. I took me eye off the ball. You was right to give me a bollocking. I should've sorted him out long ago, soon as Nat went back to him. None of this would've happened.' He shot an appealing look at her. 'But we're all square now, 'n't we? Doctor Iqbal'll take her back to the clinic. She'll be right as rain in no time.'

Kaz folded her arms, turned and walked into the kitchen. She took a glass from one of the cupboards and filled it with water from the tap.

Joey followed her. 'You pissed off with me?'

Kaz drank down half the water then placed the glass on the worktop. She fixed him with a penetrating stare. 'I dunno. What do you think?'

'You was right to have a go, I'm not saying you wasn't.'

'Jesus wept Joey – you killed a man! Now you're trying to make it look like I wanted you to do it.'

He stared at her, the little-boy-lost look, the little Joey. 'Well how else was I gonna sort it out? She was never gonna get clean while she was with that toerag. He fed her the stuff!'

Kaz picked up the glass and tossed the remaining water down the sink. 'Then you drove off and left us there. What the fuck did you think we were gonna do?'

Joey looked puzzled, for all the world like a misunderstood schoolboy. 'I knew Ash'd take care of you. And I had Yev and Tol riding shotgun. I needed to get out of there, make arrangements. Get things properly sorted, like I shoulda done before.'

As Kaz glared at him, his chin quivered, he wiped his hand across his face. Was he doing a number on her? She couldn't tell.

'I wouldn't upset you for the world babes. You know that.'

'Upset me? I just got out on licence and you make me an accessory to murder. What d'you think's gonna happen when my probation officer hears about that?'

A relieved smile spread over Joey's features. 'If it's the old bill you're worried about, that's all in hand. I already talked to Neville.'

'Who the fuck's Neville?'

'Neville Moore. At the lawyer's. He's the head honcho there now. I told him to speak to your one too. Give her the heads-up so we're prepared if the filth come calling.'

Kaz felt her stomach lurch, she reached out and gripped the sink to steady herself. 'Helen knows about this?'

'Well yeah. I also got a line on the old bill in Southend. I'm waiting for my contact to get back to me, let me know what CCTV they got on us. So you see I haven't been pissing about.'

He beamed at her like a kid expecting a pat on the head. Kaz felt the bile rising in her throat. She couldn't stop it, she turned and vomited into the sink.

17

Neville Moore sat, elbows resting on his vast black ash desk, fingertips steepled, deep in thought. Since becoming managing partner four years ago he'd occupied the impressive corner office with views on two sides of some of the City's more imposing landmarks. With Fred Sheridan's demise and the subsequent retirement of Henry Crowley he'd added his own name to the letterhead and promoted four of his brightest associates, including Helen Warner, to full partners. Still in his early forties, his head shaved to disguise a balding pate, Neville regarded himself as a man whose moment had come.

Under his guidance, the firm had changed tack, become more of a liberal campaigning outfit, taking on cases that gave them a media profile, doing pro bono work for worthy causes. Gradually the reputation of villains' brief was being superseded by a more palatable image. They'd become the scourge of the establishment, champion of the little guy. He'd even written the occasional op-ed piece for the *Guardian*.

However Neville Moore was also a pragmatist. Replacing the firm's seedy East End shopfront with a plush city address had increased his overheads tenfold. Retaining the services of a sharp go-getting team meant paying top whack. None of them wanted a drone's life in a massive corporate law firm. But still they had school fees, as did he, plus a hefty mortgage on a detached Edwardian villa outside Godalming, which all added up to a need for a healthy balance sheet and for clients like Joey Phelps.

Neville had ruthlessly pruned some of the more unpleasant gangsters from the client list. Still, being a criminal firm meant representing criminals, making sure they got a fair trial. There was no shame in that. Neville had known Joey since he was sixteen. Terry Phelps he'd never liked, the man was a boorish thug with a very short fuse. But Neville had taken immediately to Joey. Watching the lad grow up, Neville had tried to persuade him that he had the brains to take a different path in life to his old man. And Neville's argument had to some extent succeeded, but not in the way he intended. Joey needed instant gratification, he had huge energy and enthusiasm, but the villain's life really did suit him better than anything else. He simply learnt to be much better at it than his father. And he paid Neville a hefty retainer to be on call and keep him out of jail.

Neville's reflections were interrupted by Helen Warner appearing in his open doorway. He smiled and beckoned. 'Helen, come in.'

Her face was troubled, she perched on the end of his white leather sofa. 'Your email said there's a problem with Karen Phelps.'

Neville tapped his fingertips together and scanned her face. Helen's level of involvement with this particular client was starting to cause him a little concern.

'Joey Phelps phoned me. The story is they went to visit the sister Natalie in Southend. Natalie has a drug problem and was somehow persuaded to leave with them to enter a rehab programme. Unfortunately her boyfriend was upset about this and took a suicidal leap to his death from the thirteenth floor. Anyway, that's the version of events Joey's peddling.' Neville added a sceptical shrug.

Helen nodded slowly and sighed. 'And Karen was there? Oh dear.'

What she was thinking was oh shit. Neville was still scanning her. She was aware of the tense knot in her stomach. This was all getting out of hand. She was a lawyer, clients messed up all the time, that was normal. What was abnormal was her feeling like this.

Neville got up from his desk and strolled round it, hands in trouser pockets. 'My feeling is we take the bull by the horns. Go to the police before they come to us. They've probably got the evidence to place our clients at the scene, but without witnesses the suicide story will play as well as any other.'

Helen pushed back her hair in annoyance. It helped to channel her feelings into something for public consumption. 'I told her to stay away from the family. I'd better speak to her probation officer, don't want them to get shirty.'

Neville gave her a penetrating look. 'I hope you're not getting too wound up with this girl, Helen. She's simply another client. You can only give her your best advice. End of the day she makes her own choices. If she goes back to jail, it's not your fault.'

Helen met his eye with a steady gaze. The last thing she needed was for him to twig the real state of her emotions. She'd been struggling with them ever since Karen got out, she was involved, she was far too involved. It was already causing problems in her private life. She'd just about got to the point where she could admit that to herself. But Neville must never know. No one must know.

Helen turned her palms outwards and shrugged. 'It's annoying, that's all. Karen's supposed to be going to art college. She's reasonably talented. I had some plans to use her for a bit of PR. She makes a career of it, it's a great story for the

Sunday supplements, a good way to enhance the firm's profile, I thought.'

Neville nodded. 'We can always do with a bit of that. Anyway, I'm going to set up an interview with Essex Police, take Joey in myself.'

'You want me to do the same with Karen?'

'Yep, I think so. They may be thinking, given Joey's reputation, that they're on to something here. But it'll all be circumstantial. With a bit of luck we'll kick it into the long grass.'

She got up, gave him her best smile. 'Right, well I'll get on with it.'

Neville watched her stroll a little too casually out of his office. His wife took the view that Helen batted for the other side. Personally he couldn't see it; she was very good-looking, a leggy blonde, plenty of blokes would jump at the chance. But he had to admit she was a bit of a cold fish. In his experience, most women he'd ever worked with, however hard-nosed and professional, would turn on the charm at some point. A hint of flirtatiousness over coffee, a solicitous stroking of the male ego, especially to get what they wanted. Helen never indulged in any such behaviour, but that didn't make her gay. Still, he pondered, his wife was a far better reader of people than he could ever hope to be. And if Helen had got herself romantically entangled with Karen Phelps, that was the kind of PR he could certainly do without.

18

Nicci Armstrong and Mal Bradley arrived at Southend nick around ten o'clock. They took the train down from London and found it was only a short walk from the station along Victoria Avenue. They showed their warrant cards at the desk and were taken upstairs to meet the DCI who was conducting the interviews. The Phelpses were due to present themselves, lawyered up, at eleven.

Cheryl Stoneham was a small, stout woman in her early fifties, an SIO from crime division, usually based in Chelmsford. She was laughing and joking with the District Commander and a couple of other uniforms and kept them hanging about like spare parts long enough to make it clear they were on her territory. But when she finally came over and held out her hand she was all smiles.

'Cheryl Stoneham. Sorry, only just got here myself. Traffic was a bugger. I've been sorting out an interview room.'

Nicci beamed back, accepting the firm handshake. 'DS Armstrong. This is DC Bradley.'

'Well, this is a very interesting situation we find ourselves in. An apparent suicide, but one of Essex's premier villains is coming in voluntarily to be interviewed.'

Bradley shook hands too. 'His brief's probably assuming you've got CCTV that can place him at the scene.'

Stoneham sighed. 'Yeah well no such luck. The council sticks these sodding cameras up all over the shop to deter the hooligans, but most of them don't work. We've got ANPR on Phelps's vehicle and bugger all else.'

Nicci smiled. 'Proves he was in Southend at the relevant time.'

Stoneham gave her an arch look. 'I gather your lot had him under surveillance.'

Turnbull had instructed Armstrong and Bradley to 'give these bastards nothing'. He was referring to his esteemed colleagues in the Essex Police. But Nicci didn't reckon dancing to Turnbull's tune was her primary role. She looked Cheryl Stoneham up and down, judged the woman to be a decent and competent officer. 'Yeah I'm really sorry ma'am. We should have let you know we were on your turf. But it was a difficult surveillance. Things were moving very fast.'

Stoneham gave her a reproachful look. 'Too fast for you to keep up, I gather.'

Nicci shrugged. 'Unfortunately we only had one vehicle. Turns out he had backup and his boys stitched us up like the professionals they are. We lost Phelps before we ever got into town.'

Stoneham shook her head ruefully. She knew how arrogant the Met could be, but Nicci's contrite manner placated her. 'Bloody cuts! How we're expected to deal with villains like Phelps with a one-man-and-a-dog operation beats me. It's no different here. Bosses come up with all these strategy papers – we haven't got enough boots on the ground to carry them out.'

The two women shared a cynical laugh. Bradley watched them. He could see that some kind of female bonding was going on here and he was determined not to be cut out of the loop. So he joined in with the laughter, giving Stoneham his best smile.

'Our so-called strategy is to get Karen Phelps to inform against her brother.'

Nicci gave him a sidelong glance, wondering how the hell she'd got landed with such a dickhead. She turned to Stoneham. 'He's the bait.'

Stoneham gave him a wry look. 'Let's hope you're man enough for the job.' She checked her watch. 'Talking of which, I don't know where my bloody sergeant's got to.' She gave Nicci a speculative glance. 'Fancy sitting in with me? Then we can both go home and tell our rivalrous bosses that Essex and the Met cooperated fully.'

Nicci grinned. 'That'd be great.'

'Let's get ourselves a coffee then. Canteen here does jam doughnuts. Fatal for my diet. But I figure if I'm going to take on Joey Phelps and his high-priced brief, a sugar rush might give me the edge.'

The women grinned at each other in mutual accord. Stoneham led the way, Nicci by her side.

'With me it's the fags.'

'Aww, tell me about it. I used to smoke forty a day. Then my old man and my kids ganged up on me. Forced me on to the patches. Took me three goes to quit.'

'Only three? That's brilliant.'

As the two women sailed out of the open-plan office and down the corridor Bradley was forced to bring up the rear. He felt very much like an afterthought. He'd seen this before, women talking rubbish yet communicating on another more subtle level. They could've discussed Joey Phelps, the questions to ask him – which would've been the professional approach in his view – but none of that seemed necessary. They'd met less than five minutes ago, already they were mates. The analyst in Bradley marvelled at this. It also pissed him off royally. It was a trick he was desperate to learn.

19

Kaz sat on a low wall at the edge of the car park. She was pulling on a Silk Cut as if her life depended on it. It was the lowest-tar brand on the market and her pathetic concession to the fact that after a year off cigarettes she'd cracked. Overnight she'd smoked herself from nausea to a sore throat, but none of it brought her the release from anxiety she craved.

Joey and Ashley were on the other side of the car park larking around beside the Range Rover. They were playing 'Call of Duty Black Ops Zombies' on an iPad and arguing about whose turn it was. Joey was wearing a three-piece tailored suit; he certainly looked the business, although Kaz thought it unlikely this would cut much ice with the police.

After Doctor Iqbal had left with a quiescent Natalie, she and Joey had sat down at the kitchen table and constructed a plausible story to explain how Jez Harris had come to take his own life. Joey even seemed to enjoy the process; to him it was another game, a chance to outwit the filth. But Kaz felt sick to her stomach. She refused to eat the plate of lasagne and salad that Ellie placed in front of her. Finally, at about half nine, she escaped from the house and walked. It was country lanes, a few large houses, but mostly dark fields and brooding woodland. She ended up at a jovial Tudorbethan pub festooned with fairy lights several miles down the road. Just the sight of it brought on an overwhelming desire for alcohol. She stood outside for about ten minutes wrestling with a desperate craving to soak herself in booze. In the end she went in, ordered a Coke and bought forty cigarettes from the machine in the corner of the bar. This was the best she could manage in the circumstances, she told herself. She chain-smoked three fags on the way home and ended up retching into a ditch.

This morning, as they drove down to Southend, she'd sat in the back of the Range Rover and spoken as little as possible. Joey was in a sparky mood, insisted on playing her the latest tracks he'd downloaded. She let him and Ashley rattle on, they were doing their we're-a-couple-of-ordinary-lads act. Kaz may have been taken in by this before, but now she knew better.

It was a quarter to eleven when a dark blue Jaguar XK turned into the car park and drew up a couple of slots away from the Range Rover. Kaz watched as Neville Moore climbed out of the driving seat and stretched. Joey went over immediately to shake his hand. But Kaz's attention was on Helen Warner, who emerged from the passenger side. Helen glanced in Kaz's direction and caught her eye. She was too far away for Kaz to read her expression. Then Neville opened the boot of the car and she became preoccupied with collecting her jacket and briefcase.

Kaz ground the remains of her cigarette into the tarmac with her heel, then she started to walk slowly towards Helen, who had slipped on her jacket and was still rearranging her shirt cuffs and collar when they finally came face to face. Helen gave her a tight smile.

'Morning.'

Kaz returned the greeting with a pleading shrug that she hoped the others wouldn't notice. 'I'm sorry.'

Helen raised her eyebrows. Then she glanced at her boss. 'Neville, we'll follow you in. I want a word with Karen.'

He nodded. 'Fine.'

Joey was hovering, he shot a look at Kaz. 'You all right babes?'

Kaz turned on him. 'Just fuck off inside Joey and let me talk to my brief, okay?'

Joey threw up his palms defensively. 'Whoah!' He gave Neville a puzzled shrug.

Neville shepherded him and Ashley towards the main doors, leaving Kaz and Helen standing beside the Jaguar.

Kaz took a deep breath. 'Look, I can explain . . .'

Helen held up her hand. She was so annoyed it took her a moment to speak. Why couldn't the stupid girl have stayed out of trouble? 'Don't tell me what I can't hear. You know the rules. I'm an officer of the court.'

Kaz stood facing her, shoulders hunched. She stared at her feet, colouring up like a schoolkid caught out by a favourite teacher. 'I was going to say that the only reason I came down to Southend with Joey was to see if Natalie was okay.'

'And she wasn't. But you knew that Karen. You knew she was going to be in a mess. Still you went looking for trouble.'

'What would you have done if it was your sister, eh? Your sister wouldn't have turned into some scabby drug addict though, would she? No, she's probably at fucking Oxford, drinking champagne with the toffs.'

Helen took a deep breath, glanced around to check if they were being observed. 'This is not the place for an emotional audit of our respective families. And anyway, I don't have a sister.'

'Lucky you.'

Helen huffed, this was getting ridiculous. She had been determined to remain detached and professional, but she could see how wretched her client was. She reached out and put her hand on Kaz's arm. It was an awkward gesture for both of them, but Kaz was grateful at least for the attempt to comfort her.

She met Helen's gaze directly. 'I'm being a total wanker, I'm sorry. But you don't have to be angry with me. I'm angry enough with myself.'

Helen squeezed her arm. 'Listen, let's just go in there and do this. Anything else can be discussed later. I presume you and Joey have got your stories straight?'

Kaz nodded, wiped her hand across her face.

Helen smiled. 'Ready then?'

Kaz took a deep breath. 'Yeah.'

Helen gave her a penetrating look. 'For what it's worth, I don't believe for one moment that you were a party to anyone's death.'

Kaz shot a look straight back at her. 'You sure about that? 'Cause I'm not.'

20

A uniformed PC ushered Neville and Joey into the interview room. Joey's hands were shovelled in his trouser pockets, he took a turn about the room.

'Kaz'll be fine, she's a bit . . . y'know . . .'

Neville let his eyes travel significantly in the direction of the wall-mounted camera.

Joey picked up on this immediately, he gave a small giggle. 'Oh yeah. Nearly forgot.' Then he waved in the direction of the lens. 'Morning all.'

In the adjacent room, watching the monitor, Cheryl Stoneham stood, arms folded. Armstrong and Bradley were either side of her. Stoneham smiled.

'Always such a cheerful chap, our Joey.'

Nicci glanced at her. 'You interviewed him a few times then?'

'Oh yeah, since he was a juvenile. I was DI on the team that sent his sister down. We were convinced that it was him who half-bludgeoned the cashier to death. We tried every which way to get her to talk, but she wouldn't dob him in.'

Bradley inclined his head sadly. 'Hardly surprising. Probably scared stiff. Plus she was a junkie.' The two women gave him sideways glances. 'I've studied her file. Don't see how anyone could've survived unscathed in that family.'

Stoneham put on an indulgent maternal smile. 'And they say women are the romantics. I think blokes can be far worse.

Plenty of people suffer a childhood of abuse Constable, without growing up to be armed robbers. Personally I regard that as more of a career choice.'

With this Stoneham headed briskly for the door and was off down the corridor.

Nicci grinned at Bradley. 'You try too hard.'

Then she followed Stoneham, leaving Bradley feeling even more like a spare part.

Cheryl Stoneham entered the interview room at a clip, file in hand, flanked by Nicci. Neville Moore immediately offered his hand to shake.

'How are you Chief Inspector?'

'Very well Mr Moore, but somewhat surprised to be seeing you and Mr Phelps this morning. What can we do for you?'

Joey held out his hand to shake too. He gave Stoneham a dazzling smile. 'You're looking well Cheryl. Lost a bit of weight, I reckon.'

A look of pleasure quivered round Stoneham's lips, even she wasn't totally immune to Joey's charm. 'Must be from worrying about you and your exploits Joey. This is DS Armstrong.'

Nicci was aware of the blue eyes coming to rest on her. He'd been her target for nearly a year, he'd murdered one of her best friends, but this was the closest she'd ever got to Joey Phelps.

At Stoneham's invitation they all sat at the bare table, Joey and Neville facing Stoneham and Nicci respectively. Stoneham beamed and waited.

Neville Moore glanced at the tape deck at the end of the table. 'Aren't we recording this?'

Stoneham let her gaze travel to the tape deck too, she affected a look of mild surprise. 'Oh, I thought this was just an informal chat. Am I to assume that your client wishes to make a statement or answer questions on a particular matter?'

Joey started to fidget in his seat. His left leg was already tapping, still he beamed at Stoneham. 'Aww come on Cheryl, we're old mates, let's not play games. My sister's boyfriend topped himself and I'm here to make it clear, 'cause I know you lot've got suspicious minds, that I had nothing to do with it. Okay?'

Stoneham held his intense gaze for several seconds, then she reached over and clicked the tape deck on. She glanced at her watch. 'The time is eleven fifteen. I'm Detective Chief Inspector Cheryl Stoneham. With me in the room are . . .' She glanced at Nicci.

'Detective Sergeant Nicola Armstrong.'

She tilted her head towards Neville.

'Neville Moore of Crowley Sheridan Moore, representing Mr Phelps.'

Joey laughed out loud. 'I love this bit. Joseph Patrick Phelps.' He jumped up from his seat and took a bow. 'Taaadahhh! In person and for one night only. So make the most of it ladies.'

Stoneham watched his antics. 'Like the whistle Joey. Is that for our benefit?'

Joey stroked the lapels of his Italian hand-tailored suit as he sat down. 'Not bad, is it? Got it made special. In Milan.'

'Is that what all the drug dealers are wearing this season?'

Joey caught Stoneham's eye and smirked. 'Now you're just trying to wind me up, aren't you Cheryl?'

Stoneham gave an innocent shrug. 'Not at all, it was a friendly enquiry.'

'I'm a businessman. Suit's only a uniform really, innit? It's what I wear all the time now.' Joey leant back in his chair, seeming perfectly at ease, not a care in the world. Everyone else sat quietly, waiting for the next move; the score, fifteen all.

Kaz Phelps and Helen Warner had been shown to a bench in a draughty corridor. It was a busy thoroughfare, people coming and going, with automatic doors at one end that were slow to open and close. They sat in mutually agreed silence, too many people to eavesdrop and too much tension between them. Mal Bradley came strolling along with a file under his arm. Kaz didn't notice him at first, she was lost in her own thoughts. But when he stopped right in front of them she looked up.

'Morning Karen.'

It took a moment for her to register. 'Well well, PC Malik, my new best friend.'

Bradley smiled, turned to Helen Warner. 'Detective Constable Mal Bradley.'

Helen gave him a tepid smile.

Kaz looked him up and down. 'Thought you was Met. What you doing down here?'

'Nowadays we go all over the place. But today, I'm here 'cause you're here.' He glanced around him with a dissatisfied look. 'Don't know why they stuck you in this horrible corridor. Probably trying to soften you up. It'll be ages yet. Fancy a cup of tea? 'Cause I happen to know where the canteen is. And they have doughnuts.'

Bradley held out his hand, inviting them to follow.

Helen sighed. The prospect of a shot of caffeine definitely appealed. 'Why not?'

She got up, Kaz followed suit and Bradley led them towards the canteen that he'd visited earlier with Stoneham and Armstrong.

*

While Bradley was being served at the counter Kaz had the opportunity to tell Helen who he was.

A frown gathered on Helen's brow. 'I did call Turnbull after our last conversation. He gave me a load of flannel.'

'When is that nasty ponce gonna stop hassling me?'

Helen gave her a withering glance. 'At the rate you're going, not any time soon.'

Bradley carried a tray over and placed it on the table in front of them. He'd adopted the role of attentive host. He placed a cup and saucer in front of Helen. 'That's the espresso. I think you made the best choice. It's all done by the one machine.' He placed a cappuccino in front of Kaz. 'But it doesn't froth the milk separately I'm afraid.'

Kaz pulled her cup towards her. 'It'll be fine.'

Bradley unloaded a cup of tea for himself and sat down opposite the two women. 'Sure about the doughnuts? I had one earlier, they are good.'

Helen shook her head, but her attention was focused on the file Bradley had been carrying with him throughout. He placed it carefully on the table beside his cup. She gave it an appraising look. There was something about his body language, the way he handled the file. She had a shrewd idea of what was coming next, but wasn't sure how she was going to deflect it. She cursed herself for accepting his invitation to the canteen. She should've said no and if she hadn't been so pissed off with Karen she would've done.

Bradley sipped his tea and smiled. 'How's Natalie?'

Kaz ignored the question, she wasn't getting into that.

Bradley fingered the corner of the file. 'Got something here I'd like to show you.'

Helen knew she had to intervene quickly. 'This is not an appropriate place for this Constable.'

Bradley looked up, all innocence. 'Only a couple of pictures I thought Karen might like to see.'

'Absolutely not.'

But Bradley flipped open the file before Helen could finish. He swivelled it round with a flick of the wrist and Kaz found herself staring at a full colour print of a small black girl, maybe five years old. She was flat on her back on a piece of concrete, eyes wide open and staring, a gaping, bloody cavity gouged in the centre of her small chest, pools of blood all around her. Kaz gave an involuntary gasp.

Bradley nodded. 'Yeah, it's pretty shocking. Her name's Zara . . .'

Helen's hand shot out to push the file away, but Bradley was too quick for her. He pulled it to one side, leaving the image of Zara's little corpse on the table between them.

Helen got up. 'You are bang out of order Constable. Come on Karen . . .'

Kaz's eyes were riveted on the photo. She gave Bradley a puzzled frown. 'Why you showing me this?'

She felt Helen's hand on her shoulder. 'Leave it Karen . . . let's go . . .'

Bradley held up his hand. 'She wants an answer. I think she's entitled to one. I'm showing you this because before you go and lie for your brother yet again, I thought you should see some of his other handiwork.'

Kaz stared at him, her gorge rising. 'You saying Joey did this? Killed this . . . this little kid? No way!'

Bradley pulled two more pictures out of the file, two more bullet-ridden corpses. 'This is Zara's father. Hackney drug dealer. Came up through the gangs. Joey took over his patch about a month ago. Took out him, his girlfriend and his kid.'

Kaz shoved back her chair, got to her feet. She wanted to

fling her hot coffee in his stupid face, but Helen's hand was on her arm.

Bradley smiled. 'See, this is your brother's very special MO. Most gang violence, gang members target each other. Occasionally civilians get caught in the crossfire. When Joey moves in, he targets the whole family. Wipes them out. That's how he makes his point: Don't mess with me, I'm not some teenage posse, I'm a serious villain and I'm taking over this turf. Fear is a powerful tool. It works.'

Kaz was aware of Helen tugging her arm, but her eyes bored into the copper's pompous face. Her mouth was dry, she swallowed, ran her tongue over her lips. 'You'd say anything, any lie, to nail him. You show me some random picture, some poor little kid, and you say it was Joey. Where's the evidence? You ain't got none, have you? 'Cause if you did, you'd be arresting him.'

Bradley nodded. 'You're right of course. No one will give evidence against him, all too scared. No one will stand up to him, no one will stop him. That's why we need you Karen. Unless of course you're shit-scared of him too?'

Their eyes remained locked. Kaz refused to be the first to look away. She'd been doing this all her life, arguing with them – teachers, coppers, shrinks, screws – listening to their lies. She realized that, whatever she did, however law-abiding she became, the battle lines would always be drawn. All the so-called respectable people, they were on one side; she and Joey, her whole family, they were on the other. But she realized Joey was right, posh people were no different, everyone was at it. They just got away with it, like this lying slag in front of her.

She pulled her arm free from Helen's grasp, still glaring at Bradley. 'I'm not scared of him. I got no reason to be. So get off my back copper. He's worth ten of you.'

She turned on her heel and strode out of the canteen.

Helen looked at Bradley and exhaled through her nose. 'Turnbull's not going to be happy with you.'

Bradley's jaw was set, he was annoyed with himself. Maybe he had gone in too hard. The murder of Zara Kingston and her parents was definitely down to Joey's firm, who'd used it to gain control of a swathe of territory from Dalston up to Stamford Hill, plus the gangs who operated there. As to whether Joey himself pulled the trigger, he had no way of knowing that.

'He's a psychopathic killer. When's she going to figure that out?'

Helen sighed. 'He's also her little brother. When are you going to take *that* into account?'

21

Kaz had found her way from the canteen to the main desk and exit; she was heading through the door when she saw Joey outside the interview room. He waved at her and smiled. She stopped. She just wanted to get out, out into the air, maybe run for it. But he was coming towards her.

Strolling along, hands in his pockets, he looked like the cat who'd got the cream. He waited until he'd come up close, his tone was confidential: 'Piece of piss. They got nothing. Absolutely sweet FA. They're having a word with Ash – as if he's gonna say anything.'

Kaz forced a smile. She couldn't quite look at him. The image of the murdered child was etched on the back of her retina. 'Good.'

He gave her a sidelong look. 'You okay?'

Helen appeared on the stairs Kaz had come down. And several paces behind her was Mal Bradley.

Joey glanced up at them, then his gaze stopped on Bradley and recognition dawned. Joey turned a puzzled frown on his sister.

'In't he the fella from the hostel? What's he doing here?'

Kaz shot a look up at Bradley, who was following Helen down the stairs. He was still carrying that file. She put her hand on Joey's forearm and whispered. 'Leave it. I'll explain later.'

But Joey was staring at her in disbelief as he put it all together. 'You slept with a fucking copper?'

'No Joey, no I didn't! But it's too complicated to explain right now. Just trust me.'

Joey's smug attitude had evaporated, he was glaring at his sister. 'What the fuck's going on here?'

'Trust me, okay? You and me, in't this what it comes down to? Trust.'

He blinked several times, confusion and anger engulfing him. Helen had reached the bottom of the stairs. She was about to join them. Kaz gave her brother a direct, pleading look. Joey scowled at her, folded his arms across his chest.

Mal Bradley got to the bottom of the stairs too and walked past them without any acknowledgement. He headed in the direction of the interview room.

Helen noted Joey's barely disguised fury, she gave him a polite smile. 'Where's Neville?'

Joey turned to her. His look was tight and blank. 'Still inside. They're interviewing Ashley. You been having a nice private chat with that copper, have you?'

Helen looked puzzled. Joey didn't wait for a response, he strode out of the main doors into the car park. Helen glanced at Kaz, she was fighting back the tears.

Nicci watched Karen Phelps closely as she took her seat in the interview room. Her shoulders were hunched, tension rippled through her jaw, she was close to the edge. Bradley had popped in before the interview and filled Nicci in on his little scam; looking at the state of Karen, Nicci was beginning to think it might've worked. So Bradley did have a brain after all. Was this about to be the moment they finally turned Karen Phelps? Cheryl Stoneham switched the recorder on, noted the time and started the namecheck. Nicci sat back calmly, assessing the chances.

Once everyone had introduced themselves, Stoneham smiled equably. 'Well Karen, I gather you'd like to tell us about the visit to your sister . . . yesterday morning? What made you decide to go?'

Kaz stared at Stoneham, then sighed. She felt suddenly weary, her throat was sore from the fags, her head was throbbing. The image of Zara, the huge bloody wound in her chest, was spinning on a loop in her brain. Kaz became aware of Helen beside her, looking at her. She took a breath.

'My sister was twelve when I went inside. I hadn't seen her since then.'

'Were you aware of her drug problems?'

Kaz coughed, shot a sideways glance at Helen.

'Yeah, I guess.'

Stoneham picked up a piece of paper from the table.

'I received a signed fax this morning from a Doctor Iqbal, your sister's psychiatrist, outlining her condition and why she's not fit to be interviewed at present. Did you speak to Doctor Iqbal before going to Southend yesterday?'

Kaz's head felt as if it had a metal band round it, it was biting into her skull. Her brain was about to explode, she wanted to escape. She took a deep breath. Helen had told her she just had to do this then she'd be free.

'My brother spoke to Doctor Iqbal. We arranged with him that we'd collect Natalie from her flat in Southend and then she'd go back into rehab at his clinic in Yorkshire.'

Nicci rubbed the side of her nose. 'If Doctor Iqbal was coming all the way from Yorkshire anyway, why didn't he accompany you to the flat?'

Kaz stared straight back at Nicci, her eyes dark and brooding.

'He's a busy man. We was grateful that he was prepared to come in person, but we didn't know exactly what time he'd arrive. So we thought it best to take Natalie to my parents first. Also it gave my mother a chance to see her.'

Stoneham nodded, glanced at Nicci. It was a look between two experienced officers who knew they were playing the long game. Stoneham let her eyes travel slowly back to Kaz.

'So . . . what happened when you got to the flat?'

Kaz was warming to the tale, as she spoke she was loosening up. Lies were easy to tell once you got in the swing of it. She'd learnt this as a child. No one could see inside your head. The trick was to think of it as a story, make sure all the details fitted together. But the crucial thing was how you felt. If you felt you were doing something wrong, you'd mess it up. If you felt justified, it was fine. For Kaz, most of the time it felt justified, she'd spent a lifetime telling lies to save her own skin. Growing up in the violent shadow of Terry Phelps, honesty was a luxury she couldn't afford. She'd followed her mother's example, telling tales was simply how you survived.

Kaz let her shoulders relax, she glanced from one detective to the other and began her tale.

'Her boyfriend Jez let us in. He went back in the sitting room downstairs, carried on watching telly. Place is a sort of maisonette. We found Natalie in bed upstairs. She was pretty much out of it. Joey had to help me get her dressed. He carried her downstairs. I went into the sitting room, I told Jez we was leaving. He was crashed out on the sofa, can in his hand, drunk, stoned, I dunno, probably both. I told him we was taking Natalie and she was going back into rehab.'

Stoneham dipped in. 'Where was Joey whilst you were doing this?'

'He carried Natalie straight out the flat, Ashley went with him to help. They had to carry her all the way to the car.'

'What did Jez say to you?'

'Nothing. He stared straight through me, like junkies do. So I left, caught up with the others by the lift.'

'Jez didn't follow you, attempt to stop you?'

'He looked at me for a minute, then he changed channels.'

Stoneham nodded thoughtfully. 'So you were the last to leave the flat and Jez Harris was sitting watching television?'

Kaz nodded. 'Yeah. We went down in the lift. We was getting Natalie in the back of the car when it happened. There was like this crash. Sort of heavy thud. We all looked round and saw this body had landed on the bins . . .'

Kaz paused for effect, then she exhaled softly. 'When we saw it was Jez, we didn't know what to do. I thought Natalie sees this she'll freak.'

Nicci chipped in. 'But you said she was out of it, had to be carried.'

Kaz looked at her. 'She wasn't completely unconscious. She was dopey, like a rag doll. We wanted to get her away from there. Various other people come running, someone got on their mobile to call an ambulance. There wasn't nothing we could do, so we left.'

Stoneham glanced at Nicci then back at Kaz. 'So how do you think Jez Harris went from sitting on his sofa watching the television to throwing himself off his balcony less than five minutes later?'

Kaz shook her head. 'Beats me. Junkies do funny things. I know, I been one. Time gets all out of sync, slows down. You don't react for ages, then you do.'

Nicci frowned. 'So you think it took time for it to sink in

that Natalie was gone. But when he realized, he decided to commit suicide?'

Kaz shrugged. 'Who knows?'

Nicci inclined her head. 'Seems a bit impulsive even if he was high. You take his girlfriend off to rehab, so he kills himself. Why would he do that?'

'I've no idea. I'm only telling you what happened.'

Stoneham smiled, linked her fingers loosely in front of her, rested her elbows on the table. 'C'mon, haven't you spent enough of your life lying to protect Joey? Where's it going to end Karen? You've just done six years, you've got six more on licence. Did you really rob that petrol station all on your own and beat the cashier half to death?'

Kaz shifted in her seat. 'That's water under the bridge.'

Helen leant forward. 'That case is closed Chief Inspector. Karen's come here voluntarily to tell you what happened at her sister's flat. Unless you have any more questions on that subject I think we're done.'

Cheryl Stoneham pushed her chair back. 'I'd say you went to see your sister, found her in a right state and you lost your rag. Jez Harris was a small-time dealer and general low-life. According to a social worker who tried to help Natalie a couple of years back, she got clean before. Then she went back to Jez. She was dependent on him and he fed her habit. I'd say that's a pretty good motive for murder.'

Stoneham fixed Kaz with a direct look. 'If I hadn't seen my baby sister for six years, I come home and I find she's gone down more or less the same path as me, I'd be pretty gutted. So why don't you tell us what really happened Karen?'

Kaz met Stoneham's look and held it. 'I have told you.'

Stoneham gave Kaz an appraising stare. 'Plausible but not convincing. There's no emotion in it.'

'Yeah all right, when I saw the state of Nat I was upset. But it made me feel I wanna get her out of here, get her home, get her to the doctor. That was my priority and that's what we did.'

Kaz locked on Stoneham's gaze, Helen watched. It was a battle of wills between the two women. There had been a time when her client couldn't even make eye contact for more than a few seconds. All that had changed. Helen wondered what had really happened in that flat. Stoneham was right, the story was plausible but hardly convincing.

The detective shook her head slowly. Her tone was rueful. 'You look strong and fit enough. But Jez Harris was a good six foot, albeit a streak of piss. So I'm guessing it was Joey picked him up and chucked him over the balcony for you. All in a day's work for Joey, he wouldn't blink, would he? But you're the one that got mad, aren't you Karen? Jez Harris is dead because of you.'

22

The life drawing course was part of a summer school run by the Slade and was being held in studios off Woburn Square. Kaz had a place on a full-time art foundation course at London Met starting in the autumn, but she knew that the art classes she'd attended inside were more therapy than the real thing; when it came to proper drawing she needed some practice.

She stood outside the building for a few moments finishing her fag. The police had simply let her go; Stoneham clearly didn't believe her story, but as Joey had pointed out, they had no evidence to contradict it. She'd travelled back to London in Neville Moore's car. Helen and her boss had chatted between themselves, Kaz had sat behind them, said little and got them to drop her near the tube. She went back to her room at the hostel, flung herself on the bed and sobbed. She felt wretched, the pictures of that kid, Stoneham's accusation ringing in her head. She must've cried herself to sleep. When she woke up, it was the early hours and she was freezing. She crawled under the duvet fully clothed.

The next morning she took a long hot shower and contemplated her options. Helen had undertaken to explain the incident to Jalil Sahir. With the story they'd told there were no grounds for a recall. She'd merely acted out of concern for her sister and the probation service would have to accept that. She knew Helen would convince them.

That left Joey. Should she see him, explain about PC Mal and why she'd lied? But keeping Joey happy, was that her priority? Underneath it all was she scared of him? Kaz dismissed this notion out of hand. Joey would never harm her, he loved her. If anything he loved her a bit too much. She decided he was the one who'd been unreasonable, kicking off like that because he recognized the cop. He'd caused this mess, it was up to him to come to her. Kaz was done with dancing to everyone else's tune. She was going to her art class.

She ground the cigarette butt into the pavement with her heel, picked up her sketchpad and headed into the building. A series of spidery handwritten notices directed her to the lift, ancient and clunky, and up to the fourth floor. She wandered through several large, white-walled studios until she came to the one where the course was being held.

About a dozen wooden studio easels were grouped in a semi-circle round a small dais. A couple of students were already setting up, putting boards on the easels and taping paper to them. A skinny old geezer in a faded denim shirt and even more faded jeans was arranging cushions on the dais. He glanced at Kaz speculatively, tossed the last cushion on the pile and strolled over. His narrow face was sculpted and bristly, he gave Kaz a lop-sided smile.

'Mike Dawson. Welcome to Life Drawing.' The name came out with the rasping growl of a forty-a-day man.

Kaz returned his smile. 'Karen Phelps.'

Dawson picked up the register and flipped it open. 'Ah, the elusive Ms Phelps. We were beginning to think you'd run for the hills.'

Kaz noticed his eyes, almost obscured by lines and wrinkles, they were the dark grey of wet slate and the gaze didn't waver.

'Sorry, couldn't get here before. I've been having a few problems.'

Dawson nodded, concern or amusement, Kaz couldn't tell. 'Nothing . . . medical I hope.'

Kaz caught the twinkle in his eye. Was he taking the piss? Or was this how artists behaved? He looked about ninety, his fingers curled like claws, the nails rimmed with black. Kaz had met villains who were less intimidating.

She forced a smile. 'No, nothing like that.'

Dawson turned abruptly and seized one of the easels. 'Ever used one of these beasts before?'

She shook her head.

'Well, they have a habit of defeating the novice. So I will demonstrate.'

He picked up a drawing board from a stack against the wall, hoisted it on to the crossbar support, which he ratcheted into place and fixed by tightening several paint-spattered wing nuts. Kaz nearly jumped out of her skin when his bony fingers suddenly clutched her arm as he manoeuvred her into position beside the board. He raised his hand, forming his fingers into a flat, horizontal plane about three inches from her left eye.

'Here is your eyeline, which wants to be two thirds up the board, so you can look back and forth, continually back and forth from the drawing to the model. Got it? Here to there.'

He jabbed his finger in the direction of the dais. A fit young man in a bathrobe and odd socks had appeared and was re-arranging the cushions. This attracted Dawson's attention. He tutted and strode over to the young man.

'No no, we don't want a neat pile, neat is boring Leo. What we need is disarray! Disarray!'

Kaz gazed around the room, it was filling up with other

students. A small oriental girl took the easel on her left, they exchanged polite nods. This was the normal world, away from police stations and prison cells and trouble. It was where Kaz so desperately wanted to be. It was freedom. Kaz started to unpack her bag, getting out her box of charcoals and tin of pencils. Her first proper art class and here at the Slade, of all places. She had to admit she was feeling nervous, but also excited. She opened her sketchbook, tore out a sheet of cartridge and started to tape it to the board.

'Is this easel taken?'

She glanced to her right and did a double-take. Mal Bradley had dumped his bag beside the adjacent easel and was beaming at her. She stood rooted to the spot just glaring at him. She really couldn't believe it. She wanted to punch him.

'What the fuck you doing here?'

He looked offended. 'That's not a very friendly way to greet a fellow student.'

Kaz was about to respond to this when Mike Dawson returned.

'Aah great, this is Mal. He can show you the ropes. When we started the week he was an absolute beginner, but he's coming on in leaps and bounds. He's really loosened up. Though when you didn't show yesterday, Mal, I thought you might've thrown in the towel.'

Bradley grinned. 'No Mike, you've converted me. Something came up at work, had to pop in.'

Mike gave a gravelly laugh, which dissolved into a fit of coughing. 'Problems on the money markets eh? Fucking wanker bankers. Still, you're going to buy one of my paintings, aren't you Mal?' Chortling to himself, he wandered off.

Bradley grinned at Kaz. 'Bit of a weird bloke, but he knows his stuff. Even got me drawing and I was completely crap before.'

Kaz stared at him, her chest was tight, she felt she might choke. She picked up her bag and headed out.

'Where you going?'

'To the bog. Gonna follow me there too?'

Kaz discovered that the women's toilets were on the ground floor. She booted open the door of an empty stall and locked herself in. She realized she had tears in her eyes. Was it rage, frustration? She couldn't decide. Would she ever be free of these bastards? She got out her phone, she should call Helen, get this scumbag off her back in a proper, legal way. But she hesitated. She'd had no chance to really talk to Helen the day before. She'd wanted to explain, she'd wanted to feel that Helen was still on her side. But everything had started to unravel.

That fat cop Stoneham was probably right, she was to blame for Jez's death. She'd completely lost it when she saw what had happened to Natalie and she'd turned that anger on her brother. She'd accused him, she'd really had a go. Like when they were kids and the old man used to lay into them for some trivial misdemeanour. Kaz remembered letters coming from school, the ponce of a head teacher going on about Joey playing truant or some schoolboy prank. Terry Phelps would be mad at the school, but he also hated the way it reflected on him. He would thrash Joey, knocking the boy round the room until he was bruised and bleeding. Then he'd tell Joey that the punishment wasn't for what he'd done, but for getting caught and showing up his family as a consequence.

It dawned on Kaz that she'd behaved just like the old man; she felt so bad in herself, so responsible for what had happened to Natalie that she'd dumped it all on Joey. She'd used him as her punch bag, much as the old man did. And she'd made him feel ashamed, as if he'd let her down. But Joey wasn't a kid any more, he wasn't going to curl up in a ball and take the kicking and to make that point to her he'd killed Jez Harris. He'd done it, but it was her fault.

Kaz sat in the wooden cubicle, staring at the graffiti hacked into the door, wondering how on earth she was going to explain any of this to Helen. Could she ever? How would Helen understand? How could anybody who hadn't lived their life in the Phelps family?

She wasn't surprised when she came out of the toilets to find Mal Bradley leaning against the wall. He smiled at her.

'Class is about to start. Mike asked me to make sure you hadn't got lost.'

Kaz gave him a sceptical glance. 'As if.'

'Actually I was worried. Thought you might be considering jacking it all in.'

This stopped Kaz in her tracks. ''Cause of you? Don't flatter yourself.'

'I do genuinely want to help you. That's why I'm here.'

'You're stalking me, how's that help?'

Bradley pondered this. 'Well, it's more honest than covert surveillance.'

Kaz headed for the lift, Bradley followed. The heavy metal mesh gate stood open, Kaz stepped inside.

'The stunt you pulled with those pictures, that was sick.'

Bradley hauled the gate shut, it clanked into place, he hit the button and with a shudder the lift started to rise.

'You're right, I owe you an apology. I was trying to manipulate you, play on your conscience. Why? Because I know you have a conscience. You're not like him Karen.'

Kaz took a step forward, Bradley was maybe an inch taller, but she was right in his face. Her eyes bored straight into his. 'Sure about that? How d'you know I'm not gonna get pissed off with this, borrow a gun from one of my brother's "associates" and shoot a fucking hole in the middle of your chest? 'Cause that's what us villains do, innit? Least in your book.' She jabbed her finger into his sternum.

Bradley smiled. His dark liquid eyes rested gently on her face. 'I'm not the enemy Karen.'

'Don't look at me like that. I'm not some stupid poncey girl who's gonna swoon in your arms.'

He laughed. 'Yeah, I think I already figured we're on a hiding to nothing with that.'

'My lawyer could have you for sexual harassment y'know.'

He held up his hands. 'Be fair, I never laid a finger on you.'

'Why the fuck should I play fair? You lot are out to make my life a fucking misery 'til you get what you want. I'm being stalked by an undercover cop. Maybe I should take my story to the papers. That'd piss Woodentop off I'll bet.'

The lift clunked to a halt. Kaz seized the handle to the gate and hauled it open. She was straight out and striding down the corridor. Bradley had to trot to catch up with her.

'Strictly speaking I'm not undercover, 'cause you guessed I was a cop as soon as you saw me. So I'm not lying to you about who I am.'

Kaz glared at him. 'You're lying to people here though, ain't you? To the tutor, what's-his-face, Mike?'

Bradley fell into step beside her. 'To tell you the truth, it's my first attempt at all this and you're right, I am crap. Total crap.'

They'd reached the door to the studio, the class had already begun. Leo was striking an action pose, balancing a ball in one hand, leaning on a stick with the other. The muscles in his back rippled with the strain. The room was silent but for the furious scratching and scraping of charcoal on paper.

Kaz turned and eyeballed Bradley, she kept her voice low. 'Know how hard it's been for me to get here, to a place like this, to a proper college, where you can just draw all day? Actually learn something. I don't give a monkey's about you, Woodentop; bring the whole fucking Met down here if you like, you're not robbing me of this as well.'

Bradley sighed. 'No one's trying to Karen. But people have been murdered, including, I suspect, Jez Harris. My job is to find a way to stop it.' His look was deadly serious now, any hint of flirtatiousness gone. 'So however much you or your lawyer huff and puff we're not going to go away. Sooner or later we'll get the forensics or the witnesses to convict Joey and send him to jail. What you have to decide is whether you're going down with him.'

Bradley's eye travelled in an arc round the quiet studio.

'You go on backing him you'll lose all this, all your dreams. It's your choice.'

23

The bar was close to Hoxton Square and at six thirty it was standing-room only. It was a new venue building a reputation on arty cocktails at City prices and the last place Kaz wanted to be after her first gruelling day in the studio. Joey had bombarded her with texts and voicemails insisting that she should come down. He had a surprise for her. It would blow her mind. She was reluctant but she hadn't spoken to him since he walked out of Southend nick in a huff.

Dog-tired, it was an effort to drag herself, her bag and her unwieldy A3 sketchpad through the chattering crush. Bradley was right about one thing, Mike Dawson knew his stuff. His students may be a bunch of amateurs, hobbyists and wannabes like her, however, Dawson paid them the compliment of treating them exactly the same as his proper art students. That meant half a dozen lightning poses, followed by a four-hour study of Leo lounging on the mountain of cushions like a dozing pasha.

Kaz had never spent so long on one drawing before. It was hard but exhilarating. She forgot about everything: Joey, her sister, the cops and their machinations. She even found herself glancing over at Bradley's drawing and feeling a competitive buzz; he became just another student.

Dawson toured the room offering each of them comments and advice. The first time he came to Kaz he stood at her shoulder for several minutes, his eyes half closed, scrutinizing the drawing. Then he glanced at her, looked her up and down, assessing, pondering. He gave her a small smile. 'Yeah . . .' Nodded his head slowly and wandered off. She didn't know what to make of it.

Bradley gave her a mocking glance. 'Well look at you. Teacher's pet eh?'

Kaz caught sight of Joey at a corner table. Ashley was in attendance, but Joey was lording it. A bottle of Cristal in his hand he was topping up champagne flutes held by two giggling girls, a blonde and a brunette, shoulder-length hair, thigh-high skirts. Kaz huffed to herself, she hadn't come all this way to watch Joey pull. Her hands were filmed with charcoal, probably her face too, she felt a mess. She wanted to get home to her snug room at the hostel and take a long shower.

But at the sight of her Joey was on his feet waving her over, drawing her into the group.

'Hey, this is my sister. She's an art student too.'

Joey pointed at the girls, trawling his memory for names. 'Chloe and . . .' Kaz didn't catch the rest, it was drowned out by the general cacophony.

The blonde gave Kaz a superior smile, flicked back her shining mane.

'Awesome. Where you studying? I'm at Goldsmiths.'

Kaz considered telling her the truth for about five seconds. But as she took in the posh accent, the mix of designer labels and ethnic accessories she changed her mind. She returned the smile.

'Doing an MA. At the Slade.'

The blonde nodded, trying not to look outgunned.

'Cool.'

Kaz dumped her bag and sketchbook at Ashley's feet.

'Look after these Ash, I need a word with my brother.' She

beckoned to Joey, he put down the Cristal and followed her obediently out of the bar and onto the pavement. They picked their way through the huddle of smokers crowding the doorway and found a quiet spot.

Kaz scowled. 'So what you got to say to me now eh? Still pissed off, are you?'

Joey put his head to one side, gave her a sheepish grin. 'I was out of order babes . . .'

'Yeah, you were. I got the filth on my back, fucking stalking me, thanks to you . . .'

'It took me by surprise is all, seeing him down the nick. And you said you'd slept with him.'

'I didn't say that. You assumed and I let you. Why? 'Cause you had plans to set me up with Ashley! Stud fucking muffin Ashley.'

Joey couldn't help laughing. 'He ain't that bad.'

'I ain't that desperate.'

Joey chuckled some more. 'Well if you put it like that . . . Look, I knew you wouldn't've slept with a copper really. I, y'know . . . well. I dunno . . .'

He gazed at her, gave her the innocent little-boy look, which she knew was the nearest he was ever going to get to an outright apology. 'That's why I wanted you to come down here. So I could make it up to you.'

'Joey, I'm knackered. All I want is to go home.'

'I got a surprise. Me and Ash been doing a bit of research. Talking to a few contacts round here. You're gonna love this. Ready to be really surprised?'

Kaz exhaled. Joey in Santa Claus mode was not what she needed. He beamed from ear to ear, held out his hands. 'I got you . . . an exhibition.'

Kaz stared at him. 'What?'

'Some fellas I know own a bit of property round here. Mate of theirs runs a gallery. Literally just up the road from here. Been to see him, explained about you. He's agreed to give you an exhibition.'

Kaz blew out her cheeks, then she laughed. 'Joe, I'm starting college. I haven't got anything to put in a fucking exhibition.'

'Well, you could knock up a few bits.'

'I'm not ready yet. I'm a student.'

Joey seemed nonplussed. 'I tell you, them girls you met – Chloe and her mate, can't remember her name – well, they're students too and I can tell you they'll shag anyone or anything they think can give them an exhibition.'

Kaz laughed out loud, patted his arm. Any tension between them had evaporated. He meant well, she could see that. He genuinely was trying to make it up to her.

She smiled at him. 'Look babes, I appreciate the effort. I do.'

Joey opened his arms. 'Then gives us a hug.'

'I'm all mucky with charcoal.'

'So?'

He wrapped his arms round her, lifted her off her feet. She could tell he was being careful with her, his arms were gentle. She smelt his aftershave, something expensive no doubt.

He set her down, grinned. 'Actually you do look pretty mucky.'

She batted him with her hand. 'Fuck off!'

'Seriously babes, you're smart y'know. I been looking into this art game. Me and Ash, we spent the day going round these galleries. We seen paintings a kid of five coulda done and they're asking thousands for them. I tell you it's a right old racket. I never knew or I'd've been in it before.'

Kaz smiled. His boyish enthusiasms always had the power to charm her. It helped erase the other Joey from her mind, the one who'd tossed Jez Harris off a balcony as if he were a bag of garbage.

'There is a bit more to it y'know, if you wanna do something good.'

Joey grinned. He was off on one of his flights of fancy. 'Course. I know it ain't all a con. Or if it is it's a legitimate con. And that's what we need. Paintings are a great investment if you pick the right ones. And you got the eye. One more string to our bow babes. We'll clean up.'

Kaz fixed him with a thoughtful look. It was now or never. In a mood like this she had the best chance of making him listen.

'Before we get into any of that, there's something else we need to talk about.'

He cocked his head, she could see the suspicion surfacing. She'd had plenty of experience of Joey's lightning changes of mood. But she ploughed on.

'What happened at Natalie's – I'm not prepared to sweep that under the carpet.'

Joey shot an irritable glance at her, a warning of choppy waters ahead. 'It's sorted. On all levels. Natalie's in rehab, the filth's got nothing. What more do you expect?'

Kaz gazed into those baby-blue eyes, she could see the anger rising, but she held her course.

'Jez ain't the only one you killed, is he?'

Joey puffed himself up defensively. 'What? What bollocks you talking?'

Kaz took a breath. She hooked his gaze, waited until he was looking right at her. 'I want you to stop killing people.'

There, she'd said it. It was out there. Her words hung between them for maybe thirty seconds before Joey guffawed.

'Jez Fucking Harris! Why you so hung up on him? He was a fucking waste of space in anyone's book.'

She stood her ground, Joey took a step back from her, anger fizzing into a physical need to just move. Kaz tried to hold on to eye contact. She needed him to look at her.

'Joey, listen to me. I'm not talking about Jez Harris. I'm talking about you, what you do. It has to stop babes. For your sake.'

'What d'you mean, my sake? What the fuck you talking about?'

'No one else knows what it was like for you growing up. But I know. Okay, we did stuff, we did what we had to to survive. Those days are gone. You said you wanted a new start. Well now's the chance. But you gotta change too. 'Cause if you don't . . .' Kaz had to swallow hard to keep her feelings in check. 'If you don't . . . you're gonna turn into him. And I don't think I could bear that.'

Joey stood there, arms clutched protectively round his own chest. His face was blank, there was no emotion in his eyes. 'You saying you think I'm like him?'

Kaz blinked. She was close to tears, the idea of Joey turning into their father was a corrosive acid burning inside her. 'No. But you gotta start looking at what you're doing Joey.'

He looked straight at her. He seemed calm, but defeated.

'What, you think I'm turning into some kind of psycho?'

'No. 'Course I don't.' In her head there was a fine line between reassurance and lying, she wasn't sure if she'd crossed it. Joey looked so forlorn. If a demonstration were needed of the effect she could have on him, this was it.

'Someone called me that – a psycho. I thought he was a mate. People let you down Kaz. You trust 'em, they let you down. Is that what you're gonna do?'

He looked so small and vulnerable now, turning in on himself, imploding. Kaz moved forward, put her arms round him. He let his head drop on her shoulder and the tears started to flow.

'I never . . . never meant to hurt anyone. Even fucking Jez. I was just trying . . . I dunno . . . just sorting things out. You got to keep on top of things, y'know, or they get out of hand.'

Kaz stroked his hair, even cut short it was so thick, as it was when he was a boy. She let her fingers ripple through it. 'Sssh, it'll be okay.'

'He's . . . he's a fucking monster! I don't want be like him. No fucking way!'

'You're not gonna be. But you have to listen to me Joey.'

She could feel the heat of his breath, the wetness of the tears on her neck. A shudder quivered through him.

'I am listening. See, this is why I need you in my corner. Tell me what to do . . .'

She lifted his head from her shoulder, wiped the tears and snot away with the back of her hand, as she'd done so many times before. She waited until he was gazing straight at her.

'Okay . . . we follow your plan. Use the Net, move into the mainstream, make the business totally legit. But . . . no more killing. 'Cause the police ain't idiots. They'll keep going and in the end they'll nail you. So it all stops, stops now, then they got nothing.'

'They'll try and fit me up.'

'That's what you got lawyers for. You have to put yourself out of harm's way babes. Avoid trouble.'

He nodded. He seemed to be taking it in.

'And that's the deal between you and me. It all stops now. We go totally legit, stick to business. You agree to that, then we're partners.'

Joey stared at her. He seemed flabbergasted. He started to

chuckle nervously. 'You mean that? We're really gonna be part-ners?'

'Yeah, if you accept the deal.'

He didn't reply, just beamed from ear to ear, seized her round the waist and whisked her off her feet.

'Come here partner!'

24

For Helen Warner Sunday mornings were sacrosanct. Maybe this was the result of growing up in a church-going family. Her parents were good people and robust Christians, which meant she and her two brothers had to be washed and scrubbed and paraded every Sunday morning in the pews of their quaint village church. They had no choice in the matter until Helen was sixteen and, as the eldest, felt duty-bound to rebel on behalf of them all.

Now her Sundays were all about doing exactly as she liked. Living alone had, in her view, many advantages. She only had herself to please. And what pleased her was to get up on a Sunday when she wanted, throw on an old pair of joggers and a sweatshirt and go out for the papers. During the week she relied on digital media, but the rituals of her new religion required she spent Sunday mornings immersed in the broadsheets, with a pot of good coffee, catching up on the week in politics.

She was lounging on her sofa doing just that when the doorbell rang. She thought it might be her neighbour. Henry was in his nineties, long ago widowed, a retired doctor. He had family who called in regularly, but Helen tried to keep an eye on him. He occasionally locked himself out and his daughter had given her a spare key. In return, Henry gave her plants for her window boxes. He liked to chat and was a bit of a flirt.

The flats were on five floors of a very elegant Edwardian mansion block in Bloomsbury. The rooms were high-ceilinged and spacious, and Helen had only been able to afford such a desirable apartment with a sizeable legacy from her grandmother and some help from her parents. It was her home and her haven.

She opened the front door with a smile, ready with a quip for Henry. Then she blinked with shock and the colour flooded up her neck and into her cheeks.

'Karen? What are you doing here?'

Kaz smiled. She had spent some time weighing up the pros and cons of surprising Helen at home. In the end desperation got the better of her. Helen had given her the address years ago, during a prison visit; Kaz had wanted to send her a Christmas card she'd designed herself. When she started the art classes in Woburn Square and realized she was in Helen's neighbourhood, she'd done a recce and searched out the flat. This morning she was about to ring the entryphone from the street, but someone coming out had held the door open for her. So she found herself standing on Helen's doormat, feeling slightly awkward. The tone in Helen's voice didn't improve matters. Kaz knew at once that she'd made a mistake, crossed an invisible line. Now she had to front it out.

'You said you wanted another drawing.' She held out her sketchbook. 'Thought I could show you a few. My life drawing class is round the corner in Woburn Square.'

Helen gave her a sceptical look. 'It runs on a Sunday?'

Kaz had a ready-made lie, only a small one. In the circumstances it felt justified. 'I had to pop into the studio, pick up some stuff. But you're probably busy . . .'

Helen painted on a smile. 'No no, I'm just slobbing about. Sorry, do come in.'

She stepped back from the door and Kaz followed her into the hallway. The floor was old-fashioned wooden parquet blocks, the smell of wax polish rose up from them. Helen was bare-footed, Kaz watched as she walked ahead, her feet seeming to skate over the shiny floor. It was almost a shock to see Helen this naked. But isn't that why she'd really come, to infiltrate her lawyer's private life?

Helen led her into the kitchen. Though the rest of the flat retained its prized Edwardian features, the kitchen was ultra-modern; the high-gloss surfaces were pristine and, with the exception of a matching kettle and toaster, the worktops were bare.

Kaz gazed around. 'Wow, you're neat.'

Helen filled the kettle. 'Tidy home, tidy mind. Coffee?'

'Thanks. Listen, I probably should've called first . . .'

Helen returned the kettle to its base and flicked the switch. 'Let's see then.'

Kaz was momentarily puzzled, the fact she was actually in Helen's flat was absorbing all her attention.

'Your drawings.'

Kaz became aware of the sketchbook she was clutching. 'Oh yeah.'

She plonked the heavy pad on the kitchen counter and flipped it open to the first page. Leo was resplendent on his cushions, head flung back, legs akimbo, one hand suggestively close to his rather large penis. Helen looked the drawing over and smirked.

'He looks . . . rather pleased with himself.'

'His name's Leo. He's got a tendency to fall asleep, must have these wet dreams, 'cause he gets a hard-on like you wouldn't believe. At one point, Mike, he's the tutor, kicked his foot. Apparently it's . . . unprofessional.'

Helen laughed. 'A model with an erection? I should think it is!' She turned to Kaz, her gaze had warmed up. Leo had proved an unexpected icebreaker. 'It's very good, but I'm not sure I'd want him on my wall.'

'I wanted you to see what I been doing.'

Helen found it difficult to remain annoyed, she gave Kaz a diffident smile. 'I'm sorry if I seem . . . I dunno, I am pleased to see you. You took me by surprise.'

Kaz nodded, inclined her head towards the sketchbook. 'So whad'you think?'

Helen turned her attention back to the drawing and gave it some serious scrutiny.

'It's good . . . it's, well don't get me wrong, but it's different.'

'No one gave me the chance to draw naked men before. Or naked anyone for that matter.'

Helen laughed. 'What I mean is, you're drawing with far more confidence. It's bolder. Sharper.'

Kaz grinned. 'That's what I thought. So I should thank you.'

'What for?'

'For telling me to become a proper student.'

Helen pondered. The kettle was boiling. She opened a cupboard and took out a cafetiere. 'Did I tell you that? Surely Becky was the one encouraged you to do the A-level?'

Kaz folded her arms. 'You were the one I wanted to impress.'

Helen didn't reply. She busied herself spooning coffee into the cafetiere and pouring boiling water into the pot. Kaz could see the tension in her shoulders, the taut sinews running down her neck. Without her office uniform and her make-up she seemed much younger, more Kaz's age, more of a peer. And Kaz could feel Helen's discomfort; she needed rescuing.

'Joey's got one of these coffee-making machines. Froths milk. Does all sorts.'

Helen picked up this thread gratefully, adopting an overly cheerful tone. 'Yes, my parents have got something similar. Espresso machine. They were on at me to get one.' She grinned, indicated the empty worktops. 'Thing is, where would I put it?'

Kaz chuckled. 'I'm guessing you'd have to put it in a cupboard.'

'Exactly. And then you'd be forever getting it in and out, wouldn't you?' She produced two bone china mugs and a tray. 'Do you take milk?'

'Black's fine.'

Helen loaded the tray and carried it through to the sitting room. Leaving her sketchbook, Kaz followed. The room was large and airy, with windows on two sides; considering its size there wasn't much furniture: two pale cream sofas, a glass table, a plasma screen. Kaz noticed that there was already a drained coffee pot on the table, together with an empty mug and a pile of newspapers. Helen glanced at it as she put the tray down.

'Now you've caught me out with my private addictions. Coffee and more coffee.'

Kaz smiled. 'There are worse things.' She sat down on the opposite sofa, giving Helen plenty of space.

Helen began to carefully fold up the newspapers, she ended up with a small stack; she was buying time, getting over the shock. Kaz turning up like this, invading her private space, it was dangerous. It was also exciting.

Kaz watched the paper-folding with curiosity. 'How many Sunday papers do you get through?'

'I usually buy at least a couple. I like to get an overview.'

The tension between them was palpable, dressed up in a politeness that Kaz had never experienced in their previous encounters. Helen seemed entirely focused on pouring the coffee and Kaz couldn't help but watch. Both their gazes converged on the tilt of the pot, the steaming black liquid swirling into the white ceramic mugs. Finally Helen handed one to her. Kaz took it and sighed.

'I'm sorry, coming round like this. I shouldn't have. But I had to talk to you.'

Helen gave her a rueful look. 'Southend?'

Kaz put the mug down carefully on the table in front of her. The tears had started to come. She put her hand over her mouth in a vain attempt to cram them back down.

Helen got up, went to the bedroom and returned with a box of tissues. She put them on the table and sat down beside Kaz. Kaz plucked a tissue from the box, then somewhere inside a dam burst. Bent double, she sobbed. Helen placed a hand on her back and gently rubbed it.

Kaz had cried a few times inside, in her bunk, in the dead of night. But she'd always kept it to herself. She'd managed a few therapy tears, but that was an act. Now, for the first time in her adult memory, she really cried, her entire body shuddering as convulsive waves rose up from a well of pain. The last time she had allowed herself to collapse like this she'd been about six; Joey had been playing with her guinea pig and came to announce it was asleep in its cage. Kaz had found the little creature lifeless under a pile of straw. And she had howled. Ellie had tossed the animal in the dustbin and given her daughter a clout. Joey had simply watched with a grin on his face; it didn't occur to Kaz until years later that her four-year-old brother might've done for the guinea pig.

Gradually the waves subsided. Kaz blew her nose, her eyes were red-rimmed, sore. She glanced at Helen. 'Sorry.'

'Stop apologizing.'

Kaz dipped her head wearily. 'All my life I been telling lies. I mean everybody does it, don't they?'

Helen shrugged. 'Sometimes.'

Kaz started to shred the damp tissue. 'But . . . you have to draw the line. Get straight with the world or least with the people that matter, don't you?'

'You'll probably feel better if you do.' Helen rubbed Kaz's shoulder. She was administering comfort, at least that's what she was telling herself.

'What about this officer of the court, don't tell me what I don't wanna hear, three monkeys bollocks?'

A small smile crept over Helen's face. Yes there were boundaries but she knew in her heart that at this moment she simply didn't care.

'Well, it's Sunday and I'm at home and this is just two friends having a private conversation.'

'You mean that?'

Helen nodded. She sat gazing expectantly at Kaz. When they'd talked before, Kaz had always left large chunks out or skated over certain facts, Helen knew that. Getting Kaz to really trust her, this was the intimacy she'd always craved. So it might compromise her professionally, but hey, what the hell? In spite of Neville's efforts they were still regarded as villains' briefs. A thrill was rising in her, partly sexual, but also secret and forbidden; she was on a threshold, they were stepping into high-risk territory. But that was the reason she'd become a criminal lawyer, this stuff gave her a real buzz.

Kaz was sitting quietly. She seemed nervous. It took several moments for her to gather her thoughts.

'I had to do something about Natalie, didn't know what, so I forced Joey to go to Southend with me. That copper was partly right. When I saw the state of her I was mad as hell, and I took it out on Joey – gave him a right earache. And he lost it.'

Helen listened intently. The naked truth excited her, this

transparent window into the Phelps's world. Kaz was uncomfortable but she pressed on.

"Fore I knew what was happening, he'd got hold of Jez, picked him up and chucked him off the balcony. Then he walked out. Me and Ash got Natalie out of there fast as we could. I was gobsmacked, I never dreamt . . .'

More tears started to flow. Helen reached over and took Kaz's hand.

'Okay, I could grass him up, probably should. But then what? Joey wouldn't survive in prison, not in himself, as a person. He'd use his fists and he'd use drugs. It'd turn him into a brute. And he's not that. Not yet.'

Helen was entranced by the rawness of Kaz's confession. But she knew she had to choose her words carefully or the shutters would come down again.

'You sure about that?'

Kaz nodded vigorously. 'Yeah, I am sure.' She fixed her with an imploring look. 'Helen, I can stop him. I'm the only one who can. Locking him up ain't gonna do it. It'll make him worse.'

Helen turned Kaz's palm over in her own, stared down at it. 'Maybe you're confusing the boy he was six years ago with the man he is now.'

Kaz shook her head savagely. 'No, I'm not. That picture of the little girl, Joey wouldn't have done that. Not a little kid. Okay, the firm . . . he's got blokes working for him, ex-military. Stuff like that, it'd be down to them. I know it don't make it any better, but Joey's not . . . he's not a real killer. I known real killers, my old man for starters. And Joey ain't like that.'

Helen absorbed this with a sigh.

Kaz tried desperately to read her face. 'You think I'm being stupid, don't you?'

Helen met her gaze. What she was thinking needed to stay locked in her own head.

'I think . . . you're in a very difficult position. You haven't spent that much time with him and so there's a danger of being naive about him. About who he is now. The police think he's very dangerous.'

Kaz pulled her hand away angrily. 'Oh, what the fuck do they know?'

Helen tilted her head. 'I worry about you. Not just as a client . . .'

'Joey would never hurt me. Never. He's . . . we're . . . I dunno if I can even explain it. But it's not his fault how he's ended up.'

Helen pushed back a frond of dark hair from Kaz's forehead. Thoughts, notions, were rushing through her mind: she was helping Kaz, doing her job, it wasn't about personal feelings. And yet she had to touch her, she wanted so badly to touch her. She gazed into Kaz's eyes.

'You can't save him.'

'But that's the whole point – I can. He's made a deal with me.'

'What sort of deal?'

'I help him, the killing will stop.'

'Help him do what? He's a drug dealer.'

'Yeah. But we're gonna turn the business totally legit . . .'

'We? Thought you were going to college?'

'I am. But y'know, if I can steer him in the right direction . . .'

Helen shook her head angrily, got up. She raked back her hair with both hands. 'Karen . . . this is crazy. You'll get recalled. Do you want to spend another six years in jail?' Her voice carried a tone of grief and desperation.

Kaz got up too. She felt Helen was slipping away from her. And Helen was all she wanted. Kaz took a step towards her. She could feel the warmth of her body, her sweatshirt carried a hint of the perfume she habitually wore.

'I'm sorry. You're disappointed in me.'

Helen sighed in annoyance. 'No . . . the fact you want to help him is to your credit. But people don't change that easily.'

'I changed. I got off the drugs, I saw how stupid it all was.'

Helen gazed at her beseechingly. 'Yeah and this is going to get you right back in that world. Don't you see?'

Kaz huffed in exasperation. 'It's not a separate universe. C'mon, we're all closer to the edge than any of us'd like to think. You, Neville, given some of the types you represent, can you say you're squeaky clean? I can't walk away and abandon Joey. I thought I could, but I can't.'

Helen stood stock-still and exhaled. Her whole body seemed to deflate. Tears were welling up. 'Oh Karen . . . I just . . .'

Kaz met her gaze and held it.

'I just . . .'

Kaz took another step forward. If she was going to make this happen, it had to be now. She gazed into Helen's eyes, soft grey with a fleck of hazel. She remembered the first time she'd been close enough to notice their unique colour. Now she was so near she could feel Helen's breath, she could see the tiny pulse in her neck. She could smell her hair, skimming the soft skin of her shoulder. It was all so tantalizingly close. For several seconds neither moved. The tension held them, like the invisible skin on water. Then Kaz leant forward and their lips met, nervously at first. Helen's arm went round Kaz's shoulder and she pulled her close. This is what she'd wanted since the day Kaz had walked into her office, no, since before that, since way before that.

The kiss turned into an eruption of passion and need that took them both by surprise. Kaz's jacket, her boots, were dumped on the floor. Helen's discarded sweatshirt was soon added to the pile. Fingers, tongues, urgently exploring and caressing. A shudder of ecstasy convulsed Kaz's whole body as Helen's soft fingertips found her clitoris.

Kaz had had plenty of sex in her life before, quite a lot of it against her will, but this was something else. It swept her away. There was no fear or panic, she realized this was how it was supposed to be. This was about how she felt and what she wanted, not about what someone else needed from her. The smell of Helen, the touch and taste of her, suddenly everything was right. All that mattered was being there with Helen in that instant, the rest of the world fell away.

When Kaz awoke several hours later, long shafts of bright afternoon sun were streaking across the floor and up and over the snowy white duvet. She'd ended up in Helen's bed. She felt almost light-headed, it didn't matter how often she'd dreamt of this moment, the reality was surreal. She found herself staring up at the ceiling, its elaborate coving and cornices; like the walls, the bed, the paintwork, it was white. Kaz didn't think she'd ever been in such a white room before, but it felt pure and safe rather than clinical.

The door opened and Helen entered carrying a tray. She wore a pale blue bathrobe, her fine blonde hair was pushed back and decidedly ruffled. She smiled, a much softer and more intimate smile, Kaz thought, but maybe she was imagining it. Maybe she'd dreamt the whole thing. Then Helen placed the tray on the bed, lifted Kaz's hand and kissed her fingertips.

'Tea and crumpets. Sunday afternoon – seemed the right thing.'

Kaz returned the kiss. 'Dunno that I've ever had crumpets.'

Helen gave her a sidelong glance. 'Seriously? Never?'

Kaz shook her head.

'You are in for a treat. Loads of butter, that's how my granny always served them, so it drips everywhere.'

Kaz manoeuvred herself into a sitting position as Helen climbed on to the bed beside her. Kaz picked up her first crumpet and took a bite, melted butter ran down her chin.

Helen grinned, leant forward and licked it off. 'See? Granny knew a thing or two.'

Kaz smiled impishly. 'Wanna hear a really mad thing?'

Helen gave her a suspicious glance. 'More madness? Probably not.'

'Nah, this is mad in a good way. This is the first time I can remember when something really good has come from 'fessing up and telling the truth.'

Helen gazed at her and the tears started to well. Without the tough facade, the attitude, Kaz seemed very vulnerable and very young.

'I don't know what to say to that.'

Kaz brushed a tear from her lover's cheek. 'Hey, don't cry. It ain't a bad feeling.'

A phone buzzed in the pocket of Helen's bathrobe. She pulled it out.

'Oh I nearly forgot. Your phone was going berserk. Somehow it ended up on the floor behind the sofa, so I picked it up.'

Kaz took the phone, turned it over in her palm and started prodding the screen. 'I've had this bloody thing three weeks, still can't get the hang of it.'

Helen giggled. 'Give it here. You want to answer it?'

'Not really.'

'Well then you . . . oh but you've already pushed the button.'

Helen held out the phone, a voice could be heard on the end of the line.

'Kaz?'

It was Joey. Kaz gave Helen a guilty look, took the phone, put it to her ear. She folded her arms around her naked breasts, her tone was clipped and tough.

'Yeah, what's going on?'

'Thought you was never gonna answer. What you doing?'

'Nothing.'

'Well where are you?'

'Whad'you want Joey?' Kaz huffed, irritation creeping into her voice. 'I'm busy. Having tea and crumpets if you must know.'

She glanced at Helen who gave her a cheeky smile. Joey's tone was flat, devoid of emotion. It felt as though he were a million miles away.

'Oh well, I had a bit of news. Thought you should know . . .'

Kaz gazed fondly at Helen. Helen edged towards her, stroked her cheek, Kaz had to drag her attention back to the phone. 'Yeah, I'm listening.'

The line was quiet for several seconds. Then Joey sighed. 'I just heard. Sean's got parole. They're letting the fucker out. Can you believe that?'

As Kaz absorbed his words the joy drained from her face.

'Well, it was bound to happen. Listen, I'll give you a bell later, okay.' She clicked the phone off, tossed it on the duvet.

Helen looked at her with concern. 'What's happened?'

'Nothing. Yet.' Kaz sighed. 'But they're letting my cousin out of jail.'

'Will that mean problems in the family?'

Kaz nodded ruefully. 'You could say that.'

25

Sean Phelps sat, eyes closed, head tipped slightly back, listening to the taped music in the multi-faith room – a posh name, in his view, for what had always been the prison chapel. There might not be a service, but on Sunday evenings he always went there for his own version of evensong. His upbringing had been in no way religious, although his family was nominally Catholic. His belief system was simple: when you're dead you're gone, so get it while you can. However Sean was a con serving life with a tariff of twelve years and working on his parole had become a habit; 'finding God' was simply part of the package.

Private time in the chapel was something he looked forward to, it gave him the headspace to think. His cell he regarded more as an office; his various lads were always in and out, deals were done, instructions issued. And of course the screws could walk in anytime, although the bush telegraph that operated along the landing usually gave him ample warning.

Third time lucky everyone was saying. Sean had been receiving congratulations all day. Considering the form he had, he'd played a blinder, he knew that. Back in the mid-nineties the police had charged him with the drive-by shooting of a uniformed PC in Basildon. Miserable little fucker had taken a bung then failed to deliver, so in Sean's view he'd had it coming. It looked as if Sean would go down, but Terry put it about that anyone who gave evidence would end up regretting it; the CPS had to drop the case. After that the old bill got the bit between their teeth. Sean was finally convicted on forensics for the murder of a small-time drug peddler who'd pissed him off in a pub. But with a copper's murder 'lying on file' the parole board had knocked him back twice. Fourteen years he'd served, played the game, been a model prisoner; in the end even they had to accept that he'd done his whack.

Sean had taken it all in his stride and largely without resentment. The law had two sides, and he knew which he was on. He was a career villain. The filth were bound to get arsey if they thought you'd beat the system. And let's face it, if he'd got life for that copper, he'd have been lucky to be out in less than twenty. So he was definitely ahead of the game.

The prison's musical selection wasn't that broad. Sean liked a bit of country and western, the raunchier the better. It amused him to go into the multi-faith room on a Sunday evening and slap that on the tape deck, especially if there were some ragheads in there trying to say their prayers. But tonight he had the place to himself, Dolly was singing one of his favourite ballads and he had plenty to think about because tomorrow morning he'd be walking out of those gates.

Being banged up hadn't been all bad. At forty-five he was fitter than a bloke twenty years younger. He was six two, worked out every day, never backed away from a fight and was the main supplier of drugs to his fellow inmates. As a result he'd risen to the top of the prison hierarchy. Everyone deferred to him, even the screws. Now he was getting out they were queuing up to pay him court.

The door at the back of the room opened quietly and a slight, blond lad slipped in. Other cons knew not to disturb him at this hour, but as his 'boy' Darryl had special privileges. Darryl was only twenty-two, had the soft skin and silken lashes of a girl, he was serving three years for burglary and possession with intent to supply. His life inside would've been hell if he hadn't been lucky enough to hook Sean.

Darryl padded softly down the aisle between chairs and sat down next to Sean. Sean glanced at the boy, saw he had tears in his eyes.

'What the fuck's up with you?'

Darryl snivelled, wiped his nose with the back of his hand. 'Gonna miss my big cuddly bear.'

Sean shifted irritably. 'Don't fucking call me that. You know I don't like it.'

'But I know what you do like, don't I babe?' Darryl reached out and stroked Sean's thigh.

Sean gave a spluttering laugh. 'Not in here! It's the fucking chapel, for chrissake! Ain't you got no respect?'

Darryl gave him a mischievous grin. 'God loves and accepts all his creatures. I had a regular who was a vicar. I use to blow him in the vestry between Holy Communion and Matins, that's what he told me God understands.'

Sean grinned. 'You are a dirty, filthy little whore, ain't you?'

'Isn't that what big bear likes?' Darryl's hand was creeping towards Sean's groin. Sean slapped it away none too gently. Darryl shot him a petulant glance. 'Ouch! That fuckin' hurt.'

'Yeah and I'll hurt you even more if you don't stop playing up.'

'All I'm saying is I'll miss you. But I'll be out in six months and we can—'

Darryl didn't get a chance to say more because Sean seized him by the jaw and twisted his face round until they were eyeball to eyeball.

'Now you listen to me boy, 'cause I ain't gonna say this twice. What happens in here stays in here. I ain't no queer, I'm a married man. I don't want my Glynis finding out about this. She'd be disgusted.'

Darryl wrenched himself free, he was stronger than he looked.

'What d'you think she's been doing all these years? Painting her nails and waiting for you?'

Sean glared at the boy. Nostrils flaring, he wagged his index finger in Darryl's face. 'She's loyal my wife. I won't have a word spoke against her. Once I'm out, I don't need none of this and I certainly don't want it. Got that?'

Darryl's eyes began to brim with tears. 'Don't you like me any more? I thought you liked me. I understand business, on the outside I could be very useful to you.'

Sean took a deep breath, then exhaled. 'Look you're a good boy Darryl, but let's get real here. Once you get out you'll go back to your fairy friends and our paths won't cross, not ever. You got your world, I got mine.'

Darryl wiped his nose with the sleeve of his sweatshirt. 'What's gonna happen to me in here once you're gone?'

Sean huffed, this was beginning to get on his nerves. 'I've had a word, Jimmy and the other lads'll keep an eye on you. That's the best I can do mate. Take a tip from me, you got a talent, use it.'

Now Darryl really started to blub. 'But I'm in love with you.'

Sean got up angrily, that really was the last straw. 'Oh don't be such a stupid little prick! You faggots, you make me sick to my stomach. Always bloody whining. Worse than a bloody woman.'

He went over to the tape deck, cut Dolly off in mid-flow, strode back up the aisle and was gone, slamming the door behind him.

26

Kaz watched from the kitchen window as the electronic gates swung open and the white stretch limo drew up in front of the house. Ellie and Brian were already outside waiting with Terry in his wheelchair. A huge bunch of yellow ribbons was tied round one of the maple trees in the garden. Kaz was damned if she was going to participate in this farce. She was only there because Joey had begged her.

Ashley got out of the front of the limo, opened the back door. Joey was first to emerge, then Glynis, Sean's wife, followed by the man himself. Kaz watched as he enveloped Ellie in a hug. His short cropped hair was peppered with grey, but apart from that he seemed much the same as she remembered him. He leant over Terry, patted his shoulder, then enveloped him in a brief manly hug. Terry remained oblivious, his glassy eyes staring into the distance.

Kaz took a deep breath and walked with as much nonchalance as she could muster into the hallway. Sean came through the door, his arm round Ellie's shoulder, his face sombre.

'I dunno what to say mate, seeing him like this breaks my fucking heart, I can tell you.' Then his eye alighted on Kaz and his features broke into a broad grin. 'Blimey O'Reilly! What we got here? Little Kaz. You certainly grown up. Being banged up's done more for you than it done for me. All I got is grey hairs.' He guffawed, Ellie and Brian joined in.

Kaz returned his look with a hard and cold stare. She'd decided to be polite, but that's where she drew the line. 'Welcome home Sean.'

He moved in on her, the physical power of him as intimidating as it had ever been.

'Come on then little cousin, don't I get a kiss?' Without waiting for a response, he dragged her into a hug, planted his wet lips on her averted cheek, then released her with a slap on the arse. He clapped his hands together. 'Now where's the fucking bubbly?'

As Ellie escorted him through into the sitting room Kaz caught Glynis's eye. She was a petite, bird-like creature, blonde and fragile. On their first acquaintance years ago she'd put the young Kaz in mind of Barbie. Now in her early forties too many cigarettes and too many sunbeds had turned her lined and leathery. She flicked a nervous smile in Kaz's direction.

'All right Kaz? Your mum said you was out. Been meaning to give you a bell.'

Kaz returned the smile with some sympathy. She knew from Joey that Glynis had spent the last ten years living with a betting shop manager called Dave. She'd broached the question of a divorce with Sean, but he'd angrily refused her, insisting he was a Catholic and he still loved her. Mortally afraid of him, she had moved to Eastbourne with Dave in an attempt to break free. But Sean's reach was long. Probably the only reason Dave was still living and breathing was that no one had felt brave enough to tell Sean the truth. Glynis had visited regularly, kept up the pretence. Now she put Kaz in mind of a hunted animal as she clipped across the tiled floor in her four-inch heels and leather mini skirt following in Sean's wake.

Ellie led Sean through the sitting room, out into the conservatory and from there into the garden. A marquee had been erected containing half a dozen round tables, a large buffet and a small country and western band. As Sean emerged from the house with Ellie the thirty or so assembled guests raised their glasses on cue, the band struck up and everyone started to sing 'For He's a Jolly Good Fellow'. Sean stood, grinning from ear to ear, lapping it up and pretending to be surprised.

Kaz and Joey emerged from the house together. Kaz glanced at her brother, his face was a mask.

'How the hell d'you dig this lot up at such short notice?'

'Free booze, grub, word got round pretty fast.'

Kaz shot a look at Terry, being manoeuvred into place at a table by Brian.

'Wonder what he makes of it all?'

Joey turned to her. Suddenly his look was intense, penetrating. He kept his voice low. 'I know what he done to you Kaz, when you was a kid. "Uncle" fucking Sean. You want me to take him out, I will.'

Kaz stared at Joey. She certainly had her own private feelings about the return of Sean, but the simmering fury coming off her brother took her completely by surprise. She laid her hand gently on his arm and returned his gaze.

'What I want is for you to stick to our agreement. Far as I'm concerned, nothing's changed.'

He took a deep breath, reined himself in, nodded. 'Well, it's your call babes.'

The buffet lunch comprised of spare ribs, southern fried chicken, burgers, all known favourites of Sean's, with salad as the only concession to health. Bottles of champagne, wine, an avalanche of beer were chilling in plastic dustbins crammed with ice. The three waiters and two caterers were run off their feet serving food and refilling glasses. The band played, there was much strutting and posing on the tiny dance floor. Several former colleagues of Terry and Sean attempted a Cossack dance and wrecked two tables.

As the afternoon sun moved across the garden and shadows lengthened, the party went from raucous to mellow by way of alcohol and exhaustion. Glynis sat on Sean's knee, drank her way through two bottles of champagne, ate nothing and told anyone who'd listen how overjoyed she was to have her old man home and how they planned to have kids. Ellie became maudlin drunk and sobbed over Terry, who remained glassy-eyed in his wheelchair, sucking champagne through a straw.

Kaz watched the whole cavalcade with a detached eye. It was the first time she'd ever attended a party stone-cold sober, certainly the first family knees-up. These had traditionally been about alcohol and excess, usually ending in a brawl.

She noticed that Joey was toying with a beer and keeping a wary eye on the proceedings. Their eyes met, he inclined his head and she followed him into the house.

He went to the tap in the kitchen and poured himself a glass of water. She watched him drink, the tension in his shoulders, the blank expression in his eyes.

'You okay?' She stroked his arm.

Joey put the glass down. 'According to Yev, Sean's recruiting muscle. These Russian army blokes all know each other. Sean's put the word out he's hiring.'

Kaz absorbed this with a nod. 'Well he ain't about to go straight and get a job as a drugs counsellor, is he?'

'He's a slippery sod. I wanna know what he's up to.'

'I know but that needn't affect our plans.'

'And what are your plans little cousins?'

The enquiry was conversational, friendly even. Kaz and Joey still swivelled round in surprise to find Sean leaning against the door jamb. He took a long swig from the bottle of single malt in his hand. His face was flushed and sweaty, but it was hard to tell just how drunk he was. He held up the bottle.

'Bubbly's all very well, but frankly it tastes like piss. Now give me Scotch every time. Proper man's drink. But maybe I'm just old-fashioned.'

Kaz glanced at Joey, she didn't entirely trust his mood. His face was calm, still she could feel the aura of anger.

She smiled at Sean. 'My plans are I'm going to art college. I start in October.'

Sean sniggered. 'What, you gonna be a fashion designer? Could model your own stuff then, couldn't you?'

He took a couple of unsteady steps forward, he was leering quite openly at Kaz. He licked his lips. 'As I recall you had quite a talent for getting your kit off, didn't you? You liked a bit of fun.'

Joey moved like lightning. He grabbed a carving knife from the wooden block beside the cooker. The eight-inch steel blade flashed up and stopped within inches of Sean's nose.

Sean gave the knife a bemused look, then laughed. 'Whoah there boy! You always did have a short fuse, even as a kid.'

But Joey was completely calm, he even started to smile. 'You're a guest in this house and I expect you to treat my sister with respect.'

Sean put the whisky bottle down, held out his open palms.

'No offence Joey. You've put on a lovely spread for us. And to tell you the truth I'm bladdered. Kaz knows I don't mean no harm, don't you love?'

He glanced at her appealingly. She could see the sweat on his upper lip, feel the heat of his breathing. The booze-sodden smell of him turned her stomach. She glanced at Joey. 'He's pissed. Let it go.'

Joey lowered the knife, slotted it back into the block.

Sean grinned, reached out to pat Kaz's shoulder. 'You're a good girl, always was. Come here and give us a kiss, show there's no hard feelings.'

Kaz took a step backwards. 'Sean, let's get a few things straight. I'm not a good girl, certainly not *your* good girl . . .'

Sean lurched towards her. 'Awww come on, we're family. Look at your poor old dad out there – he wouldn't want us three to fall out, would he?'

He managed to wrap one arm round Joey and the other round Kaz.

'Now I'm out, we can really get cracking.' He squeezed Joey's shoulder. ''Cause you and me boy, we got a business to run. And I'm grateful for what you done. Keeping the seat warm for me since your dad was took bad.'

Joey jerked free from Sean's grasp. He looked him up and down with some disdain. 'When you've sobered up we need to talk.'

Sean laughed but a nasty glint had crept into his eye. 'I done more business pissed than sober. And I was doing it while you was still crapping your nappy. You got something to say, spit it out.'

Joey put his hands in his pockets, leant back casually against the kitchen counter.

'Okay. You need to get real Sean. You been inside a long time and the world has changed . . .'

Sean raised his hand. 'Hold up here, hold up. Three years ago your dad had his stroke. You come to me and you was practically wetting yourself. You needed my advice. And my contacts.'

'Wetting myself? Do me a favour.'

Sean raised his index finger and jabbed it at Joey. 'I put you in touch with people – the right people. You think any of those players'd take a kid like you seriously if I hadn't vouched for you?'

Kaz watched Joey, the more Sean needled him, the more cool and contained he became. She realized he was enjoying himself.

He removed his hands from his pockets, lounged against the countertop. 'Stuff we're doing now you wouldn't even understand. The Net's changing everything.'

'Bollocks!' Sean seized the whisky bottle, took a long swig, wiped his mouth with the back of his hand. 'It's still about product – and that's what I gave you boy, access to top-quality gear. Even a fucking chimp could make money if he got his hands on the product.'

Joey cracked his knuckles, weighing his options. 'I'm not trying to deny you your due Sean . . .'

'Bloody right you're not!'

'I think a hundred K should cover it. Little retirement nest-egg. I'll get the cash for you tomorrow. Then we're square.'

Sean stared at him gone out, then he burst out laughing.

'You think you can buy me out of my own fucking firm for a lousy hundred K?'

Joey considered this. 'I think I'm being very fair.'

'You are joking.'

Joey continued to smile. 'You're an old lag Sean, time to retire. Put your feet up, play golf. Kaz and me have got our own plans.'

Sean spluttered. 'Kaz? What the fuck's she got to do with any of this? I mean – pardon me love – she's a fucking *woman*!'

Joey turned to Kaz, shot her a cheeky grin. 'He's an observant old fucker, you have to give him that.'

Kaz smiled at her brother's sarcasm, but Sean wasn't amused.

He launched himself at Joey, seizing him by the throat. 'Think you can take the piss out of me you little prick—'

The booze had robbed him of his edge. Joey twisted himself deftly out of Sean's grasp and threw a choke-hold round his neck. He dragged him several paces across the kitchen, squeezing the breath out of him. Sean gasped, lashed out wildly but to no avail, his face turning puce as Joey tightened his iron grip.

Kaz watched, mesmerized. She had to admit that watching Sean suffer was enjoyable. But was she really going to stand there and let Joey choke him to death? That would hardly be sensible. She was about to step in when her mother appeared in the doorway. Ellie was three sheets to the wind, she swayed slightly, but still rapidly absorbed the scene before her and immediately took charge.

'Fucking hell! Joey, put your cousin down! Now! Why is it every sodding party we have in this house ends in a sodding fight? I'm sick of it!'

Joey released Sean, who collapsed in a gasping heap on the floor.

He looked up, pointed an accusing finger at Joey. 'You little wanker!' His voice was hoarse, but the rage was unmistakable. 'I'm gonna teach you a lesson you won't forget.' His bleary gaze travelled to Kaz. 'You and her – miserable little slut! I'll take you both down. I fucking swear!'

27

Turnbull took his place at the head of the conference table. He removed his jacket, slotted it neatly on the back of his chair and started to roll up his sleeves. It was a politician's trick, often performed for the news media, a symbolic act, a way of saying to the assembled company, 'I'm a grafter, I mean business.' But since the only other person present was Bill Mayhew the gesture was somewhat redundant.

He sat down and picked up the file in front of him. 'Presumably you've read this?'

Mayhew looked up, blinked several times, an owl suddenly caught in the headlights.

Turnbull gave him a critical glance. 'The parole board's report on Sean Phelps? I'll take that as a no, shall I?'

Shifting his bulk awkwardly in his chair, Mayhew sighed. He didn't need to read it, he'd got the gist. 'Can't imagine how they ever came to the conclusion it was safe to let him out.'

'Well let's see if we can gain some insight into their thinking, since they've chucked him back in our lap.' Turnbull flicked briskly through the pages until he found the passage he was searching for. 'Ah, here we go. Listen to this. "And we feel that the general attitude demonstrated by Phelps, particularly in the mentoring of younger offenders, provides ample demonstration of his determination to relinquish the criminal lifestyle."' He slapped the document down and sighed. 'Where the hell do they get these people and what planet are they living on?'

Turnbull got up, scanned the rooftops out of the window as though some clue might be found out there.

Mayhew scratched his head and cleared his throat. 'Well you know what they say, silver lining and all that.' He caught his boss's eye and deduced from his expression that Turnbull hadn't tumbled to the obvious benefits that might accrue from the turn of events.

Mayhew allowed himself several seconds of private pleasure; a small smile hovered on his lips. 'I was just thinking, a power struggle in the Phelps clan can only make them more vulnerable. Things get heated, risks'll be taken, mistakes made. With any luck we'll get Sean back inside and we'll nab Joey.'

Turnbull appeared to ponder this. What most people didn't realize about him was that he loved to perform. Fooling people was an art but you didn't have to be an actor. There was plenty of scope in other professions and Turnbull had built his early career as a detective on his talent for playacting. Letting suspects, or indeed fellow officers, assume he was an arrogant fool ensured they would lower their guard and underestimate him. And with his current scheme it was crucial to keep Mayhew off the scent.

Turnbull allowed very little to emerge that revealed the inner man. His great strength had always been that he'd never stopped learning. He watched, he listened, he was always reading faces, analysing motives. He knew that every man – and it was men that mostly interested him – had his own secret vanity, the private story he told inside his own head to bolster his ego.

In the case of Bill Mayhew it was the belief that under his bumbling exterior he was the smart one, the real detective. Turnbull knew this about his subordinate and used it to manipulate him. Playing on his vanity, allowing him to believe he'd thought of something Turnbull hadn't, was how he squeezed the maximum effort out of Mayhew. It kept him slaving all hours, doing the donkey work, it also kept him quiescent when Turnbull took the credit.

He put on his sincere, honest face, as if Mayhew's words had come as a revelation. 'Good point Bill. Joey's not about to step aside, is he, just because his cousin's got out?'

Mayhew smiled sagely, concluded he might be on to a winner. 'There'll be trouble. I'd bet my pension on it. Couple more surveillance teams boss, we could tighten the net on them – might get a result.'

Turnbull exhaled noisily, started to pace the room. He was warming to the role. 'Bloody budget cuts! How the hell am I supposed to mount an effective operation on a bloody shoe-string?'

He rubbed his knuckles over his well-shaven chin, glanced at Mayhew. The fat little DCI was sitting there, oblivious as usual to Turnbull's real agenda. Too easy really. Now it was time to go fishing.

'How's Bradley getting on with Karen Phelps?'

Mayhew shrugged. 'It's a game of patience.'

'What's Armstrong playing at? Can't she get things moving?'

'She's come up with a promising notion of her own. Thought I'd let her run with it.'

Turnbull frowned. 'Is that wise?' He'd suspected something was afoot. 'She strikes me as a bit too pushy for her own good.'

Mayhew blinked at him a couple of times. 'Nothing ventured, nothing gained boss.'

Turnbull fixed him with an appraising stare. Now they'd got to the nub of it. Mayhew was plotting. He was hoping to present Turnbull with some kind of stunning breakthrough, proving to himself yet again that he was the real detective, forced to work for a stupid, power-hungry boss. When Mayhew was on this tack he occasionally came up with something useful. In a nanosecond Turnbull had the entire situation sized up. He gave Mayhew a benevolent smile. 'Just keep me posted Bill.'

The DCI smiled and as he rolled out of the door Turnbull took out his phone. He scrolled through the contacts list and gazed out of the window. The day was fine, blue sky and a few scudding clouds, which suited his mood. The fact that Bradley appeared to be getting nowhere was entirely predictable. And Armstrong was pursuing her own agenda instead of backing him up. Another useful piece to the jigsaw. Turnbull smiled to himself, it was all progressing quite well really.

He pressed call and was answered on the third ring.

'Duncan, it's Alan Turnbull. I think it's time we had lunch again. Perhaps invite Marcus Foxley ...?'

28

Nicci Armstrong had been up since six, making Sophie's packed lunch, putting some washing on. Her ex, Tim, had agreed to come over and take their daughter to school, although, as usual, he made it clear what a big favour he was doing her. Even so, Nicci still didn't get away until nearly nine. She picked up Mal Bradley at Finsbury Park tube and they headed north. Bradley wasn't much of a travelling companion, dozing off in the passenger seat as soon as they passed Brent Cross. Weary and in need of a coffee, Nicci took the slip road and pulled off the motorway into Northampton services.

As she manoeuvred into a parking slot, Bradley woke up.
'We there?'

Nicci huffed. 'I wish.'

They zigzagged through the windswept car park and made for the coffee shop.

While Bradley queued at the counter, Nicci sat down and sent her daughter a text. Sophie was eight; having a mobile on in school was forbidden and it was possibly frying her child's brain anyway, but Nicci was a divorced mother trying to hold down a career and remain emotionally connected to her child. Just keeping all the balls in the air was a daily challenge. Tim's idea of fatherhood was taking Sophie off on a jolly every other weekend with his new girlfriend. They went to Alton Towers, canoeing at Center Parcs. Sophie was rapidly developing the notion that fathers were fun, whereas mothers were for everyday and stopped you from watching telly, texting your mates after bedtime and doing the stuff you really liked.

As Bradley approached with the coffees, Nicci pointed her camera phone at him.

'Make a funny face.'

'Sorry?'

'For my daughter. I'm sending her some pictures, telling her what I'm up to.'

Bradley put one of the coffee cups down, took the other and carefully balanced it on his head, pointing to it while wearing a gormless expression, index finger several inches from the cup.

Nicci snapped him. 'Very good. Thanks.'

'I do party tricks for my nephews and nieces.' Bradley rescued the cup from his head, sat down.

Nicci typed under Bradley's mugshot: 'My coffee arrives.' She pressed send and smiled warmly at Bradley.

'She'll like that.'

'Didn't even know you had a kid.'

He did know. But it seemed too good an opening to pass up, a way to get beyond the professional facade and the fuck-you attitude that Nicci Armstrong cloaked herself in.

She put her phone away. 'I don't tend to advertise the fact – bad for one's promotion prospects.'

Bradley sipped his coffee and frowned. 'What, nowadays? Strikes me everyone has to fall over backwards to be politically correct.'

Nicci laughed. 'Oh poor Bradley, how hard it is to be a bloke.'

He grinned back, gave his coffee a stir. 'I know you think I'm a complete twat Sarge, but my parents love me and maybe a couple of mates.'

She gave him an arch smile. 'Perhaps I'm a sad old hag who

doesn't respond as she should to your gorgeous looks and your lovable boyish charm.'

Bradley reddened. His face settled into a scowl. 'If you want to know, I hate all that. Always have.'

'Oh boo hoo. Get over yourself. So Turnbull's trying to pimp you out – happens to women officers all the time.'

'That doesn't make it right.'

'No it doesn't. But I haven't noticed you striding into Turnbull's office and telling him to stuff it. 'Cause you think it's your fastest route up the greasy pole, don't you?'

Bradley gave her a sidelong glance. She made him feel adolescent and transparent, whereas in reality there was only six or seven years between them.

Nicci started to laugh. She gave his arm a pat. 'You're right. I do think you're a twat, but . . . I'm getting used to you.'

What she could've said was that he was nothing like Alex Marlow. She missed Alex's acerbic take on the world, the cynical banter they'd shared. Bradley couldn't begin to compete. But she'd come to the conclusion that was a good thing.

She pulled a file out of her bag and slapped it on the table.

'Right, I don't plan to drive nearly two hundred miles for nothing. So let's work out how we're going to put the screws on this fucker.'

The driveway up to Woodcote Hall was long and winding, some of the magnificent horse chestnuts dotted across the park were already showing the first golden tinges of autumn. Nicci followed signs to the car park, which took them through an arch into an old stable yard at the side of the building.

They were kept waiting about fifteen minutes in an oak-panelled library until a nurse in a pale mauve tunic appeared and ushered them through into Doctor Iqbal's office. Iqbal was writing, he capped his Mont Blanc fountain pen, rose from behind his desk and offered his hand. He was a slight figure, the suit was tailor-made, charcoal grey with a discreet stripe. He peered at them from behind the narrow rectangles of his rimless glasses as he motioned them to the two chairs placed in front of the desk.

'You've had a long drive. Can I offer you coffee?'

Nicci smiled. 'We're fine. Thank you for sparing the time to see us Doctor Iqbal.'

Iqbal spread his open palms. 'I fear you've come a long way for nothing Sergeant. As I said to Detective Chief Inspector Mayhew on the phone, Natalie Phelps is currently undergoing our intensive detoxification programme. Her mental state is extremely fragile. Any kind of police interview at this stage could easily tip her over the edge into psychosis. I really can't risk it.'

Nicci inclined her head and continued to smile. 'We do understand your position Doctor Iqbal, but this is potentially a murder investigation.'

'And I would love to help.' Iqbal sighed. 'But it's my duty to put my patient's interests first.'

Bradley pushed back in his chair, letting it scrape the polished wooden floor as he got to his feet. He didn't get to play bad cop that often, usually he was the young sympathetic one. Shoving both hands in his pockets, he eyeballed the doctor.

'I'm sure you would love to help. But the thing is, Joey Phelps is paying you a shedload of cash to keep his sister under wraps, isn't he? Also he's not a bloke you'd want to cross.'

Iqbal puffed up his chest and adopted an expression of horror. 'If you're suggesting—'

Bradley rested both knuckles on the desk and leant forward. He was right in Iqbal's face.

'Joey Phelps is a gangster, Doctor Iqbal. Currently under investigation for several murders including that of a police officer. What do you think is going to happen when it comes out that you're involved with him? Possibly even aiding and abetting his crimes? A full-blown media shit-storm is going to engulf this place and your high-priced clients, your pop stars and bankers – they'll be running for cover. Best-case scenario? One of the regulatory bodies closes you down and you go broke. Want to hear the worst?'

Iqbal was a small man, but he had some backbone. He glared straight back at Bradley. 'This is intimidation, pure and simple. I shall be reporting you to your superiors and contacting my lawyers.'

Bradley returned his hands to his pockets. 'That's your privilege sir.'

Nicci cleared her throat. 'I apologize Doctor Iqbal. We have no wish to intimidate or even upset you. My colleague was merely trying to make you fully aware of the serious situation you're in.'

Iqbal blinked at her, got up from his desk. He was feeling decidedly hemmed in. He strode over to a side table, picked up a water carafe and poured himself a glass.

'I'm merely attempting to fulfil my duty of care to a very vulnerable patient. I have no involvement in any criminality. And I refute the suggestion most strongly.'

Nicci and Bradley exchanged a covert glance. They had him on the ropes. Bradley strolled over to the window, folded his arms and gazed out. Nicci got to her feet and faced Iqbal.

'Doctor Iqbal, no one expects you to be able to vet the families and connections of every patient you try to help.' She spread her hands wide. 'But when we come to you and tell you that you are dealing with a serious and dangerous criminal, we expect your full cooperation.'

Iqbal sighed, replaced the glass on its tray. 'I'm not lying to you. Natalie is in an extremely poor state.'

'And we wouldn't dream of subjecting her to a police interview.'

Iqbal's gaze met Nicci's. 'Well, what do you want then?'

A small smile spread across Nicci's face. She inclined her head. 'This is a delicate situation for you and for us. We mean Natalie absolutely no harm. We simply want to get to know her, easily, gently, we want to gain her trust and we want you to help us do that.'

Iqbal scrutinized Nicci's face. Now he was curious.

'So you would meet her not as police officers, because that would frighten her?'

'That's the last thing we want.'

Iqbal pondered, his restless fingers strayed and he started to rearrange the glasses and carafe on the tray.

'And if I facilitate this, it would be an . . . entirely confidential matter between us?'

Nicci moved towards him. Her tone was gentle and reassuring. 'If and when the case comes to court Joey Phelps will never know that we got to Natalie through you. We were thinking that perhaps I could pose as a volunteer, maybe a former patient that you've treated, who comes back on an occasional basis to help out?'

Iqbal backed away from Nicci and took refuge behind his desk. He removed his glasses, took a tissue from the box at his elbow and started to polish them.

'This really is most unethical you know.'

Bradley turned from the window and strolled back to his chair. Iqbal gave him a wary look, but Bradley smiled. 'Thing is Doctor Iqbal, Natalie probably witnessed her boyfriend Jez Harris being murdered by her brother. Once she gets clean and sober enough to remember that, what are you going to do with her? You can't help her with that. In order for her to be protected and to really recover and find any kind of life for herself, Joey needs to be behind bars. That's what's in your patient's best interests.'

Nicci nodded. 'DC Bradley's right. The ethical choice here is the one that'll achieve the best result for Natalie.'

Iqbal glanced from one to the other. He knew he was snookered. If he didn't cooperate and the papers got wind of his connection to Phelps he would indeed be facing the media shitstorm Bradley had promised. Phelps had paid him well, but not enough for this.

Woodcote Hall was a leading addiction facility, known for its results and its discretion. Many of its clients came from the families of the great and good. Moreover the equity fund that backed Doctor Iqbal would take a very dim view of any adverse publicity. These were things a man in his position had to take into account. Natalie was a sad and difficult girl, damaged and full of self-loathing. He felt for her, as he did for all his patients. But at the end of the day she was one patient. He had to act for the greatest good. And maybe if her brother went to prison it would help her.

Iqbal leant back in his chair, steepled his fingers, a gesture he hoped would make him feel he had regained control of the situation. He stared straight at Nicci. 'The fact of the matter is Sergeant, I've only met Joey Phelps a couple of times. He describes himself as a businessman, something in the City. I was totally unaware of any criminal connection. Obviously, now you've explained the situation, I wish to give you my full cooperation. And I think your scheme does offer a way of helping

Natalie, whilst of course maintaining the strictest confidentiality, which is essential to our work here.'

Nicci gave him a deferential nod. 'That goes without saying.'
She smiled, glanced at Bradley, then back to him.
'I think we understand one another Doctor Iqbal.'

29

Kaz had been waiting in the coffee shop for over half an hour. She clicked on her phone for the umpteenth time. It was five minutes later than the last time she looked. Helen had warned her she might be late, she was in court, but hoped they'd break early for lunch. Ordinarily Kaz would've settled down, got out her sketchbook and used the time to explore all the visual possibilities of the place, but today she was too jittery.

Sean's release from jail had thrown her totally off balance. The party had ended badly. Joey had stormed off, Ellie berated Kaz for not stopping the fight sooner. Sean himself had sat slumped on the kitchen floor, mumbling more threats, swearing to 'teach that little prick a lesson he won't forget'. When Glynis tried to drag him to his feet to take him home, he landed her a heavy punch, which sent her flying. They left him in the kitchen to sleep it off.

Kaz had taken Glynis to the massive upstairs bathroom and bathed the gash on the back of her head. She'd caught the edge of one of the worktops as she went down. She sobbed hysterically, perched on the side of the Jacuzzi. It was several minutes before she could manage to speak.

'What am I gonna do? He's gonna fucking kill me . . .'

Kaz dabbed gently at the oozing wound with a wet towel. 'I think he's more interested in killing Joey right now. And me.'

Glynis grabbed a bit of bog roll to wipe away the tears and

snot, then fumbled with the straps on her shoes. 'Hate these bleedin' things. I got more corns than an old granny.'

Kaz knelt down in front of her and unfastened the shoes. Glynis kicked them off. The heel on one had cracked when she fell.

'What am I gonna do Kaz? I can't live with him. All these years, he ain't changed. He's still the same bastard he ever was.'

Kaz sat down next to her on the side of the Jacuzzi. 'How much money you got?'

Glynis seemed taken aback. 'I've got a bit put by.'

'What about Dave?'

Glynis shot her a nervous glance. 'How d'you know about that?'

Kaz patted her hand. 'Don't worry, no one's gonna tell on you. Runs a betting shop, don't he?'

Glynis nodded. Her eyes were bloodshot with booze and ringed with claggy mascara, but she still looked like a frightened child.

Kaz watched her; on the surface they couldn't be more different. Glynis had always been the daft dolly bird, tottering everywhere on spiked heels. Even as a teenager Kaz had despised her. But scratch the surface and the same fear and desperation had blighted both their lives. Kaz could see that now and she made a decision. Sean wasn't getting his own way, not with Glynis, not with any of it. She took Glynis's hand and squeezed it.

'Listen to me. Sean's got enough on his plate. So for now all you gotta do is disappear. You leave here tonight. You got somewhere?'

Glynis nodded. 'Me and Dave've got a flat in Eastbourne. But he'll soon find that.'

'Don't worry, I'm gonna talk to Joey and we'll sort this out.

I'll get you some money. We got business contacts in Ibiza. You go out there for the winter, we'll find Dave some kind of job.'

Glynis stared at her in frank disbelief. 'Always thought you hated me, you and your mum. I tried to be mates with Ellie, but she always made me feel so stupid.'

Kaz gave a dry laugh. 'Mum became a junkie and I ended up in jail. I don't think you're the stupid one Glynis.' She pulled out her phone. 'Right, give me a number where I can reach you . . .'

Kaz scanned the coffee shop. It was beginning to fill up with the lunchtime crowd. Her phone trilled and she pulled it out, expecting it to be Helen. What she found was a text from Glynis informing her that she was back in Eastbourne and hiding out. Kaz had been big on promises after the party, when she hustled Glynis into a taxi and sent her off into the night. But now she had to deliver and that wasn't so easy. Joey had done his usual disappearing act and wasn't answering his phone.

Kaz tapped out a reassuring reply to Glynis and as she looked up from her text she saw Helen sweeping across the room towards her. She was towing a large, wheeled case stuffed with files and legal briefs. Her cheeks were pink, her blonde hair slightly awry. At the sight of her a nervous ripple swept up from Kaz's stomach, she could feel her neck and face reddening. She thought about standing up in the hope that would make her feel more in control of her own body, but she couldn't quite manage it. All she could focus on was Helen.

No one else in her life had ever had this effect, caused this mixture of desire and confusion. Was this what was meant by 'falling in love'? And would Helen notice and be scared off?

Helen brought the trolley to an abrupt scraping halt, plonked down on the chair opposite to Kaz and swept her hair back angrily with one hand.

'Bloody judge! Misdirected the jury utterly and completely. They were out for all of half an hour – not even time to review the evidence. My client gets four years. He's nineteen years old with a mental age of about eight.'

Kaz sat and watched, mesmerized by this display of energy and passion.

Helen exhaled heavily and finally looked at Kaz. 'Sorry. You must've been waiting ages.'

Kaz smiled. 'Not a problem. You want a coffee?'

'I want a large vodka and tonic.' Helen's brow puckered into a frown as she realized what she'd said. 'Sorry! I can't seem to get anything right today.'

Kaz reached across the table and put her hand over Helen's. 'Stop saying sorry. I'm just . . . pleased to see you.'

Helen checked her watch. 'Shit. I've got a case conference at two.'

'Then you should at least have a sandwich. Let me get you something.'

'Never took you for the mother hen type.' Helen had smiled as she said it, but her tone was sharp, almost a rebuke.

Kaz sat back in her chair, she felt as though she'd been slapped, gently, but a slap nonetheless. She dropped her gaze to the table top. 'I was only trying to help.'

Helen took a deep breath, scrunched up her face in frustration. 'Karen, I'm sorry, I . . . I don't know . . .' She sighed, raked her fingers through her hair.

'Bad morning. Happens to us all.' Kaz longed to touch her, stroke that hair, soothe her. But she didn't think Helen would take kindly to such a display of affection in a public place. She watched Helen paint on a smile.

'So what have you been up to? How was "Uncle" Sean's homecoming?'

'Fine.' What Kaz wanted to say, what she'd hoped and planned to say was that she was in a mess. Sean's return had thrown everything into chaos. War was about to break out in the Phelps family and she was slap-bang in the middle of it. She needed to talk it through, chart a sensible course. Above all she needed to know that Helen really cared about her. But she said none of it.

As she watched Helen checking her phone she imagined tracing a line with her finger over the contours of Helen's face, easing the furrow between her brows, stroking the straight, perfect nose, running down across the slightly parted lips.

Helen clicked the phone off, turned to Kaz with her professional lawyer's face.

'Listen, there's something I need to tell you. I don't want there to be any misunderstandings.'

Kaz could tell from the tone that what was coming wasn't going to be good. Also, unusually for Helen, she wasn't meeting Kaz's eye. Her gaze seemed to be focused somewhere off to Kaz's left.

'What happened on Sunday was . . . well, it was lovely.'

Kaz could feel the body-blow coming, moving towards her in slo-mo. Trying to ward it off was a reflex action. 'But? There's always a but, is that what you're gonna say?'

Helen shook her head apologetically. 'The thing is . . . I'm seeing someone.'

Kaz felt her stomach lurch.

'What, you mean a bloke? You're seeing a bloke?'

Helen managed to meet Kaz's intense gaze. She gave a slightly dismissive laugh.

'No no, nothing like that. Her name's Julia. We've been together for about a year. She works in PR. She's very up on the arts. You should meet her, she's got some very useful contacts. Galleries, that sort of thing. She knows loads of artists.'

Kaz's face remained totally impassive. She'd had a lifetime's practice masking her emotions. Even though she wanted to scream and howl, she inclined her head to one side and released her breath in a quiet sigh.

Helen watched her; she was annoyed with herself, annoyed with everything. She should never have got into this situation. 'I think what happened on Sunday took us both by surprise. I should never've ... I'm not saying I regret it. But ... Well, I didn't want you to be thinking it was the start of something ... I feel really bad and I wanted to be honest with you.'

Kaz nodded, tipped her chair, balancing it on the two back legs. She was retreating into the tough jail persona, hiding behind the intense, intimidating stare. Helen watched the metamorphosis with a sinking heart. Kaz disguised her desperation with a flippant shrug. 'Okay, so dump her. I mean why not?'

Helen blinked in surprise. 'That's hardly fair on her.'

Kaz laughed. 'Since when was life fair?'

Helen couldn't hold Kaz's look. The hard-eyed resentment took her back to their earliest encounters, the junkie kid who hated everyone. Okay, Helen had made a stupid mistake, given in to an impulse she should've resisted. But she couldn't take responsibility for every fuck-up in her client's fucked-up life. As for the notion she'd dump Julia for Kaz, it was too ridiculous to contemplate. Julia suited her, understood her. Julia was partner material. After all, being in a civil partnership was acceptable nowadays. If at some time in the future she decided to go down that road, Julia wouldn't compromise her potential political career.

Helen looked at her watch, she had to wind this up. 'I'm going to be late for my meeting.'

'Why didn't you tell me about her before?'

It was the obvious question, Helen felt cornered. But she wasn't going to go there. No way.

'I meant to. I . . . the opportunity never came up.'

'That's bollocks.'

Helen caught Kaz's sullen gaze, got up, grasped the handle of her trolley. 'I don't know what to say except I'm sorry. And I don't want this to alter anything between us. In fact I'd like you to meet Julia. She knows all about you. You've been a big topic of conversation.'

'You told her about Sunday?'

Helen hung her head. 'No. Not that. Obviously not. Look, I've got to go. Phone me later and let's talk about this properly. I . . . don't want to lose you.'

Kaz shot her a savage look. 'But you don't want to lose Julia more?'

Helen's chin quivered. She looked as if she might cry and Kaz was glad.

When Helen finally spoke, her voice was a whisper. 'I'm really sorry.' She turned and walked away, towing her legal paraphernalia behind her. Kaz watched until she was swallowed up by the crowd. She didn't look back.

Kaz sat stock-still for at least five minutes. She was hardly breathing. Her mind was blank, at least her thoughts seemed very distant, her body felt odd, the limbs loose and unconnected. Then she took out her phone and clicked on Joey's number. It rang a couple of times and surprisingly he answered.

'All right Kaz.'

At first she didn't speak.

'Kaz?'

She took a deep breath and this seemed to energize her. 'Joe,

I been thinking. That bloke you talked about, does loft apartments or flats or whatever. Maybe he could find me a place.'

There was a chuckle on the other end of the line. 'So you don't wanna live in a scabby hostel any more? I'm glad you finally seen the light.'

Kaz exhaled slowly, she felt as if her legs had been kicked from under her.

'Yeah, I seen the light.'

30

Natalie Phelps had been in lock-down since she arrived at Woodcote Hall. She was on strong medication to help with the withdrawal. Mostly she lay in bed, staring at the ceiling. She kept dreaming about Jez; one minute he was preparing a fix for her, then he went out of the room, simply disappeared. She shouted and shouted, but he wouldn't come back. Then this woman appeared. She looked a bit like Kaz, only Kaz had run away long ago, so it couldn't be her.

Natalie's dreams were usually full of dread, but the stuff they'd given her helped. Not as good as crack, but almost. She was still floating, up there somewhere, not down in the deep, frightening places. Trouble was, they kept waking her up. They wanted her to eat. A thick glutinous soup was spooned into her mouth. Was it chicken? She'd been a vegetarian since she was twelve; it made her want to throw up. She tried to refuse it. They asked her what she would like to eat instead and she said candyfloss. She and Jez would go down on the front some days if it was sunny and he'd buy her candyfloss. It stuck to her fingers and her cheeks, pink and sweet and tacky, she loved it. Candyfloss was definitely her favourite food.

She was sitting in her armchair watching the afternoon sun slipping across the sky and down behind the trees on the far side of the park. She liked the armchair, it was old-fashioned, well-worn leather with a high back; the wings of it hugged her and kept her safe. She could sit there all day staring out of the window and mostly she did.

The door opened and Doctor Iqbal entered. There was a nurse behind him and then someone else. She didn't know the nurse's name, but she recognized her. She was middle-aged and motherly and always patient. She never told Natalie off, never hassled her. She was as unlike Ellie as it was possible to be. Natalie's attention went immediately to her and they exchanged smiles.

Doctor Iqbal pulled up a chair and sat down in front of Natalie. He reached out, lifted her hand from her lap and enclosed it in his.

'Much more colour in your cheeks today. Have you been eating your dinner?'

Natalie nodded then grimaced. 'But not the Brussels sprouts. They're gross.'

Iqbal smiled. 'My daughter's like you. She hates Brussels sprouts.' He released her hand, adjusted his glasses. 'There's someone here I want you to meet Natalie. She's a friend of mine. And she's going to help you get better.'

Natalie glanced beyond the nurse to the younger woman standing behind her. There was no mauve tunic; she was wearing a nice shirt and smart grey trousers. Natalie was rubbish at people's ages, but she guessed the woman was quite old, maybe thirty. As Doctor Iqbal turned to her, she stepped forward and smiled.

'This is Nicci. She knows a lot about the things that have happened to you. She understands how hard it's been.'

The woman squatted down, rested her elbow on the arm of Natalie's chair.

'Hello Natalie. Doctor Iqbal says we can go outside, have a bit of a walk round the park. It's a lovely day. Do you fancy that?'

Natalie thought for a moment. 'Is it cold? I always feel the cold.'

Doctor Iqbal got to his feet. 'Don't worry, we'll wrap you up nice and warm. And I think maybe today we'll use a wheelchair, so you can ride a bit and walk a bit. How does that sound?'

Natalie glanced from him to Nicci. She had a kind face. Her eyes rested gently on Natalie and the smile carried reassurance, a sense of safety.

Natalie nodded slowly and her eyes drifted to the window and the blue sky beyond. 'Yeah. Nice.'

Nicci stood up, glanced at Iqbal. Their eyes met and he gave her a curt nod. 'I'll leave you to it then.'

The nurse wrapped a soft blue blanket round Natalie's shoulders as Iqbal disappeared out of the door.

Nicci turned back to Natalie; though her eyes were underscored with dark shadows and her face drawn, she still looked like a lost kid, eighteen going on eight. An image of Sophie flashed through Nicci's mind. Woodcote Hall was like the childhood haven Natalie had never had. Nicci watched her snuggling into the blanket and gazing up gratefully at the nurse. The Phelps family between them had done a lot of damage in the world, but that wasn't Natalie's fault. Whatever happened now, Nicci resolved, she had to make her bosses remember that.

31

Kaz had never tried to follow anyone before. She'd spent a sleepless night crying and plotting. Who was this fucking bint that Helen was 'seeing'? Julia? What kind of poncey name was that? Kaz had wandered the streets all day, now she was sitting in the coffee shop in the foyer of Helen's building hiding behind a copy of the *Evening Standard*. She was consumed with raging jealousy so she didn't realize how ludicrous she looked: a baseball cap, a newspaper, an empty cup, it was like a scene from a bad thriller. In the early hours, as she'd tossed and turned, she'd come up with a plan that would teach Helen Warner a lesson she'd never forget. She was a Phelps after all, she was Terry's daughter and she wasn't about to let some posh slag break her heart and get away with it.

The plan she'd formulated at four a.m. involved Joey's Russian minders and the kidnap of Julia. When the old bill fished Julia's stinking corpse out of the Regent Canal then Helen would realize that she'd fucked over the wrong woman. The only problem was all Kaz had was a first name; she didn't know who Julia was or where to find her.

It was six thirty when Helen finally came out of the lifts and through the security scanners. She had a raincoat on and was towing her little trolley with its overstuffed briefcase. Her face looked pinched and pale. She headed straight out into the street. As Kaz got up to follow it dawned on her how mental this was.

She hadn't thought it through at all. What if Helen took a taxi or a bus? How did she normally travel home? By tube? Kaz had no idea. And would she even be meeting Julia? Probably not.

Kaz was coming out of the coffee shop when she realized that less than a yard away a vaguely familiar figure was staring at her and beaming.

'Karen, how are you?' He held out his hand.

It was Neville Moore. As he shook her hand he gave her a concerned look. 'Are you all right? You look upset.'

Kaz took a breath. She struggled to focus on him. 'I . . . er, I've been having a bit of hassle from the cops . . .'

He nodded earnestly. 'Helen told me. We're going to have to do something about that. Can I buy you a coffee and you can fill me in on their latest antics?'

Kaz felt close to panic. Helen had disappeared and she found Neville Moore vaguely intimidating. What if he rumbled her? Maybe he'd already guessed that she was stalking Helen.

'Nah, it's okay.' She forced herself to smile. 'I was gonna leave Helen a message. She told me to keep her updated. But I know she's busy.'

Neville Moore appeared to be scanning her face. He had that dead-eyed lawyer look, although he continued to smile. 'Well unfortunately I think you may have just missed her.'

'It'll keep. You must be on your way home. Don't wanna hold you up.'

He nodded. His expression was bland, unreadable. 'I'll have a word with Helen in the morning. She's got a lot on, so I'll see if I can maybe come up with a new strategy for you myself.'

'Thanks.'

'No problem.'

Kaz finally managed to escape. She got out into the street and didn't know which way to turn. Helen was long gone. She felt lost, abandoned, and a primal fear engulfed her. She hurried down a narrow canyon of towering office blocks and broke into a sprint. She ran as if her life depended on it. She only slowed down when she reached Cheapside and had to weave around homeward-bound commuters and the crush of pavement drinkers outside every pub.

Heart thumping in her chest, she was attracting curious glances. She felt scrutinized, judged. Who were these fucking people anyway? The world seemed to be full of them. Her moronic probation officer and the scummy cops. What right did they have to manage her life, tell her what she could and couldn't do? And Helen? Why had Helen done this to her? She had opened her heart, she had trusted this woman. But Helen didn't want her, she wanted fucking Julia, whoever she was.

Kaz stopped to catch her breath. She leant against a wall, pulled off the baseball cap and hurled it over some railings. Her sides were heaving, her lungs stinging from exhaust fumes. She found herself in a small square facing the heavy wooden door of what looked like a church. Desperate to get off the street, find a quiet corner, get her head straight, she tried the door handle.

The church was St Mary-le-Bow and inside two blokes in overalls were setting out chairs. On the raised dais in front of the altar a young man was playing a grand piano. He stopped abruptly, a look of frustration on his face, flexed his fingers and repeated the piece. The blokes were ignoring him, clattering the chairs as they heaved them from their stacks and into rows on the black-and-white tiled floor.

Kaz sat down at the back and took in her surroundings; she found observing detail, sketching things in her mind's eye, helped calm her. The walls were white with the capitals on the Corinthian columns and the cornices picked out in gold. It was a bit gaudy for her taste, but she could read the message: money and religion. You can't buy a place in heaven, still there were plenty out there willing to give it a try.

The blokes in overalls finished the job and wandered off. The pianist got up, shut the piano lid with a snap and opened a bottle of Coke. Kaz found their lack of reverence for the place irritating. Yet as the pianist disappeared through a side door a sense of calm descended like a soft blanket. The traffic noise was muted. Kaz could hear her own breathing, it had slowed to its normal rate.

Killing Julia was a mad fantasy. She knew that. It wouldn't make Helen love her. Okay, unlike most people, she had the possible means to make it happen. But where would that get her? She wondered about uncontrollable rage – was it a trait you inherited? Had she got it from the old man? Was it in her genes? Behaving like him, being remotely like him, that was the last thing she wanted.

She thought about scoring some gear and getting wasted. The temptation had been niggling at the edge of her consciousness ever since Helen had delivered her bombshell. But then what? Back to jail? Give in, give up, let the fuckers know they'd finally got you. She thought of Fat Pat, her toxic hatred. Pat and Terry Phelps had a lot in common.

The phone in Kaz's pocket buzzed with an incoming text. She pulled it out, clicked it on. The sender was Helen.

hope U R ok. I feel like a total shit. I never meant to hurt U. Sorry. xx.

Kaz stared at the screen, tears started to well. She brushed them away. She wasn't going to fool herself. This wasn't a change of heart, it was just Helen being Helen. Feeling guilty. Helen didn't know how to shut her feelings down, but Kaz was an expert. It suddenly occurred to her that she could do it, flick the switch in her head. She didn't actually need the drugs and booze to achieve it.

She took out a tissue and blew her nose. Joey was right about one thing: everyone's at it. He was talking about making money, but as far as Kaz could see it applied on every level. Doing your own thing, call it what you like. Most people were plain selfish.

Kaz was done with playing by other people's rules. They could all go fuck themselves. She'd learnt her lesson; she wasn't going to give a shit for anyone ever again.

32

Joey pressed the button on the battered metal intercom, at the same time glancing up at the small camera mounted on the wall above and angled down at him. The door clicked open.

They'd driven up Seven Sisters Road and turned into a side street shortly before the tube station. The building itself was grimy, faced with crumbling yellow London brick. It gave the appearance of being deserted and vacant. But as Kaz passed through the rotting wooden door she saw that the back was reinforced with heavy steel. She followed Joey up the narrow dingy stairway, Ashley brought up the rear. At the top of the stairs there was a short corridor. The walls had recently been treated to a lick of white paint. They stepped through a doorway protected by several layers of black plastic sheeting and into a large industrial space.

Joey turned to Kaz. 'I lease the place off a couple of Lebanese brothers. Old geezers, were in the rag trade thirty years. Made jeans. Not rubbish either – posh jeans for designer labels. They had fifty machinists in this room 'til they went bust. Now of course it's all made in China.'

Kaz gazed down the long rectangular room and her jaw slackened. The clatter of sewing machines was long gone; the only noise now was from the large oscillating fans, which kept the air circulating over a sea of cannabis plants. Hundreds of them.

Joey watched her reaction with pleasure. 'Neat, innit? We grow it all hydroponically. You control the nutrients more accurately, get a better crop.'

He led her down the main aisle between the rows of plants, each one with its roots wrapped in a kind of fibre, sitting in a tray, fed with water from a plastic pipe. Long fluorescent tubes were slung low over the lush forest of bushes. Joey beamed at her like a schoolkid showing off his science project.

'We started off using rockwool as a growing medium, but that gave us some problems on the absorption front, so we switched to coconut fibre.'

Kaz stopped in her tracks, turned to him. This was a new side to Joey, one she'd missed out on in the years she'd been away.

'How d'you learn about all this?'

'Did like any businessman, hired a consultant. Come on, I'll introduce you.'

'What about the old bill?'

'Too busy chasing kids who're trying to knife each other.'

'Yeah but haven't they got all this high-tech kit nowadays?'

Joey grinned. 'Oh yeah, they got helicopters, heat cameras – all kinds of stuff. End of the day, it's still people running it. And what with the cutbacks, there's more pissed-off coppers than ever who'll take a bung. We get plenty of warning if they're headed our way.'

At the end of the room was more black plastic sheeting, Ashley held it aside for Kaz and Joey to pass through. In the corridor beyond were several glass-panelled offices. In the first one a gym-fit black kid in a baseball cap and vest sat watching a bank of security monitors while sucking a frappuccino through a straw. He paused in his slurping to give Joey a respectful nod. Kaz noticed an assault rifle propped in the corner behind him.

In the next office a small, bespectacled Vietnamese man sat working at a laptop. His face was lean yet smooth and deceptively unlined. He could've been in his sixties, but possibly older. At the sight of Joey he looked up and smiled.

'Quan, want you to meet my sister Karen.'

Quan got to his feet, inclined his head and held out his hand formally. His English delivery was staccato and hard to understand. 'Good to meet you.'

Kaz shook his hand, both she and Joey towered over him. Quan nodded again. His smile seemed fixed, polite rather than warm.

Kaz inclined her head towards the old machinists workroom. 'Quite an operation.'

Quan acknowledged the compliment with a terse nod.

Joey beamed, he was bursting with pride. 'Me and Quan, we set up four more just like it in the last six months. Quan and his family all got green fingers when it comes to growing this stuff. We're building up a brand, we got ourselves a little logo goes on the packet. That way people know they're buying the best weed in London.'

Quan's narrow face broke into an unexpected grin and he nodded vigorously. 'Best weed in London.'

Joey turned to his sister, but the smile had faded, suddenly his look was deadly serious. 'Which is one reason why that fucker Sean can go and take a long run and jump.'

Kaz nodded thoughtfully. 'Well, we need to talk about that. I got an idea.'

Joey gave her a sceptical glance.

She shrugged. 'We're partners, then I have some input, right?'

He beamed, patted her arm. ''Course you do mate.'

33

It wasn't until late in the evening, when Ashley took himself off to his room to watch the latest gross-out comedy he'd downloaded, that Kaz had a chance to talk privately to her brother. She and Joey sat on opposite sofas taking in the vast panorama of the night-time city that filled the wall-to-ceiling windows of Joey's flat.

They'd spent the afternoon on the road. After the cannabis factory Joey was determined to show her the rest of the firm's assets. He called it 'bringing her up to speed', but there was a definite element of showing off. Joey wanted his sister to see for herself that he wasn't all talk.

Ashley had driven them out of town on the A12 to a village on the fringes of Chelmsford. It was prime commuter territory, rural enough to be quiet, but still with the urban mindset: people got on with their lives and ignored one another, which was exactly what Joey needed. He'd bought a barn conversion that had been developed to include plenty of workshop space. The bank had foreclosed on the previous owners, a ceramics artist and a reflexologist, and Joey had bought the place at auction.

As the Range Rover drove through the electronic gates and crunched to a halt on the gravel drive, Kaz noticed the state-of-the-art surveillance cameras dotted at intervals under the overhanging eaves.

They got out and she turned to Joey. 'All this security, don't people get suspicious?'

He laughed.

Ash smirked and filled her in. 'Round here, no. Most of them got as much themselves, case someone tries to nick the tumble dryer or the plasma telly.'

The heavy oak front door swung open and the perfect couple emerged. He was tall, very lean, ruffled blond hair and a rugby shirt. She was smaller, pretty, her dark hair drawn back into a tight bun. Joey made the introductions.

'Marko, Leysa, my sister Karen.'

Leysa beamed and enveloped Kaz in a hug. 'So plezzed. Joey speak of you all time. Can't wait for you to come home.'

She sounded vaguely Russian, but Kaz couldn't be sure. Marko held out his hand to shake, he was nervous, gave Kaz a small smile. Leysa ushered them all inside.

The open-plan living area was modern but homely. The exposed brick walls of the barn were covered with several large woven tapestries in striking abstract designs.

Kaz gazed up at them. 'Wow. I like that.'

Leysa grinned, exposing her small, perfect teeth. 'I make them myself. A skill I learn in my family. I have a loom.' She glanced at Marko coyly. 'It's useful complement to Marko's business.'

Kaz continued to scrutinize each of the tapestries in turn. 'So is this like a Russian thing?'

Leysa laughed politely, but Kaz sensed immediately she'd hit a nerve.

'Oh no no, we from the Ukraine.'

Joey laughed. 'Touchy subject babes.'

Marko managed to open his mouth for the first time. 'Your sister not to know. My father was a professor in Lviv. The Soviets did not treat him well.'

Joey caught Kaz's eye. 'Not well as in dead.'

Kaz raised her eyebrows. 'Sorry, I'm not very good with accents.'

Leysa grinned. 'We do not take offence. I make some coffee while Marko show you the lab.'

Marko led them down a short corridor to a plain door. It looked as if it might lead to a study or laundry room, except for the keypad on the wall beside it. Marko tapped in four digits, which unlocked the door. Kaz stepped into a large, full-functioning laboratory. It had originally been built on to the back of the barn as a workshop. The windows were covered with heavy venetian blinds, but diffuse sunshine flooded the room from a row of skylights.

A young man in T-shirt, jeans and latex gloves looked up, he was working at one of the benches.

'My assistant Danya. He was student of mine back in Ukraine.'

Danya gave them a deferential nod.

Joey glanced around speculatively. 'How's the new project coming on?'

Marko inclined his head and smiled. Kaz looked him up and down. He was handsome but round-shouldered from the habit of standing with both hands scrunched in his pockets. It gave him an awkward, bashful air. She could see why Leysa did most of the talking. However this was his domain, his eyes sparkled as he pointed to a cardboard box in the corner.

'We have the first batch for you. I think it's good.'

Joey clapped him on the back and laughed. 'He don't big himself up enough Kaz, but this bloke is a fucking brilliant chemist. He's made us three variations on Mephedrone, all of which sold like hot cakes. But the new stuff, that is gonna be top product. Explain it to her Marko.'

Marko couldn't quite meet Kaz's eye, he smiled shyly. 'Well, club scene is always changing. Cocaine and alcohol, that's been it for a long time. But Joey say to me, all this smuggling, so expensive.'

Joey chipped in. 'Yeah and like we said before you're dealing with some pretty difficult types and they all want their cut. If you can make the gear yourself, it gets round all that.'

'We do well with Mephedrone, but I think to myself, what if we make MDMA only more like cocaine?' Marko was clearly warming to his theme.

Kaz watched the two of them dipping in and out, both eager to explain, two mates talking about their shared passion. She cocked her head. 'MDMA, that's like Ecstasy?'

Joey nodded. 'Yeah, basically. But people've gone off it 'cause most tabs got piss-all in them.'

Marko grinned. 'Not the stuff we make. High potency. And now . . . we make it powder, like cocaine.'

They both looked at Kaz expectantly. She realized this was the big idea, the new project.

'So you mean people got to snort it?'

Joey nodded excitedly. 'Yeah. And that's what they want. Chopping out a line with the old credit card, sharing it with their mates. It's like a social thing. I'm talking upmarket stuff here, for people who got money. I ain't interested in selling to junkies no more.'

Marko took her on a mini tour of the lab, explained the manufacturing process in highly technical terms she couldn't really understand. Then they went back into the house. Leysa served them coffee and home-baked chocolate brownies.

Kaz watched her and Marko together and she felt envious. She'd never had a proper relationship, much less been part of a couple. She wondered what it would be like, waking up every morning with that person, having friends round, cooking, watching telly together, making chocolate brownies. But that train of thought took her straight back to Helen, so she pushed it firmly away.

She'd survived her family, jail, she'd survive Helen Fucking Warner. She was getting her life sorted. Only now she was doing it on *her* terms. Joey wasn't a petty gangster like her father, he had a good business brain, Kaz had seen the evidence of that. As a result she had a clip of fifty-pound notes in her pocket and she was beginning to enjoy the notion that she could have whatever she wanted. Without Helen breathing down her neck, why not?

She'd had two more meetings with her probation officer and she'd taken along some sketches to show him. The drawing of Leo that had amused Helen sent Jalil Sahir into a bit of a spin. But Kaz had got him figured. She talked about college, eventually taking a degree; it really wasn't that difficult to keep ticking the boxes. Jalil had even started to relax with her a bit. He didn't know much about art himself, but he regarded cultural pursuits generally as a good thing. The hostel were sending in excellent reports, she'd passed all her random drug tests. From their point of view her rehabilitation was being successfully managed. But Kaz knew in reality she was the one in the driving seat.

Avoiding recall, getting the things you wanted, it was all a balancing act. The tricky part of the equation was, and always had been, Joey. Keeping him to his word, moving him away from the criminal life. He insisted he was keeping the dangerous side of the business at arm's length. But he was going to have to do more than that and Kaz was going to have to persuade him.

Lounging on one of Joey's vast, squidgy sofas she watched the red twinkling lights on the cranes across the river. They'd picked up a chinky on the way home and eaten it in front of the telly. Joey and Ash had downed a few beers, but one thing she'd gradually realized about her brother, he wasn't much of a drinker. Nor had she seen him indulging in any of the drugs that made him such a handsome living. He liked girls well enough, and he and Ash went out on the pull, but he never seemed that bothered about any of them. Clearly to him they were all interchangeable. He went clubbing, would chat to anyone, liked a laugh and a joke. But there was something oddly detached about this large, good-looking man that her little brother had grown into. They'd spent a lot of time together since she got out and she still didn't have the least clue about what really rocked his boat. He was enthusiastic enough about business and all his plans, but as she glanced across the room at him now, his features were entirely passive, his eyes fixed and blank.

'Joe?'

He blinked at her a couple of times, as if returning from a faraway place. Then smiled and jumped up. 'Want a cup of tea or something?'

She shook her head. 'No, I'm fine. I been thinking about all the stuff you showed me today.'

'Good. That was the idea.'

'It's impressive.' She folded her legs up under her on the sofa. 'But you're still growing weed and making drugs. How's that ever going to be legit?'

'They're just products Kaz. We take the profits, reinvest it in property, in whatever.'

Kaz considered this; it struck her he was a little bit too fond of his products to let go of them and replace them with another investment.

'Yeah, but in the meantime you're still paying off the old

bill and there's still a danger some ambitious idiot comes along, wants to make a name for himself and busts in on you?'

Joey laughed. 'You worry too much. All that stress babes, ain't good for you.'

Kaz smiled wearily. 'You don't worry enough.'

Joey strolled over to the fridge and took out a bottle of beer. 'Okay, so let's say some random plod stumbles across one of the cannabis factories. Even if they get hold of Quan or one of his boys, they ain't about to drop me in it. The lease is owned by an offshore company that's owned by an offshore company . . . As for Marko and Leysa, old bill would need a tip-off to sniff them out.' He flipped the top off his beer. 'And I run a very tight ship.'

Kaz watched him sipping his beer. No one could deny he exuded a confidence that was attractive, he still had charm to burn just like the little Joey. She'd watched him with Marko and Leysa, they were totally under his spell. But when he wasn't performing, rolling out the spiel and keeping everyone entertained, there was an edge to him, an underlying hardness. There was only the occasional glimpse of it, but when he said 'I run a very tight ship' she certainly got a whiff of it. She knew it was there. And then there was his temper. It was in a fit of temper that he'd killed Natalie's boyfriend and Kaz knew, even though she wanted to deny it, that Jez Harris wasn't his only victim. She fixed him with a direct look, but kept the tone deliberately casual.

'You seen Sean?'

Joey took another sip of beer. 'He's on my list.'

'That's what I'm afraid of.' Kaz got up from the sofa and walked over to Joey. 'Listen, why don't you let me deal with Sean?'

Joey chuckled. 'No babes, he's a dangerous fucker, you leave him to me.'

'I thought we had a deal, no more killing.'

Joey huffed, then reined himself in. 'Who said anything about killing?'

Kaz took a step closer to her brother and rested her palm on his chest.

'Okay, I said I had an idea, here it is: we set him up for the old bill and send him back to jail.'

'Grass him up you mean? You'd do that to your own flesh and blood?'

Kaz stared at him gone out. 'What, that's worse than killing him?'

'I never said I was gonna kill him.' Joey turned away, put his beer bottle down on the kitchen worktop. 'Anyway, I go up against Sean, it's a fair fight. But grassing, that's the coward's way out. He's a complete toerag, granted, but he's still our cousin.'

Kaz sighed in disbelief. 'All your talk about being a businessman, going legit. When push comes to shove you're still thinking like the old man, like some macho thug. You want to fight it out with Sean man to man? Swords, pistols – what did you have in mind? You know and I know how it'd be, you'd get tooled up, try and catch him unawares and blow his brains out. What's fair or honourable about that, eh?'

Kaz realized she was shaking, the ridiculousness of Joey's attitude made her mad. He stared right back at her, his blue eyes shone, his face inscrutable. They stood only inches apart, Kaz could feel the heat of his body. She was beginning to realize that behind the fun and the japes this was the real Joey. She didn't think he was about to hurt her, but for the first time in her life she had a sense that he might, he was certainly capable of it.

Suddenly he threw up his hands and laughed. 'Okay, have it your way. You wanna deal with Sean, you deal with him. All that matters to me is that he's not running round mob-handed making trouble.'

Kaz gave him a penetrating look. 'You mean it, you'll leave it to me?'

Joey hunched his shoulders. 'If I've said it, I mean it.'

Kaz folded her arms and took a turn about the room. 'Okay, first up we need to help Glynis. Get her and her bloke out of Sean's reach. Thought we might use your contacts in Ibiza.'

Joey started to smile, Kaz caught his look. 'What you grinning at?'

'You babes. This is what I've always wanted – us working together as a team. You're gonna be brilliant at this. It's what you was born for.'

34

Nicci Armstrong decided to make a day of it, take Sophie out of school, prepare a picnic, turn the whole thing into a mother-and-daughter adventure. She'd come to the conclusion that she'd made things way too easy for Tim; he got to do the fun stuff with their daughter, while she struggled to hold down a stressful job and still be a proper mum. But this was an opportunity to put the two together, do the job and steal some extra time with her child.

Sophie was over the moon, a day off school and she was helping Mummy. They were going on a secret mission, she couldn't even text her friends, but she was so excited she didn't care. They got up at six to make the packed lunch, jam sandwiches as well as egg, plus Nicci had bought some gingerbread men and chocolate-covered marshmallows from the special bakers. These were Sophie's favourites. It was like a birthday tea but without the birthday.

Nicci was in charge of driving and the satnav, Sophie was in charge of music. But she didn't bombard her mother with JLS, she tried to widen things out, including Justin Timberlake and Robbie Williams to accommodate Nicci's antiquated tastes. For the first hour as they drove north they sang along to every tune, Sophie was amazed at how many songs her mother knew. She had only a ghost of a memory of the long ago Christmas when Dad got Mum a karaoke machine and they'd made so much noise the neighbours complained.

They stopped at the motorway services for a drink and the loo. Sophie had a strawberries and crème frappuccino with masses of whipped cream on top; she kept getting a blob on the end of her nose. Nicci never usually let her have this sort of stuff, but today was different. It was like going out with Dad only better. Nicci took a video clip of her trying to drink it and they both had a fit of giggles.

Once they were back in the car Nicci told her a bit about the girl they were going to visit. Sophie knew she had to pay attention, this was a briefing for the mission. It's what the police did. The girl was Natalie and she'd got very poorly from taking too many drugs, Sophie knew all about that. They'd had a special talk at school and watched a film. She felt immensely proud and important, she'd never been asked to help her mother with work before. In fact Nicci rarely spoke about her job. So this was a double first if you counted the frappuccino.

It was the police's job to help Natalie. But first she had to be persuaded to trust Nicci and that wasn't going to be easy. Natalie had been unhappy for a long time, her parents had been cruel to her and she didn't have any friends. Sophie tried to imagine what a cruel parent might do, undoubtedly something worse than take away your phone. A boy in her class kept coming to school with loads of bruises so he had to see the school counsellor every week. Some people said his mum's boyfriend hit him. Sophie thought that was probably cruelty so helping Natalie was clearly a good thing.

As they drove up the sweeping drive to Woodcote Hall Nicci glanced across at her daughter's radiant face. Her happiness was plain to see, it was simple and infectious. Getting pregnant with Sophie had been an accident and definitely not part of Nicci's career plan. Yet as soon as she gazed at her baby's red, bawling features she was hooked. No one, least of all her own parents, had expected her to be a natural mother. Unlike her they'd read all the books; depression, sleepless nights, problems were to be expected. But Nicci adored her child, went back to work and simply coped. She was tired, she rowed with Tim, but from the word go she and Sophie were a love match. Even after the divorce there was not a moment of regret, Sophie was the jewel in her mother's life.

Nicci found a parking space in the old stableyard next to the Hall. But even as she backed into it she was developing worryingly ambiguous feelings about bringing her daughter with her. Sophie was having such a good time and somehow that made it worse. Nicci started to wonder to what extent she was exploiting her own child. Was this a ploy to come over as more sympathetic? She hadn't mentioned the plan to anyone at work – and with good reason. She could hear Mayhew tutting at her. Bad move. But what was she going to do, turn round and go home?

Sophie's eyes darted around the stableyard; she was alert to everything and well informed. A man from the National Trust had come into school and they'd done a project on Hatfield House. As they got out of the car, Sophie's brow furrowed. 'Well, this isn't Jacobean.'

Nicci grinned with delight. She was only just getting used to the adult words that were starting to pepper her child's vocabulary.

'Built a bit later I think. But you know much more about this stuff than me.'

Sophie nodded. 'Used to be only one family lived in a place like this, but they had loads of servants.'

'I think this is where they kept their horses.'

Sophie shot her mother a sidelong glance. 'Dad said maybe I could go horse-riding when we go on holiday.'

Nicci smiled. The kid was whip-smart and knew exactly how to play her parents off against each other.

'Did he now? Well I'd hold him to that if I was you.'

They waited for Natalie in the magnificent hallway supported by Palladian columns. She came down the stairs escorted by a nurse. She still looked pretty fragile and was wrapped in an oversized hoodie, which she clutched tightly round herself. Nicci made the introductions and was surprised by the confidence with which Sophie took charge.

'We've brought a picnic. Gingerbread men and chocolate marshmallows, two each.'

Natalie gave her a wary smile. 'Cool.'

This was Nicci's second visit but Natalie's drug-addled brain was clearing. She'd had time to consider the situation and she'd got her visitor sussed. Volunteer? That was a fairy story. She didn't come over as the type who went visiting junkies as a hobby, it didn't add up. Now she'd brought her kid, either that or she'd borrowed someone else's.

The three of them wandered out of the front door and round to the back of the house. Then Sophie caught sight of a small gazebo sitting on a raised hillock and she ran towards it. The two women followed, Nicci lugging the coolbox and a canvas bag of goodies. Natalie shot a suspicious glance at her new friend.

'You don't hardly look old enough to have a kid.'

'Sometimes I don't feel old enough. But we take care of each other.'

'What about her dad?'

'Divorced. Everyone, especially my parents, lectured us. You should stay together for Sophie's sake . . . blah blah blah.'

'Nah, kids know if you're miserable. Just makes things worse.' Natalie's gaze drifted off into the distance.

Nicci nodded. She wanted to come back with a question, a torrent of questions, it was the detective in her. But she had to be patient. Still she regarded lies and deception as counter-productive. She reckoned Natalie had experienced enough of that in her life, she wasn't stupid and she wasn't about to trust anyone who played the same game.

Nicci put the coolbox down and transferred the canvas bag to her other hand. 'You know I'm a police officer, don't you?'

Natalie gave a cynical shrug. 'Really?' But the straightfor-ward approach did surprise her. A thin smile spread across her face. 'Yeah, I figured.'

Nicci grinned. 'What gave me away? The big boots?'

Natalie returned the look, her eyes were pale and blank. 'No one's interested in me. Why would they be?'

'They might be.'

'Nah, I'm just a nuisance. People here are getting paid to look after me. You're here 'cause you wanna know who killed Jez.'

Nicci inclined her head. 'But Sophie's here because she gets to skive off school for a day and she loves picnics. So where shall we sit?'

Natalie cast her eye over the short springy turf. 'Dunno. Wherever.'

Nicci started to unpack the canvas bag. Natalie stood watching at first. But Nicci tossed her a corner of the brightly coloured rug and together they spread it out on the grass.

Sophie came running down the hill from the gazebo, her cheeks were pink, she was slightly breathless. 'This place is awe-some. You're so lucky Natalie.'

Natalie blinked at her a couple of times. She rubbed her forehead, as if trying to wipe away some interior pain. 'Is she really your mum?'

Sophie looked puzzled. 'Yeah. 'Course she is. Sometimes she tells me the hospital gave her the wrong baby. But that's a joke.'

Nicci smiled. She was kneeling on the rug, unloading foil-wrapped sandwiches from the coolbox. Natalie glanced from one to the other, her expression tight and pinched. Some unknown force within seemed to be churning her guts over. She swallowed hard and pulled her hood up.

'Dunno that I want a picnic, not today.' She turned abruptly on her heel and started to walk away.

Nicci and Sophie exchanged looks. Immediately Sophie was on her feet skipping after Natalie.

'Hey! Wanna hear my playlist?'

Natalie stopped in her tracks. She shrugged. 'All the music they got in here's crap. Like supermarket music.'

Sophie held out her headphones. The tiny square nano dangled from one end. 'You can borrow this for now?'

'Yeah?'

'Yeah. And . . . you tell me the stuff you like, I'll download it, make you your own playlist.'

Natalie gave her an appraising look. 'You're a nice kid.'

Sophie pulled up her own hood, unconsciously mirroring the older girl. 'Mum wants to help you. So do I.'

Natalie turned her head away. Her eyes were brimming with tears. 'You don't understand. There ain't anyone or anything can help me.'

Nicci joined her daughter. 'It may feel like that now. But there's always a way out Natalie. And there's a way out for you. You just have to look around until you find it.'

35

It was the last day of the summer school, classes were winding up in preparation for the return of the real, full-time students in October. Mal Bradley had dipped in and out, having discovered that others in the class had work and family commitments that forced them to do the same. He'd seen Karen Phelps there a few times, but she'd ignored him completely and spurned all his attempts at mateyness. The only reason he'd kept going was to put off the moment when he would have to tell Turnbull that he was getting nowhere.

He'd offered to accompany Nicci Armstrong to Yorkshire again. Her plan to befriend Natalie Phelps was progressing at a snail's pace. The notion she'd ever make a credible witness against her brother struck him as far-fetched. However Nicci was a dog with a bone, it was how she operated. She was making the drive once, sometimes twice a week, and insisted on going alone so as not to freak Natalie out. On top of a regular workload, that struck Bradley as ridiculous. Still he found some consolation in the fact he wasn't the only one on a hiding to nothing.

For the final life drawing class Mike Dawson had invited all the students to pin up their drawings to create a small exhibition. The atmosphere was celebratory. On a table in the middle of the studio Mike had provided several bottles of cheap plonk and some bags of crisps. The students had added their own contributions and soon the table was piled high with cans of beer, Jaffa Cakes, biscuits, one student had even baked a cake.

Mike led the class, glasses in hand, on a tour of the room, viewing and commenting on the work and progress of each individual student in turn. As the group gathered round Bradley's patch of wall, he noticed Karen Phelps watching him from the back of the huddle. Mike Dawson peered at the drawings intently, then cleared his throat.

'Well, Mal started out as a complete beginner, am I right?'

Bradley nodded. He felt the question was slightly redundant. Anyone could see that he drew like a seven-year-old.

Mike nodded thoughtfully. 'But what we see here is definite progress. A more confident line developing and more accurate observation. A sense of the essence of the figure is definitely emerging. Anyone care to add anything?'

A woman at the front of the group, who'd taken a shine to Bradley, raised her hand tentatively like a schoolgirl. 'I think what Mal's done is lovely. It's full of feeling.'

Bradley gave her a small nod. He placed her on the wrong side of forty and the far side of desperate. There was no way he wanted to give her the least encouragement. He caught Kaz's eye, she was watching his discomfort with amusement.

She glanced in Dawson's direction. 'Yeah, I got a comment Mike. That one at the top there looks a bit like one of them photo-fit pictures. Y'know, the kind the police make.'

Heads in the group swivelled from Kaz back to the wall and the drawing in question. Mike narrowed his eyes and scrutinized it intently, then he turned to Bradley.

'What d'you make of that Mal? You a secret fan of *Crimewatch*? D'you think there might be an influence here?'

Bradley pondered. 'It's possible. I do read a lot of crime novels, especially about gangsters and psychopaths.'

Mike chuckled. 'Ummm what you've done with the eyes – they do look a bit manic. D'you think Leo's got the look of a psychopath about him?'

A ripple of laughter went round the group. Bradley shot a challenging look at Kaz. 'Problem with psychopaths Mike, is that they look just like you or me. They fool us by seeming to be ordinary.'

Mike Dawson nodded sagely, then ushered the group on to the next student.

Bradley brought up the rear and positioned himself next to Kaz. She gave him a sideways glance.

'Don't know why you didn't 'fess up to being a copper. They'd probably love you even more. 'Specially your number one fan over there.'

Bradley adopted a stage whisper. 'Cougars – definitely not my style. Anyway as we both know, I'm supposed to be under-cover.'

'You still trying to persuade me what a friendly, funny bloke you are?'

Bradley sighed. 'No I've accepted I'm crap at that.'

Kaz eyed him speculatively. 'Maybe not totally. Once this is over, fancy buying me a cup of coffee?'

Bradley stared at her in disbelief. His brain was scrambling to catch up. Had he missed something? Was she being serious? He didn't have to paint on the smile, it surfaced naturally.

'Yeah. Of course.'

Kaz nodded. 'Shut your mouth Bradley. You look like a teenage boy who's copped off for the first time.'

36

Bradley bought two take-away coffees and they wandered into Russell Square. There was a smattering of people and pigeons all enjoying the afternoon sunshine. They found an empty bench and sat down a decorous foot apart. Bradley wasn't sure what had caused Kaz Phelps to perform such a volte-face. But he decided to play along with her and see how things panned out.

Back in the studio Kaz had been the last one to have her work reviewed by Mike and the group. Everyone had just stood round and gawped. It didn't require much expertise to see that she was streets ahead of any other student in the class. The compliments flooded in. Kaz received them awkwardly. She wasn't used to praise, certainly not in a setting like this.

Mike Dawson scanned the dozen or so drawings Kaz had displayed and rubbed the stubble on his chin. Then when the rest of the students dispersed to chat and drink the wine and beer he strolled over to her. He pulled a rather dog-eared business card from his back pocket and fixed her with his direct and penetrating gaze.

'You still got a lot to learn, you know that, don't you?' Kaz nodded. 'But you've got a rare talent.' He handed her the card. 'Keep in touch. If I can do anything to help you on your way, I will.' And with a curt nod he went off to pour himself a glass of wine.

Bradley sipped his coffee and glanced at Kaz.

'So what did Mike say to you at the end?'

'Nothing much.' Kaz lounged on the bench.

Bradley laughed. 'Bullshit. I may be crap at drawing, but I'm quite a good detective and that man thinks you're the dog's bollocks. The way he looked at your stuff was totally different to how he looked at anyone else's.'

'Yeah well you don't have to keep buttering me up, because I've decided to help the police.'

Bradley gave her a scrutinising look. 'Okay. What's brought this on?'

'I dunno. Maybe I do want my life to be different.'

He nodded. 'Have you and Joey fallen out?'

Kaz took a deep breath. 'What I'm offering you doesn't concern Joey. This is about my cousin Sean Phelps.'

Bradley tilted back his head and smiled. Now it all made sense. 'I see. You want to give us Sean. Not Joey.'

'Basically yeah.'

He began to chuckle. 'I know you think we're all plods, especially me. But come on Karen, we're not totally daft.'

Kaz gave him a blank, cold stare. 'I dunno what you mean.'

Bradley shook his head, but he was still smiling. 'Okay, let's try this for size. Sean gets out of jail. He's been away for a goodly stretch, meanwhile your dad's had a stroke and Joey's taken over the firm. But Joey's young and ambitious, he's not about to step aside for Sean. So you and your brother have cooked up a neat little scheme to send Sean straight back to jail. Am I warm?'

Kaz looked straight at Bradley. The cheeky smile had been packed away, his expression was deadly serious. She acknowledged his point with a tilt of the head. 'Yeah. But that's only part of the story.'

'Okay, I'm listening.'

She sipped her coffee, then turned to Bradley. 'Y'know Sean shot a copper and got off.'

'I've heard that, yeah.'

'Well it's true. When it happened, years ago, I heard him boasting to my old man about it.'

'And you're gonna get up in court now and say that?'

Kaz inclined her head to one side. 'No, you're gonna need more than one bit of testimony to get Sean tried for that murder.'

Bradley sighed. 'So what are you offering?'

'We both know that by rights Sean should still be in jail. He's a murderer.'

'So's Joey.'

Kaz inhaled sharply as she tried to keep a handle on her exasperation. 'I'm not gonna give you Joey. You can have Sean or nothing – that's the choice. That's still a result for you and your smarmy boss, innit?'

'I'll have to put it to him. So let's get down to the nitty-gritty. If you're not going to testify, presumably you're going to set him up. How?'

'I'm not gonna go into that now. But y'know Sean's business has always been drugs and that's what he's getting back into.'

Bradley shook his head dismissively. 'So all you're really offering us is a drugs bust?'

Kaz stared in disbelief. 'Fuck me, whad'you expect Bradley?' She spat the words at him. 'You know why I want Sean back in jail? Well, I'll tell you. I was ten years old when he started to come after me, touching me up, trying to kiss me. You grow up round men like him and my old man, you know if you don't give 'em what they want, they'll beat the shit out of you. Every time he come round to my parents' house, he'd find the opportunity to grab me, take me in the garden or upstairs and fuck me. When that bastard went down I thought it was the best day of my life. I'm doing this for me, not for Joey.'

She turned her head away, she didn't want Bradley to see the tears. They both sat in silence for several moments, then he patted her shoulder, gently, unobtrusively.

'I'll talk to Turnbull.'

37

Turnbull sat in his high-backed leather chair, a panorama of London rooftops framed in the window behind him. Mayhew's tubby frame was crammed into one of the chairs facing the desk, Bradley sat in the other. Turnbull rubbed his eyes, glanced at his phone, picked up his fountain pen and started to turn it over, end to end, repeatedly.

'How many weeks have you been on this Bradley? And this is the best you can come up with?'

Bradley was mesmerized by the pen, the barrel was marbled, it had a gold clip. He had to drag his eyes away.

'I think the thing is sir, we should regard this as a way in. She'll have become our chiz. We get one Phelps back behind bars and we gain her trust. That gives us something to work with. It's a win-win situation.'

Turnbull pushed the chair back in disbelief. 'She tells you some sob story about being raped as a kid and you fall for it. This is Joey trying to eliminate the competition. She's playing you.'

Bradley jutted his chin out. 'With all due respect, I don't think so. If Joey wanted rid of Sean, I think he'd take him out. This isn't Joey's style, it's coming from her.'

Turnbull sighed, glanced at Mayhew. 'What are we going to do with him Bill? Boy's had his head turned.'

Mayhew ran a thumb round his belt, easing the pressure on

his paunch. He agreed with Bradley, it was an opening, he couldn't really fathom why the boss was so dead against it. 'Maybe. But we could play along, see what she is prepared to give us.'

Turnbull slapped his palm firmly on the desk. 'No. I think we need to apply a bit of lateral thinking here.' He pondered. 'What this gives us potentially is leverage.'

Bradley shot a covert glance at Mayhew, who blinked a couple of times, he was looking rather sleepy. Turnbull was back to twiddling his pen, his eyes were focused off into the near distance, he seemed to be plotting. After a moment or two he zeroed back in on Bradley. 'Presumably you recorded the conversation you had with her?'

It was standard practice, Bradley knew it. His heart sank. 'No . . . I, er . . .'

Turnbull gave him a withering look.

'Sorry sir, I didn't really get the chance.'

'Well, she's not to know that, is she? You think she's frightened of Sean Phelps.'

'Probably. She certainly hates him.'

Turnbull got up from his desk, put his hands in his trouser pockets and started to jingle the change.

'Right, this is what I want you to do. You go back to her and tell her that you made a digital recording of the conversation you had and Sean Phelps will be getting a copy unless she agrees to inform against her brother.'

Bradley's jaw slackened, he glanced at Mayhew for support. 'Is that . . . strictly ethical sir?'

Turnbull laughed out loud. 'Who do you think we're dealing with here? These are violent organized criminals. I don't give a toss about the ethics of it. Anyway, what d'you think she's going to do? Take us to the IPCC?'

'Her lawyer might.'

'Then you'd better hope, Bradley, that you're right and she is shit-scared of Sean Phelps.'

Bradley sighed. The more encounters he had with the boss, the more he regretted his chosen course. Turnbull was staring right at him but Bradley managed to hold his gaze.

'What am I supposed to tell the Assistant Commissioner? That you've had an attack of conscience?' Turnbull shook his head. 'You knew what was being asked of you at the outset. Civil liberties and ethics are fine on the telly – unfortunately the likes of Joey Phelps don't subscribe to that code.'

Bradley took a deep breath. This time he wasn't about to be cowed by Turnbull. 'Yeah, but we're talking Karen Phelps here, not her brother. Sir.'

Turnbull settled back in his chair, placed his fingertips together and smiled. 'Really. They're so different, are they? Cop killer, convicted felon. I told you at the outset, this is policing at the sharp end.'

'I know sir, but—'

Turnbull gave the desk another dramatic thwack. Mayhew could see he was enjoying himself. It was clearly a charade, what Mayhew couldn't figure was what lay behind it all. Why was he bullying Bradley like this? It wasn't his usual style, Turnbull was far too slick an operator. The boss had another agenda, that much was obvious.

Turnbull fixed Bradley with an unremitting stare. 'I've heard enough. Just be a good lad and go out there and do what you're told.'

'You want me to threaten her. In effect blackmail her?'

'I don't want Sean, I want Joey. That clear enough for you?'

38

The flat was in Limehouse and modest compared to Joey's. It had two separate balconies overlooking the river and was part of a portered development on Narrow Street with underground parking and a gym. The agent, Hayley, was a lizard-eyed blonde in her forties and canny enough to hang back and let the place sell itself. Joey opened the French doors and stepped out on to one of the balconies while Kaz stood bathed in airy sunlight in the large open-plan reception room. She already knew where she'd put her easel.

Hayley joined Joey on the balcony. The sweep of the river was before them, a rippling metallic sheet of water curving south round Limehouse Reach. She scanned his profile, ticking the boxes: young, affluent, worked out, expensively dressed, Rolex Oyster, and she'd clocked the Range Rover Evoque they'd arrived in. She had him pegged as a City boy. Her guess was a new relationship and he'd just got his bonus.

She put on her professional smile. 'Speaks for itself really, doesn't it?'

Joey nodded.

'I think you two could be very happy here. Lots of young couples like you in the block. Good bars, restaurants, all on your doorstep.'

Joey turned towards her with a grin. Hayley caught the full force of his keen blue eyes.

'Flat's not for me, it's for my sister. She needs somewhere right away.'

Hayley was momentarily thrown. She'd read them as a couple and she didn't usually get these things wrong. 'Well, it's the perfect buy for a single woman. Very secure. Once contracts have been exchanged, she could be in in a matter of weeks.'

Joey inclined his head. 'Nah, she needs a place now.'

Hayley blinked at him. 'Obviously we'd do all we could to expedite . . .'

He held up his palm. 'Nah, while the lawyers sort out the paperwork, she moves in. In the meantime she pays rent.'

'I'm not sure that would be possible Mr Phelps. The vendors would never—'

'But you'll persuade them, won't you Hayley? 'Cause then you'll be picking up a five grand cash bonus, which no one need know about 'cept you and me.'

Hayley fixed him with a look of frank amazement. 'You'll be paying the asking price?'

Joey nodded. 'I don't quibble over a few quid. My sister's had a rough time lately. I want to make things easy for her.'

Hayley pondered. The only other people interested in the flat had offered twenty thousand under the asking price. She wasn't about to look a gift horse in the mouth. She scanned his amiable, smiling face. She still couldn't quite figure it.

'Wish I had a brother like you.' She took out her mobile. 'I'll go and make some calls.'

Joey rejoined Kaz, she was wandering from the main bedroom into the en suite. 'Whad'you reckon babes?'

Kaz turned to him, she had the look of a kid in a sweetshop. 'Well it's a step up from my old gaff. No steel pan in the corner, or bars on the windows.'

Joey tipped his head to one side. He was trying to appear

nonchalant, but Kaz could feel his excitement. He loved playing the benefactor; the power of money, serious money, that was his second favourite buzz.

'Move in in a couple of days if you like it.'

'Seriously? I thought this was for sale, not rent. Don't that take longer?'

A smile flickered round his lips as he savoured the moment. 'Yeah, but I've fixed all that.'

She reached her arms round his neck and gave him a hug. He beamed with pleasure. 'Lawyers'll put it in your name. All above board, like I said.'

She kissed his cheek. 'Thank you little brother.'

'It's only what you're owed.'

She patted his arm. 'Plenty of people think they're owed.'

'You mean like fucking Sean?'

'Well, I'm on the case with that.'

Joey gave her an enquiring look. 'Yeah? What's the plan?'

Kaz hadn't wanted to tell him anything until it was all set up. But on the other hand she didn't want him to think she was being cagey.

'Early days, but I've had a word with the copper that they've had following me about.'

Joey shook his head. 'Sean's a crafty old bastard. They can watch him all day long, ain't about to catch him with his fingers in the till.'

Kaz looked at him and considered her options. Should she say something? He was in a good mood, so what the hell. They had to have this discussion sometime.

'Thing is Joey, the old bill ain't daft. They know we want him out the way. If we're gonna give them Sean, he has to be wrapped up in a tasty enough package to tempt them.'

'How d'you mean?'

'Okay, this is only an idea. We give Sean one of the cannabis factories.'

Joey stared at her gone out. 'What? You know how much investment I put into them?'

Kaz nodded. 'Yeah, but it'll be worth it to get shot of Sean. You transfer the lease to some shell company that can be easily traced back to him. Let him get his feet under the table, doing business, feeling secure. One day old bill just walk in. Big drugs bust, they're happy. He's back in jail for at least another ten.'

Joey absorbed this, exhaled.

'Still expensive.'

'I know but . . .'

Kaz stopped in her tracks as Hayley came bustling in; she was all smiles.

'I've spoken to the vendor.' He was a small-time buy-to-let landlord hit by the recession and desperate to offload the place to stave off bankruptcy. When Hayley had told him she'd got the asking price, he was over the moon. The rest was easy. 'He's accepted your offer. And, since the place is empty, he's happy to facilitate an early move. My office can draw up a short-term lease that you can sign today. Then you can move in.'

Joey glanced at Kaz, raised his eyebrows. 'Well? Wanna do it?'

Kaz giggled like a kid. All thoughts of Sean had evaporated. 'Yeah!' She spun round, the white walls, the big windows, whirled past her. After all these years, her own place with her own front door. A door she could lock from the inside. She drank it all in, it was heady stuff.

Hayley held out her hand. Kaz took it and they shook on the deal. Hayley was thinking of that juicy cash bonus, the easiest five grand she'd ever earned. She flicked a covert glance at Joey and smiled.

'Everybody wins.'

39

Kaz went furniture shopping with a company credit card provided by Joey. The name on the card was someone she'd never heard of, but Joey assured her it was all above board. The card wasn't stolen or cloned, the company was entirely legit and the card holder fronting it worked for his accountants. She was indeed the company secretary as it said on the card and very well paid for her services.

As Kaz strolled in and out of various furniture stores on Tottenham Court Road she tried on her temporary identity for size. Alice Ogilvy – it had an unmistakably posh ring to it. She walked through several shops, browsing and pretending to be Alice Ogilvy. Then she wandered into Heal's; she sensed it was the kind of place Alice would feel comfortable.

As she drifted through the bed department, a young sales assistant homed in on her, his smile polite and deferential.

'If I can be of any help madam, do let me know.'

Kaz smiled back at him, a twenty-something boy on a shop worker's wage, no different to her in many ways. But they were both playing a game. She adopted a slightly bored expression.

'I've been working out in Dubai for the last five years, just come back and bought a flat in Limehouse. I need to furnish it.'

The boy's eyes lit up, it had been a slow week, his sales figures were crap and the manager was on his case. He straightened his drooping shoulders, painted on a look of enthusiasm. 'Well, a bed is a very good place to start madam. Queen or king size?'

Kaz pretended to ponder. 'King size. I think that would be best.'

An hour and a half later she hit the pavement with a sheaf of receipts in her bag and a delivery time-slot between ten and one the following day. She'd bought a bed, two bedside tables, a lamp, a very elegant chest of drawers, two leather sofas, a glass-topped coffee table and a round dining table with four chairs. It was all quite easy once you got into the swing of it.

But she couldn't help thinking of Helen's flat, the spacious, minimalist feel of it. The sofas she bought were cream and kid-soft like Helen's. For Alice Ogilvy's taste was as good as Helen's, possibly superior. In fact Helen would've thought twice before she dumped the likes of Alice Ogilvy – at least that's what Kaz told herself.

As the anger and the shame of Helen's rejection broke the surface once again, Kaz could feel the familiar tension gripping her stomach. She'd been fighting it all week. The fantasy of killing Julia kept returning to her intermittently. She imagined borrowing a gun from Yev or Tolya, tracking Julia down, she skipped over the details of how, and taking her out. Single head shot, simple as that. But then she'd have to face Helen, witness her pain. And that's when the fantasy turned to nightmare. Helen would hate her, recognize her for the slag she was. All hope would be lost. She'd be back inside again.

More than once Kaz had ended up curled in a foetal ball, sobbing. But now, as the familiar loop started to play in her head, she pushed it away. She wasn't going down that route today, she was out shopping, getting her life back on track and Helen Warner could go fuck herself.

Kaz crossed the road and was setting her mind to deciding

whether to get a laptop, a tablet computer or both, when her phone trilled with an incoming text. She opened it up and read a message from Mal Bradley: *can we meet? need to talk urgently. things moving fast.* Kaz texted back and after a short exchange she agreed to see him an hour later in a pub he suggested on Charlotte Street. She didn't much like pubs, but she figured she'd get there early, settle herself with a coffee, then he'd be walking into her territory.

He'd obviously had the same idea, appearing ten minutes short of the hour and with Nicci Armstrong in tow. Kaz had positioned herself in a corner booth, but with a good view of the door. The place was relatively empty, a few early lunchers and serious drinkers. Bradley clocked her immediately and came straight over, looking slightly put out.

'You're early.'

'Been doing some shopping.'

Bradley inclined his head in Nicci's direction. 'You may remember my colleague Nicci Armstrong.'

Kaz gave her a curt nod. Flipping back to the interview in Southend it was no real surprise to learn that she wasn't the local plod but one of Woodentop's people.

Bradley smiled. 'Can I get anyone a drink?'

Kaz pointed to her coffee. 'I'm fine.'

Nicci put a casual hand on Bradley's shoulder. 'Sit down, I'll get them. Pint?'

While Nicci headed for the bar, he slid into the booth beside Kaz.

Kaz decided to open the batting. 'Thought you lot weren't s'pose to drink on duty.'

Bradley laced his fingers in front of him. 'Yeah, but most coppers are alkies, aren't they? We're no exception. Get it when we can.'

He was turning on the charm, the cute smile, the attempt at humour. Kaz took it all in. She waited. He glanced down at the several shopping bags she had next to her, saw the famous logo.

'New laptop? Nice.'

'I need it for college.'

Nicci Armstrong returned to the table, placed a pint of lager in front of Bradley, she had a gin and tonic for herself. Kaz recognized the smell, an old familiar fragrance from long ago, like a scent she might've remembered her mother wearing. Except with Ellie the memories were more of vomit and piss, of days when she laid on her bed without budging, while Kaz, Joey and little Natalie went hungry.

Nicci sat down opposite Kaz, took a sip of her drink and glanced at Bradley. He turned the pint glass round, tracing a line with his finger through the cold dewy beads of moisture clinging to the glass. Then he looked up, straight at Kaz.

'What we need to talk to you about Karen, is politics.'

'I don't vote. They're all as bad as each other.'

Bradley smiled. He liked that she always whacked everything back at him. 'Not that kind of politics. Sean's an old lag, he's done his time. There's no real mileage for us in arresting him five minutes after he gets out. Makes the system look stupid, makes us all look stupid. That's the politics of this.'

Kaz knew what was coming next. She also knew Sean would be a hard sell. But she waited. Bradley opened his palms.

'Still, it's good that we're having this conversation. It's a start. A good start.' He smiled broadly.

Kaz fixed him with a penetrating stare. 'I'm not giving you Joey. Not now, not ever.' She picked up her cup and drained it. She'd get nowhere unless she pushed them to the edge. 'So, end of discussion.'

Nicci leant back in her chair, folded her arms.

'Tell me this Karen, what kind of life do you want?'

Kaz looked the other woman up and down. Everything about her was less obvious than Bradley. And Kaz suspected she was a lot smarter.

'I want to go to college, get a degree, become a painter.'

Nicci sighed. 'You know that's only really going to be possible once Joey goes to jail.'

'Why? 'Cause you lot're gonna hound me 'til I give in?'

'No.' Nicci smiled ruefully. 'Truth is we'll give up, move on to other targets eventually. But you're gonna spend your life taking care of Joey, dancing to his tune, covering up his mistakes. He's a killer, Karen. Probably a psychopath. You saw what he did to Jez Harris. He doesn't care about anyone else. It's the way his brain's wired. You may think you can help him, but he will use you up.'

Kaz blinked a couple of times, still she held the eye contact. She'd learnt long ago, never let them face you down. The image of Zara, the little kid with a gaping bloody hole in her chest, flashed through her brain. She shook her head, dislodging it, flinging any doubts away.

'Nah, you got it all wrong. Sean's the psycho – believe me, I know. But what, it ain't good politics for you to nick him? Even when it's given you on a plate? Joey's a wuss by comparison. He's a businessman. Money, that's what he's about.'

'He murdered a police officer.'

'You were there? Saw it, did you?'

Bradley watched the duel between the two women. He'd been reluctant to bring Nicci with him, but Mayhew had insisted. Bradley had taken this as a measure of how little he was trusted to get the job done. Now, however, he could see the value in it. Nicci was simply telling Karen Phelps what she needed to hear; it sounded authentic because it was true. It may not be enough to convince her quite yet, but this time she hadn't gone ballistic and walked out.

He smiled. 'Who's paying for the laptop? Joey?'

'None of your fucking business.'

'You're right, it's not my business. Then again if the money was derived from the proceeds of drug dealing, it is. What did you use, cash or credit card?'

'I don't have to tell you that.'

Nicci picked up the baton. 'That's true. But we take you down the nick, we search you, we marry up the laptop you've bought with a credit card that isn't yours . . . we call your probation officer . . . That would be a serious breach of your licence. You know the drill after that.'

Kaz opened her bag, pulled out a receipt. She slapped it on the table in front of Nicci.

'Cash. You think you can prove it was the proceeds of drug dealing? Go on, have a try. Meanwhile I'll call my lawyer.'

The two women stared at each other for a long moment. Then Kaz turned to Bradley. 'I told you why I wanted Sean to go down. I also told you he killed a copper. Now politics or no fucking politics, why ain't that enough?'

Bradley sighed, but it was Nicci who answered.

'Turnbull wants your brother. It's as simple as that. "Drug baron's evil empire overthrown", that's the headline he wants.'

Kaz exhaled in disbelief. 'You ever smoke a spliff? Or when you was a kid and went clubbing, you never done a tab of E?'

Nicci shot a glance at Bradley. He took a gulp of beer to avoid the necessity of lying. Kaz watched them both and smiled.

'You don't have to answer, 'cause we all know that most people've tried it, tried something, crossed the line somewhere.

If Joey was selling whisky or fags he'd be businessman of the year. They'd be giving him awards. He sells people what they want, that's why it's profitable. He's not conning old ladies out their pensions or sending the country broke. When you lot gonna start going after the real villains?'

Nicci started to laugh softly. 'Nice speech Karen. And if you're asking me personally I'd say legalize the lot. So would most coppers.'

Bradley nodded his agreement as she continued.

'The thing is, it's not legal. There are no rules to the game. But there's big bucks to be made, so people fight over territory, over customers. They threaten and maim and murder to get their slice of the action. Biggest thug wins. And you're naive if you think your brother isn't in all that up to his eyeballs. But I don't think you're naive, so maybe you don't care.'

Nicci leant back in her chair, picked up her glass and took a sip.

Kaz watched her, she realized it wasn't going to play out. She picked up her shopping bags and stood up. 'You're right, I couldn't give a toss. But I'm a slag in your eyes, so it's only to be expected innit?'

She skirted round the back of Nicci's chair and strode towards the door. In a moment she was gone.

Bradley glanced at his colleague. 'That went well.'

Nicci sighed. 'She's hearing us all right, that's why she's so petulant. It's going to take time. In the end we put her testimony together with her sister's, we got a case.'

'You actually getting anything from the sister?'

'Not yet. But we're mates.'

'Turnbull's going to go apeshit when he finds out we didn't threaten her with Sean.'

'Then don't tell him.' Nicci drained her glass. 'You want to be Turnbull's kind of copper?'

Bradley shrugged. 'Not really, no.'

'Then take my advice, draw your own line and stick to it.'

40

Kaz turned the key in the lock and let herself into her new home. Sunshine was streaming in through the enormous windows. As she started to roll up the plastic sheeting put down to protect the wooden floors small motes of dust rose up and danced in the light. The deliverymen had already rung to say they'd be there within the half-hour. She sat down, back against the wall, and opened up the takeaway coffee she'd bought from the deli on the corner. As she sipped she savoured the pleasure of finally being alone behind her own front door. For this was the first place she could really call home, free of the taint of the past and the shadows of childhood. Okay, Joey had bought it for her, but there were no strings attached. She'd made that very clear to him, wouldn't have accepted otherwise. Bradley's sidekick could accuse her brother as much as she liked, but the fact was she'd offered them real evil and they weren't even interested. Sean wouldn't get them the right headlines, it was all just crap.

After she'd walked out of the pub Bradley had texted her a couple of times. He wanted her to call him back. She'd ignored him. Then he'd started ringing. She'd still ignored him. Finally, around eleven, as she was about to go to bed, she picked up. He sounded surprised and also drunk.

'Karen? Listen I'm sorry ... Nicci can be a bit ... well y'know ...'

'Whad'you want Bradley?'

'I . . . I don't . . . we need to talk . . . I need to warn you.'

'Warn me about what?'

'Turnbull . . . he's . . . you need to watch out for yourself.'

'I been doing that all my life.'

'It's just politics this.'

'Yeah, I got that.'

Kaz heard a deep inhalation of breath on the other end of the line. 'Fact you've talked to us Karen, that can be used against you, y'know.'

'How d'you mean?'

There was silence, she could hear him swallowing; he needed a drink to answer. Or not to answer.

'Look I told you, it's all about deals. Turnbull has to deliver to his boss. And the deal is Joey.'

This was really starting to irritate Kaz. Was the point of this drunken phone call to warn her or threaten her? She couldn't work out which, but she'd had enough.

'Bradley, it's late and I'm tired. So stop ringing me and fuck off.'

She'd hung up and crawled into bed. Her last night at the hostel, she fell into a dreamless sleep and woke shortly after dawn.

By the time she'd finished her coffee, the deliverymen were at the door. They rang the intercom and she buzzed them in. Three large lads who looked as though they lifted weights when they weren't lifting furniture. In less than twenty minutes they'd brought in all her purchases, carefully unwrapped the heavy-duty plastic and disappeared with it plus a generous tip. Having watched her brother splashing the cash, Kaz followed suit; she could see the sense in it and the pleasure. Everyone was happy.

Removing her shoes she lay down on one of the soft cream sofas. She'd got the lads to position it opposite the balcony window. From her reclining position she could see the wharves opposite, long since converted into luxury apartments, and the glittering surface of the river. The tide was high, the water slapping up the side of the far embankment. She leant over to her bag and pulled out her sketchbook. She opened it to a fresh page and was gazing intently out of the window when her phone trilled on the kitchen counter. Her first impulse was to leave it, but it was probably Joey, phoning to check that everything had gone smoothly. She got up, retrieved the phone, glanced at the screen. It was an 07 number, but he changed his SIM cards frequently, never kept one for any length of time. She pressed to answer.

'Hello.'

'Kaz? Kaz, it's Glynis.' She sounded breathless and frightened, holding it together – but only just. She and Dave should be at Gatwick by now, ready to board the lunchtime flight to Ibiza. Joey had made all the arrangements, found them a small apartment in San Antonio.

'All right Glynis? What's going on?'

The reply was a muffled scrunch. Either someone had grabbed the phone or it had been dropped.

'Glynis?'

A couple of gasped breaths, then her quivering voice came back on the line.

'I gotta talk to you Kaz. You at your new place? Can I come round?'

'You'll miss your flight. You should be at the airport.'

'We can't risk it. He knows Kaz. He saw the tickets. We given him the slip, but I don't know where else to go.'

Kaz had a list of questions, but it seemed unlikely that Glynis was in a fit state to answer any of them.

'Okay, where are you now?'

'We're ... I dunno, up west somewhere. We been driving round in circles.'

'Dump the car – too easy to follow. Get on the tube, take the DLR to Westferry. I'll meet you at the station, say three-quarters of an hour.'

'Aww thanks Kaz.' The relief in her voice was palpable. 'Look ... I'm really sorry ... I ...'

'Don't be. Just do like I said.'

Kaz clicked the phone off, chucked it on her pristine new sofa in exasperation.

Bloody Sean. What was she going to do about him?

Kaz reached the station five minutes before the appointed time. She'd spent the interim trying to contact Joey. He hadn't been home the previous evening, at some girlfriend's she supposed. He wasn't answering any of the numbers she had for him, Ashley's phone was off, the landline at the flat went straight to voicemail. She left messages. She was frustrated more than irritated. Joey's habit of going AWOL just when he was needed was beginning to get on her nerves.

As she approached the station she saw the slight figure of Glynis standing alone on the pavement clutching her handbag. There was hardly anyone else about so Kaz concluded that the train must have come in some time earlier. But where was Dave? Glynis turned as soon as she saw Kaz, still she remained rooted to the spot. She didn't move forward or hurry towards her, which seemed odd. Kaz was still yards away, but her eyesight was keen enough to see that the whole left side of Glynis's face was battered and bruised. One eye was completely closed up.

Her shoulders were shaking, she was sobbing. Suddenly she crouched down like a small child and began howling.

'Sorry Kaz, I'm so sorry! So sorry!'

That was when Kaz saw the blue Mondeo parked kerbside behind her. The back door opened and Sean got out. He had his hands in the pockets of his leather jacket and a smug smile on his face.

'Think you and I need to have a chat little cousin.'

It took Kaz less than two seconds to decide how to respond. The flat wasn't far, Sean was fit enough, but she was fairly certain she could outrun him. If she could only get home, safe behind her own front door. She turned tail and ran.

She made it halfway down Limehouse Causeway before the Mondeo caught up with her. She heard the underside of the car whacking a speed bump before it screeched to a halt behind her. A quick glance over her shoulder told her that Sean was out of the car and coming after her. To her left was a ten-foot chain-link fence, she was up and over it in a trice and found herself in the playground of a primary school. She scooted round the buildings, scaled another wall at the back and landed in a tiny cobbled side street.

Although she'd walked round the area a couple of times she still didn't know it. She paused for breath and to get her bearings. It was hardly more than an alley and in one direction she could see it led to the river: a dead end. Maybe she could find somewhere to hide and wait him out. Then she saw a man appear at the other end of the alley, taller than Sean and much younger. He seemed to be beckoning. She looked hard and recognized Tolya. Her heart leapt, Joey must've picked up one of her messages and come looking for her. She immediately headed up the alley towards him at a fast trot.

Tolya was grinning. She almost felt like flinging herself into his arms.

'Why you run?'

'My bloody cousin, that's why.'

They turned the corner out of the alley and the Mondeo was parked right there. Sean was leaning against it, arms folded.

Tolya put a firm hand on her shoulder. 'No run. Only want talk.'

'Where's Joey?'

Sean sighed and stepped forward. Kaz found herself trapped between the two men and a brick wall.

'Thing is Tol works for me now – don't you Tol? He saw that things was changing, shall we say, in the management structure of the firm. He's an ambitious lad, he wanted to improve his prospects.'

Kaz took a deep breath. She was determined to front this out. Although she was scared of Sean, particularly if he had Tolya to back him up, she was determined not to show it.

'What the fuck you playing at Sean? If you got issues with me and Joey then we should all sit down and talk about it like adults.'

Sean burst out laughing. 'Oh that's rich. That's fucking priceless. He tries to kill me in his own mother's kitchen. You're trying to put my slag of a missus on a plane to Ibiza. I think I'm the innocent party here little cousin. I ain't laid a finger on no one. And now, to top it all . . . a little bird tells me you been trying to grass me up to the old bill.'

Kaz's stomach lurched. Bradley. That's what the miserable drunken shit was trying to tell her. Deals. The police wouldn't make a deal with her. Instead they'd made a deal with Sean. They thought Sean would give them Joey. Now she was seriously in trouble.

She glared at him. 'Bollocks. Some slag's telling tales and you believe 'em?'

Sean smiled. 'Get in the car little cousin, take us all back to your nice new flat and make us a cup of tea. And you and me'll have a little chat about it. Just like old times.'

Kaz shook her head vehemently. 'I know you think all women are stupid, but I'm not a kid any more. You ever try and lay a finger on me again, I'll kill you Sean. I swear.'

He laughed. Her attitude seemed to please rather than annoy him. 'Always the feisty one, weren't you? And that's what I admire. Bit of spirit. I come home to my slag of a wife and it's like fucking a rag doll. But you, little cousin, you was always much more fun. Much more my cup of tea.' He licked his lips. He was standing inches from her now. He smelt of an acrid mixture of booze, nicotine and cologne. 'Don't want to take us to your place? Fair enough. I know somewhere else we can go, just you and me, we'll be nice and cosy.'

Sean grasped her by the elbow. Tolya was heading back to the car, he got in the driver's seat. Kaz knew if she was going to make her move it had to be now. She was still holding Sean's gaze, fiercely, defiantly. Without warning she swung back her foot and kicked him hard in the shin. He yelped, but before she could break free he pulled back his fist and landed a pulverizing right hook squarely under her jaw. The force of the blow sent her reeling. Her head cracked into the brick wall behind and she went down in an unconscious heap at his feet.

Sean flexed his knuckles and rubbed his shin. He bent over her, the back of her head was badly gashed, her lip was bleeding. She was out cold. Tolya got out of the car again and came round. He looked concerned.

'She dead?'

Sean huffed. 'Nah, she'll wish she was, time I finished with her though. Vicious little bitch. Open the boot.'

Tolya seemed about to speak, but he struggled to find the right words. Sean glared at him.

'You heard me – open the fucking boot!'

41

Kaz opened her eyes into darkness; everything hurt. She was lying on her left side, cheek pressed hard against rough carpeting, the floor beneath was rumbling and rolling. A moving vehicle? A car boot? She could smell petrol and taste blood. Suddenly her whole world careened to the right, flinging her feet first against thinly covered metal. Her right ankle buckled over and was rammed by the weight of her whole body into the side of the boot. The pain shot up her leg like a bolt. She howled, wrapped her right arm and hand around her head reflexively as the vehicle swung the other way, flinging her head-first at the opposite side of the boot. Her knuckles and fingers, clutching the top of her head, took the brunt. Again pain stabbed from her hand up her arm and she realized she was going to be sick.

The vomit flew up into her mouth, into the back of her throat and nose; she made a supreme effort to lift her head in order not to choke. At the same moment her bowels went into spasm. Her jeans filled with a surge of hot shit, while a milky, coffee-flavoured puddle of puke engulfed her mouth and nose. She spluttered, struggling to raise her head a little more. The vehicle lurched, she was thrown on to her back. Then it stopped. As the engine faded all she could hear were keening sobs. It took a second to realize they were coming from her, shuddering up from some subconscious well she never knew existed. The boot opened and she was engulfed in what seemed dazzling sunlight.

'Fucking hell, she's shat herself!' The voice was unmistakably Sean's. 'Phoar, what a stink! Get her out of there.'

Kaz held her hands and arms protectively in front of her face. Someone grabbed her arm, then her shoulders, half lifting, half dragging. She guessed it was Tolya.

'Fucking state of this boot. Look at it, shit and puke everywhere. I should make you clean it out. Not so cocky now little cousin, are you?'

As soon as her feet hit the ground her ankle crumpled and the pain shot up her leg. She collapsed in a heap. Sean was looming over her.

'And to think I wanted to fuck you. State of you, you're disgusting.'

She gazed up, focusing on his face. He was wearing aviator sunglasses, the black leather jacket was brand new, his sparse grey hair freshly razored to a number one. A middle-aged gangster from a bad Brit-flick, though he obviously thought he looked cool. Kaz's heart was still pounding, her breathing was sharp and shallow, she managed to hold her head up and stare right back at him. Despite the throbbing in her jaw, she forced herself to speak.

'He's gonna kill you, you know that?'

Sean laughed. 'What, little Joey? Nah. I don't think you know him as well as you think.'

The Mondeo drove off leaving Kaz lying on rough concrete. She could see from the markings it was some sort of car park. She rolled over on to her hands and knees and began to crawl. The surface was pitted and gritty, her palms were soon red and sore. Somehow she made it to the nearest wall and used it to haul herself to her feet. Her right ankle was either broken or badly sprained. Any amount of weight on it was too painful to bear. She dabbed her mouth with her sleeve, a crust of vomit had already dried into the blood on her chin.

Looking around she realized she was several floors up on the deck of a multi-storey car park. She could see City buildings, part of the dome of St Paul's, but from the south side of the river. As she turned slowly, clutching the wall for support, her heart soared: she was in the car park behind Joey's building. She could see the back of it. She fumbled in her pocket, pulled out her mobile. The screen had a small crack across one corner, but as she pressed the button it still lit up. A keystroke gave her the shortcut to Joey's numbers. She called them each in turn. The landline in the flat clicked to voicemail after two rings, the mobiles rang and rang somewhere out there in the electronic ether. There was no answer.

Kaz leant on the wall and the tears started to come. Blood and snot bubbled from her nose. As she tried to wipe it away with the back of her hand she became aware of the pain in her jaw. Even moving her mouth slightly was excruciating. Then through the blur of tears she saw someone staring at her. A woman had emerged from the lift ten yards away. She wore the neat blue uniform of a cleaning company, the same one Joey used, and she was struggling to carry a vacuum cleaner, a bucket, a mop and tray of cleaning materials. She stood looking at Kaz, tottering under the weight of her burdens.

'You all right love?'

Kaz tried to speak, but there was something in her mouth. In spite of the pain, she managed to spit and two teeth ended up on the concrete in front of her with a trail of bloody saliva dripping from her lips down onto her shirt. The woman dumped her equipment and rushed over. She was in her fifties, small and rotund with a Jamaican accent.

'Oh my Lord! What in the world has happened to you child?'

Kaz took a deep breath and tried to answer. But shock had kicked in, her body was shaking all over. She could tell from the appalled expression on the woman's face that she didn't look good. Her exploring fingers found the gash on the back of her head. She started to sway. The woman pulled out a phone and began to press the buttons. Kaz wanted to shout, but her voice came out in a croaky whisper.

'No police.'

'Don't fret. I'm calling an ambulance, get you to hospital.'

Kaz nodded her gratitude, then she allowed her pain-racked body to slowly sink into a sitting position, back against the wall.

The woman stayed with Kaz for the fifteen minutes it took the paramedics to arrive. She said her name was Delia, she lived in Elephant and Castle. She didn't ask what had happened. It was apparent the poor girl was the victim of some species of violence, presumably a mugging. It didn't require discussion. She sat down beside Kaz and gently took her hand. She exuded an easy, natural empathy and spoke with a tone of motherly concern that Kaz had never encountered in her own family. She bemoaned the envy and the anger on the streets, the youth saw what they wanted and took it. They thought the world owed them a living. But the blame couldn't be laid just at their door – greed was a poison that had spread from top to bottom. Greed and drugs, she saw it every day and she prayed.

When the paramedics arrived in their green jumpsuits and lifted Kaz on to a stretcher, Delia whispered a silent prayer for her deliverance. Then she returned to her vacuum cleaner, mop, bucket and tray, loaded them into her battered Nissan Micra and went on her way.

*

The nearest A & E was at St Thomas's, across the bridge from Westminster. Kaz arrived in the afternoon lull and was seen by a doctor almost immediately. They cleaned her up, put her soiled clothes in a white plastic bag under the trolley and sent her for X-rays. Examination of her ankle convinced the doctor it was probably a very bad sprain, he was more concerned about the blow to the back of her skull. She admitted she'd been punched and had lost consciousness, she was unsure for how long. They didn't press her for details, but the Sister had forms to complete and asked for someone, family member or friend, they could contact. Kaz gave them Joey's number, then after a moment's hesitation, she added Helen Warner's contact details.

The X-rays and the waiting around took the best part of an hour. Kaz dozed intermittently on her trolley. In hospital she felt safe and her brain could start to unscramble the events of the morning. Sean had come after her to punish her and it was clear how he'd planned to do that. Fortunately her incontinence had put him off. Even as her head, jaw and ankle throbbed she found this vaguely amusing – she'd defeated a rapist by filling her pants with shit.

But there were more serious questions she needed to ask. How did Sean discover she'd been trying to grass him up? Had he indeed made his own deal with Woodentop? Was that what Bradley had tried to tell her?

When they wheeled her back into the main department to see the doctor again, Helen was waiting. There had been a shift change and a nurse she hadn't previously seen escorted Helen to the cubicle.

'What the hell happened?' Helen's face was tense and pinched with concern, she raked one hand through her hair. 'Was this Joey?'

Kaz shook her head. 'Sean.'

'Why?'

''Cause he's Sean.'

'I'm calling the police.'

Kaz grabbed her hand. 'No . . .'

'Karen—'

'You wanna know how I ended up like this? Turnbull's made a deal with Sean.'

'I don't understand.'

'Not sure I do. But I'm not making myself any more of a fucking hostage to fortune by running to the police. Got that?'

Helen stroked Kaz's hand. 'Okay okay, don't get upset.'

The curtain of the cubicle was pulled back and a doctor appeared. He wasn't the same one Kaz had seen previously. His appearance was oriental, his accent American.

'Karen, I'm Doctor Chen.' He smiled broadly as he flicked open the file. 'And the good news is your head is harder than we thought – no skull fracture. The jaw is badly bruised, but also fine. You have concussion and so the next few days you need to take it real easy. We're going to put a couple of stitches in the back of your head, some tube on that ankle then you can go home. Also we'll give you painkillers. Any questions?'

Kaz glanced at Helen; she had a shedload of questions, but none he could help her with. 'No. And . . . thanks.' She managed a smile.

Chen nodded amiably. 'Your friend's right. You should go to the police.'

42

Marcus Foxley's appointment as Deputy Mayor for Policing and Crime had initially attracted a slew of negative press coverage. He was too young and inexperienced, that was the line most commentators took. Foxley regarded this as unfair, he'd simply started young, becoming the leader of an outer London borough in his twenties. Foxley's dad was a shopkeeper, like his heroine, the blessed Maggie. But Foxley senior had run a string of sports goods shops, sold out to a big chain for a tidy sum and educated his kids privately. Marcus had hoped for a well-paid job in the City, but a third in Economics put paid to that. So he got on his bike, literally, and built himself a career in local politics. Frequently pictured astride his cycle in a jaunty helmet, he campaigned for road safety.

He was the first to admit that at the outset he didn't know much about the police or fighting crime. All he knew was the voters worried about it. But he found the Met's senior officers to be a friendly and helpful bunch. He always welcomed the opportunity to hear their views, and informal lunches were a good way to do that.

Checking his watch he was surprised to see it was already four o'clock. The waiters were clearing tables, most other diners had already left. He was feeling pleasantly replete; they'd got through several bottles of wine and port between the three of them, although Detective Chief Superintendent Alan Turnbull had stuck to mineral water. Foxley was glad that he wouldn't be picking up the bill. Expenses were always a political hot potato. But what did the voters expect? A trip to the local burger bar?

Their host, Duncan Linton, had a waiter at his elbow and was tapping his pin number into the card reader. Foxley smiled to himself. Okay, the restaurant was Michelin-starred, making it quite pricey, but old Duncan could afford it. He could afford quite a lot if the *Sunday Times* Rich List was to be believed.

Foxley became aware of a voice to his left. Someone was speaking to him. It was Alan. He found he had to concentrate hard to pick up the words. Something about his bike?

'. . . so Duncan's called you a cab, okay? You with me Marcus? Leave the bike here.'

Foxley turned his head to focus on his companion. He liked Alan Turnbull, he was one of the best. Turnbull's boss was Fiona Calder, the Assistant Commissioner, but she was a bit scary – reminded him of a fearsome teacher he'd had in primary school. Small women could be like small dogs, dangerous and unpredictable. He preferred Alan. Alan was a bloke you could talk to. Foxley let his weary brain float back to the early part of the meal. He'd ordered scallops as a starter. And what had they been talking about? Oh yeah, outsourcing. Just how much of the police service should be privatized. A touchy topic. In public everyone agreed. Behind closed doors a vicious political brawl was in progress.

Duncan Linton ran a private equity fund. He explained to Foxley that really he was a facilitator, a bloke who looked for money and opportunities and introduced them to each other. Alan of course was a policeman, which is why it was a bit odd for him and Duncan to be such good mates. Or maybe it wasn't. Foxley had to be honest with himself, he'd had a tad too much to drink. So he probably wasn't quite as sharp as normal. But he knew that it was his job to listen to all points of view and that's what he'd done. Linton had done most of the talking, but he and Turnbull were involved in some kind of private scheme. That was the nub of it, although temporarily Foxley couldn't recall the detail.

He must've dozed off for a couple of moments because the next thing he knew Alan Turnbull was helping him into a taxi. But he remembered his manners, thanked Linton for the lunch.

As the taxi drove off bearing the sozzled Deputy Mayor, Linton turned to his companion.

'Let's hope he remembers what he's agreed to.'

Turnbull grinned. 'I suppose I could've nicked him for being drunk in charge of a bike and used that against him.'

The two men laughed. Linton shook his head wearily; tall and patrician he had a full head of white hair and the ramrod stance of an ex-army officer.

'Politicians, they're a sorry breed at the best of times.'

'I wouldn't want to spend my life brown-nosing the great British public, would you?'

Linton gave him a thin-lipped smile but his astute gaze was scanning the younger man. 'I think Marcus'll play his part. Massive cuts are being called for across the board, privatization suits their ideology. So . . . all that's needed now is the right kind of push. A situation we can use to our advantage. Question is Alan, can you provide us with that?'

Turnbull returned the look directly. He knew he had to choose his words. Duncan Linton hadn't been born a City grandee, he'd made his eye-watering fortune through intellect and balls. It was time to put up or shut up, they'd danced round the possibilities long enough.

'Honest answer Duncan, I don't really know. What we're talking about here involves a hell of a risk for me.'

'All business involves risk; usually higher risk means bigger profits.'

Turnbull acknowledged this with a nod. 'Well, it'll take some doing but I think I've got a plan that'll work.'

Linton smiled, gave him an avuncular pat on the shoulder. 'You're our man on the inside. Pull this off and we're talking shares in the company . . .'

'A seat on the board?'

'Certainly. Don't worry – you're going to be a very rich man Alan.'

Turnbull beamed, he couldn't help feeling slightly giddy. 'Good. It's about time.'

43

Helen went out and bought a cheap pair of trackie bottoms from a sportswear shop near Waterloo station. By the time she returned Kaz was stitched, bandaged and ready to be discharged. They took a silent taxi ride to Limehouse, where Kaz managed to fish the keys to her new flat out of the pocket of her stinking jeans.

'Think I'll bin these.'

Helen gave her a thin smile. 'Good idea.'

The hospital had provided Kaz with a pair of crutches, for which Helen had had to fork out a hefty deposit. Kaz was still very shaken but her years in the prison gym had given her much more upper body strength than the average woman. She wielded the crutches with comparative ease, propelling herself forward at a fair pace, her knee bent to hold her injured ankle clear of the floor.

As she opened the door to her flat sunlight flooded out to embrace her. She hopped inside and felt immediately better. Although she'd only just got the place it already felt like a sanctuary. Helen followed her in, glancing around, taking in the space and the brand-new furniture.

She raised her eyebrows. 'Very nice. You're renting presumably?'

Kaz shook her head. 'Buying.' She clocked Helen's critical frown. 'How? That's what you're thinking, innit? How can a slag like me, just out the nick, afford a place like this? The sort of gaff you and Julia'd go for.'

Helen sighed. 'Why don't I make you a cup of tea? You got a kettle?'

'No, no kettle.' Kaz stood balancing on the crutches, glaring at her. 'Got beaten up, so I haven't got round to that yet.'

'Would you prefer me to just go?'

'If that's what you want.'

Helen pinched the flesh between her brows, she was exasperated and angry in equal measure, but she was also determined not to let Kaz wind her up.

'What I want is for you to sit down and tell me exactly what happened. For chrissake Karen, I've been calling you for days, leaving messages. I even went to the hostel. They told me you'd moved out, which is not going to make your probation officer happy, is it?'

'I've talked to Jalil. He knows all about this place.'

Helen scanned the room. 'Well I'd like to know how you explained it to him.'

Kaz hopped over to the sofa and lowered herself into one corner. 'How d'you explain your place?'

'What d'you mean, how do I explain it?' Helen pulled out one of the dining chairs and sat on it. 'I don't have to. I'm not an offender released on licence.'

'So how did you get the money? It's a flash part of town. Not exactly your average first-time buy, is it? Even for a lawyer.'

Helen sighed.

Kaz cocked her head to one side. 'You wanna ask me how I bought this – I'm just asking you the same question.'

'Okay, I inherited some money from my grandmother. And my parents helped me.'

'And where did Granny get her dosh?'

Helen huffed, this was getting ridiculous. 'She married my grandfather.'

Kaz gave her a dismissive look. Helen was hanging on to her temper by a thread. She'd been through guilt, regret, anxiety, when she realized Karen had left the hostel. She'd been evasive and off-hand with Julia. She'd just taken a mad, fear-drenched cab-ride across town, when she got the call from the A & E at St Thomas's. But she was determined to remain in control of her feelings and the situation. She took a deep breath.

'She was also quite independently wealthy. Her father owned a tea plantation in Ceylon.'

Kaz gave a low whistle. 'Tea plantation, eh? Seriously posh family then.'

'He worked bloody hard, died of a heart attack at fifty.'

'Having gone to someone else's country and made a fucking mint working the natives into the ground.'

Helen laughed out loud. 'Oh come on! It was a different time.'

'So you can buy a flat with dirty money, but I can't.'

Helen got up, strode over to the window. The tide was high, the river fast-flowing and mercurial. She stared out at it for a few moments while she reined in her temper. Then she turned back into the room.

'Where exactly are we going with this? A lecture on the evils of British colonialism? I did that course at uni, read all the books. What do you want me to say? You can live off your drug dealer brother because my family were a bunch of villains too? But that was three generations ago. And anyway it's irrelevant, because I don't have to justify my actions to the probation service.'

Kaz smiled, her eyes were burning bright. Helen couldn't

tell if it was anger or a touch of fever, but the sarcasm was unmistakable.

'Jalil's obviously got more faith in me than you have. I told him I'd come into some family money. He was all in favour of me getting my own place. He wants to see the papers when they're signed, to confirm it's in my name. Apart from that he's got no problem.'

The two women glared at each other. Neither wanted to be the first to break eye contact. But Kaz had the edge, her look remained hard and glassy. Finally Helen looked away, ran her fingers through her hair, one of her habitual gestures, then she laughed.

'You are a total bloody pain in the arse Karen Phelps.'

Kaz gave her a lopsided smile. She felt like shit. The painkillers the hospital dispensed had left her with a dull ache all over. Yet being with Helen was a shot in the arm, the hit she'd been craving. She wanted to hate her, but couldn't.

She let her own eyes soften. 'Yeah but I'm still more interesting than Julia, aren't I?'

'What do you want from me? I could've lied, I could've led you up the garden path, but I tried to be honest.'

'I don't care about honest. What I want is you to dump your fucking girlfriend and be with me.'

Helen walked over to the sink, rinsed out Kaz's old take-away coffee cup and filled it with water from the tap. She took several large gulps and placed it on the counter.

'You and me? How on earth do you suppose that would work? I've got a career, a life, things I want to do. You've got a criminal brother you think you can somehow save, your cousin's just beaten you unconscious – and you won't even go to the police.'

Kaz wrinkled her nose. 'You forgot to mention I'm an

ex-con and I probably don't even know which knife and fork to use.'

'I don't care about those things. It's not who you've been, it's what you're doing now.'

Kaz huffed, more in amusement than anger. 'That's a fucking lie for starters.'

Helen was about to argue with this, but instead held out her hands in submission and walked over to the other window. Kaz watched her. All she wanted was for Helen to come and sit beside her on the sofa, put her arms around her and stroke her hair. But she knew that wasn't going to happen.

Helen stood, arms folded, staring out of the window. She didn't turn. 'So . . . you going to tell me what happened?'

'Sean punched me in the mouth, knocked me out cold, chucked me in the boot of his car, where I shat myself.'

Helen swivelled round, a look of horror on her face. 'I'm sorry Karen, but we have to go to the police with this.'

'And it'll be my word against his. He'll have been in some pub or club at the time with ten fucking witnesses. Get real Helen. I know how my family operates.'

Helen came towards her, perched on the opposite end of the sofa, then reached out her hand. Kaz took it.

Helen gave her a sheepish smile. 'Don't hate me. I'm still . . . I care about you, I want to be your friend.'

Kaz clutched her hand, she didn't want to release it, but she made herself let go. She didn't want to appear needy; there was pride involved.

'Yeah I know.'

'Why the hell was Sean after you? I don't get it.'

Kaz sighed. 'Well, he didn't appreciate the fact that I was helping his wife get away from him. Me and Joey tried to arrange for her and her boyfriend to leg it to Ibiza. He found out.'

Helen nodded, waiting for Kaz to continue.

'There were a couple of other things, too . . .' Kaz hesitated. 'Mainly old family stuff.'

Helen painted on an optimistic smile. 'It's possible we could find grounds for some kind of injunction.'

Kaz gazed at her. Helen's irritation had evaporated. Her eyes were soft, slightly moist. She was out of her depth, Kaz could see that. But she desperately wanted to help. Kaz wondered about her and Julia, what they did in their safe, respectable life together, cushioned by professional jobs and money and parents who loved them.

Kaz smiled. 'You wanna help, you could get me a kettle. Maybe some mugs and plates – a few basics until I can get out myself. I can order food online.'

Helen nodded and beamed. 'No problem.'

She picked up Kaz's hand, gave the back of it a brisk kiss. There were tears in her eyes. 'Seeing you like this . . . is so . . . painful.'

Kaz gave a dry laugh. 'Tell me about it.'

Helen smiled and drew her into a gentle hug. Kaz felt a surge of relief, at last they were connecting. Then she felt something on the arm of the sofa beside her. Her mobile was on silent, but it started to vibrate. She wanted to ignore it, hang on to this precious moment with Helen, but she glanced at the caller ID: Joey. As usual his timing was impeccable. She stared at it for a full moment, it seemed vaguely unreal. Then she answered.

'Where are you?'

Joey's tone was light and jovial.

'We're at Schiphol. On our way back. We had a blast – you should've come.'

'You're where?'

'The airport. Amsterdam.'

'Amsterdam? Last time I saw you, you said you was going clubbing.'

'Yeah. In Amsterdam. Couple of bits of business over here, so I said to Ash why not? I told you babe.'

'You never told me.'

There was a pause on the end of the line and muffled voices.

'Ash reckons I told you, but you was all busy on the Net, looking at stuff for the flat.'

'Whatever. Did you know Tolya's working for Sean now?'

'No.'

'Well he bloody well is.'

The lightness in Joey's tone was replaced by concern. 'Babe has something happened?'

Kaz realized from the crack in her voice that she was close to tears. She was also aware of Helen watching her. She swallowed hard. 'Yeah, you could say that. Me and Sean have had a run-in.'

'A run-in? What kind of run-in? You okay?'

'Bit battered. Helen just brought me home from the hospital.'

For about thirty seconds the line was silent then Joey erupted. Kaz had to hold the phone away from her ear.

'That fucker! He's a dead man! He's a fucking dead man! I'll rip his fucking heart out I swear.'

Kaz and Helen exchanged looks; Kaz put her face in her hands and started to cry. Her life was spiralling out of control and there wasn't a thing she could do about it.

44

Nicci Armstrong sat at her desk reading over the witness statement. After Karen Phelps had walked out of the pub on Charlotte
Street she'd called Mayhew, who'd agreed to follow her hunch.
He'd sent her a couple more DCs and between them they'd
walked the length of Tottenham Court Road, showing Karen
Phelps's mugshot in every shop. At first they'd concentrated on
the electronics outlets. It hadn't taken Nicci long to figure that
Karen had practised a simple sleight of hand on them. The
receipt she showed them was some random printout she pulled
from her bag, it didn't relate to the laptop she'd bought. But a
stream of shop assistants in all the stores they visited simply
shrugged their shoulders or shook their heads. Had they sold
a laptop to this woman? They couldn't remember – or didn't
want to.

Working their way up the street they'd got as far as Heal's.
Having drawn a blank and with Bradley whingeing on about
how he should've said this or that to Phelps, Nicci called a
break. While Bradley and the DCs crossed the road to the nearest
coffee shop, Nicci took a stroll round Heal's. Most of the furniture was way beyond her price range, but she mooched round
the kitchen department for a bit, wandered into lighting and
saw a table lamp that she really fancied. Even when she and
Tim were still married they'd had little spare cash for such luxu-
ries. Now, as a single parent, every penny she earned plus the

small amount of maintenance he paid, went on rent, childcare and bills. She survived on her credit cards and the odd handout from her parents. The lamp was tempting, but she was already close to her overdraft limit and it was a few days before her monthly pay cheque went in, so she turned resolutely away. To distract herself she decided to focus on the job in hand. She pulled out her warrant card and started to show Karen's mugshot around. The third shop assistant she approached was Damien Brown.

Damien worked upstairs in the bed department, but Nicci caught him on his way out to lunch. At the sight of Karen's picture he grinned broadly, she was a lovely lady, he remembered her well, back from Dubai. He could tell immediately from the eager look on Nicci's face that the biggest sale he'd had in ages was about to go pear-shaped. He closed his eyes. It'd been a rough few months, now they'd be bound to sack him. Nicci thanked him and asked to see the manager.

It took her less than five minutes to whistle up Bradley and the DCs, one of whom took Damien Brown's statement. The store manager escorted Nicci to his office and pulled up the details of all Karen's purchases on his computer. From there it was a short hop, skip and jump to Alice Ogilvy.

Alice Ogilvy was older than Nicci had expected. Early forties, gym-fit, expensive suit with a pencil skirt. She sat alone in the interview room unfazed by her surroundings. Her eyes were closed, she appeared to be meditating. Nicci and Mayhew watched her on the monitor.

Mayhew pursed his lips. 'Tip of the iceberg?'

Nicci nodded. 'May well be. But will she talk to us?'

Mayhew ran a hand over his saggy jowls. He was dreaming about the weekend, a bit of respite, feet up in front of the telly watching some Twenty20 cricket. 'Have you checked the firm?'

'Old mate of mine from Hendon works at the Serious Fraud Office. I gave him a call. On the face of it they're a perfectly respectable medium-sized City accountants. But they've got a lot of overseas clients and they specialize in tax havens.'

Mayhew's eyes lit up. 'Really? Want me to sit in with you?'

'Bradley's asked if he can. Seems to be chasing his tail over how we handled Karen Phelps.'

'No skin off my nose.' Mayhew swallowed a belch. 'Good experience for him – if you're happy with it.'

'He's harmless. Most of the time.'

Mayhew nodded. 'Well, I'll give Customs a bell. Tax havens and evasion, might give us a way in.'

Nicci collected Bradley from the canteen where he was brooding over a cold cup of coffee. She entered the interview room with a broad smile.

'Sorry to have kept you Ms Ogilvy. This is my colleague, DC Bradley.'

Alice Ogilvy directed a half smile at Bradley but kept her focus on Nicci. 'Will you be recording this?'

'No no, we just wanted an informal chat really.'

Ogilvy nodded. She was sitting up very straight in her chair, almost a yoga pose with her spine perfectly aligned. Her breathing was slow and regular. Nicci already knew she'd be a tough nut to crack.

'We're interested in some furniture purchased at Heal's in Tottenham Court Road. Your credit card was used. Do you remember the purchase?'

Ogilvy frowned as she thought about this. She wasn't about to be rushed. 'My personal credit card was used?'

'A credit card with your name on it.'

After pondering this for several seconds, Ogilvy sighed and gave Nicci a confident smile. 'Ah, I think I know what's happened.'

Nicci didn't return the smile, she just waited for Ogilvy to go on.

'As well as being an accountant I'm a company secretary. Some of our clients, usually those with small private companies, don't need to employ someone full time, so we provide that service for them.'

Nicci nodded and waited some more. She was aware of Bradley next to her, fidgeting. He was getting impatient.

Still smiling, Ogilvy continued. 'As company secretary my name does appear on the company credit cards of some of our clients.'

Nicci considered this. 'But you don't use those cards personally?'

'We have them in case of emergencies.'

'What kind of emergencies?'

Ogilvy hesitated. 'Well, it could be anything really . . . if a director has lost their own card, we could access funds for them.'

Bradley pushed his chair back abruptly, he fixed the accountant with a hard stare. 'Joey Phelps, is he a client of yours then?'

Nicci shot a glance at him, but it wasn't enough to shut him up.

''Cause his sister has bought a shedload of furniture with a credit card in your name. I don't think that's strictly legal, is it?'

Ogilvy's eyes widened, she opened her mouth and shut it again. She seemed surprised, shocked even, but to Nicci it was all a little too rehearsed.

Ogilvy finished by tutting. 'Well, my goodness. I'm really glad you've drawn this to my attention. It's certainly something that shouldn't happen. And I shall look into it with the utmost urgency.'

'You haven't answered my question.'

Bradley wasn't about to let go. Nicci folded her arms, sat back and watched. The DC had blown it, there was nothing she could do.

'Is Joey Phelps your client?' He slapped his hand on the table.

Ogilvy held out her palms in supplication. 'As I'm sure you're aware, there are issues of confidentiality here. I couldn't possibly discuss any client without their prior consent. If you wish to pursue this, I'm only too happy to come back with my lawyer.'

Nicci gave her a long look. 'You said a moment ago you think you know what's happened. What did you mean?'

Ogilvy sighed. 'Well I meant that somehow one of the company cards must've got used. And as I also said, I shall be looking into it. But at the end of the day it's a matter between us and the credit card company.'

Bradley glowered at her. 'Not if fraud's involved.'

Ogilvy's gaze remained unflinching. 'The use of the card by a person other than the card holder is of course a technical breach of contract, though plenty of people do it. I think that what the credit-card company will be interested in is whether or not the funds were available to cover the purchase. They haven't flagged up any problems to me. I doubt they'll be interested in launching a fraud investigation for a minor infringement of the rules.'

Nicci tried again to subdue Bradley with a look. But he was fuming.

'You know what Joey Phelps is, don't you? We're talking

drugs and money-laundering here. Now either he's lying to you or you're lying to us and your oh-so-respectable firm is up to its neck in it. Which is it?'

Nicci had to admire Alice Ogilvy. Bradley's rant simply rolled off her.

She smiled at him serenely. 'Your accusations are entirely unfounded Constable. But I understand that at times your job must be very frustrating, so I won't take offence.'

Nicci got up. They were getting nowhere fast. 'This is a difficult case and we were hoping for your cooperation Ms Ogilvy.'

Ogilvy smiled. 'And I'm more than happy to give it – so long as I'm not being asked to breach my professional obligations to my clients.'

Nicci walked over to the door and opened it. 'Thank you for coming in.'

Alice Ogilvy rose to her feet in one fluid movement. She smiled at Bradley and offered her hand to shake. He ignored it and turned away. Nicci sighed, he was being a petulant boy. She shook Ogilvy's hand and watched her sail off down the corridor. Then she turned on Bradley.

'What the bloody hell is the matter with you?'

'She was taking the piss!'

'Y'know, I've had it with you Bradley. You're arrogant, you've got no patience, and if there's a way to fuck up, you'll find it.'

Nicci turned on her heel and strode off too.

Bradley slumped down on a chair. He knew she was right. Through luck and solid police work they'd happened upon the firm of accountants Joey Phelps was using to front his business dealings. And true to form he'd behaved like a rookie DC with a bug up his arse. He wanted so badly to get a result, to prove to Nicci, Mayhew, Turnbull too, that he did know what he was doing.

Nicci was right, if there was a way to fuck up he'd find it. He wanted to go after her and apologize, but he didn't think she'd listen.

45

Helen Warner had to admit to herself that she was relieved to have a reason to escape from the flat. She walked towards Canary Wharf, where she knew the underground shopping mall would provide all she needed. Karen was trying to be resolutely independent but it was clear that she needed help. Helen had been both shocked and enraged when she'd seen the state of her. Of course she wasn't getting the full story, that was obvious. With Sean's release from jail an eruption of violence within the Phelps clan was entirely predictable, but Helen had thought Karen would've had the sense to keep out of it. It seemed she'd been wrong.

She found a kettle, some mugs and decided to add a cafetiere, but was that going over the top? She stood in the kitchen shop debating the point with herself. Why was she even doing this, running round after Karen? She could've simply delegated the task to someone in the office. That's what PA's were for. But was her connection with Karen more personal than professional now? They'd only slept together once. Still, seeing her, and seeing her hurt, had stirred up a hornet's nest of dangerous emotions. Helen put the cafetiere back on the shelf, paid for her purchases and headed for Waitrose.

The previous evening she'd taken Julia out to dinner at a smart new bistro in Soho in order to propose; it was supposed to be a romantic tryst but had turned into a strategy meeting.

She'd had a call from one of her policy advisor mates at Party HQ. It hadn't hit the news feeds yet but a Northern Labour MP was about to die of cancer and his death would trigger a by-election. The leadership was keen on a female candidate; someone modern, telegenic and on-message. Helen's mate reckoned it was her big chance.

Helen was excited, she'd thought she'd be sitting it out until the next general election. But if this seat was up for grabs she was certainly going to go for it.

She realized there was no point being ambiguous about her sexuality or relationship status, the red tops'd sniff out any perceived weakness in a nanosecond. So she and Julia would celebrate their civil partnership openly and joyously, make it a real family occasion, and she'd defy the selection panel to hold it against her.

The real skeleton in her closet was Karen Phelps. Being Karen's lawyer was one thing, but she needed to take a large step back from anything more than that. As she selected tea bags, milk, cereal and fruit from the supermarket shelves she told herself this was positively the last time she was riding to the rescue.

Loaded down with supplies Helen jumped into a cab for the short ride back to Narrow Street. She was at the front door to Karen's building, paying the cabbie off, when she noticed a man in a parked car opposite watching her. For a moment she racked her brains, she couldn't quite place him. Then he got out of the car and walked towards her. It was the cop with the photos who'd tried to lean on Karen.

As the cab drove off, he joined her. All smiles he reached down to pick up one of her plastic carriers. 'Need a hand?'

She glared at him. 'Do I know you?'

He pulled out a warrant card. 'Sorry. DC Bradley – I bought you a cup of coffee in Southend.'

'What do you want? I'm rather busy.'

'Is Karen at home? I was hoping to have a word.'

Bradley gave her his most winning smile; it wasn't an effort because the sight of the lawyer had cheered him up considerably. He'd been sitting in his car for the last quarter of an hour wondering how, without ringing every doorbell in the block, he was going to find out if this really was Karen Phelps's new home. The probation service in Basildon might know, but they could be awkward bastards to deal with and had already made an official complaint about Bradley's ruse at the hostel.

After some argument about cost, Mayhew had got authorization to have Karen's mobile phone tracked. The signal location had led him to this residential block in Limehouse.

Helen looked him up and down. 'Why are you here? Did the hospital get in touch?'

He frowned. 'The hospital?'

'Clearly not.' She sighed deeply. 'Oh what the hell, I think you probably should see what that bastard's done to her. She's been beaten up.'

'By Joey?'

'By her cousin Sean.'

Bradley's face fell. The drunken phone call, the threat, all flashed through his mind. Oh shit. He thought it but didn't say it.

Kaz had spent the latter part of the afternoon dozing on the sofa covered with the brand-new duvet, delivered with the furniture that morning, which now seemed an age ago. The back of her head around the gash was extremely sore, the local anaesthetic they'd given her in order to stitch it had worn off. Her jaw was a dull ache. She'd sleep for a bit, then wake abruptly thinking she was in the car boot again.

The light was fading, the river ebbing. Helen had taken a door key to let herself back in. Kaz heard the front door open. She wanted to call out, to check, but that seemed childish, absurdly uncool. She waited a moment. The shadows in the room were lengthening, the hallway running off it was already dark, a sudden fear gripped her stomach. Why hadn't Helen announced herself? She could hear footsteps in the hall, two voices, someone fumbling for the light switch. Suddenly she was close to panic.

'Helen? That you?'

The light in the hall went on. Helen appeared round the corner, saw Kaz's anxious face. She smiled. 'It's okay.'

Except it wasn't okay, because behind her was Mal Bradley with two plastic carriers of shopping. At the sight of Kaz his jaw slackened.

'Jesus wept. What happened?'

Kaz sat up abruptly and shot an accusing glance at Helen. 'What the fuck's he doing here?'

Bradley put the carriers down on the kitchen counter. Helen went over to the sofa and sat on the end.

'I found him on the doorstep. And I think you do need to talk to him. You can't let Sean get away with this.'

Kaz was close to tears. She glared at Helen. 'They was behind it, don't you understand? To put the frighteners on me. 'Cause they don't want Sean, they want Joey.'

Helen turned to Bradley. He was standing, hands in his pockets, with a sheepish look on his face. She cocked her head. 'Well? Is this true?'

'No no, 'course it isn't ... you got it all wrong Karen. I'm really sorry ... this is terrible.'

Kaz glared at him, her face was tight and angry. 'Sorry? He

knew I'd talked to you. That's why he did this. So who the fuck told him, eh?'

Bradley held out his hands in supplication. 'It wasn't us, I swear.'

But even as he spoke Bradley was thinking of Turnbull. Was he up to something? With Turnbull you could never tell.

Kaz's tears were flowing now but she ignored them. 'Remember what you said to me on the phone? Or were you too pissed?'

He turned away, ashamed. 'I was pissed but I didn't mean—'

'You said the fact I'd talked to you lot could be used against me. Next thing Sean's after me and he's accusing me of offering to grass him up. Don't take a genius to work out who told him, does it?'

Bradley shook his head. 'Whatever Sean found out, it didn't come from us.'

Helen took two steps across the floor until she and Bradley were face to face. 'Let's see if I'm understanding this. You thought it was a legitimate tactic to put pressure on my client by threatening her with Sean Phelps?'

'Yeah, well sort of.' Bradley sighed. 'But it was just that – an empty threat. We didn't actually do anything.'

Kaz hugged the duvet around her. She wiped away the tears with her hand. 'He's fucking lying. Look at him. Get him out of here, will you?'

Bradley tried to edge round Helen. She was standing, arms folded, making sure he kept his distance. He tried to get Kaz to meet his gaze, but she wouldn't. 'Karen please . . . you've got to believe me. If Sean Phelps did this to you, I'll go and arrest him myself.'

Kaz sniffed wearily. 'You'll have to find him first.'

'I can do that.'

'He'll have a lawyer and a rock-solid alibi. Anyway, I ain't making a complaint, there's no point.'

Helen and Bradley exchanged looks. She felt torn. Bradley was offering a solution of sorts to this mess. She moved towards Kaz.

'Listen to me Karen. If what you say about the threats is true, then I'm going to the IPCC. No question. In the meantime, a crime has been committed and Sean needs to be arrested.'

Kaz looked up at them both. Helen, her brow furrowed with anxiety, Bradley, gazing at her like a sad puppy.

'You two make me laugh. I don't know what world you're living in, but it ain't the same as mine. You nick Sean, his lawyer'll have him out, couple of days tops. You know that Helen. Then what do you think he's gonna do? He'll come looking for me again – and I don't think I'll be getting off with a beating.'

Bradley was shaking his head. 'We can protect you. We've got safe houses, a witness protection scheme . . .'

Kaz laughed drily. 'I just got out of jail. I don't fancy going back.'

Helen returned to the sofa. She sat down on the end of it, put her hand on Kaz's good ankle.

'What are you going to do then?'

Kaz shrugged. 'Do what the doctor said, rest up, get better.'

Bradley shovelled his hands in his pockets, strolled over to the window. Lights were now twinkling in the buildings on the far bank. He was annoyed, he was being made to feel responsible for something that wasn't his fault.

'It's obvious what she's going to do. Well isn't it?'

Kaz fixed him with a hard stare, Bradley returned it. Any softness had gone from his features. He felt sorry for her, she looked a mess. But he had a job to do. People had been murdered, there was still the question of justice, not to mention the law. And the law was what he'd sworn to uphold.

'You got a choice here Karen. Trouble is you don't want the hassle and the difficulty of doing the right thing, acting within the law, do you? So you're going to leave it to Joey. Let him sort out your little problem for you, deal with Sean his way. Even if that makes you an accessory to murder. But hey, you'll probably get away with it. And anyway Sean deserves it, right?'

He pulled a business card from his inside pocket and dropped it on the kitchen counter.

'You have a change of heart, call me. I can't guarantee we'll succeed in putting Sean away, but you'll have done the right thing. That's got to be the way you get your life back surely.'

He gave them a thin smile and headed out. They heard the front door close behind him.

Kaz glanced at Helen, she raised her eyebrows and sighed. Kaz pulled the duvet up to her chin. 'Pompous prick.'

46

Joey Phelps strode through the doors from Customs at Gatwick's North Terminal carrying a light leather holdall. Ashley was two paces behind. The flight from Amsterdam had been subject to a three-hour delay, some kind of security alert, which hadn't improved Joey's temper. Many flights had been disrupted and the Arrivals Hall was crowded and chaotic. Yevgeny was waiting behind the barrier in a crush of bored taxi drivers and anxious relatives. Joey scanned the crowd, their eyes met and Joey gave him a curt nod. Yevgeny pushed his way forward, took the holdall and they headed for the short-stay car park.

As Yevgeny waited in the long queue at the ticket machine, Joey became increasingly impatient. Finally he snapped, barged in front of an elderly man who was taking an age to work out what to put in which slot.

'Sorry mate, bit of an emergency here. Yev!'

Yevgeny stepped up, slotted his ticket and some coins in the machine.

A woman two places behind them in the queue started to object. Her tone was upper class and commanding. 'Well, if everyone jumped the queue there'd be anarchy.'

Joey turned, in less than a second he was in her face. He towered over her.

'You talking to me love? 'Cause if you want a bit of anarchy, I can certainly arrange that for you.'

Ashley was at his elbow. 'C'mon Joe, leave it. We don't want no trouble.'

Joey continued to fix the woman with a cold, intimidating stare until he was satisfied that she was scared stiff. Then he turned abruptly away, following Yevgeny across the car park.

Ash glanced at the woman. 'Sorry. He's had a bad day.'

She pulled out her mobile, her hand was shaking. 'I'm calling the police.'

Ashley sighed and trotted after the other two. Yevgeny clicked the door lock to the Range Rover, Joey climbed into the front passenger seat and folded his arms.

'Fucking security alerts. And what is the government doing about these bloody terrorists? They should stand 'em all up against a wall and shoot 'em. I'd do it for 'em if they asked for volunteers.'

The Range Rover navigated the tight turns of the exit ramp and emerged from the multi-storey car park into darkness and rain. The wipers started to slap across the windscreen. Joey glanced at Yevgeny.

'You track him down then?'

The Russian nodded. Joey checked his watch.

'How long?'

'Satnav say one hour fifteen minute.'

Joey folded his arms and settled against the headrest. 'Maybe I can get a bit of kip then.'

He closed his eyes. The Range Rover negotiated two round-abouts then headed south on the M23. Low cloud made the night very black, the taillights ahead of them were red pinpricks, the glare of oncoming headlights spiked and refracted in the rain.

Ashley sat with his feet up in the back. For an instant he

caught Yevgeny's gaze in the rear-view mirror. The Russian was alert and ready, every inch the professional soldier. He might not wear a uniform any more, but he remained focused and disciplined. Ashley understood why Joey relied on him so much nowadays, but it still left him feeling a little jealous.

An hour down the road and several miles from their destination Yevgeny pulled into a lay-by. The rain had eased off and a waxing crescent moon could be glimpsed behind scudding clouds. Joey had been heavily asleep for the whole journey, his breathing low and steady. Ashley put a hand on his shoulder.

'Joe.'

Joey opened his eyes, blinked, rubbed his face.

Yevgeny got out of the car, went to the boot and returned with a small backpack. He opened it and pulled out a pistol. It was the latest version of the Russian SPS, a powerful and deadly handgun capable of penetrating most Kevlar vests not to mention titanium plate. Yevgeny looked it over with an expert eye and loaded a clip. He glanced at Joey. 'You want me to do this?'

Joey shot him a look. 'Nah. I can manage.'

Yevgeny handed Joey the gun, reached into the backpack and brought out a pair of latex gloves. Joey took them.

'Hope you haven't got the powdered ones. They make me itch.'

Yevgeny shook his head. 'No powder.'

Joey glanced from him to Ashley. 'Don't know what you two're looking so fucking gloomy about. This is the fun part.'

Ashley gave him a half smile. 'Don't enjoy it too much, 'cause we don't want no forensics.'

Joey huffed. 'I know. I'll put on the plastic suit and the hat. Happy?'

Ashley nodded.

The Range Rover pulled up across the street from a small

parade of shops. Yevgeny indicated some steps at the side of the building leading to the flats above. 'Up there. Number four.'

Joey put the beanie hat on, pulling it low over his forehead and ears. The plastic suit was white, disposable, polyethylene coated. Joey zipped it up to his chin. 'Anyone sees me, they'll think I'm a right prat.'

Ashley was wearing the ghost of a smile. 'That's the idea.'

Joey slipped the SPS into the pocket slot at his hip, got out of the car and trotted across the road. He mounted the steps three at a time. As he went along the walkway in front of the flats he drew on the latex gloves.

The door to number four was half glazed and Joey could see a faint glimmer of light through the frosted glass. He rang the bell, waited. A shadowy figure appeared behind the glass, the voice was anxious.

'Who is it?'

'Joey. Joey Phelps. Come on mate, let me in. I'm freezing my nuts off out here.'

The door opened a crack on the chain. Dave Harper had seen pictures of Joey, family snaps of the Phelps clan that Glynis had shown him, but they'd never actually met. He stared at Joey for a moment, Joey beamed back.

'Open up Dave, I need a word.'

Dave peered at him from behind rimless glasses. 'You on your own?'

''Course I am.'

'You know he's got Glynis?'

'That's what I'm here about.'

The door shut followed by a rasping as the chain was unhooked. Then it opened wide. Dave Harper was short, a small paunch hanging over his trousers and large dark eyes blinking rapidly behind his glasses. He was as unlike Sean Phelps as it was possible to be, which, Joey figured, must be the attraction as far as Glynis was concerned.

Joey followed Dave down the short hallway to the living room.

'Nice place. Cosy.'

Dave glanced over his shoulder. Joey was wearing a white plastic suit, which struck him as decidedly odd, but it seemed rude to comment.

'Comes with the job. Bookies is downstairs. You want a cup of tea or something?'

'Nah, you're all right. This won't take long.'

They reached the sitting room. Dave picked up the remote to turn off the television. It was a football match, a UEFA friendly between Brazil and Ukraine. They were already into injury time and things weren't looking good for Ukraine.

Joey glanced at the screen. 'Leave that mate. In fact turn it up a bit.'

Dave looked at him. 'Thought you wanted a word.'

Joey pulled the SPS out of his pocket.

'Not really. As I said, turn it up.'

Dave's eyes widened, his nervous fingers fumbled on the volume control button as he stared at the gun in disbelief. 'I don't get it. Glynis said you wanted to help us.'

Joey held the gun at waist height, his grip was easy, his hand steady as a rock. 'My sister wanted to help you and I went along with it. But you should've got on that plane to Ibiza mate. I had everything worked out nicely. You missing that plane has caused me no end of stress.'

Dave took off his glasses, wiped his hand over his sweaty face.

'We was packed and ready to go. Then Glynis got a call. It was her next-door neighbour from the old place. He kept an eye on things for her. He said the alarm was going off and he sounded really anxious.'

Joey shook his head and tutted. 'What? And it didn't occur to you two fucking knuckleheads that it was Sean?'

'Oh yeah Glynis knew. But she was worried about her neighbour. Poor old boy has terrible arthritis and his wife's in a wheelchair. They'd been really good to Glynis. She was scared Sean'd hurt them if she didn't go back. I begged her not to go.'

'She should've listened to you.'

'She didn't want them to suffer because of her.'

Joey sighed. 'Ironic really, 'cause it means you're gonna suffer instead.'

Dave was shaking, the sweat trickling from his receding hairline down his forehead. 'Don't shoot me Joey, I'm begging you. I'll do whatever you want. Go to Ibiza, stay here, disappear, whatever. You just say.'

Joey gave him a sympathetic smile. 'That's all very well Dave and I appreciate the offer. But what I want now is for you to be dead, so that when your body's found there's a good chance the old bill'll go knocking at Sean's door. Sorry mate. You seem to me like a decent bloke, so I'll make it quick and clean.'

Dave fell to his knees, sobs racked his body. He crawled towards Joey. 'No please, I'm begging you . . .'

Joey extended his arm, took aim. 'Keep still and look up.'

Dave's dark myopic gaze met his. Joey could see the fear, smell it, it was exhilarating. He squeezed the trigger. The gun's report coincided with the final whistle and cheering fans on the television. The bullet struck Dave squarely in the front of the forehead, his eyes froze in shock as it passed through his brain and blew off the back of his head. Blood and brains exploded over the sofa, carpet and wall behind him.

Joey lowered his arm with a satisfied grin. As the body slowly came to rest in a heap on the floor, he glanced around. He hadn't touched anything. The blood spray had missed him, and any tiny particles would've hit his disposable boiler suit. He slotted the gun into his pocket and headed for the door.

The sense of elation he felt was like no other experience in his life. He wanted to join the Brazilian fans on the telly and shout with joy, he restrained himself. Tonight it was business. This killing was a strategic move, but it was also a pleasure, one day Kaz would understand that. It was the key to any kind of real success in the world. Natural selection, ensuring the fittest survived. And Joey knew he was special. He'd never suffered from the maelstrom of debilitating emotions that seemed to paralyse most people. He could always stand back, remain detached and see the bigger picture. It was a huge advantage.

But in the meantime there was no harm in him having a bit of fun along the way.

47

Kaz spent the best part of a couple of days on her new sofa. She became intimate with its soft creamy undulations and the sharp smell of the leather. Making the bed up felt like too much of an effort. Helen had offered to do it for her, but Kaz had declined.

After Bradley had made his exit Helen used the new kettle and mugs to make tea. Then she paced the room. Her phone trilled a couple of times, she checked it and avoided Kaz's eye.

Kaz watched her from the sofa; tense and awkward she was obviously looking for an excuse to escape. Kaz decided to put her out of her misery.

'I'll be fine. You don't have to stay.'

'I can't leave you like this.'

'Yeah you can. You're my lawyer, this is family stuff. It ain't your problem.'

'I still want to help you.'

'Go home Helen. Nothing's gonna happen tonight.'

'You sure?'

Kaz scanned her face, she wanted to say no, stay. She wanted Helen to insist, to put her to bed, to lie down gently beside her and protect her. But maybe it always was a fantasy. Helen hadn't told her about Julia because she wanted to keep her options open. A walk on the wild side, that was her buzz. Kaz felt stupid, duped. Power and control – she'd met plenty of blokes who mainlined on that particular aphrodisiac. But Helen?

Kaz struggled to her feet and, swinging along on her crutches, escorted Helen to the door. She shut it and locked it firmly behind her. Then she returned to the couch.

She was dozing when a text pinged on her phone. Joey. His plane had been delayed, but he'd be with her soon as and he'd get everything sorted. Kaz thought about what that meant. Bradley's accusation rankled. Did she really want her brother to go out and murder Sean on her behalf? She certainly hated him enough, but to have Sean's death on her conscience . . . how would that make her feel?

She'd grown up in the world of Terry and Sean Phelps, where killing was just part of the way things were done. It wasn't spoken of that much, but it was the ultimate threat. You stayed in line or you paid the price. Violence and fear were the currency of family life. Lies and denial were what held it all together. Except underneath it didn't, you felt like shit inside. Had she spent six years in jail, struggled to get clean and sober, to find some measure of dignity, simply to go back to all that?

She fell asleep cocooned by the sofa and when she woke early morning sunlight was flooding into the room casting a warm glow over her new home. She got up and discovered that the swelling in her ankle had gone down considerably. She could just about hobble if she didn't put too much weight on it. Realizing she hadn't eaten since breakfast the previous day – most of which she'd barfed into Sean's boot – she made herself a large bowl of cereal and fruit. She had consumed most of it when the entryphone system buzzed, she hobbled and hopped across the room, pressed the button and her heart soared as the tiny screen displayed Joey's grinning face.

He breezed into the flat but his smile dissolved into an angry frown at the sight of her.

'Fucking hell!'

'Do I look that bad?'

He drew her into his arms, cradled her. Her head sank on to his shoulder and the tears came.

Ashley closed the door behind them, stood watching, waiting, like an obedient hound.

Joey glanced at him. 'Got a tissue or something?'

Ashley rummaged in his jeans, came up with a pocket pack, handed it over. Joey swept Kaz up in his arms and carried her, without apparent effort, over to the sofa. He opened the pack of tissues and handed her one. His jaw was tense, his expression fierce. 'Bastard's gonna pay for this.'

Kaz dabbed her nose, blowing was still too painful. 'Yeah well, we need to talk about that. Bottom line is Sean's not worth going to jail for.'

'You seen yourself babe? You need to take a good long look in the mirror before you start going soft on him.'

'I don't need to look in the mirror. And I'm not going soft.'

Joey took a deep breath. 'Sorry. Just ... gets me in the gut seeing you this way. Looks like you been in a cage-fight.'

She laughed drily. 'Feels a bit like that too.'

Joey shook his head wearily. 'Well, Ash has got something for you.'

At Joey's nod, Ashley reached into his pocket and pulled out a plastic bag. He opened it to reveal a medium-sized pistol.

Joey took it from him and turned it over in his palm. 'SIG P220, semi-automatic, eight-round mag – one of the most reliable handguns you can get.'

Kaz stared at him. 'What the hell am I supposed to do with that?'

Joey held out the gun. 'Get any more unannounced visits from Sean you shoot the fucker, that's what.'

'Don't be daft! I don't know how to use a gun.'

Joey gave her a reassuring smile, patted her hand. 'Don't be frightened of it. You put the clip in here.'

Ashley handed him a cartridge magazine, he slotted it into the base of the handle, clicked it home with the heel of his hand.

'Pull back the slide, make sure your decocker's off.' He indicated a small button on the side. 'Point. Hold your arm out straight, two hands.' He aimed the gun at the opposite wall. 'Shoot. Bit of kick, but provided you got it firmly with both hands, you'll be fine.'

Kaz took a deep breath and fixed him with a hard stare. 'Remember what happened last time I had a gun? No way.'

'That was a long time ago. We was stupid kids. This is just a sensible precaution.'

'I don't want it.'

Joey flicked the decocker back on, turned it over admiringly in his hand. 'Swiss design, German made.'

Ashley took what looked like a short metal gun barrel out of his other pocket and smiled at Kaz. 'We got a suppressor too, so if it does go off no one'll hear it.'

'Fuck off Ash. I don't want it.'

Joey took the suppressor and screwed it onto the barrel of the gun. Once he'd assured himself it was firmly attached he handed the whole thing back to Ashley.

'Put it in one of them kitchen drawers, case she changes her mind.'

Ashley wrapped the gun in the bag and glanced at Kaz. 'I made you up a couple of extra clips so that's twenty-four cartridges in all.'

Joey laughed. 'That should be enough, even for a dinosaur like Sean.'

Ashley put the gun in a kitchen drawer.

Kaz huffed. 'Am I talking to myself or what?'

Joey put his arm round her, pulled her into a hug. 'Only want you to be safe babe. Now what else d'you need?'

She grasped his large paw in her own hand. 'I need us both to be safe. I don't want you going after Sean, getting hurt, getting arrested. Remember what we talked about, making the business totally legit? That's what I need – to be free of the old life. For us both to be free. You're smart enough Joey. Sean's a two-bit drug dealer. It's all he'll ever be. The law'll get him, or he'll piss someone else off. The bottom line is he hurt me but I don't want his death on my conscience. Got that?'

Joey pondered this. He gazed out of the window, banks of fluffy white clouds were racing across the sky. Finally he turned, gave her a lop-sided smile.

'Okay, we'll try it your way. See what happens.'

For a moment she got the full force of his dark, unnerving stare. Did she believe him? She was getting used to his mercurial changes of direction. Much as she hated Sean, she wasn't about to let him mess up her life any more than he already had.

Joey was looking out of the window again, he seemed very far away, but then his gaze flicked back to her and he smiled.

'Just remember the gun's in the drawer if you need it. Okay?'

Kaz sighed and nodded. It was pointless arguing, her body was weary and sore. 'Whatever.'

48

It was still dark, a good half-hour before dawn, when Nicci Armstrong pulled into Thurrock services at the junction of the A13 and the M25. Traffic was already building up, taillights forming a red flickering arc across the Dartford Bridge. In a quiet corner of the lorry park there were a couple of patrol cars parked up plus an armed response team getting togged up and ready to go. DCI Cheryl Stoneham was chatting to detectives beside one of the vehicles, hands cupped round a hot coffee. As soon as she saw Nicci draw up she walked over. Nicci got out of her car. Stoneham looked remarkably cheerful considering she'd got out of bed at four.

'Morning Nic, glad you could join us.'

Nicci smiled. 'Thanks for the heads-up. We appreciate it.'

'Anything to do with the Phelps clan, we thought you'd be interested. Sussex have asked for our help, they're obviously the lead on this because the murder happened in Eastbourne. You want a coffee? We got a flask somewhere.' She swivelled her head to locate one of her uniformed officers. 'Jimmy, can you get DS Armstrong a drink?'

The PC acknowledged the request with a nod. Nicci smiled. 'Cheers. So who's the victim?'

'A bookie, name of Dave Harper. Turns out Sean Phelps's missus had been shacked up with him for years. Neighbours all knew her, assumed they were a couple.'

Nicci nodded. 'Sean gets out of jail and he's not happy about it?'

'That's the theory we're working on. Confirmed by the fact that it looks like Dave and Mrs Phelps had planned to do a runner. Two plane tickets to Ibiza found in the flat.'

Jimmy the PC trotted over, handed Nicci a styrofoam cup of coffee. She thanked him, sighed. 'Sean's likely to be expecting us then?'

'Hard to say. We got a surveillance unit tucked up near the house and according to them everyone's in bed.'

Nicci inclined her head in the direction of the armed response team.

'Still treating it as an armed digout though?'

Stoneham laughed. 'Victim had his head blown apart by some kind of serious Russian handgun. They pulled the bullet out of next-door's wall.'

The police convoy headed eastwards on the A13 then turned off north into Langdon Hills. Cheryl Stoneham coordinated their approach until they reached a suburban cul-de-sac. The target, a detached chalet bungalow sitting on a corner plot, looked a bit run down, garden full of weeds. A Mondeo was parked on the drive. Stoneham handed over to the skipper of the armed response team, and as the first hints of a grey dawn started to break in the eastern sky, they went in. Nicci sat in the back of Stoneham's car and watched.

Two swings with the Enforcer brought the front door off its hinges and four officers armed with MP5s piled into the house. In less than five minutes a dazed-looking Sean Phelps was brought out in handcuffs and pyjamas. He was put in the back of a patrol car.

The skipper of the armed response team came towards Stoneham's car. She lowered the window.

He squatted down to her level. 'All clear. First we thought it was just him and the wife. But then we found another woman locked in a back bedroom.'

Stoneham frowned. 'Interesting. Thanks John. You can stand your lads down.'

He patted the side of the car. 'Watch out for the wife, she's got a gob on her.'

As Sean Phelps was driven off to the local station to be interviewed by the officers who'd come up from Sussex, Nicci followed Stoneham into the house. Even before they crossed the threshold their ears were assailed.

'You fuckers! Bust in with your fucking guns! I ain't done nothing! Let me out of here! Let me out of here!'

They stepped into the sitting room where two of the armed officers had the screaming woman boxed in a corner. She was in her twenties, clad only in a thong and she was picking up ornaments from the mantelpiece and hurling them at the armed officers.

Stoneham paused in the doorway, sighed, glanced over her shoulder. 'Will someone get her something to wear?'

She nodded to the armed officers. 'Thanks lads, we'll take it from here.'

The two armed officers beat a hasty retreat. The woman was sobbing and cursing, she had a gold plated carriage clock in her right hand ready to fling.

Stoneham took a deep breath. 'I'm Detective Chief Inspector Stoneham. You going to chuck that at me or what?'

The woman met Stoneham's gaze, hesitated, then dumped the clock on the floor. One of the officers in the hall handed Nicci a jacket, she offered it to the woman.

Stoneham looked her up and down. 'I take it you're not Glynis Phelps.'

The woman snivelled as she slipped the jacket on. 'Who the fuck's she?'

Stoneham turned to Nicci, raised her eyebrows. Nicci nodded. 'Back bedroom.'

Nicci found Glynis Phelps curled in a foetal heap on the bed. She was wearing a silky pink dressing gown with a torn sleeve. One side of her face was a great livid purple bruise, oozing blood close to the eye. Nicci stepped through the doorway, turned on a lamp.

'Glynis, I'm DS Armstrong. You all right?'

Glynis didn't look up. She was staring into space, her eyes red-rimmed and vacant.

Nicci squatted down beside the bed. 'Did he beat you up?'

There was no reply. Nicci gently stroked her hand. 'You're safe now, you're going to be okay.'

As Glynis tried to move she winced in pain, she clutched the lower part of her left arm and cradled it.

Nicci felt her gut muscles tightening as the anger rose. What kind of man beat his wife like this, locked her up and then went to bed with another woman? Unfortunately she'd seen enough domestics to know the answer. There were plenty of blokes out there capable of it; they came in all shapes and sizes, most of them wouldn't even be classed as villains.

Using one finger, Nicci gently pushed back the strands of hair from Glynis's forehead. 'I'm going to go and call an ambulance, then I'll be straight back.'

Finally Glynis met her gaze. A voice emerged that was barely a whisper.

'He's dead, 'n't he? That's why you're here. Dave's dead.'

49

Bradley woke late with a toxic hangover. His phone was dancing manically on the bedside table. He groped for it, discovered he had three missed calls and instructions to phone Turnbull's office urgently. It took him a couple of minutes to put together the events of the previous evening. He'd been in a foul mood after his visit to Karen, but he'd gone out with some old mates from uni. They'd had a few beers and then one of them, Tom, had regaled them with tales of his City job and six-figure bonuses. Bradley knew he was smarter than Tom, he got the better degree, went on to take a master's. But afterwards he'd returned home, looked at his shabby one-bedroom flat with mildew in the bathroom, thought about his shitty career and felt incredibly stupid. So he'd ended up in front of the telly doing vodka shots.

After standing under the shower for five minutes and downing half a carton of orange juice and three paracetamol he managed to call Turnbull's PA. The instructions he received were precise: meet the boss at eleven outside City Hall, wear a suit. He decided the tube was a bad idea, it would probably make him chuck up. So he took a cab and had it drop him at London Bridge in the hope that a short walk by the river would clear his head. He arrived a couple of minutes late and saw Turnbull pacing near the main entrance.

Bradley hurried towards him, flattening his unruly hair with one hand, trying to appear calm and collected. 'Sorry I'm late sir. Problem on the tube.'

Turnbull frowned, scanned the suit, the loosely knotted tie. 'You'll do I suppose. Just do something about that tie.'

Bradley did up his top button and tightened the knot. Turnbull was already striding into the building. He had to trot to catch up.

'Umm, what are we actually doing sir?'

Turnbull didn't slacken his pace. 'The Deputy Mayor has asked us to give a briefing to some members of the Police and Crime Committee on current efforts to curb organized crime in the capital. I'm going to sit behind the Assistant Commissioner, you're going to sit behind me.'

For the next two hours Bradley did just that, sitting behind and slightly to the right of Turnbull's shoulder in a large, airy meeting room. Light glistened off the river, voices floated across the table around which the main players sat. The atmosphere was soporific. Bradley fixed his gaze on the face of an elderly, balding gent directly opposite; observing his every snuffle and twitch was the only way Bradley could stay awake. He was dimly aware of the Assistant Commissioner's voice, light and melodious but with undertones of authority. Marcus Foxley, the Deputy Mayor for Policing and Crime, led the questioning and occasionally the Assistant Commissioner would turn her head slightly as Turnbull whispered the odd comment in her ear. Finally the Deputy Mayor announced a break and Bradley was tasked with fetching cups of coffee for his bosses.

He collected the coffees from a catering assistant at a table in the corner of the room. He decided to go for a tray, he wasn't too confident of the steadiness of his hand and this seemed the less dangerous option. Weaving his way back across the room, he made it without any spillages.

Turnbull smiled, lifted a cup and saucer from the tray and handed it to the Assistant Commissioner. As she took it Fiona Calder's eye alighted on Bradley. She seemed to be trawling her memory.

'DC Bradley isn't it?'

'Yes ma'am.'

Calder nodded then her face broke into a benevolent smile. 'You've done very well Bradley. Turning Karen Phelps into a chiz can't have been an easy task.'

Bradley darted a look at Turnbull, but his face remained inscrutable. Calder gazed very directly at Bradley, he sensed his cheeks reddening; he felt like a guilty schoolboy hauled in front of the head.

'I understand she's been providing you with some very useful intel on her brother and his activities. The net is closing.'

Bradley cast Turnbull a beseeching look, but he was gazing out of the far window.

'Well er, yeah. But . . . she's very difficult to handle.' Bradley was close to panic, he didn't want to fling himself into a headlong lie. So he gabbled. 'She can be unpredictable and sometimes it's hard to know if she's telling the truth. As to whether we can rely on anything she says . . .'

Calder nodded thoughtfully. 'Use of informants is always a thorny issue. Media can go off on bouts of righteous indignation all they like, but how else do they think we're going to get reliable intel on organized criminals except through informants and so-called supergrasses?'

She gave him a long appraising look. Easy to see why Turnbull had picked him. To say he was handsome wasn't accurate. He was beautiful, a complete headturner. Yet he seemed quite modest with it. Calder could see that for most women that would be a winning combination.

Bradley felt awkward under her scrutiny, which turned to embarrassment as he noticed what he took to be a hint of salaciousness creep into her eye.

'I trust there's nothing untoward in your relationship with our source.'

Bradley shook his head vigorously. 'Oh no, not at all ma'am. I can assure you of that.'

A thin, mischievous grin spread across Calder's features. She shot a glance at Turnbull. 'Because if there is, I certainly don't want to know about it. Or read about it over my muesli.'

Turnbull sipped his coffee and smiled. 'Bradley understands that ma'am. He's a very astute young man, that's why I picked him for the job.'

Calder scanned Bradley, but his discomfort made her wonder. 'This is a difficult time for us Bradley. Met's under pressure as never before. Cuts, privatization. The only way we can protect our core functions is to prove we do the job better than anyone else. Nailing Phelps is really going to help us with that. You may have some . . . reservations about what you're doing, but your contribution is vital, you should know that.'

As he stood there balancing the tray Bradley could feel the sweat trickling down into the small of his back. He knew Turnbull had set him up and for the second time in twenty-four hours he felt extremely stupid.

50

Kaz studied herself long and hard in the bathroom mirror. Under the bright halogen lights the mauves and yellows of her bruised jaw were fully exposed. But she could see some healing had already taken place, it was now possible to open her mouth without too much pain. She examined the bloody sockets of the two teeth that had been knocked out. They were at the bottom and not particularly visible. Helen had given her the number of her own dentist, he'd be able to sort her out, no problem.

She'd taken a shower, washed her hair and got rid of the dried blood caked round the gash. Her ankle was still swollen and mottled, but she could get a pair of trainers on and had managed the short walk to the small mini-mart across the road. She still looked a fright, but the important thing was she was feeling stronger.

She wandered back into the open-plan sitting room, went into the kitchen area and opened one of the drawers. The gun was still there, wrapped in a plastic bag, as Ashley had left it. She lifted it out and placed it on the counter. She'd spent half of a wakeful night wondering what to do with it. If Sean had wanted to kill her then she'd be dead. Joey had intended the gun to be for her protection, but she'd come to the conclusion simply having it in the flat put her more at risk. She had no experience of firearms, if she tried pointing it at someone like

317

Sean, more likely than not he'd take it off her. In prison she'd relied on blagging her way out of trouble and that still seemed to her to be the best and safest course.

She picked up the gun and went out on to the balcony. She was five floors up and a small patch of private garden belonging to the ground-floor flat separated the building from the river. It was low tide, the river was winding sluggishly down the middle of its course with a muddy and debris-strewn foreshore exposed on either bank. She could see immediately that throwing the gun into the river from where she stood wasn't going to work. The water was too far away. Even at high tide she'd be in danger of missing and dumping it in her downstairs neighbour's garden. Besides, there were security cameras mounted on the back of the building. She'd have to think again.

She was returning it to the kitchen drawer when her phone rang. It was a mobile number she didn't recognize. She clicked the phone on.

'Hello.'

'Is that Karen Phelps?' The voice was vaguely familiar, but she couldn't place it.

'Yeah. Who's this?'

'Hold on please.' There was the muffled sound of the handset being passed over, then another voice, low and croaky.

'Kaz, it's Glynis.'

'Glynis. You okay?'

'I'm in Basildon Hospital. Dave's dead. Old bill have taken Sean in.'

'Dave's dead? How bad are you?'

'Broken arm. Busted ribs. Cuts and bruises. Kaz I'm so sorry . . .'

Suddenly Kaz was glad she hadn't thrown the gun in the river. She just wanted to find Sean and put a bullet in his head.

'Look, I understand. You don't have to say nothing. They keeping you in?'

'They'll have to. Ain't got nowhere else to go.'

Kaz hesitated, but only briefly. 'You can come and stay with me. Or Joey. Sean won't go looking for you there, I can guarantee it.'

There was a moment's silence on the other end of the line then the soft sound of Glynis weeping.

'After what I done to you? Surprised you'll even speak to me.'

Kaz exhaled. 'I known him longer than you. I know he don't take no for an answer. You sit tight, I'm coming down the hospital.'

'Thanks . . . thanks.' Glynis's words came in gasps between quiet sobbing.

'It's gonna be okay Glynis.' Kaz was by no means convinced of this, but it seemed the right thing to say. She heard Glynis sniff and take a breath.

'There's this cop here, wants a word. Says you know her. Nicci Armstrong?'

Kaz shook her head ruefully. Well it was obvious Turnbull's mob would be in on the act.

'Yeah well you can tell her to go and take a long run and jump. I'll see you in a bit babes.'

Kaz didn't wait for a response. She hung up.

51

Sean Phelps was fingerprinted, photographed, DNA swabs were taken, he bore it all with the stoicism of an old lag. The important thing was not to let them see they'd got to you in any way. Yanking you out of bed at dawn was a favourite trick. The fact that they'd felt the need to bring in the heavy mob appealed to his vanity. It was almost a mark of respect and he appreciated it. But by the time he was trussed up in the back of the patrol car he was fully awake, calm and ready to deal with the situation.

They took him to Basildon nick, a bit of a trip down memory lane, a couple of his early busts had happened there. He listened to the custody sergeant go through his rigmarole, that's when he learnt he was being charged with the murder of Dave Harper. He laughed out loud; did they really think he'd put himself at risk by going after that clown? He gave them Neville Moore's name and number and was kitted out in a white plastic jumpsuit. He refused to say a word until his brief arrived, except to ask for a bacon butty and a mug of tea. He got an egg sandwich and a tepid cup of coffee, but he sat in his cell and consumed them without complaint.

Neville Moore finally arrived full of apologies and blaming the traffic.

Sean gave him a thin smile. 'Ain't exactly what either of us had planned for this morning is it?'

Moore opened his briefcase, pulled out a yellow legal pad and a pen.

Sean took a deep breath. 'First up this is a load of bollocks. I don't know exactly when this went down but I got pretty solid alibis for the last two, three days.'

The lawyer nodded, made a note. 'You want to talk to them then?'

'Neville, I know the advice is keep shtum, but I really didn't do this and I need to get out of here asap. I go "no comment" I'll be sat here for the full thirty-six and I ain't got time for that.'

Moore gave him an appraising look. 'You're an innocent man, anxious to cooperate fully and clear your name?'

Sean nodded. 'As a matter of fact, that's exactly what I am.'

Cheryl Stoneham and Nicci Armstrong watched Phelps being interviewed on a video screen. Phelps was relaxed and polite, playing the reformed-gangster card to the hilt. He happily admitted that his wife's affair with Dave Harper didn't please him. But he argued that the most important thing to him now was to remain at liberty. There was no way he wanted to be caught breaching his licence, much less commit a murder for which he'd be the obvious suspect. That was plain stupid and he was no kind of fool. On the night of the murder he'd been out sampling the delights of Bas Vegas. Some old mates of his ran the doors on the clubs there and he'd been letting his hair down a bit after his long incarceration. He offered a list of names – all respectable businessmen – who could vouch for where he was and what he was doing.

Cheryl Stoneham sighed. She'd already given a grilling to the young woman arrested at the house and mistaken for Sean's wife. Her professional name was Kylie, she described herself as a hostess, definitely not a prostitute, but she was a homecoming present for Sean from some of his former colleagues in the security business. They'd been partying for the last two days and Kylie's main concern was whether or not she'd still get the bonus she'd been promised for showing Sean a really good time.

Stoneham shook her head wearily. 'He's gonna walk.'

Nicci glanced across at her. 'Surely Sussex have got more than motive?'

Stoneham snorted. 'An elderly neighbour saw "someone", who she describes as a big bloke, pass her window en route to Harper's flat.'

'It's obvious Phelps wasn't going to do this himself. He contracted it out.'

Stoneham smiled. 'I'm sure you're right Nic. But how the hell are we gonna prove that?'

Nicci nodded pensively. 'Well, there's more than one way to skin a cat.'

'You mean Glynis? She's never going to dob him in.'

'She might if she thought it was the only way to put him back inside.'

Stoneham swept a hand through her hair. 'In your dreams mate. You can bet your bottom dollar he was battering her when she married him. If she was really gonna break free she'd have done it while he was inside.'

Nicci considered this. 'Well, it's worth a crack. I'm going back down the hospital.'

'You're wasting your time.'

'Maybe, maybe not.'

Stoneham glanced at her quizzically. 'You're up to something.'

Nicci paused at the door. 'I'll keep you posted.'

52

Kaz arrived at Basildon Hospital in the late afternoon. Ashley drove her. They found a space in the multi-storey car park and followed the signs to A & E. After her conversation with Glynis she'd phoned Joey; he was at home and from his airy tone and the giggles in the background she concluded he was not alone.

'Hey babe, what's up?'

'Glynis is in hospital, Dave's dead. Old bill have arrested Sean.'

He didn't reply immediately. She could hear his breathing getting heavier, he started to pant.

'Oh for fuck's sake Joey! You talking to me, getting a blow-job or what?'

His voice came on the line, laughing and breathless. 'Yeah I'll call you back.'

The phone went dead. Kaz chucked it on the sofa, she wasn't sure why she was so annoyed. She went into the bedroom, changed into jeans, a clean shirt and was searching in the walk-in wardrobe for shoes and a jacket when her phone rang.

She returned to the sitting room, she was still hobbling and not about to compromise her ankle by hurrying. She picked the phone up and heard a boyish giggle.

'You pissed off with me babe? Sorry. But something . . . came up. Had to attend to it.' He erupted into laughter, she could hear a female voice in the background going 'Shuddup Joe.'

She took a deep breath. 'Did you hear what I said before?'

'Dave's dead, yeah I know.'

'You knew already?'

'No. You told me just now. Before.' He giggled again.

Kaz sighed. 'I'm going down to Basildon to see Glynis.'

'Okay. Ash can drive you, he ain't got nothing to do.'

'Don't you want to come?'

'Nah I'm . . . y'know I'm not that good with hospitals and stuff. I'll send Ash straight over.' There was a pause. 'Oh and give Glynis my best. Take her a nice bunch of flowers or something.'

Kaz ended the call. At times she found Joey's childishness incredibly wearing. How much effort would it require for him to come with her and support her? But Joey was only helpful when it suited him to be.

Ashley picked her up half an hour later. He seemed a little glum. They drove most of the way in silence with Kiss FM providing a muted soundtrack. Kaz gazed out of the window. She was determined to wean herself off the painkillers and had cut right down. She'd also thrown her remaining fags away. As a result her body was aching and sore and she was in need of a smoke. She felt grizzly and annoyed. But if her mood was sombre it took a nosedive when she walked into Basildon A & E and saw Nicci Armstrong.

Armstrong was hovering near the reception desk and homed in on Kaz as soon as she walked through the door.

Hearing Kaz's hiss of exasperation, Ashley glanced at her. 'What's up?'

'Bloody cops! It's this stupid bint that's after Joey.'

Ashley gave Armstrong a sullen look as she approached them.

But her attention was focused on Kaz. She looked her up and down.

'I heard he gave you a pasting too. You all right?'

Kaz closed her eyes and took a deep breath. 'Look we've come to see Glynis.'

Nicci nodded. 'We found her locked in a back bedroom all busted up. Meanwhile Sean was in bed with some hooker his mates had got for him.'

Kaz inhaled, but then habit kicked in, her face remained impassive. She wasn't about to display any kind of emotion in front of a cop. 'That's sounds like my cousin.'

Nicci turned to the charge nurse. 'All right if I take these two through?'

He replied with a nod.

Nicci had taken control of the situation and there was little Kaz could do at that moment. So she and Ashley followed her through two sets of double doors into the treatment area. The individual bays were curtained off, Nicci led them across the room to the adjacent observation ward.

There were five beds, Glynis was in the end one by a window. She turned her head slowly at their approach, the sight of her battered and bandaged face sent a jolt right through Kaz. She was in a far worse state than when Kaz had last seen her outside the DLR station. After Sean had turfed Kaz out of his car boot and dumped her in the car park he must've gone home and vented his anger on Glynis.

Kaz perched on the bedside chair and took Glynis's hand in hers. 'All right mate?'

'I been better,' Glynis replied with a ghost of a smile.

'What the doctors said to you?'

'Not much.'

Kaz was very aware of Nicci Armstrong hovering over them.

She wasn't about to go away. Kaz considered just telling her to fuck off and as if Nicci had read her thoughts, she sighed, positioned herself at the end of the bed.

'Look I know you don't want me here, but I'm not the enemy. I'm here to help the both of you.'

Glynis looked up. Her voice was a whisper. 'Sean goes down for killing Dave, that'll be good enough for me.'

Nicci nodded. 'Did he threaten to kill Dave?'

Glynis looked very small and fragile in the hospital bed. 'I dunno, maybe. I don't remember.'

Kaz turned to Nicci and fixed her with a cold stare. 'She don't need you hassling her right now, okay?'

Nicci acknowledged this with a tilt of her head. 'I appreciate that. But here's the bottom line. Sean has a rock-solid alibi and we have no reliable witnesses. He's going to walk. But if one of you is prepared to make a statement so we can charge him with ABH, then his licence'll be revoked, he'll be straight back inside.'

Kaz glared at the cop. 'What about forensics? Thought that's what you lot relied on nowadays?'

'Yeah well a detailed forensic analysis of the scene is ongoing. But ... looks like whoever did this was a professional. I'm guessing Sean hired someone.'

Ashley was standing next to Kaz, he was stock-still, just watching Nicci like a hawk. He turned to Kaz and mumbled. 'Won't be a minute. Need to make a call.'

Kaz nodded. But she remained focused on Nicci. He walked off.

Nicci Armstrong followed him with her eyes. She had a sudden sense of something revealed in Ashley's abrupt departure, she couldn't put a finger on it, it was pure instinct. But Kaz was on her feet and facing the cop.

'You can't nail Sean, so you want to put us in the frame, that it? We go to court, get pulled apart by a bunch of smart lawyers, Sean goes back for a short stretch, comes out – then what?'

Nicci sighed. 'I know it's not ideal. But once he's locked up again—'

'He killed a police officer. You couldn't get him for that. If you'd listened to me before, maybe some of this could've been avoided. But you weren't interested, were you? You and your fucking politics.'

'I know. And you're right. But we're interested now.'

Well, I'm not.' Kaz folded her arms, her whole body fizzed with hostility. ''Cause I wouldn't trust you lot as far as I could spit.'

53

Mal Bradley had never really thought of himself as a drinker. At uni he'd played a lot of sport and participated in the binge-drinking sessions that went with that. But by the time he joined the police the booze culture of old had receded, certainly in the Met and amongst those with any ambition. Bradley used to keep a few beers in his fridge along with the ready meals; he drank wine when he went out with women and pints of lager with his mates. So it had taken him a while to even become conscious of the change. The bottle of Stolichnaya his brother had given him for Christmas, together with a set of shot glasses, had soon been demolished and then replaced a number of times until keeping a bottle of Stoli in the fridge had become his new habit. As had drinking alone.

Bradley washed down his chicken tikka masala with a bottle of Japanese beer. He turned on the television, channel-surfed for a bit, but couldn't settle. So he poured himself a couple of shots, just to take the edge off his mood. He didn't give a toss what lies Turnbull was dishing up to the Assistant Commissioner; the politics of the senior ranks was none of his business. But Turnbull had set him up, paraded him in front of Fiona Calder so he'd be forced to confirm the story Turnbull had fed her. As a result Bradley was implicated in Turnbull's schemes. He was a dupe, a pawn in the boss's game, and that wasn't what he'd joined the police service for. Nicci Armstrong was right, if he didn't want to be Turnbull's kind of copper, then he had to draw his own line and stick to it.

Bradley downed a third shot, or maybe it was a fourth, picked up his phone and called Nicci's number. She answered after several rings.

'What's up Bradley?' She sounded hassled.

'I . . . y'know, wanted to say sorry. You're right, I fuck everything up . . . I am one useless fuck-up in fact. And I'm sorry.'

'Well, getting pissed won't help.'

Bradley poured himself another shot. 'You're right about that too.'

'Listen, Bradley, much as I'd like to dissect your character I'm trying to put my kid to bed.'

'Sophie, isn't it?'

'Yeah Sophie.'

'Want me to sing her a song?'

'Not really.'

'I just wanna . . . make a difference Nic. Lock up a few villains. Go home at the end of a day and feel I'd made a difference.'

'Don't we all? Now I gotta go and get Sophie out the bath.'

'This whole undercover thing is fucked, totally fucked. Karen Phelps is never gonna rat out her brother, not in a million years. Turnbull's not stupid – when's he going to realize that?'

'Maybe he does.'

'What d'you mean?'

'You shouldn't take everything at face value.'

'I don't. But what would you've done in my place?'

'Told Turnbull no. Honeytraps are illegal.'

'Where the fuck does that leave me now?'

'I don't know, Bradley. You can get pissed and feel sorry for yourself or you can discover some balls. The rules are there to protect us too, they're not just a villains' charter.'

Bradley's hand was unsteady, he poured himself another shot, slopping half of it over the table. 'Irony is one time I try to make a woman like me she ends up hating me.'

'Karen Phelps hates all cops. I don't think it's personal. I saw her at Basildon Hospital this afternoon. She came to pick up Sean's wife who he's beaten to a pulp. I suggested she bring charges against Sean herself and she practically gobbed in my face.'

'She thinks we told Sean that she was trying to inform on him.'

'That would certainly explain her hostility. Now I'm hanging up before the kid turns into a prune.'

'Nic—'

The phone clicked in his ear and she was gone.

Bradley slumped back on the sofa. He must've dozed off soon after. When he woke he had a dry mouth, a stiff neck and chicken tikka masala on his left sock. He checked his watch, it was eleven thirty.

When Bradley went out he didn't really have a plan, only a vague feeling stirring somewhere in his lower gut. He wasn't Turnbull's boy and he certainly wasn't dancing to his tune, not any more. For a while he walked and the cool night air started to clear his fuddled brain. After a while he found himself on the South Bank. He started to walk east, there were still quite a few people about, spilling out of riverside restaurants, enjoying themselves, laughing and joking, something he hadn't done in a while.

He worked and he drank to cope with the job. The last actual relationship he'd had was maybe two years ago, since then it had been the odd fuck and a morning wank in the shower if he had time. He'd told himself he was ambitious, this was a period in his life to forge ahead, make his mark. It didn't matter if he had to work all hours so long as he got the promotions. DI before he was thirty, that had been his aim. Laughable really. His last performance review wasn't brilliant, his next one would depend on Turnbull, so unless he toed the boss's line he was stuffed.

As he approached City Hall, rising up like the hull of a glass ship looming over the river, he thought again about the job he was being required to do. Turn Karen Phelps into a chiz, using whatever trickery he could muster. Turnbull had never said the plan was a male honeytrap, he'd just let the notion hover in the air. He knew that an ambitious young officer like Bradley would be anxious to second-guess his wishes. Turnbull had relied on that. He'd played him with such skill and if it all went pear-shaped the boss's hands were clean. Nicci Armstrong knew it, the rest of the team too no doubt.

Bradley felt ashamed of his own naivety. What made it worse was that he'd realized all this, he'd realized it weeks ago. Still he'd done nothing. And faced with Fiona Calder he'd simply bottled and lied to protect Turnbull. If it all came out he'd look like a complete sap. And that was exactly what he was.

Bradley stood for a while watching flecks of light dancing across the dark fast-flowing current of the river. He thought about what Nicci had said: maybe Turnbull did know that Karen Phelps wouldn't rat out her brother. He knew all along that Bradley would fail. Maybe that was his plan? But why? On the face of it, it didn't make sense. Why would an ambitious and slippery shit like Turnbull go out of his way to create such a fuck-up?

The irony was he liked Karen Phelps. If he had managed to get somewhere with her it wouldn't have been a trial. She was fit by anyone's standards. But more than that he admired her.

She was trying to escape from a nightmare upbringing, although clearly she and Joey remained completely enmeshed. She simply refused to betray her little brother, although it would've been much easier for her if she did. He had a tight and protective relationship with his own baby brother. What would he have done if Dara had turned into a killer instead of a chartered surveyor?

Bradley thought back to his first year in the job. As a uniformed PC he'd helped people. He'd been on a few exciting busts, had a spell in Traffic, riding round in fast cars, blues and twos – that had been a real buzz. But since he'd become a DC, life had become greyer; it had happened imperceptibly in tiny increments.

He walked up on to Tower Bridge, looked over and down at the current as it sped under the ironwork and into the darkness. It seemed curiously inviting. He knew his life in the police was over, that's what his gut was telling him even if the message hadn't quite travelled to his brain. He wasn't the suicidal type though; the thought crossed his mind, but only fleetingly. He turned away from the parapet, glanced up the road, stuck out his arm and hailed an approaching black cab.

54

The hospital was short of beds, extremely short of staff and hadn't needed much persuasion to release Glynis into Kaz's care. Ashley nicked a wheelchair, they loaded her into the Range Rover and drove back to Limehouse. Kaz made up her new bed and settled Glynis into it. She despatched Ashley to borrow some extra bed linen and towels plus a few pots and pans from Joey's. She ordered groceries online. It was a long time since she'd done anything like proper cooking and even then her mother had never encouraged it. But she managed to concoct a passable pasta bake, using a jar of shop-bought sauce and a recipe she found on the Net.

Kaz sat on the end of the bed eating the food she'd cooked, Glynis pushed the pasta around the plate with a fork. She sighed.

'You gone to a lot of trouble. But I just ain't hungry.'

'Try and eat a bit. You need to build up your strength.'

'What's gonna happen Kaz? You heard that cop, they got no evidence. When he gets out . . .'

'He won't come here okay? Why? Because he don't even know where this place is. Tomorrow me and Joey'll put our heads together, come up with something.'

Kaz washed up the dishes, tidied the kitchen. It felt really comforting to be doing domestic chores in her own home. When she looked in on Glynis, she'd dozed off. Kaz switched off the light and quietly closed the bedroom door. Then she made up a bed for herself on the sofa.

She lay on her back staring up at the ceiling. The room was dark but curtainless, so the reflections from the river and the street lamps played across the walls. She watched the dancing patterns. She hadn't picked up her sketchbook in days. All that had gone out of the window. Her course was due to start soon, the new life she'd planned so meticulously. But was being an art student just about impressing Helen?

Whether she liked it or not she seemed to have landed back in the family business. It had bought her this flat. But she felt that was no more than her due for the time she'd served. Joey had promised to turn the business totally legit, if she stuck with him, held him to that, maybe they'd both have a new start. That still left the problem of Sean. But even if he had made some kind of deal with the old bill, he'd murdered Dave and sooner or later she and Joey would discover how. They'd get the drop on him. Knowing Joey he was on it already.

After what seemed like hours of rumination Kaz was drifting off to sleep when she heard a low tapping. At first she thought it was Glynis. She got up, limped down the hall to the bedroom and opened the door. Glynis was on her back, sound asleep, her breathing steady and deep. The tapping was repeated and Kaz realized someone was knocking softly on the front door. She hesitated, thoughts, fears, skittering through her brain. It was very late. Joey or Ashley would've called. Her heart soared, maybe it was Helen? Maybe in the middle of the night she'd realized her true feelings and rushed round to declare her love. But how would any of them have got into the building? The main doors were locked, that's what the entryphone system was for, to keep the flats secure.

Without turning on any lights, Kaz crept down the hall and

put her eye to the spyhole in the door. The fisheye lens showed the distorted nose and cheek of a man's face. He stepped back slightly and knocked again. She realized it was Mal Bradley.

Kaz opened the door on the chain, Bradley's face turned towards her. He smiled.

'Sorry, did I get you up?'

The unmistakable reek of booze wafted through the door at Kaz. Four years sober she smelt it everywhere, on people in the street, on the tube.

She glared at him. 'What the fuck d'you want?'

'I got an idea, a solution.'

'To what?'

'To all this. Just let me come in and talk to you. Please.'

'How did you even get in the building?'

Bradley grinned. 'Waved my warrant card at one of your extremely respectable neighbours. She'd been out to take her dog for a dump.'

Kaz huffed, closed the door, unhooked the chain and let Bradley in.

'Keep your voice down 'cause Glynis is asleep.'

'She okay?'

'No. She's a mess.'

Bradley followed her down the hall into the open-plan living space. Kaz picked up a sweatshirt, pulled it on, folded her arms and turned to face him. Despite the bruises from her encounter with Sean, she looked good in her jaunty PJs, comfortable in her body. There was never anything girly or fey about her, the look was straight defiance and Bradley realized this was what he liked. It didn't matter how tough things got, she stood her ground.

He ran a hand through his unruly curls. This time he wasn't

trying to con her, the dazzling smile came naturally. 'First up I want to apologize.'

'Yeah? What for?' She stared at him very directly, she wasn't giving an inch.

'For what I said about leaving it to Joey. I don't really think you'd get your brother to kill Sean.'

'Why not? Solve everyone's problems, wouldn't it? Including yours.'

'I don't think you're as hard a nut as you make out.'

Kaz laughed drily, retreated to the sofa and sat down. 'Cut the crap Bradley. Just tell me why you're here.'

He pulled up a dining chair. 'Okay, here's the idea. Mike Dawson, the guy who ran the drawing class . . .'

'I know who he is.'

'Tomorrow I go and see him. Show him the badge, tell him I'm a police officer and I talk to him about you, your family, trying to make a fresh start.'

Kaz huffed. 'What the fuck's it got to do with him?'

'He's seen your work, he knows what you're capable of. He can help you walk away from all this.'

Kaz cocked her head contemptuously. 'Oh yeah. How?'

Bradley leant forward in his seat, smiled as he warmed to his theme.

'That bloody drawing class – I spent a lot of time hanging round, waiting for you to show up, y'know. Me and Mike, we had quite a few chats. He's spent loads of time in the States, used to teach over there, various art schools. He goes back all the time to see his mates.'

Kaz folded her arms again. 'I don't see what this has got to . . .'

'Point is he could maybe help you get a place in a college over there. As a student. Get you out of this country, away from

Sean, away from Joey. Karen, this could be your escape route.'

Kaz smiled, shook her head cynically. 'You fix this for me? And what do I have to do in return? Let me guess.'

'No.' Bradley held up his palms. 'Absolutely nothing. No strings attached. I swear.'

Kaz stared at him hard. 'I don't get it.'

He held her gaze. There was only a single lamp on in the room, so not enough light for her to see the moistening of his eyes.

'I'm . . .' He swallowed hard. 'Well, I guess I'm trying to help you here. Proper help, real help. No deals, no tricks. You go to college in the States, you leave the family, Joey, the past behind you.' He sighed deeply. 'You've served your time. I reckon you deserve the chance to make a life for yourself.'

As Kaz digested this her penetrating gaze never left his face. He seemed quite emotional but he was probably pissed. What was his angle? She couldn't figure it. Finally she took a deep breath, got up.

'Want a cup of coffee? Might sober you up a bit.'

'Yeah cheers.' He smiled. 'But y'know, this is not booze talking.'

She went over to the sink, filled the kettle and slotted it back on to its base. She turned to face him.

'It's a nice idea, but you're forgetting one thing. I'm released on licence. Next six years I got to keep my nose clean and my probation officer happy. Can't see them letting me swan off to the States.'

Bradley considered this. 'I've known of instances of offenders getting permission to travel abroad, even lifers. It depends on the circumstances and the perceived risk.'

Kaz lifted down two mugs from the cupboard.

'Okay, even if I could wangle some special deal, what's it going to cost? An arm and a leg. Plus I don't think they're about to take someone like me with one AS-level she got in the nick.'

Bradley stood up, shovelled his hands in his jeans pockets. 'Yeah I know it won't be easy, but that's where Mike comes in. They'll see your drawings, but most of all they'll listen to Mike's recommendation. And there are all sorts of scholarships and bursaries available. Ex-con turns into a brilliant artist – the Americans love all that.'

Kaz smiled. 'You got it all figured out, haven't you?'

'It could work.'

'Does Woodentop know about this? Or your snotty mate Nicci?'

'No one knows. Or need ever know. This'll just be between you and me and Mike.'

'And the probation service.'

'Okay, them too. But the ones I've met go out of their way to avoid cops.'

Kaz spooned coffee granules into two mugs. 'I gotta say Bradley, I didn't think you could surprise me. But you have. I don't know what angle you're working here but it's slick . . .'

He took two urgent steps towards her. 'There is no angle. That's the angle. The lies, the deals, the tricks – I've had enough. Why should your life go down the pan so we can get Joey? I don't think the end does justify the means.'

Realizing he was looming over her, he took a step back. 'Sorry, I didn't mean to . . . y'know.' He turned away, ran his hand through his hair.

Kaz watched him and wondered: was he being straight with her? Or had they merely come up with a more astute way of wooing her? Play the long game, make her grateful to Bradley so they did really become mates? She thought about the States, living in New York. If this was the bait it was a smart choice.

She poured boiling water into the coffee mugs. 'Milk?'

'Yeah, cheers, just a dash.'

She milked the coffees and handed him one.

He gave her a warm smile. 'Thanks.'

She returned to the sofa, settled herself in one corner. 'Okay, say I buy all this – which I'm not saying I do – where's that leave you?'

Bradley took a sip of the coffee. 'I'm thinking of putting my papers in. You've said it yourself, I'm a crap cop. Maybe I'll go off and do some travelling myself. I got cousins in Australia, I wouldn't mind seeing that part of the world. After that, who knows?'

Kaz watched him as he prowled the room with the coffee mug in his hand. If this was all an act he'd suddenly become very good at it. She found herself looking at him more closely, observing with the artist's eye. He was tall and rangy with a nervous energy, the type of bloke who was never going to get fat. And he was used to women fancying him, there was a cock-sure look in his eye, an expectation that his overtures would be reciprocated. But at the same time he was totally different to the men she'd encountered in her life before. They'd simply scared or revolted her, beginning with her own father.

Bradley was a new experience, but what was it about him? If you set aside the fact he was a cop, being around him was never awkward or uncomfortable. It felt a bit like being with Joey, except there was something else, a physical tension in the pit of her stomach, a pleasant lassitude. Kaz realized with a jolt that it was sexual, a definite sexual buzz. Bradley gave off a whiff of some kind of sexual pheromone and it hit her on a purely physical level. She found herself imagining what it would be like to have sex with him. It wasn't anything to do with passion or the painful longing she had just to be close to Helen. This was happening on a completely separate plane.

It had never occurred to Kaz that sexual attraction could be such a simple animal thing. All her sexual encounters with men had been freighted with coercion and violence. But she didn't find Bradley in the least bit frightening, nor did she like him particularly. If anything she thought he was soft in the head. The whole thing was a complete conundrum.

He was aware of her watching him and he turned, gave her a nervous smile. 'So what d'you reckon? Want me to go and see Mike tomorrow, see if I can make this thing happen?'

Kaz folded her arms. The prospect of going to the States flashed through her brain, but what if it was all a con? Well, there was only one way to find out. She shrugged with as much nonchalance as she could muster.

'Yeah. You could give it a go.'

55

Sean Phelps and Neville Moore walked out of Basildon Police Station shortly after eight o'clock the next morning. Four officers from Sussex Police had taken turns to try and run Sean into the ground with a marathon interrogation session, but he'd remained calm and polite, enjoying the fact that for once he was telling the truth. Neville kept insisting on regular breaks and at the end of it all they came out looking far better than the frazzled and frustrated cops.

Sean took in a lungful of morning air, summer had faded and there was a decided autumnal chill. He clapped his hands together, the custody sergeant had kitted him out with an old tracksuit to put over his pyjamas.

He smiled at Neville. 'Fancy a spot of breakfast before you get off?'

Neville rubbed his fingers over the stubble on his jaw. He was not a man who liked to be grubby. 'Thanks, but I need to call the office and my wife.'

Sean nodded. Neville Moore was always professional to a T, but he didn't do chummy.

'Wives, yeah,' he sighed. 'Well mine thinks I tried to off her boyfriend. What the fuck am I gonna do about that?'

Neville fixed him with a direct look. 'Take my advice Sean: do nothing. The police aren't finished with this yet, not by a long chalk.'

Sean huffed impatiently. 'I know, but where's that leave me, eh? I get out the nick, find she's been lying to me for years. Okay, we have a bit of a ruck about it. I clumped her, I'll admit that. But she's my wife, I'd never do her any real harm. I gotta make this right with her Neville.'

Neville took out a linen handkerchief and wiped his face, it had been a long night, he wanted to wrap this up, get in his car and drive back to London. 'We don't even know where she is.'

'Oh I can take a guess.'

'I'd wait for her to come home if I were you.'

Sean gave him a speculative glance. 'Look, you was brilliant, done the business as always. But do me one last favour before you go.'

Neville laughed, shook his head. 'All right – as long as I can bill you for it!'

'You know me. I know how to be grateful. All I need now is for you to get on the blower to your office, find out my cousin's new address.'

'Joey? He lives in Southwark near the Tate Modern.'

'Not Joey. Karen's got herself a new place apparently.'

'And you think that's where Glynis'll be?'

'Good chance.'

Neville sucked in a long breath through his teeth. Strictly speaking he should refuse, Karen wasn't even his client. But saying no to Sean Phelps would put him in an awkward position. He was fairly convinced that Sean was telling the truth when he said he hadn't shot Dave Harper. They could all do stony-faced but he'd dealt with enough serious criminals to read the telltale body language. Sean wanted to sort things out with his wife, he could sympathize with that. Moreover, sympathizing with Sean was the more lucrative option, gangsters like him expected to pay over the odds for a deluxe service and that's what kept the firm afloat in the face of massive cutbacks in the government's legal aid budget. As to the domestic abuse, Neville found it personally distasteful, but that was part of the culture with people like the Phelpses and Glynis knew that as well as anyone.

Having taken a rapid inventory of the pros and cons, Neville sighed.

'Okay, I'll get the address. Go and talk to her by all means.' He raised an admonitory finger. 'But that's it – no rough stuff, right? Because you give this lot the least excuse, they'll revoke your licence and you're back inside.'

Sean opened his palms. 'Swear to God. She's my wife. I love her.'

Neville wondered what love meant to a man like Sean Phelps. He didn't think there'd be much kindness involved. But he still took out his mobile, rang the office and asked for Helen Warner's PA.

56

Kaz stirred scrambled eggs round one of her borrowed pans, she'd just about got the measure of the ceramic hob. The eggs set but remained light and fluffy, she felt pleased with her efforts as she spooned them on to two pieces of buttered toast. After Bradley had left she'd lain awake for some hours juggling hopes and possibilities. Part of her wanted to believe in his sincerity, but experience told her that it was probably all bollocks and she'd be a fool to even let herself dream.

Nevertheless his offer and the vista it opened up had set her thinking: if there was a real chance to walk away, would she take it? Since Helen had dumped her flat she'd been in a spin most of the time. Angry and resentful she'd turned to Joey; at least he wanted her. But she knew in her heart that he too was selling her a fairy story. All this talk about using the Net and eventually turning the firm legit: Joey was a drug dealer, that's what he was good at. She'd seen him at the cannabis factory and the lab, he enjoyed it. He was smarter, richer maybe, but it was still the old man's world and denial had always been the name of the game. Every villain Kaz'd ever met called himself a businessman; it was just part of the con.

If she'd learnt anything in the last six years, it was that she liked waking up every morning clean and sober. And she liked art. Feeling the texture of cartridge paper as her pencil skated across it, the smell of paint, mixing blue and yellow to create green – these were Helen's gifts to her. With Helen she'd also discovered what it was like to be totally honest with someone. It had given her such a feeling of relief when she'd told Helen the truth about Southend. But where did that leave her now? Caught between two worlds.

Suddenly Bradley's mad plan seemed very attractive.

Glynis was sitting up in bed sipping a mug of tea. She didn't look that good, but on the other hand she didn't look half dead and desperate any more. Kaz settled the plate of scrambled egg and toast in her lap.

'There you go. Want you to eat at least half.'

Glynis smiled, her lip quivered. She reached out for Kaz's hand. 'I meant to say before ... y'know I'm really ... really grateful for all this.'

'You did say before, now eat up before it gets cold.'

'I been thinking about burying Dave. I'd like him to have a nice send-off.'

'Could be a while before they release the body.'

Glynis took a tentative mouthful of egg. Kaz sat down on the side of the bed and started on her own plate. Glynis winced as she tried to chew. She put down the fork.

'I was only a kid when I got with Sean. I thought he was great, such a man's man. He'd've thought Dave was a right pussy. He asked me if I really loved him.'

'What – Sean asked you?'

'Yeah. We had quite a ruck about it. So I told him Dave was the love of my life.'

'Was he?'

Glynis leant back against her pillow. 'Nah, he was a lovely bloke. Kind. Being with him was easier. But I always went for the bad boys.' A wistful look crept into her eyes. 'Sean and your dad, they was always exciting to be around. You was guaranteed to have a laugh.'

Kaz gave her a sceptical look. 'Guaranteed a shedload of grief too.'

Glynis gazed out of the window, lost in memory somewhere. The side of her face was one huge mottled bruise, red, violet and yellow. The colours were vibrant, Kaz imagined painting her. Glynis looked down at her plate and sighed.

Kaz was scraping the plates and loading the dishwasher when she heard a soft tap at the front door. She checked her watch: it was nearly ten thirty. Bradley had promised to return as soon as he'd spoken to Mike Dawson, but Kaz hadn't really expected that to be before midday. And she wished he'd use the bloody entryphone. Still, she felt a secret surge of excitement as she went to answer the door. Had Mike agreed to help her? Was there really a chance she could be going to the States?

She didn't want to open herself up too much to Bradley so she was concentrating on playing it cool as she unhooked the chain. Without warning the door flew back in her face, the hinges cracking away from the frame under the impact of a heavy boot. It knocked her sideways, she had to reach for the wall to stop herself falling. As she scrabbled to retain her footing Sean Phelps filled the doorway. He'd showered and shaved, black shirt, black leather jacket and he had Tolya at his back. He beamed, grabbing her arm to steady her.

'Careful little cousin. You'll do yourself a mischief.'

Kaz wrenched herself free, anger masking her fear. 'What the fuck you playing at? Look what you done to my bloody door!'

'Sorry sweetheart. I know it's a bit over the top. But I had this odd feeling you might not be that pleased to see me. Tell me I'm wrong.'

'Wrong don't even begin to sum you up Sean. You was wrong the day you was born.'

He tipped back his head and laughed, his teeth sharp and jagged, like a small rodent. 'See? This is what I like about her Tol – more balls than any bloke.'

Tolya gave him a vague smile.

Sean sighed and turned to Kaz. 'I don't think he understands half what I say.'

'What d'you want Sean?' Kaz glared at him. She needed a way out. But Tolya was blocking her escape. ''Cause I'm expecting Joey.'

'Yeah? That why you're half dressed?' He ran his gaze down over her body. 'I'm not saying you don't look appealing . . .'

Kaz took a deep breath, both to calm herself and to create the impression she was unconcerned. 'I was just getting dressed.'

She turned on her heel and stalked off down the hall.

Sean had an amused smile playing around his lips. He gave Tolya a nod and they followed Kaz into the living room.

Sean glanced around appreciatively. 'Nice gaff. I presume I'm paying for this.'

'Joey paid for it.'

Sean grinned. 'That's what I mean. Out the firm – *my* firm.'

Kaz folded her arms. In pyjama bottoms and a thin T-shirt she felt next to naked, but she fixed him with a hard stare. 'What d'you want? 'Cause Joey'll be here any minute. When he sees your boot print in that door, he's not gonna be happy.'

It was a lie. She'd already phoned Joey a couple of times and he wasn't picking up, shacked up with some girl she'd presumed.

Sean gave her a contemptuous smile. 'You reckon?' He took

a deep breath and hollered: 'Glynis! Come out here now! Don't make me fucking come and drag you.'

Kaz's eyes darted around the room, trying to locate her phone. It was on the kitchen worktop, close to the kettle. She had to find a way of getting hold of it without being seen. But although Sean had turned his head towards the hall, Tolya's gaze remained firmly fixed on her.

Glynis appeared in the doorway. She was clutching her broken arm in its sling and shaking. Her eyes were downcast, she couldn't meet Sean's gaze. He didn't seem angry, more resigned. He stared at her. Then Kaz noticed him swallow hard. The muscles in his jaw flexed as he forced down any emotion.

'Right, first up, we need to get a few things clear. I didn't kill Dave.'

Glynis was crying, but she didn't utter a sound. The tears merely coursed down her bruised cheeks.

Sean took a step towards his wife. 'I made you a promise Glyn. Remember? You come home, we get back to normal and I'll let it go. That's what I said and that's what I done.'

Glynis raised her head, met his eye finally. 'You got someone else though, din't you? Got someone else to do it.'

Sean slapped the palm of his hand on the kitchen worktop. 'No I bloody didn't! You and the old bill, you all seem to think I'm a fucking fool.'

Glynis glared back at him, her eyes brimming with tears, her body shaking; Kaz couldn't tell if it was fear or rage.

Her voice erupted in a hoarse scream. 'Who done it then Sean? Who done it? Everyone liked Dave. He din't have a fucking enemy in the world!'

For an instant Kaz thought Sean was going to hit her. But he rammed his hands in his jeans pockets and turned away.

Kaz moved across the room, put an arm round Glynis and shepherded her to the sofa. They both sat down.

Sean paced the room. His face was flushed, he wiped beads of sweat from his forehead with the palm of his hand.

Kaz eyed her phone on the worktop by the kettle. She stood up, feigned a sigh. 'Well, I think maybe we could all do with a cup of tea.'

Sean turned on her, two strides across the room and he was looming over her. 'I din't come here to drink fucking tea. I come for some answers. And you're gonna give 'em me little cousin.'

He was right in her face, so close she could smell his sour breath, but Kaz returned his gaze fiercely. 'Answers to what? I don't know who killed Dave.'

'You must think I was born yesterday.' Sean thrust his jaw forward. 'First you try grassing me up to the old bill, when that din't work, you come up with a better plan, din't you?'

Kaz wanted to step away, put as much distance between them as possible, but she knew standing her ground was vital. She folded her arms. 'Now you're being ridiculous.'

'Am I?' He shot a glance over at Glynis on the sofa. 'Been looking after you well has she Glyn? 'Course she has. Bit of a change of heart though innit? Her and Ellie, you think how they treated you over the years. All this nicey-nicey, it's just a cover-up.'

Kaz could see Glynis out of the corner of her eye, frail and teary-eyed. But she continued to eyeball Sean. 'He's talking rubbish Glynis. I spent six years inside, before that I was out of my box on all sorts. You and me, we hardly knew each other. As for me mum, she's a right old cow and I'm the first to admit it.'

Glynis sniffed, wiped her nose on the sleeve of her cardigan.

She wasn't looking at any of them, she was retreating into herself, battening down the hatches.

Sean glanced at his wife impatiently. 'Well, you can think what you like.' His gaze switched back to Kaz. 'I ain't leaving here 'til I got the truth.'

Kaz fixed him with a steely glare. 'I don't know who killed Dave. That's the truth. So now you can fuck off out of here.'

The swingeing blow socked into Kaz's left cheek and sent her head ricocheting sideways. Sean grabbed her by the shoulders and flung her against the wall. It knocked the wind out of her, her mouth gaped as she gasped for breath.

He stood back with a satisfied smirk. 'Right, now I got your full attention let's take a look at the facts, shall we? Someone here is trying to fit me up. Now who could that be, eh? Joey, he plays games. Bit of a psycho really our Joey. But my little cousin here, she's the brains of the outfit, got the brains and balls for both. So she decides to elbow me out and take over the firm. Getting warm, am I?'

Kaz's head was spinning, her knees felt like jelly, her recently sprained ankle was making its presence felt. She concentrated on getting enough air in and out of her lungs, but she fixed her gaze on Sean. Looking away would signal that she was beaten.

He gave her a quizzical smile. 'Who did you get to do it then, eh?' He cocked his head in Tolya's direction. 'One of this lot? Some Ruskie ex-army? There's plenty of them about. Shoot anyone for a blow-job. That how you fixed it little cousin? Waggled your cute little tail? You're good at that.'

Kaz used all the muscles in her core to lift her body up to its full height, then concentrated on bringing as much disdain into her voice as she could manage. 'Y'know Sean, you spent far too long in the nick. 'Cause you really have lost the plot.'

Sean gave a dry laugh. 'Yeah? Could say the same about you darling.'

Tolya hadn't moved since he walked into the room. He stood stock-still, his muscular forearms neatly folded. He had followed the exchange with his eyes, though it was hard to tell how much he actually understood.

Sean turned to him and pointed at Glynis. 'Take her and put her in the car.'

Tolya nodded but didn't move. Sean looked at him, jabbed a finger in Glynis's direction. 'Her and you' – he pointed towards the door – 'in the car. Wait for me. Got it?'

Tolya went over to the sofa, helped Glynis up. She didn't object or resist, but he was gentle. He led her towards the door, then glanced at Sean. 'I come back.'

Sean shook his head. 'No. No need. Me and my cousin are gonna have a little chat.'

Glynis's expression was blank. She didn't look at Sean or Kaz as Tolya led her out. The broken door creaked on its hinges as Tolya pulled it to behind them.

Sean laughed. 'Fucking Russians, you never know if they can understand you or not. You found that?'

Kaz edged away from him, placing the kitchen breakfast bar between them. 'I've only ever met two: him and his brother.'

'Y'know it's a real pity you decided to go down this road Kaz.' Sean sighed wearily. ''Cause I'd've seen you all right. I believe in family, sticking together. Your dad took care of Glynis and I'd've taken care of you and your mum.'

'I can take care of myself.'

'You think you can, that's what's got you in this mess.' His eyes were skimming over her body, taking in all the curves and contours. 'Pretty girl like you, you should be making the most of your assets. It's a hard world, particularly in our game.

You got to be a bloke to survive it, women simply ain't tough enough.'

He started to move round the breakfast bar towards her. She edged away.

'I didn't have Dave killed. And I'm not trying to take over the sodding business. Anyway, since Dad's stroke what it amounts to is what Joey's made of it.'

Sean huffed in disgust. 'That little psycho? You think the sun shines out of his arse, don't you? But you should watch out for him little cousin. He comes on like he's your best mate, but he don't give a fuck for no one.'

'You don't know him.'

'Oh don't I? When he was a kid, pissing himself every five minutes, your dad used to say "that boy has got a screw loose". And he was right.'

'And whose fault is that? None of us is exactly normal.'

'He's pulling your strings little cousin. You realize it was him told me that you'd tried to grass me up to the bill?'

'I don't believe you.'

'Believe what you like. He's a twisted little fucker, you're just too blind to see.'

She glared at him across the breakfast bar. His eyes were devouring her, it was clear what he had in mind. The thrill of the chase, the prospect of conquest, it was giving him a hard on.

He adopted a soft, wheedling tone. 'Come on Kaz, I don't wanna fight with you. You and me, we had some laughs din't we, back in the day?'

'No. You laughed, I didn't. Mostly I cried.'

Suddenly his face broke into an ugly grin. 'Naaah, you want it really. You always did. You bitches are all the same. Think you can stitch me up? I am gonna teach you a lesson you won't forget in a hurry.'

He lunged forward, made a grab for her arm, but Kaz was too quick for him. She threw herself sideways, tripped and skidded on her knees across the wooden floor.

He laughed, he was loving it. 'Wanna play games, do you?'

She did a quick roll on to one side and jumped to her feet. Her back was to the window, she thought about the balcony but it was a long drop. He took off his jacket, laid it neatly over the arm of the sofa. Then he unbuckled his belt. His eyes were glassy with lust. She decided to let him move in on her, then go for the balls.

As he stepped forward she made a grab for his groin, but the material of his jeans was too thick around the crotch, she couldn't get a firm grip. She only succeeded in exciting him more.

He gasped. 'Oh yeah, you're gonna get plenty of that.'

She pulled back her right fist, punched him hard in the stomach. Her knuckles cracked against a solid wall of muscle, a daily workout in the prison gym had given him abs most blokes would kill for.

He laughed, grasped her T-shirt by the neckline and ripped it right off. They both froze for a moment. He stared at her breasts, she was skinny, but still had an ace pair of tits on her. She covered them reflexively with her forearms, then realized that effectively immobilized her.

Sean was almost drooling, so she dropped her arms, let him lean in, his lips going down towards her left nipple. His tongue lolled, she felt it warm and wet on her skin, like being licked by a dog. Then she brought her right knee up sharp and hard under his jaw. He bit his own tongue and howled.

'Fucking bitch!'

He grabbed her by the shoulders, she struggled, kicked, he grappled her to the floor and pinned her down with his superior weight. He was red in the face, sweat dripping off him, but loving every minute. Kaz jerked and twisted with all her might, trying to throw him off, bite him. Her battered body was screaming with pain, but a fury was rising in her, the anger that had always been there at the brutality and injustice of it all. She screwed up her face and started to scream. 'Get off me you bastard! Get off!'

He put his left forearm across her windpipe, choking off her screams and her breath, then he used his right hand to reach down and pull off her pyjamas. She gasped for air, her legs were flailing, but she managed to free her right arm. As he unzipped his fly she jabbed him in the eye with the nail of her index finger.

He bellowed. 'Aawww, fucking hell!'

The moment his grip on her throat loosened, she shoved him hard and he fell back with one hand over his eye.

'What d'you do that for, you bitch!'

She wriggled from under him, sucking in air in short, hoarse gasps. She scrambled to her feet and made for the kitchen drawer. She pulled it open, grabbed the plastic bag.

Sean was on his feet behind her, his tone full of indignation. 'That hurt. You could've fucking blinded me!'

'This'll hurt even more.' She pulled the SIG 220 from the bag and pointed it straight at him.

He stared at her in disbelief, stark naked holding a gun. Then he laughed. 'Come on it was only a bit of rough and tumble. You used to like all that.' He eyed the gun speculatively. 'Anyway, you got the safety catch on.'

He stepped forward, held his hand out for the gun, like a father dealing with a naughty child. Remembering Joey's instructions Kaz quickly dropped the hammer with her thumb. Sean made a grab for the barrel, he got hold of the silencer, twisting it down, trying to wrest it from her grasp. As her wrist was wrenched sideways, she pulled the trigger.

The dull snap of the bullet being discharged took them both by surprise. Sean lurched backwards as it tore through the flesh of his thigh. He landed on his backside, clutching the side of his leg. His face was puce with shock and fury.

'Now look what you done, you stupid bitch!'

It was a flesh wound and there was blood, but the bullet had gone right through, missing arteries and bone. Kaz looked down in astonishment at the weapon in her hand. Sean grimaced in pain.

'Well don't just stand there, get a towel or something.'

Kaz blinked at him. She was in shock herself. Picking up a tea towel from the counter, she tossed it to him. A blood-soaked patch was forming on the side of his jeans, he wrapped the tea towel round it. Then he pulled his mobile from his pocket and glared at her.

'You have got to be the stupidest fucking bint on the planet.' He scrolled through the numbers with one hand, keeping the other pressed hard to the tea towel on his leg. 'You are going straight back to jail and for a nice long stretch.'

Kaz considered this. The gun going off had paralysed her momentarily. Now goosebumps were prickling up on her naked skin, her throat felt sore and bruised where he'd crushed her windpipe. She raised the gun and pointed it at his head. The range was less than two metres. Her hand felt surprisingly steady.

'No, I don't think so Sean. Not for a scumbag like you.'

She took a deep calming breath and squeezed the trigger.

57

Detective Chief Superintendent Turnbull chose a phone shop in Victoria Street. It was part of a large national chain and far enough away from the office to make it unlikely he'd bump into anyone. He was skimming through the pay-as-you go display when the assistant came over and asked if he needed any help. Turnbull gave the girl an appraising look, she was mixed oriental background, a south London accent. He smiled broadly, just the ally he needed.

'My daughter, she's fifteen. You think she can hold on to a phone? Lost two – one nicked, dropped another down the toilet.'

The shop assistant giggled. 'Yeah, stuff like that happens quite a lot.'

Turnbull warmed to his theme. 'I've told her, no more smart phones. Cheap and basic, until you can learn to look after it. Any suggestions?'

He stepped out of the shop ten minutes later with a small pink handset, untraceable SIM loaded and ten pounds credit. He paid cash. He scrolled the contacts list on his own BlackBerry until he came to Duncan Linton's number, keyed it into the new phone and hit call.

Linton ran his business from an elegant address in South Audley Street. A roomful of quants, a small management team – he liked to keep a tight rein on everything himself. He was watching the BBC News channel on one of his five computer screens when the call came through on his mobile. He didn't know the number, but he recognized the voice even before Turnbull identified himself. Linton leant back in his chair.

'I'm watching the BBC news. The Commissioner's just announced the posthumous award of the Queen's Gallantry Medal to an Alex Marlow. Is that him?'

Turnbull was standing in a shop doorway. 'That's him. So now the clock's ticking.'

'You're ready to make your move?'

'More than ready. Don't worry Duncan, it'll work.'

Turnbull sounded confident. There had been a few private doubts but he'd reminded himself he was going nowhere in the Met, because there was nowhere to go. Senior officers were being axed. This was the smart move, this was about stepping up into a different league. Still he took a deep breath to calm himself. 'Make sure you sit firmly on Foxley's tail. We don't want him reneging on the deal. Remind him he's promised us the contract.'

He heard Linton laugh. 'He'll be fine Alan. I've got my eye on him.' His tone was worryingly casual.

Turnbull wondered if this were true. Linton had numerous deals on the go, if this went pear-shaped he wouldn't be the one to lose. Turnbull had to remind himself he was talking to a potential partner, an equal. Though who wouldn't be starstruck by Linton's wealth? The Learjet, the mansion in the Caribbean, it wasn't Turnbull's world.

He coughed to conceal the tension in his voice. 'This is a secure line, so I'll keep you posted. Let me know any developments your end.'

Linton chuckled again. 'I will. Good luck.'

Turnbull ended the call, slipped the phone in his inside jacket pocket. He glanced up and down the street. Buses, taxis, a taint of exhaust fumes and the bustle of the city in all its forms. Nothing had changed but to Turnbull it all seemed brighter, more vivid. He was going for gold and a surge of adrenalin was rushing through his veins. Years ago, when he was a young DC in the Flying Squad and they went out on a big bust, this is what it felt like. He smiled to himself, he'd made the right decision. Maybe there was something to be said for the God-awful school motto they'd had drummed into them: *Audentes fortuna iuvat*. Fortune favours the bold.

58

Kaz squatted on her haunches in the corner of the kitchen, naked and shivering. She felt like a small feral creature that had survived the predator's onslaught, but only just. The first bullet had merely grazed Sean above his right temple. He'd yelped, then as he'd tried to scramble to his feet Kaz had adjusted her aim. Her second shot went straight through the eye and he'd collapsed in a heap, stone dead.

Now a large puddle of blood was edging towards her bare foot. She stood up to avoid it, letting the gun clatter to the floor, turned and retched over the sink. A thin skein of saliva, laced with scrambled egg, dripped from her mouth. She wiped it away with the back of her hand and had to grasp the kitchen counter firmly to stop her legs from buckling under her.

Suddenly there was a noise in the hall. Kaz's heart lurched. The front door hinges creaked. Someone had come in. Kaz's first thought was Bradley. He'd finally turned up, too late to save her. Now she was most certainly going back to jail. But the prospect suddenly didn't seem so bad. Life inside was predictable. She wouldn't have to think any more, worry any more. She could give in, let the days and then the years simply wash over her. A sense of relief coursed through her sore, battered body and oblivious to the fact she was totally naked, she turned to face him.

But the man who appeared framed in the hall doorway was

larger and squarer. Tolya stood, hands on hips, wearing a big grin. He glanced at the corpse and nodded with approval.

'Dead?'

Kaz stared at him, completely thrown. Was he about to attack her? He simply smiled, then squatted down to take a closer look at Kaz's handiwork.

'Nice shot. I call Joey. You need take a shower, put clothes on.'

Kaz clutched the kitchen worktop for support. She knew she was in shock, still none of it made sense.

He stood up, gave her a reassuring look. 'It's okay. Go take shower. I call Joey.'

'I don't . . . understand . . .'

Tolya frowned as if it should be obvious. 'Joey, he say me keep eye on things 'til you kill him.'

'Kill him?'

'Kill him, kill Sean. Bam.' Tolya mimed the shot and grinned.

Kaz's brain was racing to catch up. Tolya's accent was hard enough to decipher. She shook her head. 'Joey? But . . . you were working for Sean?'

Tolya laughed. 'No no, Yevgeny and me, we work always for Joey. Joey say me to . . . to . . .'

He screwed up his face with frustration as he searched for the right word.

Kaz's mind was ricocheting between relief and anger. She clutched her arms round her naked torso protectively. 'What the fuck you trying to say? Joey told you to what . . . pretend to work for Sean?'

Tolya beamed and slapped his thigh. 'Yeah pretend! I pretend. I keep watch on you, wait 'til you kill him.'

As the truth sank in, Kaz's brain exploded. 'He could've fucking killed me and you stood by and watched!'

Tolya looked mortified. 'No no no! Sean, he beat women for his pleasure. He don't kill them.'

'He tried to rape me!'

Tolya nodded sagely. 'Joey say if he try rape you, you get mad enough then you kill him.'

Kaz swallowed hard as she absorbed this. Joey had engineered the whole thing? She couldn't quite believe it. Why? Why would he do such a thing to her, knowing how she felt about Sean? It was bonkers.

Tolya watched her, he couldn't help letting his eyes stray a bit over the contours of her naked body. He started grinning like an idiot, then he wagged his finger at her, as he supposed a concerned brother might.

'Go shower, get clothes. I call Joey. Don't worry. We clean this up.'

59

Bradley tracked Mike Dawson down to an office at the Slade only to discover he'd gone to an art history conference in Oxford. The departmental PA, a young African woman with an impenetrable accent, assumed Bradley was some kind of student and was less than helpful. Only when Bradley produced his warrant card and a tone of voice that promised trouble did she become marginally more compliant. He ended up exchanging texts with Mike and arranging to meet him in the early evening on his return from Oxford.

All of which left Bradley at a bit of a loose end. He sat in a coffee shop feeling like a kid bunking off school. Was he really going to chuck it all in as he'd boasted to Karen Phelps? On a sunny morning with a head free of booze his career prospects didn't look so bad. Maybe what he needed was a sabbatical? He'd never taken a gap year as a student, waste of time and money his dad had said. It was something rich kids did: help the poor for a couple of months then have an exotic holiday. Maybe he could persuade his bosses to give him some time-out now. He could travel, have time to think, reassess, pick up the job again later.

He started to muse on the places he might visit and somehow that led him to a fantasy of him and Karen in New York. What if they met in a cool bar in Tribeca? Two Brits, far away from home, untainted by past complications, falling easily into conversation, liking each other, fancying each other? If they met like that he was pretty sure he would make her laugh. It would be like some indie rom-com with a soundtrack by Coldplay. She would be damaged and difficult, fleeing the past, but his love would save her, redeem them both. They'd live happily ever after in a cool loft apartment in some transatlantic nirvana.

His phone buzzing and dancing on the tabletop dragged him back to reality. It was Nicci Armstrong.

'You really sick or just hung-over?'

Bradley smiled to himself, she didn't beat about the bush. 'Neither as it happens. I'm out and about, pursuing a line of inquiry.'

'Well if you're still pissed off with Ms Alice Ogilvy and the forces of corporate capitalism, get your arse back here because I could do with some help.'

This hooked Bradley's attention. 'Turnbull's agreed to go after them for money-laundering?'

He heard Nicci sigh and take a gulp of something, probably coffee. 'Not exactly. But we've had a small window of opportunity open up. You in or out?'

Bradley didn't think twice, the dream vaporized.

'I'll be there in twenty minutes.'

Nicci put the phone down and drained her coffee mug. Caffeine was her drug of choice, she drank it all day, usually until it gave her palpitations. The morning meeting with Turnbull had been predictable enough. She and Bill Mayhew had hung around for half an hour outside his office to be granted a ten-minute slot.

Bill had presented the case. The connection they'd dug up between Alice Ogilvy and Joey Phelps suggested that Mainwaring Grant, Ogilvy's firm, might be involved in some serious money-laundering. Bill wanted a complete shakedown: a seizure of files, computers, the interrogation of staff. He gave Turnbull his usual diffident smile.

'We line up the senior partners, put their nuts in a vice, I think that'll give us the track we need back to Joey. Probably a few others as well.'

Turnbull seemed preoccupied. While Mayhew talked he checked and rechecked his phone, he couldn't sit still. When the DCI had finished he placed the BlackBerry carefully on the desk in front of him and considered the proposition for all of ten seconds. 'A firm of City accountants, Bill – are you serious? How many man-hours do you think that'll take?'

Mayhew pondered. 'Well it depends what we—'

'Too many, that's how many. We're not forensic accountants. It could take months and we'd still come up with bugger-all.'

This was much the response that Mayhew had expected. A small smile played around his lips as he lobbed in the grenade. 'Nic's had a word with an old mate at the SFO. The firm's already on their radar, it specializes in helping clients place funds in tax havens. As soon as we mentioned Joey and the organized crime connection their ears pricked up.'

Turnbull cast a baleful eye in Nicci's direction. He might've guessed it was her stirring this particular pot.

She gave him her best smile. 'According to my contact, boss, money-laundering would be an easy score for them. As long as we're talking over a million, which we probably are, then the SFO are within their remit. They'd provide us with their expertise and we'd—'

Turnbull held up his hand. 'No. No no no! I am not about to take part in some bloody SFO-sponsored circus. No bloody way.'

Nicci and Mayhew exchanged glances. It didn't really surprise them that Turnbull was getting so hot under the collar. Letting the Serious Fraud Office steal his thunder, definitely not Turnbull's style. Still, he did seem unusually wound up.

Turnbull huffed, got to his feet, shoved his hands in his pockets. Then he reined himself in, turned to Mayhew and sighed. 'What is the matter with you Bill? Why are you trying to complicate the issue? Joey Phelps is a murderer, a cop killer, a two-bit thug. He's our target, not some posh firm of accountants who will most certainly have the sense not to keep any kind of incriminating evidence in their files or databases.'

Mayhew raised his palm in a placatory gesture. 'We just thought that getting some leverage into Phelps's drug dealing operation—'

Turnbull's index finger zeroed in on Mayhew. 'I don't want him for drug dealing, I want him for murder. Clear?' He glanced at Nicci. 'Alex Marlow's murder, that's our priority surely?'

Nicci squirmed, Turnbull had an uncanny knack of putting his finger on the sorest spot. Mayhew was nodding.

Turnbull checked his watch, he seemed edgy. He looked at Mayhew. 'Now . . . unless there's anything else?'

Mayhew and Nicci both rose to their feet. He held the door open for her. They headed off down the corridor in silence.

Mayhew stopped at the vending machine, scooped a handful of change from his trouser pocket, fed several coins into the machine and selected a Mars Duo. Nicci gave him a censorious glance.

'Does that really go with statins?'

He cracked open the packaging and sank his teeth deep into the bar. With a mouth full of melting chocolate he was barely audible. 'Turnbull gets to bully me 'cause he's the gaffer . . . wife gets to bully me 'cause she's the wife.' He swallowed and took another bite. 'But you Nic, you don't get to bully me.'

'Fair enough. So what now?'

Mayhew moved on to the second bar, chewing it slowly like a ruminant. He folded the wrapper neatly and tossed it in the bin, then he hauled the waistband of his trousers back over his paunch.

'Well . . .' His tongue scooted across his front teeth collecting up the last remnants of chocolate. 'I thought he'd say that, but we had to ask. Now we do what we've always done. We busk it.'

Nicci sighed. 'Ogilvy doesn't strike me as a woman who's that easily frightened. But I'll do my best.'

'Take Bradley with you. You were complaining about him ranting before, but sometimes playing the heavy does work. We can't follow through, so may as well go for broke.'

60

Kaz stood under the shower for what felt like an eternity. She could hear coming and going, interior doors banging, an electric drill. But she let the water cascade over her head and drown it all out. Her limbs were a dead weight, she barely managed to hold herself up. As the hot water reddened her skin the welts and bruises from her two encounters with Sean all seemed to blend into a single battered body. If there was any part of her mind that felt guilty about what she'd done she couldn't locate it. In the seconds after she'd pulled the trigger elation had engulfed her, then nausea, then shock. Now her entire system felt drained.

Through the moisture-fogged shower screen she saw the bathroom door open and a figure appear. She rubbed her hand across the glass to clear it. But before she could see she heard the familiar voice.

'Struth babes, it's like a fucking sauna in here.'

She peered through the glass at Joey. He grinned back at her.

'Gimme a minute, I'm getting out.'

Joey retreated to the bedroom. Kaz stepped from the shower and enveloped herself in a bath towel. She found him sitting on the bed checking messages on his phone. He looked up and smiled. She didn't know where to begin.

'Where's Glynis?'

'I got Ash to take her back to my place.'

'Does she know?'

He gave her a look of wide-eyed innocence. 'Know what?'

This exasperated Kaz, she wasn't in the mood for twenty questions. 'About Sean. About me killing fucking Sean. That's what.'

A mischievous glint crept into Joey's eye. 'Okay, let's talk about that. Glynis don't know and she don't need to know. In fact no one does, 'cause Sean ain't dead.'

Kaz screwed up her face, she wanted to scream. Frustration, anger, she wasn't sure which was the overriding emotion. Joey stood up, slipped his phone in his jeans pocket. He towered over her. He put his finger under her chin, turned it towards him and fixed her with a laser-eyed stare.

'Listen to me carefully babes, 'cause this is important. Sean ain't dead. Cops are after him for Dave's murder. He didn't fancy the prospect of another twenty years in jail, so he done a runner.' Joey checked his watch. 'Small private plane's taking off from North Weald airfield . . . in fact about now. Cops'll find a couple of mechanics who work down there and saw a bloke get on it, who looks a lot like Sean. Couple weeks' time someone'll see him in a bar on the Costa. Once the rumour mill gets going, there'll be sightings all over. Some lucky bastard cop might even get a trip to Spain to check 'em out.'

Joey beamed and held out his palms like a magician who'd just pulled an ace from the pack and was waiting for the applause.

Kaz stared at him. 'It ain't a fucking game Joey.'

He tipped back his head and laughed. 'Oh it is babes and the only one worth playing.'

She continued to hold his gaze. His look was hard, but behind the eyes was a blankness, an emotional void. Sean was right and in her heart she'd always known it, Joey didn't give a fuck for anyone and that included her. He only ever did things his way. She took a step away from him and sat down on the bed. Her whole body felt dislocated, her head was spinning. 'Can I ask you a question and get a straight answer?'

Joey smiled. 'You always get a straight answer from me babes, I ain't a liar.'

'Who told Sean I was trying to grass him up to the old bill?'

Joey looked mystified. 'How should I know? You said yourself them cops was playing all sorts of games—'

With a surge of energy that surprised even her, Kaz leapt to her feet. Blind fury engulfed her. She thumped his chest with the flat of her hand as she screamed in his face.

'Tell me the fucking truth Joey! You told him, din't you! You told him! You told him so he'd come after me!'

Joey's face remained impassive, neither hostile nor upset. If anything he looked curious. Then he gently gathered her into his arms. She struggled to push him away, but he was insistent. The hug became firmer and she lacked the strength to resist. She let her body go limp and he gently rocked her.

'Don't get upset babes, don't get upset. I'm gonna sort all this out, I promise.'

He pushed her damp hair back from her forehead and gently kissed it. She could feel his warmth and his strength but it was no longer reassuring. Her body might be powerless to resist him, but her mind was focusing and moving into survival mode.

There was a tap on the bedroom door, it opened a crack and Yevgeny stuck his head round.

'We done now boss. Me and Tolya, we go.'

Joey gave him a nod. 'Door fixed too?'

'Everything fixed.'

'What about the neighbours?'

Yevgeny shrugged. 'No one home.'

'Cheers mate.' Joey held Kaz at arm's length, as you would a child, and he smiled. 'All cleaned up. So that means we can go make a nice cup of tea. I reckon you've earned it.'

Kaz looked up at him, she found it hard to even focus on his face. 'Yeah but what they done with the body?'

'They'll get rid of it. Burn it most like. You don't have to worry about none of it. Sean's gone. You got the job done. Now how about that cuppa?'

61

Mainwaring Grant's offices were smart bordering on opulent. The company logo on the wall behind the reception desk was etched in gold. The building was Victorian but had been carefully refurbished to retain, in estate agent's speak, many attractive original features. Bradley stared up at the ornate ceiling as Nicci Armstrong announced their arrival to the sleek receptionist. There was a large oil painting on one wall of a pink-cheeked shepherdess in a gauzy outfit petting a gambolling lamb.

Nicci turned to Bradley, her eyes scoping the room. 'Looks like they do a lot of business with the Middle East.'

Bradley nodded, keeping his voice low. 'Loads of front, remains to be seen how much backbone.'

Alice Ogilvy came to greet them herself and she didn't keep them waiting. She led them down a carpeted corridor hung with English pastoral scenes to a spacious conference room. At one end of a vast walnut table two men were already seated. They got up as Armstrong and Bradley entered the room. Ogilvy pointed to the younger man first, he was fresh-faced with a fashionably tight suit and a Justin Bieber fringe.

'My colleague Anthony Hobbart.'

Hobbart offered a damp handshake. Armstrong felt his nervousness and his youth. She couldn't quite figure why Ogilvy had got him there. Maybe he was just ballast.

Ogilvy moved on to the older man, ginger and balding with a vaguely foxy air. 'And Nigel Puricelli, our legal adviser.'

Puricelli shook hands firmly and met both Armstrong and Bradley's eye with a sardonic gaze. They all sat down.

Ogilvy smiled. 'Coffee? Tea? We have an excellent selection of herbal infusions.'

Armstrong returned the smile. 'We're fine.'

The room settled into silence. Nicci knew they'd only get one bite of the cherry and she was determined not to rush it.

Finally Puricelli pursed his lips and took charge. 'So how can we help you Sergeant?'

Nicci took a file from her bag. 'As Ms Ogilvy knows we're interested in any dealings your firm may have had with Joey Phelps.'

Puricelli nodded slowly. 'And this . . . Joey Phelps is currently under investigation for what particular crime?'

Nicci cocked her head. 'That I'm not at liberty to discuss, Mr Puricelli. But I do want to make it clear we understand that he probably deceived you. He presents himself to the world as a businessman and most certainly lies about his criminal enterprises.'

As Puricelli absorbed this, he drew in several ostentatious breaths then he glanced at Alice Ogilvy. She was still but tense and keeping a wary eye on Bradley. She gave him a thin smile and launched her opening salvo.

'We had absolutely no knowledge that Mr Phelps was involved or indeed suspected of involvement in drug dealing. Mainwaring Grant has an international reputation for probity, which we take extremely seriously.'

Bradley raised his eyebrows but left it to Nicci to respond.

She inclined her head politely. 'We accept that. We're merely seeking information.'

Puricelli nodded. 'What sort of information?'

Ogilvy shot him a look. She seemed calm but still anxious to reinforce her point. 'I should also add that although we did a small amount of work for Mr Phelps he is no longer a client. The . . . mix-up with the credit card was not acceptable practice and we terminated our relationship.'

This amused Bradley. He wondered how Joey had felt about that given his own method for terminating business relationships. He noticed that Alice Ogilvy was looking pale. Perhaps she'd bitten off more than she could chew, found herself in cahoots with a gangster and got frightened. He wanted to sympathize with her, but maybe he was being naive. Would a woman with her experience really not have known what Joey Phelps was as soon as she met him?

Alice Ogilvy turned to the young man beside her and her voice acquired a sharper edge. 'It was Anthony who actually dealt with Mr Phelps. I had very little personal involvement. So perhaps he can answer some of your questions.'

All eyes turned to the unfortunate Anthony, whose neck started to redden. Armstrong and Bradley exchanged looks, they were being offered a sacrificial lamb, young and fluffy, much like the counterpart that hung in the reception area.

Bradley was almost enjoying himself, perhaps being a cop wasn't so bad after all. He eyeballed Anthony, put on his Rottweiler face. 'How did you first meet Joey Phelps, Anthony?'

Anthony gulped, gave Ogilvy a nervous look. 'Well . . . I've sort of known him for years. We was in the same class at school.'

Bradley nodded. They'd hit pay dirt, a direct line back to Joey. 'And school was where?'

'Basildon.'

'You still live there?'

Anthony compressed his lips and nodded.

'See much of Joey socially?'

The young man shifted in his seat, his tone was dismissive. 'Joey doesn't live in Basildon any more.'

They were about the same age, but Bradley felt he had the edge. He was enjoying getting under Anthony's skin. He smiled. 'But still your old schoolmate came to you for help? Why was that?'

Anthony shot a questioning glance at Puricelli. 'I don't know.'

Puricelli merely pursed his lips.

Anthony ploughed on. 'He just wanted some tax advice is all.'

Bradley chuckled. 'How to avoid tax on his next drug deal?'

Anthony shook his head. 'Just how to fill in a few forms.'

Puricelli quietly monitored the exchange. He read the room like a poker player. Bradley was a bit of a show-off, it was Armstrong he needed to convince to seal the deal. He put his finger on a small plastic folder and slid it across the desk in Nicci's direction.

'Anthony and I have had a chat, done some trawling through the files. And we've come up with something that seems innocent enough, but which in the light of your suspicions may prove useful.'

Nicci opened the folder, glanced at the first page and frowned.

'Marko . . .' – she struggled to pronounce the name – '. . . Dimitrenko? A Ukrainian dissident?'

Puricelli nodded. 'Dr Dimitrenko and his wife Leysa originally came to the UK seeking political asylum. But they had some problems with that and eventually Dr Dimitrenko obtained sponsorship as a skilled worker from a company belonging to Mr Phelps.'

Resenting the change of direction, Bradley fixed Puricelli with a hard stare. 'I've got a feeling, Mr Puricelli, that you think if you throw the dog a bone he'll stop sniffing around. But my present inclination is to take Anthony here down the nick and get him to tell us everything he knows about his old pal.'

Anthony looked like he was about to cry, his chin quivered. He couldn't contain himself. 'He's not my pal okay! I don't even know why you got me here.' He glared at Ogilvy. 'I've just done my job. I haven't done anything wrong.'

Ogilvy reached over and put her hand on Anthony's. 'It's okay Anthony. I'm sure that what the officers want most is our help and cooperation in this matter.'

Anthony wiped his face with the back of his hand.

Nicci looked up from the file, which she'd quickly skimmed. 'Indeed we do. So, Marko Dimitrenko?' She referred to the file. 'Doctor as in academic . . . from a family of dissidents . . . what's useful about this for us?'

Puricelli smirked. Nicci had the impression he enjoyed having the upper hand. 'You need to read to the end of the file Sergeant. Dr Dimitrenko taught at Lviv University. He was the equivalent of a senior lecturer in the Faculty of Chemistry. He also did research for pharmaceutical companies.'

Realization dawned on Nicci's face. 'A research chemist?'

Puricelli smiled, the hook was in. He opened his palms. 'Alice believed that Phelps was a legitimate businessman. She had no reason to wonder why he might employ a research chemist as a project consultant. But if he is indeed involved in the supply of illegal drugs, that casts the matter in a rather different light, doesn't it?'

Nicci knew the bone she'd been offered was large and juicy. It would certainly do for now. She nodded. 'Well . . . we'd need to interview Dr Dimitrenko.'

Puricelli smiled. 'All the details you need to find him are in there.' He hesitated. 'And really . . . that is all we have that could be of the least use. Mainwaring Grant does most of its business internationally. Mr Phelps is not the sort of client we would normally accept. Unfortunately somehow he . . . slipped in under the radar.'

Nicci glanced at Anthony, who was rubbing one sweaty palm with the other. Then she got up and fixed Puricelli with a polite smile.

'We'll be in touch Mr Puricelli.'

As Bradley and Armstrong stepped out on to Clerkenwell Road she pulled out her phone.

Bradley puffed his cheeks. 'We lean on Anthony hard enough we could bust their scam wide open.'

Nicci was scrolling through her address book. 'Nice thought. But even supposing Turnbull would let us, they'll just dump him like a ton of bricks. All we'll get is Anthony the bad apple and squeaky-clean senior management who knew nothing. That's why they were dangling him under our nose.'

Nicci found the number she was looking for and clicked on it. Her call was answered on the second ring.

'Cheryl, hi. It's Nicci Armstrong. I've got a name – Marko Dimitrenko – and an address in Danbury. Chances are it's where Joey Phelps has set up his drugs lab. Yeah, grab a pen, I'll hold on.'

62

Kaz sat on the sofa. Joey handed her a mug of tea.

'I put a couple of sugars in, 'cause that helps when you've
had a bit of shock.'

She didn't know what had shocked her more, shooting her
cousin or discovering that her own brother had set her up to
do it. She accepted the mug without comment.

Since entering the room she'd hardly been able to take her
eyes off the solid oak flooring. It looked absolutely pristine.
There was no sign of the puddle of blood that had surrounded
Sean's head. Kaz scrutinized it inch by inch. There didn't appear
to be a stain, but maybe there was the slightest discolouration.
Joey watched her. He squatted down beside her, patted her
thigh.

'What's done is done. It don't do to dwell on it babes.'

'What did they use to clean the floor? Bleach?'

Joey looked across at the kitchen area. 'I dunno.'

'All the forensics they got nowadays, they can find blood
and DNA and stuff on a fucking pinhead.'

Joey pondered. 'Okay, we'll have the whole thing up, re-
screeded, new floor laid. You moved in, but didn't like the colour.'

Kaz glanced at him, sun was flooding the room, she'd loved
the colour; like warm honey. It was one of the reasons that in
such a short time the place had become her haven.

'I don't know if I can live here any more.'

Joey folded his arms. 'Then we'll find you somewhere else. Ain't a problem. Meantime you can stay with me.'

He was in Mister Reasonable mode, Mister Loving Brother. But Kaz wasn't fooled by it any more. She glared at him. 'Fucking hell Joey, he could've killed me.'

Joey shook his head. 'Nah, I put Tolya in there to keep an eye on things.'

Kaz turned away from him; she could feel the tears welling up. She tried to swallow them down, but failed.

'I don't get it y'know. Why would you do this to me? You hate me that much?'

A pained expression came in to his eyes. 'Don't talk daft, course I don't.' He took a deep breath, his brow puckered. He gazed at her, the hard, laser-eyed stare. 'Look, you said you wanted to sort Sean out yourself. You said it, din't you? I'd've done it, or got Yev to, but you insisted. So . . . I figured after what he done to you as a kid you deserved the chance.'

'I didn't want to kill him!'

Joey sighed. 'Oh get real babe. Grassing him up to the old bill was never gonna work.'

The tears were coursing down her cheeks now. 'It could've. Better than murder.'

Joey exhaled an impatient snort of air. 'Sean was a dinosaur. It was all "back in the day" with him. He'd've caused us trouble whether he was inside or out. He had to be taken out. Simple as. You just needed a bit of encouragement to get to that.'

She stared at him in disbelief. '*Encouragement?* That what you call it? You promised me the killing would stop.'

Joey flung his arms up in the air in exasperation and walked across to the window. 'I don't know why you keep harping on that. All animals kill – it's natural. Lions kill zebras, sharks taste blood they attack – you seen them nature documentaries. It's how the world works babe, and we're just animals like the rest.'

Kaz fixed him with a steady gaze. 'That's bollocks and you know it.'

Joey glanced across the room at her, he tilted his head to one side. Then a dreamy expression swam into his eyes. 'Yeah, but . . . when you pulled the trigger, when he went down, didn't that give you a rush? That power? To me, that's the best feeling in the world. There ain't nothing else that comes close.'

She stared at him. The fervour in his gaze was disturbing.

He crossed the room, knelt down beside her, took her hand. 'I wanted you to feel it babes. I wanted you to understand. Now we're on the same page, you and me. And you know why? 'Cause we're special.'

She wrenched her hand away. 'Special? Special fucking needs more like.'

'That's cool.' Joey laughed, got to his feet. 'Special needs! Like Ashley's spaz brother?' He continued to giggle, enjoying his own joke. Kaz glared at him.

'No it's not cool. I don't want to spend the rest of my life in jail.'

'You won't. Cops've got their heads up their arses most of the time.' He grinned, a glint of pride crept into his eye. 'Wanna know how many people I've killed?'

'No! I fucking don't!'

Joey looked disappointed. He folded his arms. 'Okay, I'm gonna tell you something I've never told anyone else.' His face took on a deadly serious look. 'I am special. Joking apart. I've always known it. And I'm not talking about some ego thing. I'm not some psycho with delusions. Some of us, our brains are hard-wired differently and there's a reason for that.'

Kaz watched him, a look of serenity spread over his features as he warmed to his theme.

'Thousands and thousands of years ago, extraterrestrials visited this planet. We wasn't much more than a bunch of cavemen. But they taught us things – there's bags of evidence for it if you know where to look. And suddenly evolution took off like a fucking rocket.' He swooped his arm upwards in a forty-five-degree trajectory.

'A few of these extraterrestrials, they bred with our women. Passed on their very special genes. And some of us have got that in our DNA. We're just different. Better at surviving, tougher. Don't matter where we was born, we find a way to come out on top.'

Kaz's jaw slackened. 'You really believe this?'

Joey fixed her with his piercing gaze. 'It explains everything. Books have been written about it, people've done research. Not idiots – proper scientists. Okay, it sounds a bit bonkers to start with. But y'know all the stuff they dish up at school, baby Jesus and all that, that's the fucking fairy story.'

Kaz sat in silence staring at her mug of tea. Joey was nothing if not surprising.

He grinned at her, drained his own mug. 'Ready for a top-up?'

She shook her head. He poured himself more tea.

She studied his face. 'Okay, so have I got this right? If you're different, if you got these . . . special genes, you don't care about . . .' The image of the bullet tearing into Sean's eye socket flashed through her mind and bile shot up into her throat. She swallowed hard. 'You don't care about killing people. You don't feel nothing?'

Joey took a slug of tea. 'No. Okay, you have to pretend to be like everyone else. But the truth is it ain't no different to swatting a fly.'

Kaz absorbed this as she watched him wandering round the

room. That restless energy – he seemed perpetually wired. Realizing her own body was jangling with tension, she exhaled.

'Well, you may be special. But I'm not.' Her voice was a whisper. 'I felt it.'

He stared at her. His eyes seemed to be filling with disappointment. He puffed out his cheeks. 'Maybe you're not. So in future you'd better leave that side of the business to me, okay?'

Kaz's phone was still on the kitchen worktop beside the kettle. It buzzed.

Joey picked it up. 'You got a text. Want me to read it?'

She held out her hand, she had to concentrate to stop it shaking. 'Nah, it's okay. I can—'

She didn't get a chance to say more, he'd already clicked onto the message.

'From Mal – who the fuck's Mal?'

Kaz's heart missed a beat. 'Just . . . a bloke I met in my art class.'

Joey peered at the screen.

'He says "Probs getting hold of M. Meeting him tonite. Will keep U posted."' Joey gave her a quizzical glance. 'What's all this about then, eh?'

Kaz got up. She knew she had to hold it together, appear nonchalant. She walked over and put her mug on the kitchen counter.

'Oh, some plan a bunch of them have dreamt up. I don't really wanna be involved. Mike ran the art class. Mal and some of the others are trying to set up a little exhibition of all the work we done.'

Joey looked at her for what seemed an age then he gave an approving nod. 'Sounds like a great idea to me. You wanna be an artist babe, you gotta put yourself out there.' He held out the phone to her. 'You should text him back.'

Kaz frowned. 'I'll do it later.'

She reached for the phone, but Joey held on to it.

'No time like the present.' His thumbs hovered over the keypad. There was a definite edge in his voice. 'What we gonna say to Mal eh?'

63

Bradley clicked his phone on and a text popped up: *yo Mal count me in 4 def. kaz x*. He stared at it, it seemed very odd. But then reduced to text-speak quite a few people ceased to sound like themselves. It was the name that gave him pause. He'd only ever called her Kaz once, in an attempt to be chummy. And as for the *x*, that made no sense. But maybe her attitude to him was finally thawing.

Out of the corner of his eye he caught sight of Nicci Armstrong. She was beckoning to him. He was standing next to a squad car on the gravel driveway of a tasteful barn conversion on the outskirts of Danbury in Essex. Cheryl Stoneham and her team had secured the place half an hour earlier and detained three Ukrainian nationals: a couple in their mid-thirties and a younger man.

Bradley joined Nicci and she led him into the house. A pretty, dark-haired woman was perched on the sofa. Her eyes were red-rimmed with crying and she was wringing a soggy tissue in her hands. She gazed up at him as they passed.

Nicci led him into the back of the house, they paused outside a door to the large workshop area which had been converted into some sort of laboratory. Cheryl Stoneham was conferring with the forensic photographer and the exhibits officer.

'I want a full digital and stills recording before we bag up the exhibits.' She glanced at the photographer. 'Don't let the rest of the team hassle you. It takes as long as it takes. I want the forensics on this watertight, okay?'

The photographer nodded, already booted and suited, he entered the lab. Cheryl turned to greet Bradley. She gave him a broad grin.

'Well you two have had a score, haven't you?'

He smiled. 'We will if we can join up the dots and connect them to Joey Phelps.'

Cheryl nodded thoughtfully. 'Nic here has got you pegged as a chap with some education. Know anything about the Ukraine?'

'A bit. Mostly what I've read in the papers.'

'Well, we've taken the husband and his oppo down the nick. He's poker-faced, asking for his lawyer. But the wife . . . she's our way in I reckon. I've been letting her stew. So . . . how d'you fancy being her new best friend?'

Bradley beamed. 'I'll give it a go.'

'Her name's Leysa.'

Bradley took a deep breath. 'Okay . . .'

As he headed off into the main living room Cheryl Stoneham gave Nicci a sceptical look.

'Why you giving him a leg up? Doubt he'd do the same for you.'

Nicci shrugged. 'He's not all bad. He's good at sniffing out the psychological angle. You saw that in Southend. And he's such a pretty boy, women get fooled by that.'

Cheryl gave her a wry glance. 'Including you Nic?'

Bradley managed to bum a couple of cups of coffee off the SOCOs, who were gathered round their van waiting to go in. He returned to the house with the brimming styrofoam cups, gave a nod to the WPC who was minding Leysa. 'Go and get a drink if you want.'

The WPC left, Bradley offered Leysa one of the coffees and sat down beside her.

'DC Mal Bradley.'

Leysa met his eye, he gave her a warm smile. She responded with a sour look. 'I don't know nothing.'

Bradley nodded. 'Been in England long?'

'Year maybe.'

'Your English is good.'

She stared at him with disdain, she wasn't about to respond to cheap flattery.

He smiled again. 'How d'you get into all this Leysa? You and your husband, you strike me as smart, well-educated people. Not low-life drug dealers. What happened?'

Leysa pursed her lips. 'You wouldn't understand.'

Bradley took a sip of his coffee. 'Try me. I read the papers. Complicated place your country. I read about your ex-prime minister, what's her name, Yula . . . ?'

'Yulia Tymoshenko.'

'Right, now wasn't she a leader of the Orange Revolution? I'm guessing you had some involvement in all that. But didn't they jail her for seven years?'

A tight angry expression spread across Leysa's face, she seemed close to tears. Bradley waited. She wanted to talk, he could feel it.

She wiped her nose with a crumpled tissue. 'When we lost the election, we knew things would be bad, old Soviet ways would return.'

'And did they?'

She looked at him, trying to tough it out. She just needed to hang in there. There'd be lawyers, all the help they needed.

Joey had promised. Right now though she felt abandoned. He looked rather innocent for a cop. Maybe he would understand. She sighed.

'Marko lose his job at the university. They steal his research, we have no money, a rich "businessman" take our apartment.'

Bradley frowned as he tried to get his head round this. 'Why? Because you supported the opposition?'

Leysa hung her head. 'It was me, I work for Yulia's campaign.' A wistful smile crept over her features. 'Marko, he only happy in his lab. He don't do politics. But they come against him because of me. It's all my fault.'

'So you came to England?'

Leysa fixed him with a steady gaze, but her tone was bitter.

'Yeah England, this great land of freedom and democracy. We ask for political asylum but you say no. Too many Ukrainians like us looking for a way out.'

Bradley nodded sympathetically. 'That's really tough. So let me guess, you needed leave to remain. But for that Marko had to find work and that's when Joey Phelps came along. How did you meet him?'

Leysa's gaze didn't waver, nor did she miss a beat. 'I don't know any Joey.'

Bradley tipped out the dregs of his coffee in a plant pot.

'C'mon Leysa, don't do this. We were doing really well.'

She flashed an angry look at him. 'I told you. I don't know nothing.'

Bradley looked her up and down. She was small with the elfin physique of a marathon runner. Yet she sat slightly hunched, one arm resting protectively across her rounded belly. He watched her for a second then it dawned on him. She was pregnant. He caught her eye.

'Okay here's the reality check. Loads of people come to the

UK to get away from whatever at home. We're inundated with people who've suffered. We can't take everyone. You got an industrial-scale drugs lab out the back there. Your husband is going down for quite a stretch. But he's gonna protect you, isn't he? Say you didn't really know what he was up to.'

Leysa stared at him. 'It's true. I don't know nothing. I'm not a chemist.'

Bradley smiled. 'And we may well decide to accept that . . .' He paused for effect.

Her dark eyes searched his face for clues. The day had taken her completely by surprise. She'd returned from the supermarket and was unpacking her shopping when armed police burst through the door. She'd been led to believe that this sort of thing didn't happen in England. She'd had no chance to exchange even a word with Marko, they'd put him in the back of a police car and he was gone.

Bradley sighed. 'The easiest thing for us would be to put you on a plane to Kiev. That's what my boss is thinking. You could be home this time tomorrow.'

The colour drained from Leysa's face and Bradley knew he'd hit the target bang on. Whatever she feared most was back in the Ukraine. Jail? Poverty? A life of hardship for her unborn child? He decided to press the point home.

'Marko'll get maybe fifteen years. Then he'll be deported too on his release. That'll be when you next see him.'

Her dark eyes swam with tears. Bradley watched the threat sink in. Cruel but necessary he told himself. He wanted to take her hand, reassure her. Instead he adopted a softer tone. 'You may think I'm a complete bastard, but I'm not. World we live in today is a terrible place for many people. I know I'm lucky to live where I do. I know you're not a real criminal, you're just a woman who's trying to survive.'

Leysa's tears fell in huge droplets into her lap. She tried to mop them with her sodden tissue. Bradley pulled a fresh one from his jacket pocket and handed it to her. She wiped her eyes and then fixed him with a haunted stare. 'What do you want?'

Bradley gave a diffident shrug. 'Well, if you were prepared to give evidence in court, then obviously you'd have to stay here. Case like this could take a year at least to come to trial.' He gave her a considered look. 'By that time the baby'll have been born. It'll have citizenship, which could help you.'

At the mention of the baby she shot him a savage look. 'And you say you not a bastard. But you want me to testify against my own husband.'

Bradley shook his head. 'Oh no, I want you to help your husband. Help him reduce his sentence.'

He watched her latch on to this, hope then confusion racing across her face. This was what he'd been waiting for.

He tossed her the lifeline. 'Leysa, we know who set you up here in this place, who's behind all this. You need to testify against Joey Phelps and you need to persuade Marko to do the same. Trust me, it's your best option.'

64

Glynis sat on the long low sofa in Joey's flat staring out of the vast picture window at the cityscape beyond. Ashley had wrapped a duvet round her and an untouched mug of tea was on the glass table in front of her. In the time she'd been there the sky had clouded over, the sun disappearing behind a wide sheet of cirrostratus. Watching the clouds thicken had given her something to do while she waited. It would only be a matter of time before Sean came for her. She heard the door open, people coming in, but she didn't look round, she was too petrified. Then Kaz sat down on the sofa beside her. She took Glynis's hand. Glynis turned towards her.

'Where's Sean?'

Suddenly Joey was looming over them both. He seemed to fill the window, blocking the vista beyond.

'He's done a runner Glynis. Spain we think.'

Glynis glanced from him to Kaz. 'Spain?'

But Kaz's eyes were focused on her brother. She got up to face him. 'Joey, this ain't fair. She deserves to know the truth.'

He stared right back at her, his pupils wide and glassy. He looked about to erupt. Then he just shrugged his shoulders and sighed. 'Your fucking funeral babes – you killed him. I was only trying to help.'

Glynis's frantic gaze darted from one to the other. 'Killed? What's happened?'

Kaz turned to face her. 'After Tol took you out of my place Sean tried to rape me. I shot him. He's dead.'

Glynis's jaw slackened. A low keening sob rose from deep in her chest. She put her face in her hands and began to wail.

Joey watched her with a disgruntled look. He shoved his hands in his pockets and glared at Kaz. 'Now what fucking good has that done, eh?'

Kaz ignored him. She rested the palm of her hand on Glynis's back. After a few moments the lament subsided. Glynis lifted her head, carefully wiped the tears from each cheek with her index fingers, looked at Kaz and slowly nodded. Her voice was barely audible. 'Thanks.'

Kaz hugged her.

Joey stared at the two women with a look of complete bafflement. He turned round. Ashley was standing in the kitchen area with a phone to his ear. Joey moved towards him, shaking his head in wonderment.

'You see that Ash? I don't get it. Do you get it?'

Ashley ignored the question, his expression was tense. He held out the phone. 'Neville wants a word. Think we got a problem.'

Joey took the phone with a smile. 'All right Nev?'

As he listened his face crumpled into an angry scowl then he thundered down the phone. 'Whad'you mean you can't go yourself? What the fuck else am I paying you for? . . . No Neville, you fucking listen to me. You get down there and you get them out!'

Ashley hovered, alert, waiting for instructions. Kaz and Glynis simply watched open-mouthed. Joey didn't bother to turn the phone off. He smashed it several times into the granite counter with all the force he could muster.

'Bastards! Fucking bastards!'

Splinters of shattered phone spun across the worktop and skittered on to the floor. Then he took a deep breath and let the air flow slowly out through his nostrils. 'Right then . . .'

His intense stare zeroed in on Kaz and he gave her a thin smile.

'Got a bit of business to attend to babes. But don't go running off. I need to know where you are.'

She returned his look with a steady gaze. Somehow he didn't seem like her little brother any more. During her years inside he'd become someone else. She realized now how stupid she'd been not to see this before. Sean was right about that. Her fear had always been he'd turn into the old man, an angry, thoughtless brute. But this was something else. Something far worse.

He continued to stare at her. 'Okay?'

She nodded obediently.

He smiled. 'Good girl.' He patted her arm, grabbed his jacket and headed out with Ashley trotting behind him.

65

Mike Dawson's train from Oxford got into Paddington shortly before seven in the evening. Bradley had arranged to meet him in a bar he knew near the station, part of the redevelopment around Sheldon Square. He had taken the train back into town, leaving Nicci at Chelmsford nick slowly coaxing a statement out of Leysa.

He'd considered cancelling the meeting with Mike. Stoneham's team were all pretty psyched. It was a major bust and he was at the heart of it. It made him feel like a proper copper again. The camaraderie, the pats on the back, the belief that this really could lead to a successful prosecution. Bill Mayhew was on his way from London to join in the interrogation of the Dimitrenkos. But Bradley also felt he owed it to Karen Phelps to deliver on his promise. He didn't know why. It wasn't as if he was getting anything in return. It just felt like the right thing to do.

He texted his apologies to Mike explaining he'd be a bit late. But still he ran most of the way from the tube station to the bar. As he walked through the double doors he saw Mike settled in a corner booth nursing his pint and across the table from him sat Karen Phelps. Bradley walked towards them with a bemused look on his face.

Mike turned and gave him a mischievous smile. 'I didn't realize what a colourful pair I had in my class. Usually it's teachers and civil servants. But an undercover detective and an ex-con? Quite exciting.'

Bradley cast an enquiring glance in Karen's direction. She looked pale and tense, she gave him the ghost of a smile.

'I called Mike. My future, I figured I should be here.'

Bradley had to suppress his annoyance. He could've stayed in Chelmsford after all. 'Anyone for a refill?'

Mike shook his head, but Kaz got up, smiled at Bradley for a second time.

'I'll get them. You sit down, you look knackered. What d'you want?'

Bradley was playing catch-up in his head. Karen Phelps expressing concern like a normal person was a new experience for him.

'Umm, yeah. A pint of lager thanks.'

Bradley sat down as Kaz went to the bar. Mike watched her then inclined his head.

'I knew there was something between you two. But I thought you just fancied her.'

Bradley gave him a wry smile. 'Maybe I do. Stupid, eh?'

'She's been telling me about her family and her upbringing. Sounds like a complete nest of vipers.'

'Yeah that's quite a good word for them. Vipers are ruthless killers, aren't they?'

Mike tilted his head sadly. 'There's a whole world out there that most of us only read about in the papers.'

Bradley leant forward across the table. 'If you can help her Mike then you probably would be saving her life.'

Mike coughed, the raspy gravel from a lifetime of nicotine rumbled through his chest. But his eyes twinkled, he was excited. 'I'll certainly do my damnedest. Never expected to find the artistic equivalent of Jean Genet in my own backyard.'

Bradley laughed. 'Don't tell her that. Her head will swell.'

Kaz returned to the table with a pint of lager and a coffee for herself.

Bradley took a long draught, wiped his mouth neatly with his fingers and turned to Mike. 'Okay, what we thought is you've taught at various places in the States. You've got contacts. What are the chances of getting Karen in somewhere over there?'

Mike raised his eyebrows and puffed out his cheeks. 'The States? I've got more influence this side of the pond. Be much simpler to have a word with our own admissions tutor.'

Kaz was about to speak. She seemed to Bradley to have lost her usual stroppy attitude and the confidence that went with it. Her eyes glinted with tears, she swallowed hard; telling the truth wasn't going to be an easy habit to acquire.

'The thing is Mike, my brother . . . he's a psychopath.' She glanced at Bradley, jutted her chin, partly in defiance but also to control the quiver in her voice. 'It's taken me a while to . . . to really see this. I need to get as far away from him as I can. I'm sorry, this probably sounds like some kind of con to get into some posh American college that wouldn't look twice at me otherwise.'

Mike fixed her with his eagle eye, reached out and put his claw-like fingers over hers. 'No it doesn't.' He pondered then grinned. 'One of my oldest friends is a professor at the Pratt Institute in New York. I'll call him as soon as I get home. I'll scan some of your work and send it. I think he'll recognize your potential as much as I do.'

Kaz's jaw slackened. She couldn't believe what he was saying. 'The Pratt Institute?'

'You've heard of it?'

Kaz nodded. She'd heard of it all right. She'd found its website, back inside when she used all her allotted IT time trawling the

Net in search of dreams to inspire her. It was full of images of cool, rich students and exciting art.

Bradley glanced from one to the other. 'I haven't.'

'It's . . .' Kaz had a look he'd never seen on her face before, that of a wide-eyed kid.

Mike smiled and helped her out. 'It's a good school, as they say over there.'

'Even if I could get in how the hell would I pay for it?'

Mike took a slug of his pint, he was enjoying himself. This is what teaching was all about for him, finding the Kaz Phelpses of this world and helping them on their way.

'Good schools have big endowment funds, which means scholarships. Anyway I'm sure we can find some philanthropic bunch of Yanks who are into supporting reformed criminals.' Mike gave a dry chuckle. 'I'm presuming you are reformed.'

Kaz returned his look with a bleak smile. 'The other big hurdle is my probation officer. I'm released on licence. They'd have to agree.'

Mike pondered this then his eyes crinkled into a smile. 'Last year chap came to the summer school – as I say we get a lot of civil servants. He bought a couple of my own paintings, we've kept in touch. He's the senior, permanent head-some-thing-or-other at the Ministry of Justice. I'll give him a ring. Tell him we need his help in the interests of art.'

Bradley beamed. 'You think he'll listen to you?'

Mike gave him an impish grin. 'Haven't I taught you anything Mal? What matters is what you see, the way things look, the world of appearances. Wonderful PR coup for them, of course they'll listen.'

Bradley hailed a cab for Mike. He and Kaz stood side by side on the pavement as it drove off.

Kaz started to smile and shake her head. 'Scariest-looking geezer I've ever met. But he turns out to be the most all right bloke there is.'

Bradley gave her a teasing glance. 'That's the world of appearances for you.'

They both laughed. Bradley looked her up and down. She'd relaxed a bit, but she still looked wired and tense. Her face was pale and drawn.

He cocked his head. 'You all right?'

She sighed. 'Yeah. Stressful couple of days is all.'

He nodded. 'Is Sean still giving you grief?'

She shot him a wary look. 'No, he's . . . I dunno. He's gone off. Haven't seen him.'

Bradley seemed to be scanning her face, it made her nervous. She knew the mask had slipped and she needed time and calm in order to get it back in place. She felt like shit. Was he suspicious or was she being paranoid? She wanted to run.

He gave her a warm smile. 'Don't look so worried. I think there's an odds-on chance this'll work.'

Kaz nodded. 'And you're still not going to ask for anything in return?'

Bradley raised his eyebrows. 'Nope.'

They started to walk down the street towards the tube. He smiled. 'Although . . . purely for my own satisfaction I wouldn't mind knowing how you've come to change your mind about Joey.'

Kaz considered this. Part of her really wanted to tell him, tell him everything, come clean. That feeling of release, she craved it more than any drug. And in a bizarre way she felt he would understand. But that would be mad, he was still a cop.

'Oh I dunno.' She put her hands in her pockets. 'I've spent time with him, watched him. He thinks he's special. He don't care who he hurts. No conscience. That's the definition of a psychopath, in't it?'

'Pretty much. But you didn't used to think that about him.'

Kaz shot him a combative look, a glimpse of the old Kaz. 'You don't know what I used to think.' Then she shook her head savagely and her tone became tinged with grief. 'Truth is I din't used to think. Period. I'm stupid. He's my little brother. Or he was.'

They walked on for a few moments in silence. Bradley could see the entrance to the tube up ahead. He turned to look at her and realized she was crying. She made no sound. She seemed cocooned in her own misery. He sensed that any offer of comfort would be an intrusion. They reached the station and turned to face each other. He smiled awkwardly. 'I'll say goodbye here because I need to make a call.'

She nodded. Then abruptly she grabbed his hand and squeezed it hard.

'I'm sorry PC Mal. If I could do the right thing . . . but I want to escape. I have to escape. I know I'm as bad as him. Probably worse.'

He drew her gently towards him, wrapped her in a hug and she didn't resist.

'No you're not. You have got a conscience. Sometimes running away is the smartest thing to do.'

He didn't want to let go, but he didn't want her to feel trapped. As he released her he took a step backwards. 'You going to be okay?'

She nodded. 'I'm planning my exit. Mike comes through, I'm going. You won't see me for dust.'

He smiled, reached out for her hand, drew it to his lips and kissed it. 'Take care.'

She nodded, turned on her heel. He watched her pass through the ticket barrier and disappear.

He stood alone on the pavement feeling very flat, which made no sense. He'd achieved what he'd set out to do. He told himself he was being foolish. He'd drunk one pint in the bar, but he really felt he needed another. Probably another three or four if he was honest. He noticed there was a pub across the road. As he started to walk towards it he scrolled through his phone to Nicci Armstrong's number and rang it. She picked up on the third ring.

'Bradley, where the fuck are you?'

'I left a message for you, something I had to do. How's it going?'

Nicci was sitting alone in the corner of the police canteen trying to decipher the date stamp on a fruit yogurt. The choice had been this or a couple of tired sandwiches.

'I come out the interview room thinking you'd gone to the bog, but no, you've buggered off back to London. Where is your head Bradley? Stuck up your arse yet again?'

'I'm sorry. Promise I had to keep, it was important. Did you get a statement out of Leysa?'

'Sort of. Now we've got Turnbull on the phone throwing his weight around, arguing with Cheryl's boss about who's the lead on this. And I'm stuck in the middle. On my tod.'

'Thought Mayhew was coming down.'

'You walked out on me. I went out on a limb for you with Cheryl Stoneham. I don't know why I bothered.'

Bradley sighed. 'Nic, I wouldn't have gone if it hadn't been important.'

'Yeah, important to you. I've got a life too y'know. I had to phone up my ex-mother-in-law who hates my guts and beg her to babysit Sophie. I'd like to be able to keep a few promises myself, especially to my own kid.'

Bradley was approaching the door to the pub, it looked Victorian with hints of neo-gothic tracery in the window arches. He got a glimpse of the ornate tiled and mirrored interior, it was pretty quiet and the prospect of drinking a beer alone in peace was all he could think about. But he needed to finish the call first.

'Look, I'm sorry and I'll—'

As he stopped a couple of feet from the threshold a large bloke barged straight into the back of him sending the phone flying from his hand and clattering to the pavement. Nicci heard a loud crack in her ear as it hit, then the line went dead.

'Bradley?'

Now the fool had dropped his bloody phone, she couldn't believe it.

In confusion Bradley turned to apologize but a fist slammed into his gut knocking the wind out of him. He doubled over gasping and hands grabbed him from behind. Before he could even get his breath two men were dragging him across the pavement. A black BMW X5 was pulled up kerbside, rear door open. They chucked him on the back seat and as he struggled to sit up someone leant over from the front passenger seat and coshed him. For a brief instant he thought he recognized the face, then everything went black.

Nicci Armstrong sat in the canteen and opened her yogurt. This was dinner and come to think of it lunch too. She was irritable with hunger. All she wanted was to be at home with Sophie. She thought of ringing Bradley but what would be the point? He was probably in a bar somewhere half-cut and that's why he'd trashed his phone. Cheryl was right, he didn't give a toss about her. Had she gone soft on him because he had a pretty face? Make it all right for the boys so they'll like you? It felt as though she'd been doing that her whole life and it never worked. Tim had always been at his most charming when he was feeding her a pack of lies. She knew relying on men was a hiding to nothing. And they always stuck together. In the end Bradley was still Turnbull's boy, he'd get the credit for the bust, she'd be ignored. Well sod that. Bradley could cover his own useless arse from now on.

66

Bradley came to with the side of his face pressing against rough concrete. He could smell engine oil and brick dust. His arms were pinioned behind him, firmly bound with duct tape at the wrists. He looked up into a bright fluorescent tube that hung on a chain overhead, beyond that was an arched ceiling of bricks. A face loomed over him, young, unfamiliar.

'He wake up boss.'

The place was chilly, a draught of evening air wafting in from somewhere. A voice floated over his head, which felt extremely sore.

'Stick him on that chair Tol.'

He was lifted bodily, plonked on an orange plastic bucket chair. The frame of the chair swayed as he landed awkwardly, arms trussed behind him. A figure stepped from the shadows: Joey Phelps. It had to be. Seconds after he'd come to his senses Bradley had realized this. He was in big trouble.

'You know who was the last person to sit in that chair?' Joey smiled, but his eyes remained cold and blank. 'Your mate Marlow.'

Bradley focused on Joey. If there was any chance of getting out of this alive, fear wasn't an option. He adopted a chatty tone.

'Never met him personally. Before my time.'

Joey nodded thoughtfully. 'I always liked him. We had some

laughs. But then he was put in to lead me up the garden path, wasn't he? Like you been doing with my sister.'

'Only met her the once, when you were both interviewed in Southend.'

Joey rolled his neck around, flexed his shoulders. Bradley got the impression this was all a ritual, the build-up, and Joey was enjoying himself.

He gave Bradley a quizzical look. 'Oh, come on Mal, don't lie. I've even texted you back on her phone. How long you been shagging her?'

Bradley gave him a broad confidential smile. 'I'm not lying. I've never shagged your sister. Truth is I would've liked to. She's fit. Just never got the chance.'

Joey held out a hand in Tolya's direction. Tolya gave him an iPhone. Joey swiped the screen with his middle finger, brought up the video and held it in front of Bradley's face. 'Take a look at this.'

The short video sequence was of Bradley and Kaz outside the tube station. It had been filmed from across the road. Their voices were inaudible, drowned out by the general noise of the street. But it was all there, standing close together, her grabbing his hand, the hug, the final chivalrous kiss.

Joey grinned. 'Nice touch that, kissing her hand. Girls like that stuff, don't they?' The smile faded. 'I reckon you been shagging her more or less since she got out the nick. You was there at the hostel – saw you leaving her room meself.'

Bradley took a deep breath. 'Okay . . . I'll admit that was the brief. Get close to her, get it on with her. But she turned me down Joey, every step of the way. That's the God's honest truth.'

Joey shook his head slowly and wearily. Then his fist shot out landing a lightning blow squarely in Bradley's face. Bone cracked, Bradley cried out as blood gushed from his smashed nose. He had to spit in order not to choke.

Joey leant his head to one side. 'You really think I'm fucking stupid, don't you? Well I'm not. I'm gonna ask you again, how long you been shagging my sister?'

He stood in front of Bradley, balanced and easy on the balls of his feet, readying himself to deliver a second punch. But the door to the lock-up creaked open and Ashley appeared.

Joey turned towards him, annoyed. 'Well ... where is she?'

'Couldn't find her. Went to her place, back to your place. Phoned her – she's not picking up.'

Joey took a couple of strides across the floor until he was right in Ashley's face.

'One fucking thing I give you to do and you can't fucking do it!'

'She's disappeared Joe. So's Glynis.'

'They haven't disappeared. What are they, fucking ghosts? It's just you're too stupid to find them.'

'Well where else d'you want me to look?'

Joey started to pace. He flung his arms in the air, jabbed his finger in Bradley's direction. 'I wanted this sorted out, now, tonight. How am I supposed to do that without her here, eh?'

He glanced at Bradley, walked over towards him. 'Where's she gone? Tell me.'

Bradley's mouth hung open, it was the only way he could breathe. With some effort he raised his head and looked Joey directly in the eye. 'I don't know. You can beat me to death here and now, but the answer'll still be I don't know.'

Joey swivelled on his heel. 'Aaww fuck this.' He stormed towards the door. 'I'll find her myself.' He shot a glance at Tolya. 'Tie him up properly, I don't want him going walkabout.'

The door slammed behind him. Bradley felt the solid knot of tension in his stomach start to loosen; for the moment at least, Joey was gone.

67

Marko Dimitrenko sat at the table in the interview room. His gangling frame and rounded shoulders had the effect of making him look more downtrodden than he really was. The lawyer took the seat beside him. They'd only met half an hour previously, but he was Joey's man, a top professional; this was what Joey had always promised and indeed Neville Moore seemed to fit the bill. He'd immediately taken charge of the situation. He knew the senior cop, a rather stout, middle-aged woman; they'd exchanged pleasantries. Marko simply assumed the lawyer was bribing her and the interview was for the sake of appearances.

Cheryl Stoneham switched on the tape deck, went through the usual round of identification: the suspect, his lawyer, herself and her colleague, DS Nicci Armstrong. Then she asked Marko whether he wanted an interpreter present.

Marko felt this was a deliberate insult, designed to unnerve him. He stared at her coldly. 'I can speak to you in Russian, English, German or French. You choose.'

Stoneham gave him a tight smile. 'I'll take that as a no then.'

Neville Moore inclined his head and sighed. Nicci watched him. He was working hard at giving the impression that this was all a big misunderstanding.

'Chief Inspector, my client is a highly educated man, an

academic in his own country, and he wishes to offer you his full cooperation.'

Cheryl Stoneham exchanged a glance with Nicci. 'Well we're jolly pleased to hear that Mr Moore.'

However a sixth sense was telling her the lawyer was looking a little too smug. He had something up his sleeve.

Neville turned to Marko. 'Did you write out the formulas?'

Marko huffed, all this police nonsense was making him impatient. He wanted to get home, see what damage these idiots had done to his lab. But most of all he wanted to see Leysa. He pulled a square of paper from his pocket and unfolded it. The paper was covered in chemical formulae, strings of equations and numbers written out in a small, neat hand. Moore pushed the sheet across the table in Stoneham's direction.

'This is to assist your forensic laboratory in their analysis of any substances seized from Dr Dimitrenko's premises.'

Stoneham considered the hieroglyphics in front of her, showed the paper to Nicci. 'And the point of this, Mr Moore?'

Neville smiled, he always liked this bit and it didn't happen often. But pulling the rug out from under the police was, for him, great sport. 'Dr Dimitrenko is a scientist, a research chemist, and he is proud of the fact that he has produced an entirely synthetic compound to replace safrole, the oil that is the primary precursor of MDMA.'

Stoneham fixed Marko with a hard stare. He was sitting now with arms folded, a look of arrogant disdain on his face.

Nicci stepped in. 'So Dr Dimitrenko, you admit that you've been trying to manufacture MDMA, an illegal class-A drug?'

Marko just glanced at Neville Moore, who smiled at Nicci and inclined his head.

'No Sergeant. He categorically denies that. As you know the Misuse of Drugs Act has been extended by order to cover various chemical compounds: MDMA or Ecstasy and more recently Mephedrone. But what my client has created is an entirely new product outside of these definitions and neither a Class-A or Class-B drug within the meaning of the Act.'

Stoneham picked up the sheet of paper. Her colour was rising. 'By product you mean a new designer drug that replicates the effects but isn't the same formula as the rest of the poisonous crap that's out there?'

Moore held out his open palms. 'The law is an imperfect tool Chief Inspector. But what you have seized and what Dr Dimitrenko has created is a perfectly legal high as a full chemical analysis will show.'

Stoneham shoved her chair back and got up. She was steaming. 'Yeah, until it kills some fifteen-year-old kid in a club!'

Moore knew he'd won, Stoneham's uncharacteristic flash of temper was ample evidence of that. But he smiled politely. 'That's merely speculation. Legal highs are part of the recreational life of millions, much like alcohol. Now ... since my client has broken no laws I presume he's free to go?'

Stoneham swallowed a bitter riposte and fixed him with a cold, hard stare. 'No. We will be holding Dr Dimitrenko until his immigration status can be confirmed.'

Marko stared at her in disbelief. He turned to Moore. 'What? What's this crap? I need to go home, see my wife! Now!'

Stoneham leant over the tape deck. 'Interview concluded at twenty fifteen.'

She switched the machine off, glanced at Marko. 'Your wife has been helping us with our inquiries and will also be handed over to the UK Borders Agency.'

Marko jumped up, flung back his chair.

'No, you cannot hold us.' He rounded on Neville. 'Just pay her, pay her more!' He glared at Stoneham. 'How much you want?'

Neville's eyes closed. He placed his hand over his face in disbelief then glanced up at Stoneham with a beseeching look. 'I apologize Chief Inspector. There are as you can see some cultural differences here that need ironing out ...'

Stoneham returned the look, now the boot was on the other foot. It went some way to making up for this shambles.

'I understand that Mr Moore and I'll leave you to explain the facts of life to your client. But if I have anything to do with it he'll be deported.'

Nicci followed Stoneham out of the room. The DCI stomped down the corridor straight into the women's toilets. She slapped the door of the nearest stall. 'Jesus H. Christ on a fucking raft!'

Nicci exhaled. 'They could be trying to pull a fast one. Baffle us with science. When the lab actually analyses the stuff they could still decide it's MDMA.'

Cheryl sighed, shook her head. 'I know Neville Moore. He's a slick operator, never sticks his neck out too far.'

She ran the tap, cupped her hands and filled them with water. She splashed it on her face.

'What really gets to me is that arrogant bastard thinks I'm bribable. I've been in this job a long time, seen my share of nasty villains. But this one, he really doesn't think he's doing anything wrong, does he? He wants to go out in one of our vans on a Saturday night. Scrape up some of the kids that are full of booze and pills made of fuck knows what. Haul them down to A & E and hope that pumping their stomachs'll save their lives.'

Nicci put her hand on Stoneham's shoulder and patted it. 'I'm sure we've got enough of a case for deportation. That'll shut up the shop for now.'

Stoneham turned to her. 'Sorry. I shouldn't do this in front of you. You're the junior officer, but you're holding it together. I'm the one blowing my stack. I really thought we had them. I've been chasing Joey Phelps a long time.'

Nicci gave her a weary shrug. 'He's not your average villain. Somehow he always manages to slip the noose.'

68

The taxi cruised sedately up the winding drive to Woodcote Hall. Kaz had caught the last train of the evening to Leeds and checked into an anonymous-looking hotel in Bishopgate Street close to the station. She'd set her phone alarm to wake her at seven, grabbed coffee, fruit and a croissant at the station buffet and taken the Wharfedale Line to Ilkley. As the train climbed up out of the Aire Valley, Kaz had eaten her breakfast and communed with the sheep. Being out of London, out of Essex, in a very different landscape felt odd at first. But it also finally brought her some relief, made her realize how much she wanted to feel free. She thought about New York and the prospect of a life far away in a place where Joey couldn't follow her. Well, he could follow her, but Kaz felt that taking on America was beyond even Joey's inflated ambition.

However she couldn't contemplate running away without first seeing Natalie and making sure she was okay. She picked up the taxi at Ilkley station, the driver was familiar with her destination and chatted amiably as they wound their way a dozen or so miles north into the Dales.

Joey had described the place as seriously posh and for once he hadn't been lying. Kaz waited in the oak-panelled library. After about five minutes Doctor Iqbal entered wreathed in smiles. He scanned the room rapidly as he offered his hand to shake.

'Apologies for keeping you waiting Miss Phelps. You are on

your own I see. I thought your brother might be with you.'

Kaz returned the smile. 'No, just me. Joey's busy.'

'Well I think that might be for the best. Your sister is . . . easily overwhelmed.'

Kaz nodded but she couldn't help sense the tension in Iqbal. 'She's okay, isn't she? Only you look a bit worried.'

Iqbal shook his head. 'I have a very full schedule today, that's all. Natalie is doing well. Very well. She is out of detox, she has been participating in therapy. I think you'll find her much improved.'

'That's great.'

'Still a way to go, but . . . you can make your own judgement. I'll get one of my staff to take you up to her room.'

'Thank you.'

Iqbal inclined his head politely, but he was frowning. He hesitated, then seemed to come to a decision.

'I hope you will understand that our priority here is always to serve the best interests of the patient.'

Kaz nodded. 'Yeah, well that's what my brother's paying you for.'

Iqbal gave her a thin smile. 'Indeed.'

Natalie's room was at the end of a long corridor. The nurse who escorted Kaz was round and motherly but very neat in her pale mauve tunic. She said her name was June, she'd come to Woodcote Hall five years ago when she gave up on the NHS. Natalie was eating well, not large portions, but good food. She was improving on a daily basis.

June tapped politely on the heavy oak door and opened it. There was a large leather wing chair by the window. Natalie was curled up in it, her eyes were closed, but she wasn't sleeping. She was wearing a swish pair of headphones and her fingers were drumming on the arm of the chair to some barely audible beat.

June stood in front of her patiently until, sensing a presence, Natalie opened her eyes. Her face immediately broke into a wide smile, she removed the headphones. June leant over her, patted her arm.

'You've got a visitor lovey.'

Natalie swivelled in the chair and glanced in Kaz's direction with an expectant smile on her face. As soon as she saw Kaz, she frowned.

'Oh . . .'

June gave her another reassuring pat. 'Wrong day dear. But I'll leave you with your sister. I'm sure you've got lots of catching up to do.'

Kaz scanned the room. It wasn't large, but the ceiling was high and dual-aspect windows made it light and airy. The walls were a soft peach with fabrics and furnishings to match. There was a washbasin, mirror and vanity unit in one corner. A cork pinboard was propped in another with a large sheet of paper taped to it, part collage, part painting. Kaz's eye was immediately drawn to its riotous colours.

June picked up a high-backed chair and brought it over for Kaz. 'Now don't feel you girls have to stay inside. The grounds are lovely. And it's good for Natalie to get out in the fresh air.'

Kaz nodded her thanks and sat down on the chair, which June had placed next to Natalie's. She gave her sister what she hoped was a warm smile. The door shut behind June and they sat in silence for several moments.

Natalie's gaze was watchful and alert. She still looked young and vulnerable, but an intelligence had returned to her face. The drugged-up zombie was gone. She sighed. 'Never expected to see you.'

'I wanted to come before. But y'know how it is. Things got complicated.'

Natalie nodded slowly. She scanned Kaz's face as if searching for clues, something to connect with her memories. 'You look different.'

Kaz smiled. 'So do you.'

Natalie reached into her jeans pocket and pulled out an iPod nano. She tapped the screen to switch the music off. Kaz's eyes followed her slow deliberate actions.

'What you listening to?'

'Various bands. Mate of mine made me a playlist.'

Kaz nodded. It felt as though she was wading through treacle. 'You made friends in here, that's good.'

Natalie was carefully coiling the cable round the headphones. 'Nic's not in here. She just comes to visit. I thought you was her.'

Kaz painted on a smile. 'Maybe you'd've preferred that.'

Natalie fixed her sister with a direct stare. Kaz was shocked to realize that she had a definite look of Joey about her. She tilted her head in the same way he did.

Her gaze left Kaz's face and drifted to the window and the view beyond. 'I find it hard to remember stuff, like what happened when. But you was there, weren't you? At the flat.'

Kaz nodded. 'I came to see you at your flat, yeah.'

'Was you there when he done it?'

'Who you talking about Nat?'

Natalie didn't respond immediately, but the eyes returned to Kaz's face and the rage was unmistakable. Still she took her time. 'You fucking know who I'm talking about. Was you there when he chucked Jez off the balcony?'

Kaz took a deep breath. 'Yeah. Well . . . I actually came into the room just after. But yeah, I was there.'

Natalie took a moment to absorb this. 'You ain't gonna lie to protect him then?'

'If we're talking about Joey, then no, I ain't gonna lie to protect him. I'm not gonna lie to you about anything Nat. We're still sisters and if that's ever gonna mean anything again, then we tell each other the truth. It's the only thing that's gonna work.'

Natalie's gaze flickered suspiciously over her sister's face. 'What about the old bill? You gonna lie to them? Tell 'em it was an accident?'

Kaz took a deep breath. She hadn't expected this visit to be easy, but nor had she expected her baby sister to go straight for the jugular.

Natalie continued to scrutinize her, she saw Kaz's hesitation and the guilty look in her eye. She got up from the chair with a huff. 'Oh what the fuck, we both know the answer, don't we? You done six years to protect Joey. Lying to the filth – piece of piss. Old habits, eh, Kaz?'

Natalie stepped over to the window, folded her arms and looked out. Kaz waited. Even facing her sister's back she could feel the hostility radiating from her.

'Listen to me Nat, I don't want this to turn into me and Joey against you. I'm not on his side, not any more. You and me, we ain't seen each other for such a long time. A lot's happened to me. A lot. I had to fight to get clean myself.'

Natalie turned to look at her. 'Doctor Iqbal says we use to escape and we gotta look at what we're escaping from. In my case it's my whole fucking life and my whole fucking family.'

Kaz gave her a weak smile. 'I know what you mean.'

Natalie stared at her for several moments. Gradually her face softened, she sighed deeply. 'You're not how I remember you.'

Kaz laughed. 'That's a bonus, 'cause I was running round

out of my box most of the time. Look, I'm here 'cause I wanna help. I'm still your sister. And I know how hard it is to get clean.'

Natalie gave her the ghost of a smile. 'Do you?'

'Just talk to me Nat. Please.'

Natalie turned to face the window again, she stared out across the park to avoid her sister's eye.

'Jez used to get all our gear off Joey. I wasn't suppose to know, 'cause of Mum 'n'all that. But it was Joey kept us supplied. He always slipped Jez a few quid too, to take care of me. "Keep her happy", that's what he told Jez. Last time I was in here three months, got clean. Felt great. I got home, soon as Mum and Brian went out, Joey comes round. Brings Jez. Couple of lines to celebrate my homecoming they said, that won't do you any harm. Well . . . you can guess the rest.'

Kaz got up from her chair and gathered Natalie in her arms. Natalie remained ramrod stiff at first, but slowly she allowed herself to relax into the hug. Kaz could feel her bony shoulders start to shake. Then her whole body began to convulse with sobs.

Kaz held her tight, gently rocking her. 'It's okay babes, it's all gonna be okay.'

'Now you are fucking lying to me.'

Kaz could feel the wetness of her sister's tears on her neck, they soaked into the collar of her shirt. Or maybe it was her own tears. They stood crying in each other's arms for what seemed like an age. Finally Natalie edged away, wiped the back of her hand across her nose.

'Wanna see something?'

Kaz nodded. She pulled a wedge of folded tissues from her pocket, handed one to Natalie. Natalie blew her nose, went over to the corner, picked up the corkboard and propped it up on the bed. Kaz gazed at the oddly serpentine picture, it was a chaotic jumble of images, hard to decipher.

She smiled. 'Yeah . . . it's an interesting picture.'

Natalie shook her head. 'It's not a picture, it's like a chart. It's what we done in therapy. It's called "life events".' Natalie pointed to the top left-hand corner. 'Starts here.' Her finger snaked across and down the sheet. 'You have to put in all the big things, how you felt about them.' She pointed to a purple square, waxy impasto crayon, covered with horizontal and vertical black lines like a cage. 'That's the cupboard.'

Kaz could see the tears gathering in her sister's eyes again. 'What cupboard?'

'The big one upstairs in the hall, where we used to hide from Dad.'

Kaz nodded, gave her sister a tight smile. 'Oh yeah, that was always the best hiding place, behind the boxes and coats.'

Natalie stared back at her, the anger was gone from her eyes, leaving raw hurt. 'Joey told me that when you two used to hide in there together, 'specially after the old man had given him a thrashing, you'd give him a hand-job to take his mind off it.'

The words exploded in Kaz's brain, catapulting her back into a corner of the past that she'd firmly shut away. Her and Joey, two petrified teenagers, comforting each other in the warm, fetid darkness of the cupboard. Her immediate impulse was to deny it. Because it didn't happen, of course it didn't happen. But before she could speak Natalie beat her to it.

'After you went inside he wanted me to do the same. He never forced me. Used to give me sweets. A Crunchie and a Creme Egg for a hand-job, two bags of Haribos and a box of Maltesers for a blow-job. I was only twelve. Later on, when I said I wouldn't do it no more, he started to give me other stuff.'

Kaz couldn't speak, the revulsion that swept through her was visceral. And she knew it was her fault. It was all her fault. She'd chosen the wrong sibling to protect.

There was still morning dew underfoot as Kaz and Natalie walked out across the grass. The sweeping parkland, created by some long-forgotten Yorkshire mill owner in an attempt to perfect nature in the manner of Italian landscape painting, stretched out before them down to a curving lake and some woods. A young Sikh groundsman was raking leaves and feeding a smoky bonfire. He gave them a friendly grin as they passed.

Natalie glanced at her sister. 'Nice innit? Peaceful.'

Kaz nodded, gave her a weak smile. 'I want to apologize, but somehow that don't seem quite enough.'

Natalie looked at her. 'Let's go down to the lake. I never had a chance to take a proper look at it. They don't let us near it on our own, in case we try and top ourselves I guess.'

As they walked down the grassy slope a couple of moorhens scurried before them and headed for the water. The bank was edged with reeds, the water beyond still and dark.

Natalie turned to Kaz impulsively. 'Fancy a swim?'

'No! It looks bloody freezing. Anyway I don't think Doctor Iqbal'd like it.'

'Pity.' Natalie smiled. 'Jez taught me to swim. Used to go down the beach in Southend. It was a laugh.'

Kaz stopped in front of her sister. She shoved both hands in the pockets of her jeans. She'd promised Natalie the truth, but delivering it was something else. She took a deep breath.

'The day we came to your flat . . . I'd just got out. I really needed to see you. I had no idea that Joey would . . . would lose it like that.' Kaz swallowed hard. 'At the time I blamed myself 'cause I had a go at him about how he hadn't taken care of you. Result . . . he got angry and took it out on Jez. So yeah, I lied to the police for him. Convinced myself it was a one-off, not the real Joey. Come to think of it, he just wound me round his little finger.'

Natalie gave her a wry smile. 'That's Joey.'

Kaz reached out, took Natalie's arm. 'Listen, babes, I got a plan. I'm going to the States. New York. You could come with me.'

Natalie looked at her gone out. 'What would I do in New York?'

'Start again. Get your life back.'

Natalie started to giggle. 'New York? That's ridiculous.'

'Well what are you gonna do when you get out of this place? You can't go home.'

'My mate Nic reckons I should get a job. Train for something. Hairdressing maybe. I quite fancy being a hairdresser.'

Kaz shook her head in annoyance. 'Who the fuck is this Nic and what does she know about anything?'

Natalie gave her a sheepish look, she couldn't meet her sister's gaze. 'She's . . . someone who's been helping me. Helping me get my head straight.'

The realization hit Kaz like a bolt. 'Nic as in Nicci? Oh fuck! You been set up babes.'

Natalie frowned angrily. 'No I haven't. I'm not a fool. And Nic's been straight with me.'

'She's not your friend, she's a copper. She's only doing her job.'

Natalie screwed up her face and balled her fists. She reminded Kaz of the angry toddler she once was. 'Fuck you! She is my friend! Cares about me more than any of you lot ever have.' She turned on her heel and started to walk back up the grassy slope.

Kaz sighed. She gazed out over the lake. A duck and drake skimmed to a landing, sending ripples out across the dark waters. She turned and called after her sister. 'Nat, wait a minute. I'm sorry.'

She didn't get a reply. Natalie had stopped dead in her tracks. A tall figure was crossing the manicured bit of lawn in front of the house and walking down the hill towards them. As he strode across the grass it took Kaz a matter of seconds to grasp what her sister had already realized: it was Joey.

69

Nicci Armstrong arrived at Paddington Green police station around eleven a.m. It brought back memories; she'd served here as a rookie, her second posting after Hendon. She'd been so idealistic then, enthusiastic about the job, just starting going out with Tim, but that felt like another life now and she put it to the back of her mind.

An unremitting drizzle was falling which had slowed traffic in central London to a crawl. As she showed her ID to the desk sergeant she checked her watch and made an effort to get a handle on her anxiety. The journey should've taken twenty, it was now thirty-five minutes since they'd got the call.

PC Jason Tyler came down to the desk to meet her. He was a large, robust bloke, mid-thirties with a weight-lifter's neck. He escorted her to a small office, took a plastic bag from a desk drawer and emptied out a mobile phone. Nicci stared at it, one smartphone looked much like another.

She glanced at Tyler. 'When did you find it?'

'We took it off this homeless kid last night. Didn't really look at it until this morning. Your colleague's lucky, if it'd had a pin on it, we'd've never traced it to him.'

Nicci gave him a rueful smile. 'DC Bradley can be a bit casual, so no phone pin doesn't surprise me. Tell me about the kid.'

Tyler grinned and shook his head wearily. 'He's one of our

regulars. Thirteen. Cheeky little sod, been through more children's homes than you've had hot dinners.'

Nicci noticed the warmth in Tyler's voice, big tough street cop with a soft spot for homeless kids. She smiled. 'Sounds to me as if you like him.'

Tyler put on his professional face. 'Yeah well there's a bunch of them hang out round the mainline station. They try a bit of thieving, but mainly they're rent boys. We go out on a sweep, scoop them up, call social services. Within the week they're back.'

Nicci nodded. 'So this mugging, you think the boy's lying about what he saw?'

'Yeah, he's a right little fibber. Likes to be the centre of attention. Poor little sod hasn't had much of that in his life.'

'Well, let's take a look.'

Tyler led her through a warren of corridors. Some of the route was familiar, but she'd forgotten a lot. Too many places and too many years in between. Bradley hadn't been seen this morning, but there was nothing unusual about that. She'd called his landline, got the voicemail. Still her gut was full of foreboding. She needed to distract herself. She glanced at Tyler, with his dark shaved head, solid muscle under the uniform, he looked every inch the hard man.

'By the way I wasn't being critical when I said I thought you liked him. But most officers don't have much time for these street kids.'

Tyler gave her a sidelong look. 'Yeah well most officers didn't grow up like I did. I was just another mixed-race kid who could've fallen through the net. But I was lucky, got fostered by an ace family who knew what they was doing.'

Nicci smiled. 'We could do with more like you.'

Tyler laughed, uncomfortable with the compliment. 'Don't

say that Sarge. ''Cause I've almost certainly got you down here on a wild-goose chase.'

Tyler opened the door to an interview room. The kid was seated at the table with a PSP he'd been given to keep him quiet. He ignored their entrance, kept zapping away at the game. Tyler looped his thumbs in his belt, stood in front of the boy.

'Right, this is DS Armstrong. So put that thing down and pay attention.' He turned to Nicci with a sheepish smile. 'Meet Dollie.'

Nicci stepped forward. The boy was deliberately ignoring her, but she could see that was all part of the act. Maybe Tyler was right, this was just a teenage drama queen making up stories.

She stared at him. 'That your real name, Dollie?'

The boy plonked the PSP down and gave her a look of total disdain. 'Naah course it in't. I'm called Dollie 'cause I'm as fuckable as a girl.'

Nicci met his defiant look with a smile. He was small and scrawny, but his large liquid-brown eyes and sculpted cheekbones did make him look very girlish.

'So tell me about the phone Dollie.'

'I din't nick it.'

'No one's saying you did.'

'Found it.'

'Found it where?'

There was a Coke can on the table. Dollie picked it up and shook it, gave Nicci a mischievous look. 'Get him to get me another one of these.'

Tyler huffed. 'You'll get another drink once you've answered the Sergeant's question. Come on now, she's a busy woman.'

Dollie stuck out his chin, grinned at Nicci. 'Where you say you from? The social? 'Cause I ain't getting banged up in no home.'

Tyler stepped forward and pointed a threatening index finger at the kid. 'Listen to me boy, don't make a fool of me here . . .'

Dollie tossed his head. In the course of his short chaotic life he'd learnt one thing, to recognize his assets and trade on them. Nicci sat down at the table in front of him, folded her hands patiently and smiled.

'Okay Dollie, what do you want?'

'You mean like right now?'

Nicci nodded.

The boy grinned. 'I'll take a quarter pounder and fries and a large Coke.'

Nicci sighed. 'Trouble is, if we get you that, then we could be bribing you. So unless you want to talk to me of your own free will, I may as well get PC Tyler here to call child protection and ship you out.'

Dollie pouted. 'Fuckers, you're all the same.'

Nicci waited for a moment. 'On the other hand, if I felt you'd given us your full cooperation, then I think a burger and fries might be a suitable reward . . . before we let you go on your way.'

Dollie's dark eyes scanned her face, then moved over to Tyler's. He sucked his teeth. The boy sat up in his chair, adjusted his narrow shoulders.

'I been sitting outside the tube station begging. Not that many people about, I was thinking of jacking it in. This bloke come along with a girl. I think they was together, sort of. Anyway, chat chat, she gives him a hug and he kisses her hand. Then I see this Beamer parked across the road, bloke got the window down taking pictures of them. I thought it was your fucking lot.'

Nicci pursed her lips. 'The bloke and the girl, did they see the man taking pictures?'

Dollie shook his head. 'No. They was just looking at each other. She went in the tube. He gets out his phone, makes a call. He crosses the road to the pub. He's yattering away on the phone, so he don't see these two big blokes get out the Beamer. They come up behind him, one of 'em gives him a shove, he drops the phone. They whack him in the gut, drag him off to the Beamer. Drive off. So the phone was lying there, so I went and picked it up.'

Nicci took a deep breath.

Dollie glanced at her nervously. 'It's true, I promise.'

Nicci gave him a brief smile. 'I know it is. What sort of Beamer was it? A big one, four-by-four? Or an ordinary car?'

'Big one, black. Chrome wheels like you see on the posters. And blacked-out side windows.'

Nicci nodded. Her face was a tense mask, but she forced another smile, patted the boy on the arm. 'One more question. This was last night, what sort of time?'

The kid put his head to one side and pondered. 'Dunno. Ain't got a watch. It was dark.'

Tyler glanced at Nicci. 'We picked him up at nine thirty. How long after was that Dollie?'

The boy hunched his shoulders. 'Dunno. Hour maybe.'

Nicci absorbed this. She got up from her chair. 'Thanks Dollie. Now . . . we're going to get you a burger and fries.'

The boy grinned. 'Double cheeseburger?'

'Yeah double cheeseburger. And PC Tyler's going to sit with you and write all this down. Everything you can remember. I don't want you to make anything up to make it sound better, but I don't want you to leave anything out. Understand?'

Dollie nodded, he puffed out his chest. He could feel that what he'd said was important and he liked that.

Nicci glanced at Tyler. 'All right if I leave you with this? I need to make a call.'

Tyler's face was grave. 'Fine. Let us know anything else you need.'

Nicci was halfway out the door. 'Bag the phone as evidence.'

As soon as she was in the corridor she pulled out her own phone, scrolled the contacts list for Bill Mayhew's name. Her palms were sweating as she tapped the screen. She knew he'd be waiting for her call, but still it was a relief to hear his voice.

'What we got Nic?'

She took a deep breath. 'I think the kid's kosher. Looks to me like Joey Phelps has got Bradley. And he's had him for over twelve hours.'

70

Joey had liked Woodcote Hall from the first moment he set eyes on it. The elegant Palladian mansion in its acres of parkland was exactly the kind of place he aspired to live in. Of course he imagined it not as some poxy addiction clinic but as a private residence, restored to splendour with a few extra mod cons like a swimming pool, gym, home cinema, whole-house audio and tellies in every bathroom. Joey prided himself on being a patriotic Englishman. He hated the fact that many of the nation's stately homes, not to mention most of the truly upscale property in London, had been bought up by foreigners. In his view all these Arabs and oligarchs should be sent packing. His fantasy of himself was of the complete country gentleman, horses in his stables, a collection of vintage cars, a shotgun over his arm, a dog at his heel as he strolled down the grassy slope from his terrace to the lake, much as he was doing now.

Tracking his sister down had been easy. He'd supplied her number to a disgraced ex-cop now in the security business; the cop got onto a contact in the phone company who put a location trace on her phone. It had cost him a measly two hundred quid to discover she was in a hotel in Leeds. The rest was guesswork.

His first impulse had been to steam up the motorway after her, but he decided against it. This was about establishing who was boss. He wasn't the little brother any more, which is how

Kaz had been treating him. Family loyalty mattered, the old man had taught him that. He wanted Kaz back in the business with him, partners certainly, but with him in charge. She'd stepped out of line and he needed to put her straight. He'd be firm but fair, that's what he told Yevgeny as they drove up the M1 in the early morning. Protection and authority: women needed and expected that.

As he walked across the grass towards Natalie he opened his arms and grinned. 'All right babes. I should've been up before, but y'know – stuff to do.'

Natalie stood stock-still. She didn't resist as he folded her in a hug, she simply didn't move. He held her at arm's length, scanned her pale face. 'You're looking much better.' He glanced over her shoulder and beamed at his other sister, who was coming up the slope towards them. 'She's looking much better, 'n't she Kaz?'

Kaz stopped a couple of yards away from him. 'You following me or something?'

Joey gave her an innocent shrug. 'Nah, course not. Nice day, I fancied a drive. Thought it was time I visited my baby sister. You could've knocked me down with a feather when I seen you was here too.'

Kaz shook her head wearily. 'Why don't I believe you Joey?'

Her tone wasn't respectful, it was patronizing. She was still talking to him as if he was a little kid. And this got Joey's goat. After what she'd done she ought to be sweet to him at the very least. The sunny smile faded. He fixed her with a hard stare.

'Well, good job I run into you. 'Cause you and me need to have a little chat.'

Kaz nodded, she didn't seem that bothered, which she ought to be. She ought to be worried at the very least. Instead she just gave him a dismissive look.

'I need to take Natalie back to her room first.'

Joey took a step forward. 'No. I think Natalie should hear this too.'

Kaz huffed, she returned his look. There was no flinching, no hint of backing down. 'Joey, she's not well. For fuck's sake leave her out of this.'

Colour was rising in his cheeks, this wasn't what he'd planned. He needed to stay in control, but she was winding him up, she was doing it deliberately. He'd intended to be measured, give her a chance to explain, but Kaz had provoked him and so he blurted it out. 'Police busted Marko and Leysa yesterday. Know how much that's fucking cost me? A fucking mint. Middle of the fucking countryside, but they went straight there. How did they know where to go Kaz, that's what I been asking myself?'

'How should I know?' Kaz put an arm round Natalie's shoulder. 'I can't even remember where they live. Out Chelmsford way somewhere?'

She steered Natalie to one side in an attempt to get round Joey, but he stepped in front and blocked them. Natalie started to cry, she buried her face in her hands.

Kaz turned on him. 'Now look what you done. Back off Joey!'

Their eyes met. The tension rippled through his jaw. 'You don't tell me what to do. Not any more.' His look was cold and blank. 'I let you speak to me like this 'cause you're my sister and I love you. Anyone else, I'd fucking deck 'em. But you've let me down Kaz and we need to sort that out.'

Kaz gave him a considered look. She still didn't seem particularly scared, which annoyed him. She sighed.

'Okay, whatever you think needs sorting out, we'll sort out. But let Natalie go back to her room. Please.' She gave him a smile.

He glanced from her to Natalie. Natalie was blubbing like a baby, that's what she always did. All this money to get her clean – waste of time. She was only ever happy when she was off her head. Silly cow was completely mental, it was time they all accepted that.

Joey put his hands on his hips, puffed out his cheeks. 'All right all right, but she can find her own way, she's not a fucking invalid.'

Kaz pointed her sister in the direction of the house. She caught a glimpse of a mauve tunic on the terrace. She patted Natalie's arm. 'Look, I think that's June. She'll take you back up.'

Natalie gazed at her, the startled woodland creature paralysed with fear. Kaz gave her a reassuring smile. 'It'll be fine.' She cast a defiant look at her brother. 'Tell her it'll be fine Joey.'

'Yeah yeah, it'll be fine.'

Kaz gave her sister a gentle push, propelling her towards the house. Natalie glanced over her shoulder, her voice barely audible. 'Come back, won't you.'

Kaz nodded. ''Course I will.'

She turned to face Joey. He was staring right at her. He looked like an aggrieved, petulant kid, but she knew that didn't make him any less dangerous.

She gave him a weary smile. 'So what's going on little brother? You must've left London at the crack of dawn.'

Joey shovelled his hands in his pockets. 'Don't call me that, I don't like it.'

'It's a term of affection.'

'No it ain't. It's you trying to put me in my place.'

'Then I'm sorry.'

His eyes bored into her. She could feel his untempered fury. They'd had disagreements before and she'd seen glimpses of his rage, but somehow this was different and it was directed exclusively at her.

'Ever since you got out, haven't I taken care of you? Everything you needed. Every little thing. Flat. Money. I even took care of that mess with Sean.'

She wanted to challenge this but it didn't seem a good time to argue the toss.

'But you let me down babes. You was the one person I trusted, and you let me down.'

'How?' She held out her palms in supplication.

'And you lied to me about it.'

'Lied about what?'

'I knew all along you was shagging that fucking copper.'

This stopped Kaz in her tracks. She stared at him in disbelief. 'No, you got it all wrong.'

'Naah, I think I finally got it all right.'

He pulled an iPhone from his pocket, swiped a finger across the screen and pulled up a video clip. He handed the phone to Kaz.

The lighting wasn't that good, but a figure on the tiny screen was slumped in a chair. His head lolled, it was bleeding and he appeared to be tied up. He moved and Kaz realized with a jolt it was Bradley. She stared at her brother in horror.

'What the fuck have you done Joey?'

He shook his head bitterly. 'Naah, what the fuck have you done? Grassed me up to your boyfriend that's what! I ain't stupid, I know that's how they got Marko and Leysa.'

Kaz was simply stunned. 'This is mental Joey. I couldn't even tell you where they live.'

'You been there!'

'Yeah, but I was driven. I don't know where it was.'

Joey shook his head quickly and sharply, as if to erase any

doubt. 'Nah, you knew and you told him. He turns up mob-handed. Now the filth're threatening them with deportation. And Leysa's pregnant – bet you didn't know that.'

Kaz took a deep breath, it was vital she made him see sense. 'However they found out, it was from someone else, because it wasn't from me.' She hooked into his gaze, he turned angrily away. 'Look at me Joe, please, because I'm telling you the truth.'

He turned back to look at her, but the eyes were icy and blank. She exhaled.

'I swear to you . . . on the Bible . . . on whatever you want, he's not my boyfriend. I hardly fucking know him.'

Joey reached out and took the phone back. He fixed her with his laser-eyed stare. 'That case I might as well give Tolya a bell, get him to shoot the fucker now.'

Kaz swallowed hard. 'No don't do that. That's stupid.'

'Oh, so you do care about him.'

Kaz could feel her heart thumping in her chest. She sucked in a couple of calming breaths. 'He's a copper. You shoot a copper you'll never become legit, just a straight businessman. Thought that's what you wanted.'

Joey laughed. 'Tell you what little sister, you get in the car, come back to London with me right now, or I ring Tol, tell him to put a bullet in your boyfriend's head. Your choice babes.'

71

Nicci Armstrong stood in front of Turnbull's desk. He was looking immaculate, a pristine white shirt, blue silk tie. Gold cufflinks peeped out from the sleeves of his dark suit. He seemed to be dressed for a wedding or a job interview. He planted his elbows on the neat pile of papers in front of him and steepled his fingers. But he was struggling to hold his temper.

'Let me get this straight, you were on the phone to him, unexpectedly, middle of the conversation, the line goes dead. But you didn't follow that up for over twelve hours? Why not?'

Nicci took a deep breath. 'It didn't . . . seem necessary.'

Turnbull rose to his feet, kicked away the chair. He leant forward, resting white knuckles on the desk, his whole frame rippling with frustration and fury. His goal was within reach, one single meeting away. But he'd never anticipated this. He'd set Bradley up to fail, not to get himself killed. The last thing he needed was another death on his conscience.

He turned his wrath on Nicci. 'Necessary? You're supposed to be Bradley's backup. He goes off the grid and you don't think it necessary to find out why? I'll have your fucking job for this Armstrong!'

Nicci glared right back at him, the tension was burning off her. They were wasting so much time. 'He was off on his own, he didn't even tell me what . . .'

She realized Turnbull wasn't listening. His gaze had shot

over her shoulder, past Mayhew, a couple of paces behind, and through the glass-panelled door to where Fiona Calder was striding towards the office, a look of thunder on her face. As she seized the handle and flung the door open, Turnbull turned to them.

'You two, out!'

The Assistant Commissioner paused on the threshold, glanced at Mayhew and Nicci. Out of uniform, in an expensive charcoal-grey trouser suit and fine string of pearls, she looked like any well-heeled executive or CEO.

She fixed Turnbull with a glacial stare. 'No Alan, I think all your team need to hear this.' She checked her wristwatch. 'Shouldn't you have left for your meeting with the IPCC by now? They take a dim view of people being late.'

The colour was draining from Turnbull's face. Nicci had always seen him as tough and imperious, but confronted by this small, middle-aged woman, he seemed to shrink.

He cleared his throat. 'We have a situation here ma'am, which I need to deal with as a matter of urgency—'

In spite of her size, Calder's presence filled the room. 'I think you've dealt with your last situation as a serving police officer. You're suspended from duty.'

Turnbull blinked a couple of times, then he came right back at her. 'That won't stop me making my statement to the IPCC. You sanctioned an illegal operation – you're the one who's finished.'

Calder gave him a cynical laugh. 'You chose Bradley, not me. You set up the honey trap.'

Turnbull's jaw tightened. 'I was acting on your instructions ma'am and that's what I'll tell the IPCC. We'll see who they believe.'

'My instructions!' Calder was seething. Turnbull towered

over her in height, but she stepped forward, jabbing her index finger at his chest. 'You lied to me and you set up your own officers to fail.'

She glanced at Nicci and Mayhew, several other members of the squad were hovering near the open door.

'And for what? To mess up a major investigation and prove we're all rubbish? Hoping that'll create a big enough scandal so your friend Duncan Linton can move a private security firm in to take over major investigations?'

At the mention of Linton's name, Turnbull did indeed blanch. How the hell did she know?

The Assistant Commissioner allowed herself a triumphant smile. 'Oh, the Commissioner knows all about your deal with Linton. How? Marcus Foxley told him. Never trust a politician Alan. He may behave like a naive fool, but that doesn't mean he is one.'

Turnbull was stunned, but he was determined to stand his ground. 'Well, privatization is coming whether you and the Commissioner like it or not.'

'So you thought you'd buy yourself a ticket on the gravy train? How many millions did you hope to make?'

Turnbull shot her a defiant look. 'It's not just about money. It's about who takes over. Putting the right people in the job. You want some ex-American police chief running homicide investigations in London?'

Calder turned and with a sweep of her arm encompassed Nicci, Mayhew and the officers in the outer office.

'And that's your excuse for betraying me, your colleagues and the Metropolitan Police Service? Shame on you Turnbull. Shame on you.'

Turnbull jutted his chin.

'The core values of the MPS have got a far better chance of

survival with Duncan Linton than with some of the other outfits that'll be vying for the contract.'

Nicci glanced at Mayhew. They'd both been watching open-mouthed as their bosses slugged it out, but Nicci couldn't keep quiet any longer. The image of Alex Marlow's bloated corpse kept flashing through her mind.

'Sorry ma'am, but DC Bradley . . . well it looks like Joey Phelps has got him.'

Calder turned, her fury with Turnbull was consuming her. She stared at Nicci blankly. 'What?'

'We've only just found out. We think Phelps kidnapped him yesterday evening.'

Fiona Calder swivelled round, pointed at a stocky, carrot-haired officer standing near the doorway. 'You – what's your name?'

The officer's eyes widened, he flushed red from neck to forehead. 'DC Payne ma'am.'

'Payne, I want you to escort Detective Chief Superintendent Turnbull out of the building. You will relieve him of his warrant card and bring it to me.'

Payne's jaw slackened, he glanced at Mayhew for support. Mayhew gave him a curt nod.

Calder turned back to Nicci. 'You're Armstrong aren't you?'

'Yes ma'am.'

'You're sure about all this?'

Nicci nodded. 'Yeah. We've got a witness saw him being taken.'

Calder zeroed in on Mayhew. 'I want Joey Phelps brought in. Get SO19 to provide armed backup. Find him. Nick him. Now. I'll be taking over direct control of this operation myself.'

Mayhew nodded and scurried out. Nicci followed. Calder glanced at Turnbull. He was still standing behind the desk, hands in his pockets. He looked pale, but he'd regained most of his composure.

He gave her a contemptuous smile. 'You can't walk in here and throw me out.'

'I'm acting on the Commissioner's instructions. Your lawyer can make representations directly to him and the IPCC. Now, does DC Payne require assistance to escort you out?'

Payne was hovering in the doorway with a look of total embarrassment on his face. Turnbull let a small hiss of annoyance escape between his teeth. He reached into his jacket pocket, pulled out his warrant card and tossed it on the desk. He glared at Calder.

'This isn't over, y'know.'

72

The roadworks on the M1 slowed traffic from a twenty-mile-an-hour crawl to sporadic gridlock. Kaz sat in the back of the X5 wondering what the hell she was going to do. Joey had taken the precaution of trashing her phone, grinding it into the gravel with his heel before they left Woodcote Hall. She'd caught a glimpse of Natalie being shepherded away into the house by June as Yevgeny held the car door open for her. Doctor Iqbal seemed in his way to be a pretty canny bloke. Kaz hoped he'd find a way to protect her sister. And then there was Nic, who Natalie was convinced was such a good mate, but Kaz didn't place any reliance on that.

It was the middle of the afternoon by the time they arrived at the garage lock-up under some railway arches in Ilford. Tolya was sitting outside on an upturned crate smoking a Turkish cigarette. Joey got out of the front passenger seat and stretched, he'd spent a large part of the journey dozing.

He nodded at Tolya. 'Where's Ash?'

'I call him like you say. He not pick up. Think he went back to the flat.'

Joey yawned. 'Skiving off, dozy sod. Well let's get this show on the road.'

Yevgeny opened the car door for Kaz. She made a point of meeting his gaze, but his look remained disinterested and professional. She followed Tolya and her brother into the lock-up.

Yevgeny was close behind, making sure she was penned in.

Coming out of daylight into the gloomy interior required a moment for the eyes to adjust. But Kaz didn't have any problem seeing the hooded figure trussed up on a chair in front of her. His arms were pinioned behind him, his torso and legs were bound to the chair with heavy-duty duct tape, the chair was chained to an oil drum full of concrete. Tolya hadn't taken any chances. The hood was loose-weave hessian sacking blackened with engine oil. He pulled it off to reveal Bradley's flushed and bloodied face.

Tolya glanced at Joey apologetically. 'Nose all busted up, so if I tape the mouth he don't breathe.' He pointed upwards at the vaulted ceiling. 'Trains every five minute. No one hear him.'

As Kaz gazed at Bradley she felt rising nausea sting the back of her throat, her hand went reflexively to her mouth. He looked up at her, a hint of a smile in his eyes, but a beaten and bleeding creature. Dried blood encrusted his face, his nose was swollen to twice the normal size. She realized Joey was watching her reaction, a satisfied smile playing round his mouth.

'Right then, now we'll get the truth.'

Kaz took a calming breath and turned to face her brother. She understood enough about his psychology to know she had to front it out with him.

'Yeah you will Joey. 'Cause this is fucking ridiculous.'

Joey inclined his head, he was enjoying himself. 'Show her the clip Tol.'

Tolya got out his phone, tapped the screen a couple of times. He set it to play and handed her the device. She watched the sequence of her and Bradley in front of the tube station. She shook her head in disbelief, tossed the phone back to Tolya and glared at her brother.

'Is that it? Is that your excuse for this total fucking mess?'

Joey tipped back his head and laughed. 'I know you got balls babe. And I've always admired that. Never give up in a fight. But you're shagging him, anyone can tell that. And it was you told him about Marko and Leysa.'

Bradley coughed and spat a globule of congealed blood from his mouth. His voice was rough, a hoarse whisper. 'No. She didn't. Mainwaring Grant gave us your files. We found the place in Danbury from that.'

Joey turned and glared at Bradley. 'Did I fucking tell you to speak?'

It was clearly an effort to hold his head up, but Bradley returned his look. 'Said you wanted the truth. Well ring up your old school pal Anthony Hobbart. He'll tell you what happened, we went round there and leant on them. They gave us Dimitrenko to get rid of us. And I suspect to get rid of you.'

Joey ruminated on this. His brow darkened, he looked ready to explode. Then he simply laughed. 'Well whad'you know? Fucking accountants, eh.'

This lightning change of mood gave Kaz the opening she was looking for. She reached out, put her hand on his arm.

'Joe, listen to me. I don't blame you for jumping to conclusions.' She shot a look in Bradley's direction. 'But let me tell you the truth about me and him. Since I got out I've only slept with one person. And it ain't him.'

Joey gazed at her, a troubled look came into his eyes. His glance darted from Tolya to Yevgeny.

'Not one of them? They're fucking animals.'

Kaz smiled. She didn't want to get into this with him. It was no one's business but her own. But she figured that the truth was the only thing likely to convince him. She dipped her head.

'Not them. Helen. Helen Warner, my lawyer. You can phone her and ask her.'

Joey's jaw slackened. She was acutely aware of the four men around her, enough testosterone to start World War Three. But she didn't care about their judgement. Yevgeny and Tolya remained inscrutable. She wasn't sure, but she thought perhaps Bradley smiled. Joey turned to the others, palms outstretched in incredulity.

'You believe this? My sister a fucking carpet muncher? I mean look at her. Look at her. She's too beautiful to be a dyke.'

Kaz sighed. 'Doesn't really work like that.'

Joey gave her a shrewd look. 'Then what is going on with him?'

Kaz met his gaze. 'We went to meet my art class teacher to persuade him to help me get a college place.'

Her brother frowned. 'Thought you had a college place.'

Kaz smiled ruefully, somehow the truth had got him to listen, so the truth it had to be. 'This one's in New York.'

Joey nodded as he absorbed this. Then he pointed at Bradley. 'Why would he help you? You can't tell me he done it for nothing.'

'I was playing him.' Kaz hunched her shoulders, gave her brother an appealing look. 'I mean obviously.'

Joey turned away, he looked petulant. 'You wanna go to New York, why didn't you ask me? We could've gone together.'

'Joey, I needed him to persuade the art teacher to wangle me the college place and convince probation. These things ain't easy to arrange.'

Joey nodded, took a deep breath then exhaled. Kaz could feel her stomach knotted with tension, but she was starting to hope. He did seem to believe her. The problem now was how to get Bradley out of there.

Joey paced a couple of times, checked his watch. 'Where the fuck's Ashley? Tol, give him another call.'

Tolya produced his phone and went out of the lock-up.

440

Joey seemed to be musing to himself. 'Never been to New York. I've always fancied it.'

Kaz squeezed his arm. 'Let's go together. We'll have a great time.'

Joey glanced at Bradley and huffed. 'What we gonna do about him?'

Kaz didn't miss a beat.

'Bribe him. He wants to get out the police, go to Australia. Don't you Bradley?'

Bradley had been watching the two of them with an eagle eye. He nodded. 'Yeah, get a job with my cousins.'

Joey gave Bradley a cursory glance. His tone was oddly innocent. 'You really think you can trust him?'

'What you can trust babes is the money. You've got it, he wants it. Bent cop's not gonna grass you up. It's in his interests to just disappear.'

Joey fixed her with a penetrating look, then his lip started to tremble with amusement. The amusement erupted into hilarity and he slapped his thigh. He laughed until his eyes watered, then he wagged his finger at Yevgeny.

'You gotta admit Yev, she's good. My sister is good. Don't think I ever heard such a convincing load of old bullshit, have you?'

Kaz stared at him in surprise. 'It's not bullshit. Joey, I swear to you . . .'

Joey continued to chortle. 'Now the dyke bit, that was a stroke of genius.' He adopted a mocking tone. '"I've only ever slept with one person and it ain't him."'

Kaz shot a nervous look at Bradley. Joey giggled.

'Have you seen her fucking lawyer? Miss Prissy. Got a bug up her arse this far. And the idea of the two of them at it . . . no one'd buy that. No one.' He giggled some more.

Kaz held out her hand beseechingly. 'Call her, call her Joey. That'll prove it.'

Joey wiped away tears of mirth with the back of his hand. He took a deep breath and his expression changed.

'Nah, I got a better way to prove it. Quicker too.' He glanced at the Russian. 'Yev, you got that SIG?'

Yevgeny unzipped his jacket pocket and brought out the SIG Sauer 220 pistol. He screwed on the suppressor, handed it to Joey. Joey checked the magazine was properly loaded, pulled back the slide and decocked it. His face was completely serious now. He turned to his sister.

'Okay, let's say I decide to believe you. You and him, nothing going on. That's what you're telling me, innit?'

Kaz swallowed hard. 'Yeah.'

Joey offered her the SIG. 'Right. All you gotta do is shoot him in the head. Then I'll know you're telling me the truth.'

Kaz stared in disbelief at the gun.

Joey held it out. 'Go on, take it.'

She glanced at Bradley, his shoulder blades and arms were pulled back tight by the duct tape, his head bowed, but he was staring right at her, a look of shock and fear on his face.

Joey fixed her with his laser-eyed stare. 'Ain't as if you haven't done it before. What's the problem?' He waited a moment then turned, held out the gun at arm's length and pointed it at Bradley. 'Want me to do it for you?'

Bradley stared down the barrel and fixed Joey with his own unflinching look. 'Yeah go on Joey, you do it! You're the psycho. Murder's your job not hers.'

A slow smile spread over Joey's face, he closed one eye as he lined up his arm and took aim at Bradley's head.

Kaz stepped in front of him, held out her hand. 'No! Give it to me, I'll do it.'

For a frozen instant Joey looked disappointed.

She hooked his gaze. 'I'll do it.'

He lowered his arm and handed the gun to her.

As Kaz's palm closed around the pistol grip she didn't know what she was going to do, only that she had to do something. All eyes were on her. Joey had an amused and expectant grin, Yevgeny stood, arms folded, watching and waiting. Bradley was craning his neck to look at her, the bruising round his nose and eyes had turned a livid purple, leaving the eyes sharp and bright with fear. Kaz took a deep breath and pointed the gun at her brother.

'This stops now Joey. I ain't gonna let you kill him.'

Joey grinned and put his hands on his hips.

'Well that answers that question, dunnit? I knew I was right. But how you gonna get out of here babes, you and lover boy? By the time you shot me Yev'll be across there ripping your head off. You could take a pop at him, but then I'd do the same. So you got one shot, who's it gonna be?'

Kaz didn't move, the gun remained trained on Joey. He smiled.

'Tick tock. Made up your mind yet?'

He held out his hand and started to edge forward. 'Give me the gun babes.'

Kaz raised her arm slightly, aimed a couple of inches above Joey's head and pulled the trigger. The report ricocheted round the lock-up. The bullet tore into the wall sending shards of brick flying. Joey ducked reflexively. He seemed more surprised than unnerved.

'Fucking hell Kaz!'

Tolya appeared in the doorway, a sneaky fag in his hand. He shot a look at Yevgeny, who simply sighed. Kaz adjusted her aim, pointing the gun straight at Joey.

'Don't make the mistake of thinking I won't shoot you little brother. 'Cause like you said, I done it before. Now untie him.'

Joey shook his head wearily. 'Listen to me Kaz—'

'Untie him. Now!'

Joey cocked his head at the Russian. 'Yev—'

'Not him Joey. You. You do it.'

Joey stepped forward, gave Bradley a disdainful smile and started to pick ineffectually at the duct tape.

'It ain't designed to come off, this stuff, that's why we use it. Needs a knife.'

'You got strong hands, tear it.'

Bradley's eyes were darting between Kaz and Joey. His mouth was bone dry. He licked his lips. 'Get him to click emergency services on his mobile, put the phone to my ear, I'll call for backup.'

Joey clouted him hard across the side of the head. 'The fuck you will!'

'Joey! I'm warning you!'

He raised his palms. 'All right all right . . . but honestly?'

Joey freed the end of the duct tape round Bradley's torso and started to unwind it. He was taking his time. 'So babes, where you gonna run?'

Kaz didn't get a chance to answer, the door behind Tolya opened and Ashley appeared.

Joey turned to face him. 'About bloody time. As you can see me and my sister are having a slight disagreement.'

Ashley glanced at Kaz and then back to Joey. His face was tense and drawn. 'Joe, something I need to tell you.'

Joey huffed. 'Why are you such a fucking twat? Let me deal with this first, okay.'

'It's your dad. He's dead.'

Joey's head tipped back as if he'd been hit, he let his hands fall to his sides, he looked confused. 'Dead? How can he be dead?'

'Brian found him in his wheelchair, called me. That's where I been. Over their place. I didn't want them to tell you on the phone. Then the old bill turned up looking for you. I had to climb over the fence sharpish. They been to the flat too.'

Joey turned to his sister, tears welling up in his eyes. 'How can he be dead?'

Kaz looked at Ashley. 'What was it? Another stroke?'

Ashley nodded. 'Think so.'

Kaz lowered her arm. It seemed faintly absurd to be standing there holding a gun on her weeping brother. Joey cupped his palms over his face and sobbed.

'He's dead Kaz. What am I gonna do?'

Kaz glanced at Yevgeny, trying to gauge what his next move would be. She sighed.

'Probably for the best. He didn't have much of a life sitting in that chair like a zombie.'

Joey wiped away tears and snot with his fingers. He frowned, he seemed to be trying to put a picture together in his mind. 'So what you telling me Ash? Dad's dead and the fucking filth are all over the fucking house?'

Ashley nodded. 'That's about the size of it, yeah.'

Joey turned on Bradley, still bound to the chair trying to free himself from the duct tape, and his fury exploded. He heaved the chair on its side, Bradley crashed to the floor and his head struck the concrete.

'Fucking bastards! You got no respect!'

Joey booted him in the gut. Kaz launched herself at her brother's back, spun him round and pointed the gun right in his face.

'Enough!'

He simply stared at her, a tear rolled down his cheek. He sniffed. 'I gotta go and see Mum.'

Ashley shook his head. 'No you can't Joe, there's filth all over.' He glanced at Bradley. 'Probably looking for him.'

Joey turned, fury was still burning off him, he walked round in a circle, took a couple of deep breaths. Then he stopped, stared at the bricks overhead. It was almost as if he were counting them. The rage appeared to subside.

He looked at Ashley. 'Call Neville. He'll sort them out.' He turned to Yevgeny and pointed at the semi-conscious Bradley. 'Finish this off and clean up the mess. I gotta go and be with my mum.'

Joey headed for the door, as an afterthought he glanced at Kaz. 'You coming babes? Mum's gonna need her family round her.'

Kaz hissed in disbelief. 'What planet you living on Joey? She and Brian are probably cracking open the champagne.'

Joey stared at her, his eyes cold and blank. 'Fuck you then.'

And he was gone. Ashley scurried out of the door after him.

Kaz looked down at Bradley, it was hard to tell if he was still breathing. She glanced at the pistol in her hand, Yevgeny and Tolya were both watching her. She met their gaze, held it. Then she sighed.

'Don't you think that perhaps this particular tour of duty is over for you lads? Take a plane to somewhere hot, sit on a nice beach? Whad'you reckon?'

Yevgeny pondered this, turned to his brother, said something in Russian. Tolya nodded.

Unexpectedly Yevgeny smiled. 'You a tough lady. I like you. See you around sometime maybe.'

Tolya gave her a nod and a smile then the two Russians disappeared out of the door.

Kaz dropped the gun, rushed over to the workbench and found a Stanley knife. She used it to cut Bradley free from the chair. He was conscious but disorientated. He was bleeding from the ear.

She cradled his head. 'I got no phone, so I'm gonna have to get some help.' Pulling off her jacket, she folded it up and made a pillow for his head.

'They . . .' The effort to speak made him clutch his ribs and wince with pain.

Kaz took his hand 'They've gone, don't worry. Just lie still. I'll get an ambulance. You're gonna be fine.'

He held onto her hand and squeezed it.

73

Helen Warner was sitting through what seemed an interminable partners' meeting when one of the PAs came in and whispered that Karen Phelps was calling her collect from a kebab shop in Ilford. She gave Neville Moore an apologetic smile and slipped out of the room.

Since fetching Karen home from the hospital she'd taken a firm decision to put some space between them. But it hadn't been easy. Now she found her heart was thumping and her palms were clammy as she headed towards the phone.

She and Julia had set a date, booked the registry office. It was the sensible thing, it was the life she wanted, the life she needed. Karen Phelps was definitely not what she needed. Being with Karen would be madness; it would comprehensively fuck her up, her nascent political career would be dead in the water. And yet the scent of Karen's skin, the look of those intense dark eyes, the desire for her, niggled at the fringes of Helen's consciousness, it simply wouldn't leave her alone. Was this love? Stupid ragbag of a word. She'd loved before and look where that got her. Dumped flat to preserve the public image, to protect someone else's interests. Well she'd learnt the lesson back then: stay safe, stay in control.

She took a deep breath and grabbed the phone. Her tone was clipped, businesslike. 'Karen? What's up?'

The voice on the line was tense, hassled, even so the familiar

448

timbre stabbed Helen straight in the gut. 'I gotta be quick, 'cause I'm waiting for the ambulance.'

'Ambulance? What the hell . . .'

'Just listen. Joey got hold of Bradley. Remember Bradley the cop?'

'Of course . . .'

'Joey was gonna shoot him. I stopped him, but Bradley's beat up pretty bad. Hang on . . . here's the ambulance now.'

Helen could hear muffled chat in the background, a siren, finally Karen came back on the line.

'Romford. The A & E at Queen's. That's where we're going. Need you to call the cops, Woodentop's lot. Tell 'em. Okay?'

'Karen—'

The line went dead.

Helen could feel her hand shaking as she replaced the handset. Across the office she caught Neville Moore's gaze and he was zoning in on her. She'd had the odd barbed comment from him about professional standards and inappropriate relationships. He'd been watching her, monitoring her; maybe even checking her emails – she wouldn't put it past him.

As he approached he gave her his gimlet-eyed smile. 'Problems?'

She jutted her chin, no way was he getting the drop on her. Not now. She gave a diffident shrug. 'I think you may have a problem Neville. Joey Phelps has just tried to shoot a police officer.'

74

Nicci Armstrong walked into the A & E department at Queen's Hospital in Romford, headed straight to the front of the queue and flashed her ID at the triage nurse. She was probably being unnecessarily abrupt but the day had been frustrating in the extreme. They'd searched all the premises with known connections to Joey Phelps and drawn a blank. His vehicles had been flagged up, they'd put out an APW. With panic mounting Nicci had been rushing round in ever-decreasing circles wired on caffeine. As the hours went by the mood of the team had deteriorated, the theory gaining ground was that Bradley was already dead and Phelps had skipped the country. Then Nicci got a call from Karen Phelps's lawyer.

It was Helen Warner who told her Bradley was en route to Queen's Hospital in an ambulance with Karen Phelps. Nicci had run out of the Phelps family compound, leaving Essex Police to continue the stakeout. She was the first officer to reach the hospital.

The waiting area was in a late afternoon torpor, with a couple of unruly kids testing the patience of their vexed parents. Karen Phelps was sitting alone in one corner staring into space.

Nicci steamed straight up to her, she wanted answers and she wanted them now. Her temper was in danger of getting the upper hand. As she took a deep breath to rein it in, Kaz looked up at her.

'You got him yet?'

Somehow this was so unexpected and direct that it floored Nicci. 'Your brother? Not yet no.'

'He's on his way to my parents' place in Essex. You'll get him there.'

Nicci nodded. 'Where's Bradley?'

'Doctors are looking at him, X-raying him, whatever.'

Nicci nodded again. A small oriental staff nurse came through the swing doors in front of them. She carried a clipboard and a rather bored, supercilious air. Her eyes flicked over them. 'Which one is Karen? He wants to talk to you.'

Nicci pulled out her warrant card. 'I'm DS Armstrong.'

The nurse looked at her dismissively. 'No police interviews. He needs emergency surgery. You'll have to wait.' She turned to Kaz. 'Follow me.'

For Nicci this was the straw that broke the camel's back. She stepped in front of the nurse and loomed threateningly. 'Hang about sunshine. For your information he is a police officer. He's been missing and we've been looking for him all day. Now you go and get someone a lot higher up the food chain that I can talk to about this.'

The nurse glared at her and spluttered. 'This hospital has a policy of zero tolerance towards abusers of its staff.'

Kaz couldn't help smiling, it was like a Pekinese in a face-off with a Rottweiler.

'Really?' Nicci put her hands on her hips. 'Well, you've got one minute to get your boss or I'll be nicking you for obstruction. That's my policy.'

She didn't have to say more. A burly charge nurse and a registrar in surgical scrubs were homing in on them to defuse the situation.

*

Bradley was in a curtained-off cubicle in the trauma unit with a drip in his arm. The dried blood had been cleaned away but his face looked like a punchbag. A nurse was prepping him for emergency surgery, shaving the hair off the side of his head. She let the dark locks drop on the floor. The registrar escorted Nicci and Kaz to the cubicle. She was a horsey young woman, auburn hair scraped back in a bun and an abundance of freckles, but her manner was breezy and confident.

'He has an epidural haematoma – bleeding inside his skull – so we're taking him up to theatre immediately to deal with this. We presumed he was a victim of crime and pictures have been taken. He's lucid at the moment, but I can only give you a couple of minutes.'

Nicci nodded her thanks, she and Kaz exchanged awkward glances. Then Bradley noticed them and attempted a smile.

'Nic . . . glad you're here. Can't see that good, you need to come close.'

Nicci winced inwardly as she realized that probably meant serious neurological damage. She stood beside the trolley and took his hand. 'We've been looking for you all day.'

He gave her the ghost of a smile. 'Tell everyone I'm sorry.'

She could see he was having trouble focusing on her. 'Jesus wept Mal! How am I meant to cover your sorry arse if you don't talk to me, tell me what you're doing.'

He squeezed her hand. 'It was a secret. Wanted to help Karen but didn't want Turnbull to find out.'

Nicci shook her head, she could feel tears prickling behind her eyes. 'What, you think I talk to Turnbull any more than I have to?'

He was struggling to concentrate. He raised his hand in Kaz's direction.

'She saved my neck. Pointed a gun at her brother and stopped him from killing me. She wasn't part of this.'

Nicci glanced across at Kaz, who was on the other side of the trolley.

'Well we don't really know that, do we?'

Bradley took a breath. He was focusing all his effort on speaking. His voice was a hoarse whisper. 'Listen to me Nic, I know. Kaz and I were bloody lucky he didn't kill us both.'

The curtains were drawn back, the registrar, a nurse and some porters were waiting.

Kaz lifted Bradley's hand up gently and kissed the fingers. 'Hang on in there PC Mal, 'cause we've got a date in New York.'

Bradley smiled, then he started to cough. The cough turned to a gasp and a splutter as he fought for breath. His left arm jerked, then his whole body went into convulsions.

The registrar took charge. 'He's having a seizure. Call crash!'

Suddenly people in surgical scrubs were rushing in. A trolley with equipment appeared, the registrar was issuing instructions while injecting something into the cannula in Bradley's arm.

Kaz shot a glance at Nicci. 'What the fuck . . .?'

Nicci swallowed hard. The small oriental staff nurse took her elbow, but there was no hostility, just a professional look of concern. 'Please. You need to wait outside.'

She shepherded Nicci and Kaz to the waiting area. They stood in the middle of floor staring at each other helplessly for a moment. Then Kaz sank down on her haunches, hugging her arms round her knees.

Nicci towered over her. 'What the fuck did you two think you were playing at?'

Kaz glanced up, anger in her eyes. 'He was trying to help me get away from my brother. It was his fucking idea!'

Nicci released a hiss of air between her teeth. She took out her phone. 'He said you had a gun. Where's the gun?'

'I dunno. I left it on the floor in the lock-up.' Kaz buried her face in her knees.

Nicci was turning the phone over and over, fast, jittery repetitions.

'Where's the lock-up?'

Kaz rose up in one fast and fluid action. At her full height she was a couple of inches taller than Nicci. She fixed her with a fierce glare.

'Fucking cops! He's probably . . .' She swallowed hard. 'And all you can do is ask fucking questions!'

Nicci met her stare, raised her chin defiantly. 'I'm doing my job. Preserving the evidence to make a case – to send your fucking psychopath of a brother to jail.'

Kaz seemed to deflate, her shoulders sank. She breathed a heavy sigh. Nicci was close enough to feel the exuded air on her face. She could see the tears welling in the corners of Kaz's eyes. She watched the younger woman's trachea rise and fall as she swallowed. Then on the periphery of her vision she saw the auburn-headed registrar come through the swing doors. She stepped back and turned.

The registrar met her gaze and Nicci knew at once what was coming: the professional condolences, the sparse medical details, the official pronouncement that DC Mal Bradley was dead.

75

Kaz watched DS Nicci Armstrong disappear through the automatic doors and into the nicotine fug beyond. The doctor had explained in short, matter-of-fact sentences that the blood leaking inside Bradley's skull had turned into a massive haemorrhage. There was nothing they could do. Nicci had thanked the doctor politely, turned and walked away. Kaz had simply stood there, thinking about him, how he'd kept turning up, cajoling her, harassing her. How was it that she should feel so much pain over the death of a cop?

She concluded she was in shock. Her mouth felt dry. Although she hadn't eaten since breakfast she wasn't hungry, but she was certainly dehydrated. She walked over to the vending machine. She was peering at the contents, looking for something that wasn't entirely sugar water, when she heard a familiar voice at her back.

'Need some change?'

Her heart leapt. She turned and there was Helen. Kaz didn't want to feel so absurdly glad and grateful, but she was. They stared at each other awkwardly then Kaz stepped into her arms.

'Thanks for coming.'

Helen held onto her but only briefly before stepping back. 'I thought they'd certainly take you in for questioning. So best if I'm here.'

She fed some coins into the machine and a plastic bottle of

water plonked into the tray; she handed it to Kaz with a smile. Her manner was friendly but business-like.

'I've seen DS Armstrong outside. There are some other detectives who've just arrived. How do you want to play this?'

Kaz scanned her lover's face. Although they'd only made love on one occasion she found it hard to think of Helen as anything else. The memory of that intimacy was too precious. She longed to stroke her hair or touch her cheek. Instead she cracked open the bottle of water and took a long draught.

She wiped her mouth with her hand. 'Bradley's dead.'

'Oh, I see. That's a bit awkward. Do they know you helped him?'

Kaz stared at Helen. 'A bit awkward?'

'What d'you expect me to say? Tragic obviously. But my main concern at this moment is that you may be about to be charged as an accessory to murder and have your licence revoked.'

Kaz let her gaze rest on Helen's face. She was so beautiful it hurt to look at her. But then Kaz began to wonder, was that all an illusion, the product of confused feelings, but mostly desire? When she looked closer she could see a tightness round the lips, a prissiness, an assumption of superiority. Helen was certainly good-looking, but there was a harshness in her features, a need for control. Kaz wondered why she'd really come. To do her job? To salve her conscience? It was impossible to get behind the mask.

She took a deep breath. 'I know I phoned you, asked for your help. But y'know, all this is complicated. I've decided I'm gonna get myself a new lawyer. Your firm represents Joey. Don't think that's gonna work for me any more.'

Helen raised her eyebrows, she seemed surprised and mildly offended. 'Neville represents your brother and I'm quite capable of separating—'

Kaz reached out a hand and brushed Helen's arm. The frisson was still there, and hard to ignore, but Kaz knew she had to.

'I know what you're capable of. And I'll always be grateful to you. But I've made up my mind.'

Helen pursed her lips, it left her face tight and pinched. She wanted to be the one to draw the line, not Karen. The power had been wrested from her and she resented it. 'Well . . . I hope we can remain friends.'

Kaz gave her a sombre smile. 'Who knows? Maybe.'

Helen bit back an angry riposte.

Kaz tilted her head. 'Sorry you've had a wasted journey.'

Helen shrugged, turned on her heel and stalked off. Kaz watched her go. She still looked magnificent, very haughty and very Helen. Kaz swallowed hard but the tears still came.

76

Terry Phelps's funeral took place on a day of unseasonable autumn sunshine. The sky was cloudless, the temperature in the high teens. But even without the weather there was never any doubt that this was to be a spectacular send-off. Everything had to be top of the range, family dignity demanded it. A team of four plumed black horses drew a Victorian glass funeral carriage bearing the casket. On top of the walnut coffin a memorial ribbon wreath composed entirely of white roses spelled out two words: *The Guvnor*. This had been Brian's idea. Kaz couldn't remember anyone ever calling her father that, but the feeling was it fitted the occasion.

It took well over an hour for the horse-drawn cortège to wend its way through the Essex lanes to Chelmsford Crematorium. Sitting in the back of a vintage Rolls Royce, crawling along at less than ten miles an hour, Kaz had plenty of time for reflection.

The police had arrested her at the hospital, as she assumed they would. But before the interrogation began, she pre-empted them by laying her own deal on the table. She wanted a new identity and a place on the witness protection scheme for her and her sister. In return she'd tell them everything she knew and testify against Joey.

Fiona Calder knew a result when she saw it; Kaz's testimony would provide the evidence for a double murder conviction. It would also help scupper any allegations of illegality Turnbull might take to the IPCC. Calder agreed, released Kaz and called a press conference.

The crowd that turned out at the crematorium to pay their respects were a motley crew of superannuated villains with walking sticks as much in evidence as mirrored sunglasses. Ellie had been waiting practically her whole married life for this day and she didn't disappoint. She walked into the chapel with her two daughters in a black feather fascinator with a light veil specially commissioned for the occasion. As the priest told his sceptical audience that although Terence Albert Phelps was a man of the streets he repented at the last, Ellie dabbed her dry cheeks with a black lace hanky.

There was a discreet police presence in the chapel and a couple of armed response officers with MP5s in the Rose Garden. Kaz reflected ruefully that this was probably the one aspect of the rigmarole her old man would've appreciated. Joey sat at the back handcuffed to a big brawny prison officer. He'd been arrested on the A12 by a couple of traffic cops who'd stopped him for speeding. He didn't put up any resistance and whistled up Neville Moore to get him out. When he was charged with double murder, refused bail and remanded to Belmarsh prison, he fired Neville in a fit of pique. But then rehired him three days later.

As the mourners filed out and Kaz stood beside her mother shaking hands and accepting condolences, Joey finally caught her eye. He gave her a wink and a cheeky grin, then turned to his minder with an appealing smile. 'All right if I just give me poor old mum a hug?'

The prison officer nodded. The police had deployed more officers than he'd ever seen at a villain's funeral. Joey Phelps wasn't going anywhere.

Joey enveloped Ellie in as large an embrace as the handcuffs would allow. She wriggled free, one hand on the fascinator.

'Careful Joey! Mind me hat!'

He smiled at her, his baby-blue eyes filling with tears. 'I'm sorry Mum. I've let you down.' He glanced at the remaining family line-up: Kaz, Natalie, Brian and Glynis. 'I've let you all down. Let the family down. And I'm sorry.'

Brian shifted uncomfortably. 'Can't be helped lad. I'm sure your dad'd understand.'

Natalie fiddled with the cuffs on her jacket, she couldn't meet her brother's eye.

He glanced from her to Glynis and beamed. 'All right Glyn? I must admit I'm really surprised not to see Sean here today. Aren't you Mum?' His gaze slid along the line and came to rest on Kaz. He fixed her with a hypnotic stare. 'I mean I know he's probably a bit nervous of the old bill, but for him to miss Dad's send-off, well, I have to say I'm a bit puzzled. Aren't you Kaz? Hope nothing's happened to him.'

Glynis looked up from under the broad brim of her hat. 'Oh, don't worry Joey – he's fine. He's been moving about a lot, y'know how it is. But he calls me every week. 'Course, I told him about your dad and he was gutted. He sends you his love Ellie. We got your dad a lovely wreath: heart-shaped with lots of different colour roses. Sean picked it out himself.'

She glanced at Kaz, who returned her brother's gaze with a serene smile.

'Hope that puts your mind at rest little brother.'

EPILOGUE

Nicci Armstrong got off the train at Glasgow Central station. It was a city she'd never visited before, but using the map on her phone she found her way to Sauchiehall Street and the bar where they'd arranged to meet. It was part of a chain, but targeting the cooler, top-end of the market, not exactly a typical art student hang-out, which was the point. She took a stool at the high bar and was ordering herself a glass of Pinot Grigio when she noticed a vaguely familiar figure approaching. The hair was shorter, cut in a trendy crop, the clothes were quirky and retro. She was carrying a large A1 portfolio and a leather satchel. She gave Nicci a tentative smile.

'Found it okay then?'

Nicci nodded. 'I don't know what to call you.'

The young woman held out her hand. 'Clare O'Keeffe. Pleased to meet you.'

They shook hands awkwardly. Nicci came away with a film of charcoal on her fingers. Clare looked embarrassed.

'Bit mucky, sorry about that. Life drawing class.'

Nicci smiled. 'Don't worry. Drink?'

'Just a mineral water.'

Nicci ordered from the barman, they collected their drinks and settled themselves in a corner booth.

Nicci raised her glass. 'Well, I don't know if you'll want to drink to this or not, but we've got a trial date. Tenth of April.'

Clare raised her glass and clinked it with Nicci's. 'I'll be glad to get it over with.'

Nicci nodded. 'I'm sure. I've tried calling your sister a few times, but she never gets back to me.'

Clare sighed. 'When she left Woodcote Hall Mum persuaded her to go home. I asked her to come up here and live with me, but she wouldn't.'

'Do you think she'll manage to stay clean if she's back there?'

A look of anxiety crossed Clare's face, but she pushed it away.

'I dunno. I wanted to give her my number so she could stay in touch, but my Witness Protection Officer said absolutely not.'

'I'd agree with that. They wouldn't even give me your number, only pass on a message.' Nicci took a sip of her drink. 'The other thing I need to tell you is about Ashley Carter.'

Clare smiled wistfully. 'Poor old Ash. I don't think my brother treated him that well.'

'Seems the worm has turned. He's been separated from Joey for quite a few months now and his family have got him a smart new lawyer who wants to get some leverage on his sentence. We hope he's going to become a prosecution witness, testify about the murder of Alex Marlow.'

Clare raised her eyebrows. 'I always did think Ash was smarter than he looked. But he'd been running round after Joey since they was about ten.'

'He's also saying Joey shot Dave Harper, Glynis's boyfriend.'

Clare's eyes widened. 'No kidding! Well well.'

She pondered this for a moment, sipped her mineral water and smiled to herself. She seemed quieter and more contained than Nicci remembered. But then suddenly her eyes lit up.

'I've been reading the papers. Woodentop's making a name for himself.'

Nicci gave her a puzzled look, then she realized. 'You mean Alan Turnbull? Yeah he's certainly stirring things up.'

Clare gave her a mischievous grin. 'Did you lot really think I was gonna fall for Bradley?'

Nicci returned the smile and held up her palm. 'Hey, no one ever consulted me. It was something the bosses dreamt up.'

'Now they're all trying to blame each other.'

'Pretty much.'

Clare's gaze drifted off, she seemed lost in reverie. She rubbed her chin thoughtfully.

'I liked him though. Didn't want to. But he was a persistent little fucker.'

Nicci smiled ruefully. 'Yep, he was that all right.'

They sat in silence for several minutes. Nicci watched Clare tracing a pattern in the beads of moisture on the side of her glass. She remembered Bradley doing the exact same thing, but she quickly put the memory away.

'Did you pick the new name yourself?'

Clare nodded. 'It's after Georgia O'Keeffe, one of my favourite artists. Thought it'd give me something to live up to, keep me on track.'

Nicci sighed. 'Never heard of her I'm afraid.' She raised her chin, gave Clare a searching look. 'It must be hard, just walking away from everything and everyone. Cutting yourself off so completely.'

Nicci couldn't imagine it, never seeing Sophie again, even her parents, that would be hard enough.

Clare looked at her, smiled, then her gaze shifted off into the distance, out of the window and into the streets beyond.

'No it's not. It's not hard, it's brilliant. It's what I've always wanted. Just to walk away. Start again as a different person.'

Nicci scanned her face, she wondered if that were even possible. But if it was she hoped with all her heart that Kaz Phelps had achieved it.

Acknowledgements

Making the transition from television writer to novelist has not been an easy passage and I'm enormously grateful to everyone who's given me their support, not to mention their time and expertise. Thanks to Jill Foster, Gary Wild, Alison Finch and Dominic Lord, for always being there but also respecting my need to chase a dream.

Anne Sharp and Win Browne were both generous with their introductions. Professor Dave Barclay was informative and invaluable as he is for so many crime writers. Joan Scott, Kathy Lefanu, Brian Chapman and DCI Roy Ledingham all gave me a wealth of professional insights and procedural detail. Lisanne Radice and Jenny Parrot guided me through early drafts with their editorial skills. And special thanks to GC, whose input was indispensable.

I was lucky enough to secure the indomitable Jane Gregory as my agent, she and her team have proved excellent guides in this new world. Trisha Jackson, my editor, whilst shepherding me gently through an unfamiliar process, has brought her sharp intellect to bear on the more wobbly parts of the text. Laura Carr has provided invaluable guidance with grammar and syntax. The backup team at Pan Macmillan have all been friendly and helpful on everything from marketing strategies to social media.

And last but by no means least a very special thank you to my two first readers Sue Kenyon and Jenny Kenyon, without whom . . .

COMING SOON
The explosive sequel to *The Informant*

THE MOURNER
Susan Wilkins

If she can't get justice, will she settle for vengeance?

Kaz Phelps has escaped her brother and her criminal past to become an anonymous art student in Glasgow. But can life under the witness protection scheme ever give her the freedom she craves?

Banged up and brooding, Joey Phelps faces thirty years behind bars. Still, with cash and connections on the outside, can an overstretched prison system really contain him?

Helen Warner, once Kaz's lawyer and lover, is a rising star in Parliament. But has she made the kind of enemies who have no regard for the democratic process, or even the law?

Ousted from the police and paralysed by tragic personal loss, Nicci Armstrong is in danger of going under. Can a job she doesn't want with a private security firm help her to put her life back together?

A murder dressed up as suicide and corruption that goes to the heart of government unite ex-cop and ex-con in a deadly quest to learn the truth. What they discover proves what both have always known – villainy is rife on both sides of the law.